HOW TO BE THE BEST Third Wheel

LORIDEE DE VILLA

HOW TO BE THE BEST Third Wheel

wattpad books

An imprint of Wattpad WEBTOON Book Group

Published in Canada by Wattpad WEBTOON Book Group,
a division of Wattpad Corp.
36 Wellington Street E., Suite 200, Toronto, ON M5E 1C7 Canada

www.wattpad.com

First Wattpad Books edition: May 2022
ISBN 978-1-77729-008-5 (Trade Paper original)
ISBN 978-1-77729-009-2 (eBook edition)

Library and Archives Canada Cataloguing in Publication information is available upon request.

Printed and bound in Canada
1 3 5 7 9 10 8 6 4 2

Cover design by Cassie Gonzales

To my love life—
thank you for being so nonexistent that I had to write this.

WARNING

—

This book may cause a loss of brain cells from facepalms, premature wrinkles from periodic cringing, irregular and rapid heartbeat from character ships, occasional uncontrollable swooning, and *many* relatable moments. The author takes no responsibility for damage to books or electronic devices if you hurl yours across the room.

INTRODUCTION

*

On the front page of any great research paper are key words that should be well understood before diving into the subject matter. *This* can hardly be described as a research paper. However, my life, the life of Lara Dela Cruz, is as great as any scholarly article that has drained blood, sweat, and tears from its authors, so it deserves some key words as well . . .

Third Wheeling—an unfortunate state in which a person tags along with a couple. This may result in feeling left out and uncomfortable, especially when the couple decides to have a full-out make-out session in your face.

Third Wheel—me. (And literally everyone on planet Earth at some point or another.)

Relationship Expert—also me.

I'll humbly let you know that *I* know what I'm doing. Romantic comedies? I can recite their scripts in my sleep. Books? Those are character ships with extra words. K-dramas? *Saranghaeyo* to all the leads who almost kiss the protagonist in episode ten—obviously in the rain—and who give them a piggyback ride sometime during the first season.

Single—unfortunately also me. Alternatively, a state in which awesome people with truly excellent advice are left alone because "coaches don't play," and totally not because the last demon I summoned did not help me land a relationship. I'm obviously joking. Maybe.

So, to all the single third-wheel relationship experts out there (and anyone else who has picked up this monstrosity), I'm more than pleased to present to you the official handbook to being the *best* third wheel.

TIP ONE:
DON'T OVERREACT; UPGRADE

✱

People might consider me ever so slightly *overdramatic*.

But I pride myself on the fact that I have the perfect amount of drama *and* paranoia for the average teenager. For example, I may have performed multiple soliloquies in front of my mirror this morning, practicing what I would say to my best friends after not seeing them for the entire summer because my family and I were in the Philippines. I also may have pictured the absolute worst-case scenario that could happen at school, which is basically a zombie apocalypse preventing me from *escaping* the school (and also my friends completely ghosting me). All of the above is natural, human behavior. It has *nothing* to do with the potentially catastrophic, life-altering first day of grade twelve.

Stepping into the Keele Street–side entrance of the school, I open the infamous LKJC (a fun acronym for Lara, Kiera, Jasmine, and Carol) group chat to ask my friends if they're around.

Me: *You guys here yet?*
Kiera: *Yeah, at our usual spot*

We've claimed a particular section of the hallway near the art department on the third floor as our spot. With large windows that overlook the first-floor atrium, it's where we've been doing our morning meetups since tenth grade.

Jasmine: *Not Carol, though, she's probably going to get detention on the first day for being late LOL*

Me: *For real ha-ha*

Carol: *Wowwww I'm literally 2 minutes away!*

Kiera: *Sureee . . .*

Carol: *It's true! Watch, I'll be there in less than 5*

Jasmine: *Okayyy . . .*

I manage to huff my way up three flights of yellow-painted stairs to the third-floor landing. Needing one last moment to compose myself (and my heavy breathing) before pushing the doors open, I sweep some stray hairs away from my glasses and pull out my cell phone to take one last look at my reflection. The straightener did its job because my long, black hair is still not frizzy. The T-shirt tucked into baggy jeans looks cute enough, and my white shoes are . . . they're not white anymore, but it's *fine.*

One last breath. *Inhale. Exhale.*

Pushing the heavy metal doors open, I stride confidently into the packed hallway. By "confidently," I mean that I manage to walk without falling, tripping, or doing anything remotely embarrassing. Schedule in hand, I search for my friends, but am greeted instead by half-asleep fellow seniors and frantic, stray puppyesque freshmen heading to their classes twenty minutes early.

Turning left at the next hallway, I finally see two of the three girls. Kiera is gesturing frantically (probably talking about an anime or her own life drama) and Jasmine, leaning her head against the blue lockers, is either uninterested or sleepy.

Jasmine looks the same; her short black hair still in a bob with bangs clipped to the side. With each passing year she looks more like her mom, who has dark eyes that kiss in the corners and rosy cheeks against pale skin. The only difference between them is that everything Mrs. Zhao wears is fresh off of the runway, while Jasmine values simplicity over anything else. Today that means Jasmine's got on a light-gray cardigan with cropped denim capris.

Unlike Jasmine, Kiera's appearance has changed from when I last saw her in June. Her strawberry-blond hair, which used to be down to her waist, is cut to her shoulders, with loose curls framing her face. Nevertheless, I notice her girly style is still in place as she adjusts her lavender sundress.

Their outfits match their personalities almost exactly. Jasmine has been my best friend/neighbor since kindergarten, and even then she was the shy type. Being the true introvert of our friend group, it makes sense that she dresses to blend in. She's also the only one who's mature enough to keep the rest of us in line.

Kiera Jones is exactly as bubbly as she looks. Everything about her is bright, from her dress to her hair to her eyes to the smile that never fades. Speaking of bright, we became friends in kindergarten after she drew a flower on my hand with a neon-pink marker, for the sole reason of matching the drawing on hers. It took a week to wash off, but our friendship has lasted since then. She has a natural charm that can attract just about every type of person, making her friends with almost everyone at school, and is the girl people instantly fall for.

Yet she's never been in a romantic relationship. None of us have, except for Carol. But we like to disregard Carol's one and only ex-boyfriend because that fling only lasted a month and ended with a whole lot of Taylor Swift songs (the angry ones, not the sad ones).

Sometimes I find it weird that my friends never accept any of their suitors. Jasmine has had at least three cute guys ask her out, all of whom she accidentally ghosted because she's oblivious. Kiera simply rejects people on the spot. Carol uses an intensive interrogation process to weed out the candidates. And me? Nobody ever asks me out. I think they're either intimidated by the fact that I'm the perfect package deal or they've witnessed my early morning hallway monologues, in which I argue that real men will never live up to fictional ones. Our shared lack of interest in a partner keeps us on the same page. We're all able to keep the perfect balance between our separate lives, school, extracurriculars, and of course, each other. Best of all, there's no relationship drama to get in the way.

As I rush toward them, a sudden jolt of energy bursts through my body, like I've had one too many caffeinated drinks. I've *really* missed them.

Spending July and August in my parents' hometown in the Philippines has resulted in me now being two shades darker than usual and having mosquito-bitten legs. It was a family reunion with relatives I hardly knew existed, and if you've ever seen a complete Filipino family, you'd probably mistake it for a small village, which is funny because we were *literally* in a small village. Unlike most of our other Fil-Can friends, my parents didn't come from Manila or any of the big cities. Their home is somewhere in the rural part of Batangas, where water only runs during the early morning and late night and *butiki* crawl up the walls. For a girl who's lived in Toronto her whole life, let's just say culture shock smacked me in the face. But the biggest adjustment I had to make was the absolute lack of internet, which meant not communicating with my best friends for almost two whole months.

"Kiera! Jasmine!" I shout, waving my hands.

Their faces light up as they wave back. I am about to do that movie running scene–thing when a foot comes out of nowhere and I trip, landing on the ground and doing away with my attempt to get through the day without embarrassing myself. I maneuver my body so that I'm at least *sitting* on the floor instead of lying down on my stomach. When the culprit's eyes meet mine, the familiar feeling of disgust sets in. That *idiot*.

He holds a handout to help me up. I make the stupid decision to take it. Midway, he releases my wrist, sending me back on my butt. *Wonderful.* Stifled laughs from bystanders are met with my own glares. Annoyed, I get up, scowling at his devilish smile. By devilish, I mean that he reminds me of an actual demon that escaped from hell.

I am by no means a hateful person. I'm never a part of any school drama and honestly, aside from corrupt world leaders and conceited people, I don't hate anyone, except one specific boy I've known since birth; one I would've murdered a long time ago if his mother wasn't best friends with mine—Jameson Bryer. James for short. Or The Idiot. They're interchangeable.

Getting up from the ground, I narrow my eyes at him. "Do you wake up every day asking the underworld for a checklist of things to help make the world a terrible place?" While going to war with each other is usually our thing, I refrain from kicking him where the sun doesn't shine because it's Tuesday morning and frankly, revenge is a second day of school thing.

James runs a hand through his dark-brown hair. "Of course not. Unlike you, I am a descendant from the heavens." He presses his palms together in a prayer gesture then draws an imaginary circle above his head. "I haven't seen you in two months. How much have you missed me?"

My right eye twitches slightly. Because my love for his family is the only thing keeping me from pushing him off the nearest cliff, I say, "You know the distance between here and Jupiter? That, times negative one."

"Sad to see you haven't changed."

While I was away in the Philippines for the summer, he went on a luxury cruise in the Bahamas—and I had the pleasure of not seeing his face until today.

"I can only say the same about you," I retort. "You'd think that two months would give you enough time to plan a more *creative* greeting, but I see you're plagiarizing tactics."

He takes a step forward, closing the distance between us. "Well, sweetheart, I live by the saying an eye for an eye. You tripped me two months ago, so I'd say revenge was awfully overdue."

"That was an accident!"

He raises an eyebrow.

"Accidentally . . . on purpose," I admit. "But you were being infuriating that day and that trail was supermuddy and you know that I *don't* hike and—" I clamp my mouth shut when I notice the amusement on his face. This is what he wants. He wants me to run my mouth until I slip up and he can tease me for it. And since I am not giving him the satisfaction of doing that today, I give him a curt nod before turning around, finishing our conversation.

Walking over to my friends, I hold my head high even though everyone is looking at me. At this point, I don't feel bothered by their stares; it's the common aftermath of my James encounters. My *frustrating* James encounters. Kiera and Jasmine stand beside the lockers, both trying to look supportive, though I can sense the secondhand embarrassment radiating off of them.

"Do you think I'd get caught if I took some eggs from the caf and egged his car?" I ask.

They laugh, lightening the mood. Though I controlled myself

earlier, everyone knows that I never back down from James. Sure, he's the school's beloved star hockey player, but I'll retaliate when provoked. It's the reason why our personal attacks on each other never seem to end. Fighting is our thing. Our feud was established when it was decided that we'd both exist on the same planet. In fact, I should have been prepared for a sneak attack like that trip in the hall. I'd let my guard down and it won't happen again.

"I'm here! I'm here!" Rapid steps approach as Carol runs toward us in her Adidas joggers, bright blue cleats in her arms and her bag half falling off her shoulder.

The best way to describe Carol Gonsalves is chaotic. She's the friend who's either late, underdressed, or says something completely inappropriate out of the blue. She joined our friend group in the fifth grade when her family immigrated from Goa and has been my partner in pranks ever since. I don't think I'd terrorize James as effectively without her. "Ha! Told y'all," she says, pointing a finger at us. "I was here in less than three minutes. What did I miss?"

Jasmine says, "The public humiliation of Lara."

"What do you mean?" Carol mumbles, holding a hair tie between her front teeth as she gathers her long black locks into a bun.

"Let's just say that Lara and James's dynamic has not changed," Kiera says.

I let out a large breath. "Unfortunately, that entails him tripping me on the first day of school."

After Carol finishes wrapping the elastic around her mass of hair, she punches me in the shoulder, expecting an interesting story. "I came too late! Bro, what did you do to him?"

"Nothing." I shrug.

"No, seriously! What did you do? Did you twist his arm? Did you kick him in the—"

"I ignored him."

She stops chuckling immediately and frowns, nostrils flaring. "What happened to you on vacation that you suddenly turned to the *good side*?" Carol grips my shoulders and shakes me back and forth until I feel like I'm about to hurl. "Get yourself together, woman! I did not raise you like this!"

"Dude, *calmes-toi*, I don't want to start my day off with negative vibes," I say, and she pretends to wipe a bead of sweat off her forehead. "Now forget about him. What were you guys up to while I was gone?'

Their eyes widen like criminals that have been spotted, like deer caught in headlights. Jasmine fidgets with her fingers, Kiera bites her lip, and Carol looks ready to bolt even though she *just* got here.

"Is it about Mark?" Mark was a guy from the soccer team, and he obviously liked Carol. They'd been hanging out for a while now, but I wasn't sure if their friendship would become something more. Did something happen over the summer?

No one replies. *They're not telling me something.*

"I'm not telling her," Jasmine squeaks. Kiera shakes her head, too, following Jasmine's lead.

They both look at Carol, knowing that she always does the best at explaining situations. She approaches me and places a hand on my shoulder, frightened eyes becoming round circles. Not that I'm a scary person . . . just a bit *unpredictable*. "Don't freak out on us but . . ."

There's a new commotion behind us, distracting me from the conversation and forcing my head to turn. James yells to his friends as they emerge from the other hallway, walking over and greeting them wildly with complex handshakes and backslaps. Meanwhile, the other students stare at them like they're celebrities. In this high school setting, I suppose they are. All it takes is above average physical genetics mixed with athletic ability to create a popular person, right?

But if being popular is the same as being well known, then I suppose I'm pretty popular as well. Not because I'm athletic but because James and I almost kill each other on the daily, and if they're looking at him, they're also looking at me.

James walks with his crew following closely, drawing the eyes of *everyone*. Usually in the movies, you'd see the mean girl and her squad, but this is a guy version of that. Imagine a rock song from a 2000s coming of age movie playing in the background. Then imagine the confident Regina George stride. Now mix that with four good-looking student athletes but subtract the problematic attitudes, since James's squad consists of fairly nice people who are unfortunate enough to be friends with the idiot.

Among the unlucky, is Mark Medina—James's oldest friend from elementary school and one of mine too. He's cute in the same way that a puppy is, but shy. I always wondered how he ended up being friends with a demon, considering he's a literal angel from the heavens, or as he likes to say, *Lara, for the hundredth time, I'm from Peru.* To be fair, the top of Machu Picchu is pretty close to the sky.

Then there's Daniel Samuels. I can't say much about him because I don't know him all that well. He's the smart one of the group, and besides playing hockey, he's the president of the debate club. He's Black, with long braided cornrows and a charming smile that naturally causes people to gravitate toward him. Less shy than Mark but not as boisterous or obnoxious as James.

Lastly, we have Logan Ford, who is neither shy nor bright. I'm not saying this to be mean, but in grade nine geography class he confidently stated that Brazil was located in Europe. There's that, and the fact that he's a literal representation of the stereotypical blue-eyed, blond-haired player that you see in every other Netflix film. He's always been nice to me, but his reputation for going through girls as if the yearbook was a dating checklist has been enough to keep me away.

They all have updated looks from when we last saw them in June. Daniel's style has evolved, now playing with more color and pattern; Logan sports a summer tan, a striking contrast to his natural fairness; and Mark has a fresh haircut, chopping off his usual shoulder-length locks.

I turn back to my friends, ready to ask about why they're so nervous, when I hear the voice of one of James's squad members.

"Babe!"

Spinning around so fast that my head could fall off if it wasn't attached to my body, my attention focuses on a certain shy boy now running over to my group. *Mark*? Carol grins at me shyly as he wraps an arm around her shoulder. She brushes his dark-brown curls away from his green eyes. Nausea threatens to overwhelm me, but I keep my expression under control. "Looks like we're going to be third wheels!" I chirp to Kiera and Jasmine, who don't return my smile or laugh at my joke like they would normally.

"Darling!" another guy shouts, causing a cringe to form on my face. *Darling? Are we in the 1960s now?*

Daniel races toward us. *Who is he going—*

He wraps his arms around Kiera and kisses her forehead.

Oh my goodness, no.

"Honey!"

Whipping my head around once more (okay, I did get whiplash this time), I see Logan sprinting toward us. Pushing me out of the way, he attacks Jasmine's face with his own, as if she's in a life-threatening condition and needs immediate CPR. And this is why honey belongs in a beehive and not in a school hallway.

What the heck is going on? And where is the nearest trash can so I can vomit?

Carol, fine. We all saw that coming. She and Mark have been close for almost five months. Kiera, kind of weird. She's not really the type to date with her overloaded schedule. But *Jasmine*? Jasmine Zhao is a freaking saint! We all thought she was going to become a nun or something! *Can someone fetch me a glass of water? Actually, can you make it holy water?* Yet here she is, hand-deep in his blond hair, making out with Logan Ford, the blue-eyed mega player of the school. Don't tell me I missed the good-girl, bad-boy story arc while I was gone. Staring at the three couples for a minute, I consider all the ways that I could chase these boys off with a sledgehammer.

Breaking away from the kiss, Jasmine says, "Lara, don't freak out, we can expl—"

"What the hell is *this*?" I shout at the top of my lungs, gesturing at the three members of James's squad who have attached themselves to my best friends like leeches.

I look at Carol and Mark, Kiera and Daniel, Jasmine and Logan, and finally at James, who is, thankfully, as confused as I am about this situation.

"Guys?" he asks his friends, an eyebrow raised.

Mark says, "Sorry, bro, we couldn't reach you for the whole summer. You literally did not reply to our group chat for a month."

"Yeah, Lara, you had no signal so . . ." Kiera adds.

James and I have the exact same expression on our faces. I don't know if I'm going to go ballistic or if I'm going to faint. I turn to Jasmine. "You too? You told me that you wouldn't date until you graduated!"

"I know, I know, but it sort of just,"—she looks lovingly at her boyfriend (gross)—"happened."

"You guys are actually committing to a relationship?" James says, and I narrow my eyes at him. Classic James, moving on from one girl to the next as if they're objects. Seeing my repulsed expression, he sticks his hands up and quickly adds, "I'm just kidding, sweetheart, don't be such a buzzkill."

Oh, I could kick him right now. *Self-control, Lara, self-control.*

"Oh yeah," he adds. "Sorry about my nonexistent replies in the group chat. My phone actually fell into the ocean, and I just got a new one."

"Ocean?" Daniel raises an eyebrow.

"You don't notice a lot of things when you're salsa dancing on the deck with a hot girl." James steps forward and back with his eyes closed—a motion that seems like a dance, but I can't call it that. A smile plays on his lips as he thinks back to the event.

"*Anyway—*" I start, but Kiera jumps in before I can continue.

"Lara, we'll explain everything to you at lunch. Promise." She gives my right shoulder a reassuring squeeze before grabbing Daniel's hand and doing that nasty, romantic eye-contact thing. Lunch. Along with stressing about the line for cafeteria french fries, I'm stressing about *this*. Their boyfriends. My french fries. Boy-fries, as we'd once called them as elementary kids.

The warning bell rings, and the three couples go hand in hand into the sunset—well, to their first period classes.

James and I stand frozen in our places, exchanging glances before continuing to watch our friends' backs get farther away. We usually face very different problems, but today we're united on one common front. Our friendships are screwed. How is it possible to have upgraded to a seventh wheel?

I sit at the back of my first period English class, dumbfounded. In the two months that I was away, my friends just *happened* to bump into three hot guys, changing their relationship status from single to not-so single. I tap my long nails on the hardcover English textbook, trying to absorb the new information without hyperventilating.

Right as my breathing returns to normal, Logan and Daniel walk into the classroom. Noticing the empty seats beside me, Logan sits on my left, sandwiched between me and Daniel. They both have gleeful expressions on their faces, obviously not understanding the trauma they induced earlier. It makes me want to scream. Here I was, thinking that I was incredibly lucky to have a friend group void of relationship drama; that all of us were on the same page. Now, I'm sitting beside two people responsible for this unwanted new chapter, who shrink in their seats as I glower at them.

"Lara, I really like Kiera and I'm so sorry that we never told you until now," Daniel explains. "It just kind of happened during the summer." His dark eyes hold enough sincerity that I have difficulty keeping the angry expression on my face.

"And I really like Jas. Like really, *really*, like her," Logan says, but I'm less convinced. I'm sure he's really, *really* liked a lot of girls, considering he has a new one each week. "I know what you're thinking. And she's different. I'm different with her."

The words *she's different* and *I'm different with her* immediately activate my defensive parent mode because goodness gracious, I've read enough books to know that this foreshadows a lot of relationship bumps.

"Listen," I hiss at Daniel, "if you ever do anything to make Kiera cry, I swear on my life, I will hunt you down and beat you until you can't move."

Daniel begins to nod but pauses. "Okay, I'm not going to hurt her, but you do realize we're talking about *Kiera*, right? The other day I showed her a *car commercial* and she cried because there was a puppy. Can we negotiate this agreement? Perhaps only beat me up if her tears are caused by my *mistakes*?"

How did my overly emotional best friend end up with a guy who interprets threats using logic?

"Or not," he says, caving under my intense stare. "It's fine."

Then it's Logan's turn. "And you, I get that you think that you're a 'nice person' and all, but we all know about that speed dating crap you pull on girls. Jasmine *doesn't* need a player."

"I know," he says, shaking his head and frowning like he'd never consider hurting Jas. "I'm serious about her. I've never felt this way about anyone."

"*Sure*."

I pull out my phone just as Logan begins to respond. "I promise I've changed. I'm . . . Lara, are you listening?"

"You know, Logan, I've been thinking about capitalism lately, and how much I like money."

"*Okay*?"

"I've also been thinking about intestines and, well, how fitting that you have some." Looking up from my cell phone, I calmly ask, "Logan Ford, do you know how much intestines are worth on the black market?"

"No?"

He might not but my Google search page does. Sliding my phone to the center of his desk, I watch in amusement as his blue eyes widen with fear. I've never seen someone so terrified of numbers. His frozen stature is enough confirmation that the threat has been received, so I reach for my cell phone and shove it back into my pocket.

Finally, our English teacher walks into the room. "Good morning, everyone!" he greets us as he places his coffee mug on the desk. "My name is Mr. Garcia and we'll be spending the first period of the whole semester together. The assigned locker list is on the back wall, and at the end of class I'll be handing out the personal information sheets for you to take home and fill in. How does that sound?"

As usual, the class full of sleep-deprived teenagers does not show any sign of response. Half of them have their phones in their laps, checking their social media as if something has changed within the past minute.

"I'll take that as a yes. Now, on your desks you'll find our short story textbook, which we'll be using for unit one. Please turn to page five and take a moment to read over the first story," he instructs, and the sound of flipping pages takes over the room.

While some students begin the reading, others have her books standing upright, attempting to hide their cell phones. Mr. Garcia sighs, eyeing one of the students in the corner of the room. "Richard, can you please get off the phone."

"I'm not even on it! I'm reading!" he says defensively, pointing to the erect book, which, unfortunately for his case, is upside down.

This is going to be a long day, I think to myself.

TIP TWO:
RESTRAIN YOURSELF FROM ATTACKING COUPLES

✸

It's not that I *hate* couples.

But when I'm trying to get through a packed hallway with limited time available to get to my next class, I would rather not see space being taken up by people who are trying to copulate against the lockers. Passing the second set of PDAers, I avert my gaze immediately. As I quickly make my way to the staircase, any intention of not looking miserable is swept away once I almost bump into freshmen not yet accustomed to the rules of speed walking. Ugh.

At last I make it to the biology classroom down on the second floor. After grabbing a new textbook from the pile, I sit at a desk in the front row, near the side of the room. Unlike other classrooms, the back walls are lined with laminate countertops and cabinets holding glassware. The arrangement of test tubes and flasks pleases my inner science geek and may be the only thing giving me an ounce of joy today. However, if there's one thing in Toronto that might cause a shocking explosion, it's me in a lab. Luckily, chemistry is a next-semester problem, and the biggest danger I'll face this semester is holding a scalpel.

Setting my backpack on the floor, I begin to reach for an empty binder when there's a loud thunk of somebody sitting in the chair next to me. My eyes widen. His dark-brown hair is in messy waves and he smells like oranges: Jameson freaking Bryer.

"Sit somewhere else." I groan.

"Why? Last time I heard, Canada was a free country," James states, his face getting closer to mine.

I try not to grit my teeth to the point of erosion. "Well, maybe you should use that freedom to relocate, because your lack of distance from me is offensive."

"*Really*?" He leans back in his chair and bites his bottom lip before continuing, speaking louder this time. "You weren't saying that last night. In fact, you seemed to *enjoy* my closeness." He smirks, clearly proud of the dirty and untrue accusation, while I turn a lovely shade of pink.

I wince, narrowing my eyes at him and praying that the *tsismosas* of the school are asleep. "Please, I wouldn't have sex with you if you were the last living organism on this planet."

"Sweetheart, we need to stop pretending that you don't want a chance with—"

"What?" I stand up from my desk and head to the closest cabinet, grabbing the smallest glass test tube that I can find and raising it. "Please, James, your little friend would probably fit in *this* and there would *still* be wiggle room."

The class snickers, along with a few of his teammates, and now it's his turn to become a tomato. Before I can say anything else to him, the sound of heels clicking fills the room and Ms. Perez arrives, slamming a big binder on the front counter. "Ms. Dela Cruz, put my equipment back and return to your seat!"

I scurry back to my desk because if there's one thing that scares me, it's Ms. Perez. I had her for biology last year and she doesn't like anything fun so in her class, we get Lara 2.0: the A plus, work completing, honor roll, Catholic girl. And likely enough, James just helped ruin my halo reputation.

After class, I grab my math binder and slam the locker door shut so loudly that the dude with the locker next to mine gives me a concerned glance before escaping. Yes, James can piss me off with his name calling and tripping and dirty jokes, but *this* is another level. I simply cannot be in biology class with him because if he annoys me, I will inevitably retaliate, which makes me look bad too. And if Ms. Perez is frustrated with me like she was in class today, my grades are absolutely, positively, doomed. And if my grades are bad, I'll feel bad because I thrive off of academic validation. Plus, you can't scam universities into giving you "congratulations" money with low marks.

Oh James. Is it possible to hate a human being so much? I hate him more than Bob Belcher hates Jimmy Pesto. I hate him more than Katniss Everdeen hates President Snow. I hate him more than the girls hate each other on *The* freaking *Bachelor*.

I enter math class and for the first time today, there's a teacher supervising the seated students. As I take the nearest desk, Ms. Kelleher looks up from her salad, giving me a warm smile from behind her long blond hair. She's my favorite teacher for two reasons: she's young at heart and her lessons are anything but boring.

"How was your summer, Lara?" she asks, her British accent picking up slightly.

"Good, actually. I was in the Philippines for the summer and—"

"Lara!" James calls, throwing his bag over his shoulder and interrupting me for the hundredth time today. The bottom of his backpack hits the surface of the desk beside me, and I clench my jaw as he continues to stand there.

"Are you stalking me? Is this a new thing you've picked up? If it is, I'm afraid you'll need to get a better hobby, James."

"I *am* in this class, sweetheart."

Again, with the sweetheart business. God knows why he chooses *that* out of all insulting words, but pet names gross me out as much as the couples who use them. When he does have an actual girlfriend (or a short fling), the word babe comes out of his mouth once every two minutes. Disgusting, but at least it's never directed at me. It's selfish of me to wish for some girl to sacrifice herself and snatch him up, but he only stops calling me sweetheart when he has a girlfriend.

"You don't have math this semester," I say, my face like stone. There's no way I read his schedule wrong during second period.

"I *didn't* have math this semester."

"Exactly! So get out!"

"Ah, I thought you were good at English? I said that I *didn't* have math this semester." He props his elbows on the desk, supporting his giant head on interlaced fingers. Lips curving up into a grin, he says, "Let me enlighten you with how exactly the past tense works."

Breathe in, breathe out, breathe in, breathe out. My doctor once said that breathing exercises help calm a person's heart rate. Clearly, it's *not* helping!

Ms. K frowns. "Lara, are you okay?"

I face her and nod, trying my best not to explode into a fury. She pulls out a piece of paper and examines it. A pensive look emerges on her face.

"James, is it?" she asks. "I'm afraid I don't see you on my class list."

At those words, the tension in my brain releases and I exhale. *Yes! Yes! Yes!* I really can't handle another seventy-five minutes with him.

"That might be because I switched my classes a few minutes ago," James explains, and my hope sinks to the pit of my stomach, inevitably deteriorating from the gastric acid.

I turn to Ms. K. "Do you teach another period?"

She shakes her head and sighs. "Unfortunately, no. Besides, you two seem to know each other well. Just try to get along."

"Don't worry, Lara," James says. "I'll be nice."

I almost choke at his words. *Nice? James?* Has nice gotten a new meaning that I haven't heard of?

Question: Is James nice?
Nice (adjective)—pleasant and agreeable.

Hypothesis: if that is the definition of nice, then James is the complete opposite.

Observations:

1. James has had about six "relationships" since we started high school. This does not include the weekly flings or the girls he has probably slept with. This by itself isn't a problem, but let's get to the second observation.

2. He is the primary cause of makeup malfunctions in the girls' washroom. Do you know how many times I've almost slipped on puddles made by sad girls crying over the idiot?

3. He likes embarrassing unsuspecting people in the hallways. For example, tripping me this morning.

Conclusion: James is definitely not nice.

I stare at Ms. K, hoping that she gets the telepathic message that I am transferring to her: *James is not nice, he is a demon in a human body.*

Meanwhile, Mark saunters into the classroom as well, taking a step back when he notices James and me sitting together. His eyes say: *What happened to you? Did you guys become friends within the last two hours?* I shake my head no, implying, *I still hate him, and I wish a bull shark ate him in the Bahamas.*

I gesture for Mark to come closer, and he hesitates for a second before walking over to us. He knows that we'll start to argue at any moment now. Judging by his frequent glances at the classroom door, he doesn't want to be a part of this. Everyone knows to stay at least ten feet away from us when we go to war. He fidgets with his fingers as he looks from me to James.

"I thought you had French class third period?" he asks James.

"I did, but I realized that I wanted to have math this semester, so I went to guidance and switched," he reveals.

Mark scratches the back of his neck. "But . . . why?" James's playful smile falls for a split second, but it happens so quickly that I can't be sure if I actually saw it happen. "Don't tell me it's because you want to leech off of our work."

"*Our* work?" I snort. "You mean *yours*. James is not getting anything from me."

"C'mon, Lara," James says, batting his eyelashes like a toddler instead of the seventeen-year-old, six-foot tree that he is. "Don't you want to share your mathematical expertise with me?"

"No," I say without hesitation.

Ms. K stares at the three of us, seemingly invested in our little drama. She shrugs, the corners of her lips rising. "Lara, you're actually quite good at math. You may want to reconsider. Plus, it's always good to have more volunteer hours." She pauses to look at James. "But perhaps you'd like to cut back on the flirting."

I gag a little. "Miss, this isn't flirting, it's called being a *hindrance*."

James laughs while I turn red.

What do you do when your mortal enemy crashes your math class and your favorite teacher betrays you? Evacuate the premises. I'm moving to Alaska now. Someone help me pack my bags, change my name to Laora Maria José Fernando, and get a fake passport. I am immigrating there. Yup. That is the solution.

TIP THREE:
WALK A FEW FEET BEHIND

*

The cafeteria isn't anything special. Our school is relatively small, so there's no room for a two-tiered *High School Musical*–type lunchroom or anything similar to that. Instead, long gray tables line the center of the floor and shorter ones run along the sides of the room. Multicultural flags border the ceiling, while club posters and advertisements cover the walls.

It's only been five minutes since the bell rang, but the line for food extends halfway around the perimeter of the room. Though I was planning on buying french fries to cope with the news of the boy-fries, I decide against it because I'm far too lazy to wait in such a horrendously long queue of people. Even worse than the long line, the tables are almost full. Unlike the movies, lunchroom tables aren't based on cliques. Instead, ravenous teenagers sit everywhere, and the rule is first come, first served. I'm glancing around, looking for an empty seat, when a hand waves in the midst of swarming students.

"Lara!" Carol calls, standing up and waving both arms. They're all sitting at a rectangular table in our favorite corner. The nearby students look up from their meals and Jasmine tugs on Carol's shirt, forcing her to sit back down.

"How's the first day been so far?" I ask, plopping down on the bench beside Kiera, setting my lunch bag on the table and my backpack beside me. Of course, I need to ask a normal question before conducting an interrogation. It's called decency.

Kiera takes a bite out of her sandwich. "Nothing new. I'm excited for volleyball tryouts next week."

Nothing new? That's the understatement of the year. This day has decided to throw me into a parallel universe in which none of my friends are single. The only thing remotely normal is that James is still a nuisance.

Opening a thermos filled with grilled chicken on rice, I dig my spoon in and stuff my face. "That's cool," I say, mouth full. As per usual, I expect Kiera to make the volleyball team, Carol to make the soccer team, and Jasmine to reject the coach's offer to join the track team. And I'll probably win some sort of medal when sleeping becomes a sport.

From across the table, Carol takes out several containers of food from her backpack and beside her, Jasmine furrows her brows. "What's with all the food?" she asks.

"We had a wedding on the weekend," Carol replies. "Our family friend recently became Mrs. Selvakumar." Unexcited jazz hands decorated with Mehndi designs follow the statement.

"You seem bitter," I say, before taking another bite of my food.

She lets out a big exhale. "Nah, I'm happy for her. I mostly wish the clan of aunties would get their noses out of *my* business, with all their questions about the future. One of them even asked when I'll start going by *Dr.* Gonsalves. Like, *does it look like I want to help people*? I'm just waiting for the opportunity to overthrow this country once the world starts to crumble."

"*Carol—*" Jasmine starts.

"Relax, Jas," Carol says with a dismissive hand wave. "We probably have a couple of years left before the apocalypse. I'll be a good leader by then."

Jasmine gives her a weary nod, but we've all accepted Carol's fantastical (but frightening) schemes.

"Anyway," Carol starts. "The reason why I have so much food here is not only because I'm hungry, but because I know how much you guys like my mom's—"

"Butter chicken?" Kiera interrupts, clasping her hands.

"Biryani?" I guess.

Jasmine props her elbows on the table and rests her chin on her hands. "Whatever it is, I'm happy I don't have to buy overpriced food from the caf today."

Carol pushes black plastic containers toward each of us. "How about both?" she says. And *that* is the best news I've heard all day.

We dig into the delicious leftovers. Then I decide to ask the pressing question. "Anyone care to explain this morning?" I look pointedly at each of them; they avert their gazes and stay silent—which may be attributed to the fact that my face went from excited child to military general real quick.

Kiera and Jasmine look to Carol, who takes a breath, probably thinking of the least risky way to tell me what happened. "It was the beginning of summer, he told me that he had feelings for me, and I felt the same." She shrugs coolly, as if getting a boyfriend and not telling your best friend is a normal occurrence. It's not. Other than Carol's one other relationship, none of us have had boyfriends before. Crushes, sure. Even then, we hardly talked about guys, and if anyone had a crush, it never became the focus of our conversations. A "Look at what Mark texted me" from Carol was enough crush content for a day.

I tap my index finger on my chin and pretend to think. "And?"

Her eyes widen. "*And*? Do you want me to describe it to you in romantic teen fiction form?" she jokes.

"Yes. I'd appreciate that very much," I say, setting my food down to direct my full attention on the girls.

"Fine. Imagine this." She starts with a hand in the air, ready for a dramatic retelling. "I was on the school field. The sky was gray, and I was practicing shooting techniques for soccer."

"Tell me more," I muse.

"Mark was there and asked if he could practice with me. I was like, 'Sure.' As we were passing the ball back and forth, it started to rain. Like, really hard. I screamed because I was wearing my new cleats for the first time and—"

"You screamed because of *shoes*?" Carol could wrestle her brothers in the mud while wearing a Chanel dress and *still* not care.

"Dude," she says loudly. "I saved up two hundred dollars for those cleats. I didn't want to ruin them on the first day." *That makes sense.* "Mark picked me up and carried me across the field. I asked him what the heck he was doing, and he said that he didn't want my shoes to get muddy."

Wow. It's like something out of a movie. My brain fights my heart as I try not to react to the overload of adorableness. *Remember, be serious. I am an investigator, not a fangirl.*

"We stood under the awning of the school and waited for the rain to stop. He told me he'd had a crush on me all year, and you guys all knew I liked him so . . . yeah. That's how it began." She ends the story with a clap and proceeds to cross her arms and lean back, seeming to forget that these benches have no back. Luckily, Jasmine sticks out her arm before Carol falls backward onto the floor. "This is why we're friends," she says to Jasmine. "You always have my back."

My biggest concern was that our support system would crumble with boyfriends wedging into their lives, but maybe I'm wrong. We've been best friends for far too long, and our dynamic has hardly changed since elementary school. And right now, as Carol begins to annoy Jasmine with a series of arm pokes, everything feels normal.

Kiera clears her throat, and our attention shifts to her. "My turn! And don't worry, Lara, I am aware of the criterion you demand in terms of description." She winks. I give her a thumbs-up. "It was at the beginning of summer," she starts, with a slow wave of the forearm. "I was at the Eaton Centre, working at Hot Topic, and went to Starbucks on my break to order my favorite drink—"

"A caramel Frappuccino," Jasmine, Carol, and I finish for her. Kiera Jones only ever orders one type of drink.

"Correct!" she gushes. "So, I was walking out, and Daniel bumped right into me. The barista didn't put the lid on tight enough and my drink spilled all over my clothes. I almost died from embarrassment."

My friends having mishaps gives me pure joy. "Please tell me there's video footage of that."

Kiera glares at me but continues. "Fortunately not, *Lara*. Right after, he offered to pay for dry cleaning, but I said it was fine. He gave me his number in case I changed my mind, and even though I didn't, I *did* think he was cute, so I messaged him. After a bit of talking, he asked me out on a date! Now, here we are!"

Although her story sounds like a rip-off of some sort of Hallmark Christmas movie, I give her the nod of approval so we can move on to Jasmine. "Okay, Jas, how did *you* end up with *Logan* out of all the guys in the world?"

Ignoring my last remark, Jasmine straightens her back and places her folded hands on the table. "I was at home, practicing the violin. I had decided that I'd use the entire break to improve my skills—"

"*Improve*?" I interrupt. Jasmine is a musical genius. She plays eight different instruments, the violin being her favorite. "You've been playing since you were two, you've already been scouted by the number one music company in North America, and you were basically a child prodigy!"

"I'm okay," she states humbly.

Unlike the stereotype that Asian parents force their kids to master a bunch of things (like musical instruments), Jasmine actually loves what she does, and her mother couldn't be more supportive. The only stereotypical thing that goes on with our friend group is the collective experience of our parents holding the standard for good grades above our heads and making sure we're "A-sian" and not "B-sian." This obviously excludes Kiera because she's not Asian, but growing up, her mom was a "yell at you at the kitchen table while you learn fractions" type of tiger mom, much like all our moms.

In many ways, my, Jasmine's, and Carol's upbringings are quite similar despite our families being from totally different countries. Jasmine and I are second-generation immigrants, coming from families with strong ties to their homeland—hers from Beijing, China, and mine from the Philippines. Meanwhile, Carol's a first-generation immigrant from Goa, India. This might sound stereotypical again, but generally speaking, our parents are *strict*. While Kiera's able to head out her front door with a simple "Bye! Love you," the rest of us need to give two weeks' notice and file a defensive case to go out. Overprotectiveness seems to be a common trait among most immigrant parents, but because the four of us are practically glued at the hip, the rules bend a little for our friend group. For example, we can go out pretty easily when it's only the LKJC.

One rule I did not expect to bend was the no-boyfriend rule, but since nobody's bringing that up, I'm going to assume everyone's parents are totally okay with this.

Jasmine continues, "My mom's friend is a director at the Arts Centre on Front Street and told me that I was welcome to use the stage any time it was unoccupied. When I got there on the first Monday of July, I happened to walk in when it was occupied. By Logan. He was playing the piano and he was *really* good. I hid behind the stage curtains for a bit and . . . do I have to say the rest? It's embarrassing."

"C'mon, don't be shy," Carol says. "Tell Lara what you told us." She turns to me. "Trust me, it's good."

Jasmine cringes at whatever memory she recalls. "It's mortifying. I got so tangled up in the curtains that I accidentally pulled them off the bar they were hanging from, and I fell on the floor."

Jasmine doing something embarrassing only happens once in a blue moon. The last time something this embarrassing happened was in the ninth grade, when she almost broke into a senior boy's locker, thinking it was hers. I can't help but laugh, a small snort escaping as I do.

"It wasn't funny in the moment," she grumbles. "Logan obviously discovered me, and he helped me up. It was weird, but also cute. And I think we happened to . . . click?" She stares off with a look that I've never seen on her face before.

Is she . . . *in love*? I mean, what is love, really? It's really just some chemical reaction in our brains. Oh gosh, I am losing them to stupid chemicals.

Kiera props an elbow on the table, resting her cheek on her palm. "What do you think? I know it's a shock. To come back and we're all not single anymore. But you were gone for a long time."

I blink at her. In my books, two months is not that long, but she's correct that I am still in shock. My brain and my heart are at odds in trying to process this information. My brain argues for chasing their boyfriends away with a sledgehammer because they were not accounted for in the equation of our friendship. But my heart wants me to cave, be genuinely happy for my friends and accept the situation because I can't possibly understand how they feel about these three guys. What if they *are* in love? All eyes are focused on me, anticipating my response. I sigh. "I'll try my best not to kill them, but I'm not making any promises."

At those words, their shoulders relax, likely relieved knowing that my impulsive and protective nature is contained for now.

Our lovely lunchtime catch-up seems to be going well until James, Daniel, Logan, and Mark arrive in my peripheral vision. If I witness another disgusting make-out session today, I *will* lose the very little eyesight I have left. Though I only have seconds before they reach us, there's still hope in relocating the boys' intended targets and avoiding another revolting display of physical affection. If there is anything a seventh wheel has to be aware of, it is the deadly make-out.

Cue Plan A: Get them out of the danger zone. More importantly, get *myself* out of the danger zone.

"Hey, guys, I need to go to my locker. Can you come with?" I ask, suddenly standing and collecting my things.

Kiera's face scrunches in confusion. "Lunch has hardly started! Don't you want to sit down and relax for a bit?" Plan A is not working! Damn it!

I rack my brain, thinking of an alternative plan, but it's too late. The guys are walking toward our table. Mark sits beside Carol and kisses her on the cheek; Daniel wraps an arm around Kiera; and then there's the stage-curtain couple . . . *this* is when a curtain would be much appreciated.

While everyone else is at least trying to be modest, Jasmine and

Logan kiss like they're reenacting a climactic scene in a romance movie. I want to both throw up and pluck my eyeballs out. I have lost all will to eat—and eating is my core personality trait. I'm losing myself.

"Aaand that's my cue to leave," I say, snapping my fingers and stepping away from the overcrowded table. James doesn't even wait for me to fully leave the bench before pushing me aside and taking my seat. "Seriously?"

"You're leaving anyway." He shrugs.

"Already?" Jasmine says, during her brief gasp for air. She could change her career to deep-sea diver if she wanted.

"Yeah, I have to grab something from the library."

"What do you have to get from the library? We had most of our classes together this morning and *I* don't have to go to the library," James presses. "What?" he says when he sees my face. "I know. You're jealous! I mean, I don't blame you. It must be hard to be single, especially when it's not by choice—"

"I'm not jealous," I say firmly. "I'm busy." *And slightly nauseated*, I want to add. "I'll see you guys later."

I leave the cafeteria with my stomach in knots. I don't think I'm jealous that they have boyfriends. It just doesn't feel right that their boyfriends are sitting at our favorite table while I'm not. I could've stayed, but how awkward would that have been? I tell the stomach knot to untangle itself and proceed to roam the hallways until lunch ends.

I don't see the girls again until fourth period—the only class we have together. Unfortunately, that class is physical education, and the only "education" I'm getting from it is that basketball has complicated rules that I don't care about and my fitness declines exponentially with each year.

A few other girls and I stand chatting in the middle of the gymnasium, waiting for everyone else to finish changing, while the teacher collects some equipment from the storage room. Finally, Kiera, Jasmine, and Carol run onto the court—Kiera and Carol shoving each other while Jasmine tries to pry them apart. By the time they get to me, Jasmine mutters that I'll have to regulate the two athletes next time.

"Dude, why'd you leave us?" Carol asks, adjusting her long, black hair into a high ponytail.

I raise my eyebrows at her then look at Jasmine. "Some of us can't handle an extreme make-out session as well as others."

Her face flushes but she gives me a shy smile. "Lara, it's normal for couples to kiss."

"Not in the cafeteria, it's not. That place literally functions as an *eating* area. Where you eat *food*. Do you get what I'm hinting at?"

She playfully shoves my shoulder, thinking that I'm kidding, but I'm not.

The sound of a sharp whistle pierces the air, pausing all conversation and turning all the girls to face our gym teacher—a muscular woman with fiery eyes, dressed in a full tracksuit. In one hand is an old CD player and in the other, a CD case, which can only mean one thing: today I will die from running sprints and, during my autopsy, they're going to conclude death by beep test.

After the catastrophe called the beep test, we quickly change back into our regular clothes, thankful for the end of the day. The bell rings and students file out, finally free from the confines of school. Jasmine and I bid the other two girls good-bye and walk past the line of cars exiting the parking lot and in the direction of home, near High Park.

The main road is usually busy and loud, but once we get to the neighborhood, it's quieter, with houses lined up and large trees towering over the sidewalks. It usually takes us about twenty minutes to get to our houses, with Jasmine fulfilling her mandatory responsibility of listening to my rants. Mandatory because I can't shut up and this is her only way home.

"You don't get it, Jas. He's in two of my classes and he keeps being . . . *James*. I can't take it anymore," I whine, placing my head on her shoulder as we walk.

"At least that's only a hundred and fifty minutes of your day?" she offers.

"That doesn't help." I sigh dramatically. "If I pass away from stress, you might as well play 'Killer Queen' at my funeral."

"You want me to play a Queen song? On the violin?"

I shrug. "I want my burial to be a vibe."

As I begin to sing the chorus loudly with accompanying hand gestures, people walking in our direction turn their heads to stare at me. Jasmine places her hand on my mouth to prevent me from attracting more unwanted attention. "Lara! People are staring!"

I pull her hand off my mouth. "Who wouldn't? With a voice like this?" Jasmine rolls her eyes, and we continue walking.

"Jas! Lara! Wait up!" a voice shouts from behind us, triggering a groan to escape my lips. Logan runs up and kisses Jasmine on the cheek. At least they kept it PG this time.

"Can I walk you home?" Logan asks Jasmine politely.

Jasmine looks at him longingly but says, "Sorry. I always walk with Lara."

Yes! But her eyes don't drift from his, even for a moment. Her pupils dilate in the same way mine do when I first open a pizza box. Knowing that I wouldn't want my friend to keep me from my meat lover's pizza, I plaster a smile on my face. "It's fine. I'm not going to *die* if you walk with Logan. Go with him."

To Logan, my facial expression automatically switches. "I know that I only took *self-defense*, but I can defend my friends too." He gulps nervously.

Logan takes her hand and they walk in front of me. Since we're all walking on the same side of the street in the same direction, awkwardness never departs from my side. Imagine—a cute, young couple walking and holding hands followed closely by a loner girl trying to drown herself in sad Adele songs. *Wonderful.*

The lyrics to "Someone Like You" come out of my mouth in the form of an angelic screech, so beautiful that the couple stops and looks back. I can't tell if they're terrified or in awe. "Sorry, I thought you guys could use some background music. Like in romantic montages?" I quickly make a heart shape with my hands.

They turn back around, proceeding with their conversation, and I silently go back to my songs. Trying to give them space, I keep myself a few feet behind them. Who needs someone to talk to when I have my sad Adele songs, right?

TIP FOUR:
FOCUS ON FAMILY

✱

Jasmine's house arrives before mine, and Logan takes the extra steps to drop her at the front door. I walk past them to my own house, three doors down; neither of them bothers to look at me so I don't feel the need to say good-bye either. From my front porch, I have a perfect view of the couple—laughing at something and standing on her doorstep like main characters from a cheesy rom-com. Unlike a cheesy rom-com, it's less fun to observe the "rom" part in real life.

I only let myself feel upset for a minute because I had the chance to let Jasmine walk with me. But I don't know which would've been a worse feeling—this or the guilt that would eat me up at the sight of her longing to be with Logan. On the bright side, I didn't have to witness the extensive mushiness of their conversation.

As my old front door squeaks open, I enter quietly, hoping not to attract the attention of any family members who might bombard me with a million questions about school. The millisecond that my toe scratches the surface of the floor, the sound of loud yelling upstairs hits my ears.

"It's not my fault that it broke again!" Mom yells at Dad in her "sassy" tone, as we kids like to call it. They fight like this all the time, but I'm convinced it's their love language.

"*Sa dami ng damit mo, nasira na naman ang closet natin!*" (Because you have so many clothes, our closet broke again!) Dad sighs. My mom can't argue with that.

"*Mahal*," (Love) he continues. "*Ang dami mo nang damit. P'wede bang pass muna tayo sa pagbili?*" (You already have so many clothes. Can we stop shopping?)

I shake my head at the continuing battle and make my way upstairs to my tiny bedroom. I assume *Lola* (grandma) Nora must be sleeping, reading the bible, or—strangely enough—checking her Twitter feed, since no one is attacking me for updates about the latest school gossip.

My bedroom door locks with a satisfying click. The day's clothes find their way to the corner of my wooden floor, rather than my forgotten hamper sitting in our laundry room. Removing the snug sports bra and throwing it onto the bed, I sigh happily, reaching the absolute peak of comfort. After slipping on my gray sweatpants and an oversized T-shirt, I remove my hair from its intricate braid and clip it up with my favorite butterfly-shaped clamp.

Now dressed to lounge properly, I head back downstairs, only to find my mom at the foot of the staircase with a towering pile of her clothes in her arms, reaching to right below her chin. "*Kailan ka dumating, Ara?*" (When did you come home, Ara?) she asks. *Ara*, a nickname that was somehow formed because my younger sister wasn't able to produce the el sound when she was a baby.

"I came home, like, five minutes ago, but you guys were too busy fighting about your closet or something," I answer in English, too lazy to speak Tagalog because they understand me just fine. "Speaking of, why are you carrying all those clothes?"

"*Dadalhin ko sa basement para magka-room sa closet namin*," (I'm bringing them to the basement to make more room in our closet) she says in a matter-of-fact way. "*Akala niya mapipigilan niya ako sa pag-sha-shopping . . . No way.*" (He really thought he could stop me from shopping . . . No way.)

My mother is a smart woman. She's a five-foot Filipina with a shopping addiction, a brown balayage, and a brain wired to make sure she always gets her way.

"*Nasaan ang mga damit ko?!*" (Where are my clothes?!) Dad yells from upstairs.

So it doesn't surprise me that she'd choose to relocate Dad's clothes to the basement in order to create space for hers.

Mom winks in my direction before leaving, not bothering to reply to Dad's very valid question.

Before I can even think about going to the kitchen for food, the front door lets out another squeak, catching my attention; my little sister, Camilla (aka Illa) runs in, throwing her shoes off to the side of the entrance and rushing over the porcelain tiles, almost slipping as she hurries over to me. She's probably the most spunky and energetic thirteen-year-old girl you'd ever meet.

"OMG! I had the best day ever at school today! Ask me why! Ask me why!" she squeals, brushing her pink hair from her face, legs jittering underneath a floral maxi skirt. She beams from ear to ear, and I wonder how a human being can possess so much joy.

Turning around, I walk down the hallway, hoping to escape her hyperpositivity and finally get my snack but she follows. "Why? It's the first day of torture and sleeplessness—"

"Thanks for asking, *Ate*," she interrupts. *Ate* (pronounced ah-teh) is a Filipino word for older sister, or basically any older female figure. *Kuya* works in the same way, meaning older brother or an older male figure. "Guess who I'm paired up with in science class?"

I stop abruptly in the middle of the kitchen. Not this again. I'm not equipped to deal with her frequent crushes. "Who?" I ask unenthusiastically.

"Kaden Lee!" Her shriek causes my hearing range to drop by a few frequencies.

"What exactly is the big deal?"

The girl in front of me turns pale, nearing the color of paper. Instead of losing consciousness, she fishes her iPhone from her pocket and goes straight to her Instagram account. Pulling out a picture of this Kaden Lee, she holds it to my face, as if my eyesight wasn't bad enough. "Ate. *This* is the big deal. He's freaking hot."

"Yay?"

Suddenly, Lola Nora bursts into the room, eyes gleaming with excitement. Tsismis is the primary reason for her existence, and she can sense juicy gossip from a mile away.

"*Camilla, ano'ng balita? Si Kaden ba 'yon?*" (Camilla, what's the news? Is that Kaden?) She holds her hands up to her cheeks, grinning widely. Despite only being at home, she wears bright red lipstick and a rosy blush because it "keeps her youthful."

My brows scrunch in confusion. "How does she know about Kad—"

Illa shrieks. "*YES! Lab partner ko po si Kaden!!!*" (YES! Kaden's my lab partner!!!) in fluent Tagalog. When it comes to talking to our parents, it's okay to be lazy and reply in English. But Lola Nora's not fluent in English, so us speaking in Tagalog with her makes communication much easier. The language barrier doesn't stop her from watching North American reality television though.

They both scream like it's the end of the world and I raise my hands to my ears, trying to protect my eardrums. "WHAT IS HAPPENING?"

Illa giggles and waves her hand in the air. "Don't worry about it. I wouldn't expect you to get it."

Defensively, I say, "Excuse me? What are you implying?"

She blinks before extending a hand to my shoulder and nodding sympathetically. "You don't understand romance," she starts, and my jaw drops. *Did she just . . .* "But don't worry, you're going to be that rich, successful woman who never gets married."

Is that a compliment or an insult? And how is a thirteen-year-old assuming my relationship*less* future? "You should've stopped at a rich, successful woman."

She laughs before dragging Lola Nora down the hallway, proceeding up the stairs to spill her entire love story to our seventy-something-year-old grandmother instead of me. Sure, I might've implied that I couldn't care less about her crush, but I'm still her older sister. Shouldn't I be the first person she exposes the drama to?

The doorbell rings again and I internally groan. All I wanted to do was get a bag of chips, but my plans keep getting derailed. Heading over to our front door, I open it, only to see Tita Gia, aka the most luxurious Bryer, in all her glory. She's dressed to the nines on a Tuesday afternoon, sporting a perfectly fitted tweed dress reaching above the knee and a white Chanel purse hanging from her arm. With her natural poise and elegance, you'd never believe she gave birth to the terror named James. The woman goes in for a hug and barges in before I can say, "Come in."

"Lara! *Ineng* (dear), how are you!"

Tita translates to *aunt* in English. We're not related at all. Actually, she and Mom have been co-workers at Toronto General Hospital since before James and I were born and have been best friends since college. Mom works full time as a nurse practitioner, while Tita Gia works part time as an RN, juggling their family business endeavors on the side.

"I'm fine. Thanks."

Mom rushes up the basement stairs to greet her best friend. "Gia!" she shrieks, as if they didn't see each other yesterday (now you know where I get my overreactive genes from). Their chatter fades as they relocate to the kitchen.

I go back to close the door but as the universe has planned, her three children run in from the car, causing a wave of exhaustion to swallow me whole, even though *he* hasn't even reached the front step. His siblings are all younger: Gabriel is the same age as Illa, and Sebastian is six years old. It might be important to mention that our moms planned their pregnancies so that their kids would become best friends. While Illa and Gabe have always gotten along, James and I are the complete opposite. Unfortunately for our mothers' plans, James is now less of a BFF and more of a BWATCOM (Boy Who Annoys The Crap Outta Me).

Gabe reaches the door first. He's the one who looks most like Tita Gia with his tanned skin. Unlike Gabe, the other two boys have fairer skin that they inherited from Tito Danny. Gabe's the sweet one; the polite kid all the parents compare their kids to; the complete opposite of James. With a friendly wave, he says, "Hey, Ate Lara!"

"Hey! Come in, guys." *Except James*, I want to add, watching him make his way to the front porch, which I desperately wish was the edge of a cliff. Gabe slips his shoes off and adds them to the mat filled with footwear before walking past me and in the direction of the kitchen.

Seb runs up to me, shouting, "Ate Lara!" and I crouch down to accept a tight hug from him. With his two dimples and his cute little smile, Seb is the definition of adorable. He looks a lot like a miniature version of James, especially with the identical dimples on both sides of their cheeks.

Releasing Seb after a few seconds, I help him slip off his tiny sneakers and let him scurry into the house, to where the rest of the family is congregating. The clicking of the front door catches my attention and I stand back up with my arms crossed over my chest. James leans his back against the door, eyes scanning my choice of wardrobe.

"You look *beautiful* today," he says sarcastically, sporting an amused grin.

I roll my eyes. "And you're *so* charming, aren't you?"

"Of course, sweetheart," he says with a wink. Shoving his hands into the pockets of his jeans, he takes a couple of steps forward, but before he takes another one, he stops beside me. "What's with the intensely crossed arms?"

Suddenly the padded sports bra removal is less heavenly. "None of your business."

"No need to keep them crossed. Nothing much under there anyway." Then he walks past me, hitting my shoulder and leaving me stunned.

My jaw drops open and then I close it, gritting my teeth. How dare he insult my flatish chest like that! Besides, my boobs are just small, or *low-fat*—unlike the rest of me.

Mom yells, "Ara! Come here," preventing me from stomping off to my bedroom.

I begrudgingly follow her order. Tita Gia and Mom sit at our round marble table while the boys take the couch in the family room, which flows into our kitchen because of the open concept floor design.

"Sit down, *anak*. Tita Gia wants to talk to you," Mom says.

Oh no, Mom only calls me *anak* (child) when she wants me to do something.

Pulling out a chair, I sit down slowly, wondering what the two women are up to. Looking from my mom to Tita Gia, I brace myself for what's coming next.

"Lara," Tita Gia says, "I know this is a pretty big favor to ask, but it's senior year and soon enough universities will start looking at grades." She rests her hand on mine before the earthquake hits. "You see, James is going to be applying for a few competitive business programs and he's not the strongest math student . . ."

No, Tita, please no.

I try to hide my twisting facial expression as she continues. "You've always been so smart, and I wanted to ask if you'd tutor him? We've hired a bunch of professional tutors and none of them seem to be working. Your tito and I figured that maybe he'd feel more comfortable with a friend. Plus, remember when you guys worked together on that science project in grade eight? That turned out great!"

A friend? We're right off the dartboard on that one. And that science project was done way before our relationship took *this* wild turn. He was bearable back then!

My instinct is to deny immediately. "That would be so great, but actually—" Mom grabs my wrist under the table before she proceeds to interrupt me.

"*Bes*," she says to Tita Gia, calling her a common Filipino term of endearment for your best friend. "*One second lang*." (Give me one second.)

With my wrist in hand, she pulls me away from the table to the living room, separated from the family room and kitchen only by a single wall. Once alone, she whispers, "*Ara, mahiya ka naman. Ang bait-bait ng tita mo sa inyo, pero hindi mo man lang matulungan?*"

(Lara, you should be embarrassed. Your tita is so nice to you guys, but you can't even help her?)

I see we're using the classic *mahiya ka naman* (you should be embarrassed) . . . nice. "Mom, you know that James and I aren't friends."

"*Sige na, Ara. Sino ba ang naghahatid sa 'yo no'ng elementary pa kayo? Araw-araw pa 'yon,*" (C'mon, Ara. Who dropped you off to school before? That was every single day,) she reminds me.

I grumble. "Tita Gia."

As much as I hate James, Tita Gia has always been a second mother to me. In addition to dropping us off at school, she would lead the decorating committee at my birthday parties, attend all my elementary school science fairs, and occasionally bring me things that she would've passed down to her own daughter, if she had one. What kind of monster would I be if I didn't help her?

Sighing, I give my mom a small nod and she pats my shoulder approvingly before leading me back into the kitchen. Tita Gia is tapping on her phone screen but places her cell phone on the table when we enter. "Do you think you can do it? We'll pay you too."

When the painful *yes* refuses to leave my mouth, Mom nudges my arm. I clear my throat before inevitably agreeing to my own doom. "Sure, I can try my best to help him."

Tita Gia beams and stands up to hug me. "Thank you, ineng."

I leave them at the table to continue their conversation, joining the now two boys in the family room. James and Seb sit beside each other on the smaller couch, James glued to his phone and Seb watching his brother scroll through whatever it is. "Where'd your kuya Gabe go?" I ask Seb, taking a seat on the adjacent couch.

"With Ate Illa," he replies, sliding off of his seat and walking over to me. As usual, the two best friends—Illa and Gabe—are hanging out. At least Mom and Tita Gia's plan for their kids to be friends worked a little. James and I were the first trial, but that became a horrible failure.

Seb crawls onto my lap with a mischievous grin, gesturing for me to lean closer. "Ate Lara, I wanna tell you something."

"What is it?"

Cupping both hands against my ear, he whispers, "Kuya's looking at you funny," causing my face to heat up, embarrassed for whatever reason.

I frown before making a quick turn, eyeing James. The kid is indeed correct, he is looking at me funny. It doesn't last that long until he goes back to his cell phone. I have a few things to say to James but I don't want to do it in front of Seb. "Seb, I think Gabe and Illa are watching TV upstairs. Why don't you see what they're watching?"

He grins widely before nodding and running off, leaving James and me alone to quarrel. James looks up from his phone right away, proceeding to shove it into his back pocket. We stare at each other, me trying to ignore the annoying smirk tugging on his lips.

"Why do you do this?" I whisper because we're within hearing range of our mothers. Though they aren't paying attention to us judging from their loud laughs over discussing a *teleserye*.

He shrugs. "Do what?" he whispers back.

"First, you embarrass me in the school hallway. Then you magically show up in a class that you weren't taking before. And now you need my help in math?"

Cocking his head to the side, he places a hand on my shoulder. "Thanks for restating today's events, but I don't see any problem with coincidence."

Coincidence? "That's not the word I'd use to describe this situation," I say, slapping his hand away from me.

"Since our friends are now busy with each other, I thought you would have much more time on your hands to help a struggling student," he says with a pout.

I almost choke on my own saliva. "Okay, Bryer, what's the deal this time? Is this another elaborate scheme of yours to, I don't know, prank me in front of a bunch of people this week? I know I was feeling merciful this morning, but you should really watch your back."

"Listen, I need help with math. You're good at math. My parents think I need a good peer influence. You're a scam artist and people think of you as a good person. It's quite simple, Dela Cruz. I'm not doing any sorcery."

Before I can argue any further, Tita Gia's voice pierces the air. "Boys! We're leaving!"

Gabe and Seb run down the stairs while James and I emerge from the family room, everyone gathering at the front landing. Tita Gia slips her heels back on before asking, "Lara, what days are you available to tutor James again?"

"Fridays are pretty goo—"

My mom interrupts me midsentence. "Isn't it easier if they work on homework together daily? You guys have the same subjects after all."

Is she trying to get rid of me or something?

Tita Gia's face lights up. "That's right! That way you guys can figure out the work gradually instead of waiting for the end of the week! Does that work with your schedule, Lara?"

"Well—"

Mom speaks on my behalf. Again. "She's not busy. All she does is sleep."

"What? No, I don't!"

James buds in and I pray for his contradiction to this agreement.

"We usually have a hockey game each week but other than that I'm down."

That hardly helps. "How about practice? Don't you have to go to those at least twice a week?"

He shrugs. "Coach is a fan of morning practices."

Tita Gia claps happily. James is obviously happy because I'm annoyed, and Mom is probably glad to get rid of my ritual four o'clock nap. Social rules suppress my opposition and I hold a very uncomfortable smile. As they leave, they also leave me with a completely new schedule that makes me slightly disgusted.

Holy fishballs.

TIP FIVE:
BE POLITE WHEN THIRD WHEELING

✱

Wednesdays.

If there's anything that is almost as terrible as Mondays, it has to be Wednesdays. It's not a fresh start to a week, nor a happy ending. It just interrupts the rhythm of naturally paired days like Saturday and Sunday, Monday and Tuesday, and Thursday and Friday. Wednesday is the third wheel. I feel like that should make me enjoy the day out of empathy, but I hate it.

Other students don't seem to share my disdain for the day. They actually look alive and the third-floor hallway buzzes with conversation. It's probably because the second day of school still holds some excitement about being back. And I suppose most students didn't have a brutal, life-altering first day where they found out they were the only single person left in their friend group.

Kiera said she was already at school, so I walk in the direction of our spot, simultaneously trying to convince myself that day two can't possibly be as bad as day one. When I see James, my mood falls a couple more notches. He isn't facing my direction, which is a God-given miracle. I slowly backpedal to behind another wall, planning my detour. I might be overexaggerating, but I don't want any unnecessary contact with James, especially now that we have a mandatory schedule together.

Taking another peek at the hall, I see his figure is nowhere to be seen. The coast is clear. Finally, I can continue to my destination.

I turn around to depart from my beloved wall, but the surprise of James's sudden presence causes me to jolt backward, and I slam against it almost immediately. Ouch.

I look up to see his dark-brown eyes peering into mine, almost looking concerned, and a section of his wavy hair falls over his brows. "You good?"

"*Splendid*," I groan.

"Are you avoiding me?" he asks.

"Is it illegal to do so?"

He pretends to think, then responds. "At least tell me why."

I step to the side and begin walking away, but he follows me. "I don't know, maybe it's because I don't like you and people tend to avoid things they don't like. It's, like, an evolutionary trait."

He runs right in front of me, blocking my path. This again.

"Get out of my way. I have somewhere to be."

Taking a step forward so that our toes are almost touching, he leans down so that his smirking face hovers above mine. "Make me."

So I do.

I stomp on his foot; not hard enough to break any toes but enough for him to press his lips together in a grimace. I'm sure he's been expecting my revenge after tripping me on the first day of school and now, he doesn't have to expect it anymore.

I quickly hurry away from him but he chases me. He's the only person who can make me exercise, and I hate him for it. We look like little kids playing a game of tag, and some teachers yell at us to stop, but with James on my trail, the reprimands are ignored. Seeing the girls, I run straight into them.

Taking Kiera's shoulders, I hold her in front, in order to keep space between me and the enemy. James and I do that thing where you both go to one side and then to the other. Kiera really picked a bad time to have her hair in a ponytail because I end up catching some frizzy blond strands in my mouth.

Kiera, still sandwiched between me and James, begs Jasmine to pull her away from us, but I can't let her go.

Then the three boys approach us, waving. Logan takes his place beside Jasmine, offering to take the textbooks from her arms, while Mark points at me and James shuffling around Kiera. "What's happening *here*?" We both ignore him.

"Seems like Lara's too occupied to kill us today," Daniel jokes, removing his denim jacket and tying it around his waist. His braids are tied up in a bun, and a single earring accents his outfit.

I narrow my eyes at all three of them. "You'd be surprised at how good I am at multitasking."

Daniel begins to approach Kiera for a kiss, but I interrupt him. "Really, Daniel? Don't you see that Kiera is in the middle of helping me here!"

She pushes my hands off of her shoulders and goes to her boyfriend. This is the point in my life where I doubt our years of friendship.

A millisecond after Kiera's betrayal, James engulfs me in his arms, immobilizing my upper body. My legs become useless as he lifts me from the ground and presses my back against his chest. Like any sane person, I scream. Our friends cover their faces as students stop and stare at me. James and I are used to the weird looks.

Suddenly, Ms. K walks by with binders in her arms and stops to look at us. She adjusts her glasses before asking, "Darling, are you all right?"

I struggle against James's grip. "Considering I'm being held captive by the person I hate most, I'd say *no*. C'mon, Ms. K, I'm sure if we work together, we can get him suspended."

James laughs and Ms. K does the same. "James, I don't think this is the best way of trying to get a girlfriend."

James puts me down and lets go. "Well, it usually works."

Ms. K shoots us another smile before she goes on her way.

Kiera and Daniel leave shortly after, heading to the sign-up sheet for volleyball, while James and Logan converse about their first hockey practice this morning. Jasmine nods along to their conversation, though she's never had an interest in hockey . . . ever. Carol and Mark are the least annoying pair, so I glue myself to them.

"Wanna walk around before class?" Mark asks Carol, almost immediately when I step foot beside her.

"Good idea! Let's go!" I intervene. Before she can respond, I link my right arm with her left and begin walking quickly. Mark catches up and stands in front of us, clasping his hands before saying, "Sorry, but I think there's a third-wheel situation going on here."

Shaking my head, I look at Mark. "You're right. I didn't want to say this, but, Mark, you're kind of being a third wheel."

He rolls his eyes. "Lara, can I please walk with my girlfriend?"

"Of course," I say. "If you don't feel awkward tagging along with us, I don't mind you being here."

Mark begrudgingly accepts the situation and takes Carol's free hand as we promenade the hall.

"*So*," I start, talking to Carol and dismissing Mark's presence entirely. "For mall and movie night, I'm thinking that we have dinner at that new Korean barbeque place instead of at the mall. We can still do some window shopping before the movie, but I heard that new restaurant is really good."

The LKJC has always done mall and movie nights downtown at least once a month, ever since our parents gave us a pinch of freedom. It's a tradition that causes us to spend more money than we should.

"That's next Friday, right?" Carol asks.

"Yeah."

Mark stops in his tracks, which causes the rest of us to halt too. "Wait, is that the restaurant with the garden patio?"

I nod. "It is! Have you been?"

He and Carol look at each other before she goes, "Yeah . . . actually, we had our first date there."

Out of the blue, Carol starts laughing. "Do you remember that dude in the line?" she asks Mark. He pauses for a second before bursting out laughing too. I stand beside them, more lost than ever.

The two recount their interesting first date while I listen in, smiling when they laugh and not understanding any of their inside jokes. They don't bother to add any context for me to get what they're referencing, and when the bell rings for class, I feel surprisingly relieved to leave the situation.

After arriving late at the cafeteria and realizing that no spots are available at our table, I spend the second official lunch without my friends. Instead of having a chaotic conversation with the girls, I sit alone on a prickly carpeted floor in the back corner of the library, staring at large book spines about biology and sneaking bites of a sandwich while hiding.

I hardly expect anyone to spend their forty-minute lunch break here, which is why I'm surprised at the sound of footsteps growing closer to me. Someone has managed to find their way to my exact lunch spot. Getting up, I pretend to examine the spines of the old anatomy books, then look over and sneak glances at the tall boy beside me.

He has light-brown hair that almost reaches his broad shoulders and looks about as tall as James. From the side, his face has familiarity, but I can't be too sure. His head shifts a little, causing me to look back down at the bookshelf before I get caught staring.

A familiar voice goes, "Lara?" and I know for sure who the brunet is. *No way . . .*

"Oh my God, Xander! What are you doing here? Don't you go to St. Augustine's?"

Xander was a friend I made back in the summer after tenth grade, when I volunteered at the children's hospital for the first time. Back then he looked like an average teenage boy: short, a face full of acne, and rectangular glasses that sat on the bridge of his nose. And of course, I'll never forget his extensive graphic T-shirt collection, which revolved around Star Wars and Marvel—that was good.

Now, he's probably close to a foot taller than me and his face has magically cleared up, with only a couple of acne scars and small breakouts. The glasses have disappeared completely, and his style has evolved from Sheldon Cooper to Leonardo DiCaprio from the 90s. What a plot twist.

He closes his book and walks over to me, beaming brightly. "I did," he says, "but I'm living with my dad now and this school's closer. I didn't even remember you went here. If I had, I would've told you."

"And how's Anannya?" I ask, while fully taking out the sandwich from my lunch bag.

When I say her name, his green eyes light up and I know that they're going steady. I'm glad for that because *I'm* the one who got them together with my romantic expertise. Anannya is the nicest upperclassman I've met, and though Xander was a stuttering mess around her, I was the great wing woman who hyped up his personality and got her attention. Then I pulled the guys let's have lunch together at this place thing, then I "accidentally" couldn't make it, causing a chain of reactions leading to their relationship.

"Anannya's doing great. She started med sci at Western and is really excited about it. Hopefully, I'll join her next year." He crosses his fingers.

"I'm glad to hear that."

"How about you?" he asks. "Where are you off to next year?"

My brain turns to jelly whenever people ask me that. When you get near grade twelve, it's assumed you know exactly what you want to do and where you want to go. Everyone seems to have an idea about top choices and programs and scholarships, and that scares me because I only have a slight inclination toward what I want to pursue. It's only September, and I really don't want to think about university until it's absolutely necessary.

I let out a small laugh. "Wherever I get accepted. Maybe a science program?" It's the same answer I've given to everyone who's asked me. That summer with Xander and Anannya, I fell in love with the hospital and the patients and the caretakers, so much so that I started to think about a career in medicine. But that's something I like to keep for myself because I don't know if my mind's going to change. And even if it doesn't, what am I supposed to say to people if I don't make it?

He smiles. "You'd be great in science. You should think about applying to some type of health program, I think it would really suit you."

Comforting warmth envelops my body when he says that. "Thanks."

The warning bell rings, and I pack up my stuff, happy to have seen Xander and even happier that I was able to finish my lunch without getting caught. We walk out of the library together and out of the corner of my eye, I see the KJC packing up their stuff at our table, with their guys beside them. Their smiles are big. I pull out my phone, which has no new notifications, and I wonder if they even noticed I was gone.

Standing on James's front porch, I wait impatiently for him to open the door. Having been to his house a million times before, I shouldn't be so awestruck, but the enormity of it never fails to amaze me. I have no clue how anyone can afford a house this big, especially in the inflated city of Toronto. It screams luxury from the outside: gray stone lining the front, two large pillars beside the huge wooden door, a driveway with a roundabout, a beautiful garden, and a garage with three doors! Three! Can you believe that?

I ring the doorbell one more time and at that very second the door opens and James greets me with a cheerful grin. "Hey."

I push past him and let myself in, taking my shoes off and heading to the kitchen. It's kind of like a maze in here, but I mastered it a long time ago. I know every nook and cranny after playing endless games of hide and seek, hide and seek in the dark, and hide and weep (a game we made up that was probably more traumatizing than fun).

"Where are you going?" he asks, following me as I go through the front corridor, turn left into the living room, continue to the dining room, and eventually head close to the kitchen, where the aroma of freshly cooked food fills the air.

"Your kitchen, duh."

Maybe it's considered rude to go straight to someone's kitchen without invitation, but Tita Gia always tells me to make myself at home, and at home, I like to eat. Plus, the Bryers have an entire pantry filled with good snacks that I regularly raid.

Like every room in this house, the kitchen is huge. We enter and James's grandmother, Lola Edna (Tita Gia's mom) sings an old Tagalog song while stirring up something in a large pan. She notices my presence and her eyes light up. "*Lara! Ano'ng ginagawa mo dito? Kumain ka muna!*" (Lara! What are you doing here? Eat first!) she says excitedly.

"*Tutulungan ko lang po si James sa math. Ano po ang niluluto n'yo? Parang masarap, e,*" (I'm going to help James with math. What are you cooking? Looks good,) I respond, setting my backpack down on the floor and taking a seat on a tall stool in front of the kitchen island.

Like my Lola, Lola Edna immigrated here at an older age and doesn't speak fluent English. So I switch to Tagalog when I'm around her too. I glance at James, who's standing beside the counter and staring at me blankly. Although he's half Filipino, he doesn't speak nor understand Tagalog. But James and Lola Edna get along well because they try really hard to understand each other. For their tight-knit family, a language barrier means nothing.

"*Masarap talaga 'to! Specialty ko 'yan!*" (This is really good! It's my special recipe!) Lola Edna says, pushing a large plate of *pancit*—a Filipino noodle dish—toward me, along with a fork. I thank her while admiring the concoction of diced vegetables and chicken on stir-fried egg noodles.

"*Apo*, you want too?" she asks James. *Apo* is our term for grandchild.

"No, thank you, Lola. I'm still full," he says, patting his stomach. *His loss*, I think to myself.

The first bite is divine, and I devour the rest in under five minutes, catching James staring at me as I finish up. Creep. "What? Do I have something on my face?" I ask, wiping my mouth with the back of my hand.

He shakes his head. "Nah, but you eat like you've been starved for ages."

Unbothered by his comment (which happens to be true), I shrug and thank Lola Edna for the meal, placing the empty plate in the sink.

"*Walang anuman*," (No problem,) she says before turning to James, reaching up to pat his cheek. He leans down slightly so she can reach his face. Raising an eyebrow, she goes, "Study well, *ha*?"

He gives her one of his classically charming smiles. "Of course."

Pleased by his reply, Lola Edna walks away, leaving the two of us alone in the kitchen.

"So where do you want to study?" James asks. "We could study in the library, or the living room, or . . . my room?" he suggests with his mischievous smirk.

Ignoring his joke, I haul my backpack to the little table separate from the kitchen island, beside the French doors leading to their backyard. "Let's study here. There's nice natural light coming in through the window."

He pulls up a chair beside me. "Are you scared of my bedroom?"

I'm not exactly sure what emotion that statement is supposed to elicit. I'm getting paid to teach him how to factor, not to entertain his lewd, messed-up fantasies. "Okay, then . . . how about we start on today's math?"

"You're no fun, Lara. You do realize that a whole lot of girls would love to be invited up to my room."

I pause the stacking of my books on the table to laugh in his face—a good, hearty laugh that must sound like a donkey. "Maybe that's because they haven't seen you with snot dripping down your nose for, like, the first seven years of your life. Now please stop wasting my time and tell me what you don't understand from the lesson."

He grunts, grabbing my textbook from the top of the pile and opening it up to the first chapter. "Fine. I guess let's start with the whole even and odd function thing. Like how the hell am I supposed to know which equation goes with what graph? Isn't that what Desmos is for?"

"Yes, but during the test, the only graphing calculator you'll have is your brain, which is why you need to train it to recognize a couple of patterns."

I point out some of the key concepts from the lesson and explain them in my own words. Then we go over some homework problems together until it seems like he's got the hang of things. After a couple of hours, he seems comfortable with the material and honestly, I'm not surprised. He's smarter than he makes himself seem. Yes, he needs someone to drive the "smart" out of him, but it's there.

"Wow, I'm actually really smart," he boasts, reading my mind and standing up to stretch his arms. "I could probably score higher than you if I start trying."

I snort. "Smart is the overstatement of the year." No point in complimenting him when his ego's already as inflated as Toronto's real estate market.

"You always have to burst my bubble."

"It's my specialty." I shrug before getting up and collecting my things. "Looks like we're done here, so I'm going home."

As I'm slipping my books into my backpack, he says, "Wait, give me your number."

"Just call the landline," I say, trying to avoid any nonessential communication. "Your parents know the number since our mothers talk 24/7." The last thing I need are weird messages.

"Oh okay. I'm sure a conversation with any of your family members will be very interesting."

Don't punch him, Lara, keep your cool. Instead of freaking out, I smack my cell phone into the middle of his open palm and victory paints itself on his face. But when he opens the screen, the look of victory is immediately replaced with a frown. I am so glad that I recently changed my lock-screen wallpaper to one that says *Don't touch my phone, you stupid idiot. You don't know the password anyway.*

How fitting for this situation.

He passes back the phone and I enter my password. We do a swap of numbers, and with that his existence is forever noted on my electronic device.

"Oh, by the way, I—" he starts, but the sound of the front door opening interrupts him.

"Okay, Seb, we're home, na. You can take your backpack off now," Ate Kelly says from the foyer. She's been living with the Bryers ever since Seb turned one and is the best nanny they've ever had. When James and I were younger, his nanny was a lot more like a tyrant and that obviously didn't amount to anything good considering we were always fooling around.

"I don't wanna!" Seb whines before the sound of faster, littler footsteps gets louder. He runs into the kitchen with his tiny backpack and Gabe trails behind him.

"Ate Lara!" he shouts, rushing to me and hugging my legs.

I lift him up. "How was your day?" I ask both the boys.

Seb's eyes light up and his hands gesture excitedly. "It was so fun! At recess we played tag and I was *it* and I caught a lot of people, and I ran so much!"

"Wow! That does sound fun! How about you, Gabe?"

"Quite uneventful, actually." He yawns. "We were working on an

English essay. Illa and I are partners for a French project. That's about it." I smile and nod but on the inside I think, *Illa better not let Gabe do all of the work.* She has a track record of getting distracted and procrastinating when it comes to school.

Setting Seb back down, I hurl my bag over my shoulder.

"You're going home already?" Seb pouts, the cutest sad expression I've ever seen.

"Don't worry, bud," James says, patting his back. "You'll see Ate Lara again tomorrow and a lot more often."

Seb beams brightly and that look makes up for everything I have to endure with James. Yes, I'd rather not help my mortal enemy, but if being here means that I get to see that adorable child, my day is made.

James walks me to the front door and I slip my shoes on. "I'll drive you home," he says, and I raise an eyebrow. He's driven me once before, two weeks after he received his driver's license. That day, we both realized that we shouldn't be bickering in an enclosed space together with one of us responsible for our safety. Never again, I had said.

"No thanks. I'm trying to kill two birds with one stone and keep myself alive while avoiding you." If anything, the walk home will give me some time to de-stress.

Still, he puts his shoes on and laces them up.

"I said you don't have to drive me home, Bryer."

"Don't worry, I won't. Are you ready to go for a walk?" He offers his arm.

I roll my eyes and walk out the door as he follows me. Stupid boys trying to be cute and all. Knowing James, something is definitely up, and it isn't cute at all.

Outside, we stroll down the sidewalk in silence; the cool evening air rustles the leaves on the surrounding trees against each other. The silence is awkward because we're used to arguing loudly in each other's presence. Grabbing my earphones from my sweater pocket, I decide that listening to anything—or pretending to—will help me avoid this situation entirely. But after a minute of attempting to untangle the annoying wires, I give up and put them back.

"Why are you walking me home?" I finally ask. "My house is literally only twenty minutes away."

"Mom's gonna kill me if you get kidnapped," he answers, shoving his hands into the pockets of his jeans as he turns to smile at me. "Gotta keep you safe, y'know?" His dimples make this situation a million times more deadly than it has to be.

"*Me*? Safe with *you*?" I say, pointing a finger at myself then at him.

He playfully shoves me, causing me to step onto the grass. I push him back and step back on the sidewalk. We continue our walk until we finally reach my house. I take a step on my driveway, but his fingers wrap around my wrist, pulling me back, though they immediately release when I give him a puzzled look. Clearing his throat he says, "Thanks, you know, for tutoring me."

"I'd have thought you were being serious for once if you hadn't tried to convince me that you were an undiscovered genius half an hour ago."

He shakes his head. "No, really. I know you don't want to do this, but it actually does mean something to me. I couldn't care less about math or a business program or college in general, but my dad does. I don't want to disappoint him."

Suddenly, we both get serious. "Is Tito Danny coming back anytime soon?"

A deep sigh follows before he says, "I doubt it. He promised to visit for Christmas, but we'll see what happens. He's trying, he really is. Things are just . . . busy."

"Yeah." I don't try to reassure him or say something to get his hopes up because Tito Danny has a reputation for being busy, and it never seems to change.

"Anyway, you should go get some rest or scare people with your face," he says, "or whatever people like you do with your spare time." The idiot flicks my forehead and I slap his hand away before running to my front doorstep.

"Bye, loser!" I yell back at him.

He waves and walks back in the opposite direction. When he's out of sight, I find myself lingering at the door longer than usual. It's always been like this. James and I pester each other repeatedly and then once in a while he shares things and it makes me feel like we're friends again—but we're not, and I don't think we ever will be.

I don't know how I feel right now, and it scares me. The way I deal with most scary things is by texting the group chat and asking for advice. So that is what I do.

Me: *Is anyone able to talk right now?*

Usually, at least one of them answers. They almost always have their phones on them, and Kiera, especially, is very fast with her replies. I sit on the porch bench and wait for a bit, listening to the faint chirping of birds mixed with steady wind. No replies.

I try to FaceTime the group instead, but the ringtone plays for far too long with nobody picking up in the end. Maybe they're busy. I probably shouldn't bother them with my problems anyway.

Me: *It's okay, I got it*

I have the best friends in the world. Although I don't have much evidence of that right now, I know it must be true. We've been together for so long that it needs to be. But why does it feel like every friendship I've held has slipped through my fingertips so easily?

TIP SIX:
ALWAYS HUNT FOR THE TRUTH

✸

The next morning arrives with zero replies to my messages. Once at school, I go straight to our spot on the third floor, like usual. The only difference is nobody is waiting there. I pull out my phone and take a look at the time. I'm not early and Carol's the only one I expect to be late.

They should be coming any minute now. I send another message to add onto my previous ones. *Where are they?* I stare at my phone, pretending that I'm actually doing something when really, I'm avoiding the shame that comes with being alone in a high school hallway. After a while, I realize that nobody's going to arrive, so I decide to walk around and find some other people to talk to. The only person I run into is James, and he comes right up to me before I can even run in the opposite direction.

"Dude, you won't believe what I saw on Instagram," he says, which catches me off guard. No insult or anything annoying?

"What is it?"

He shoves his phone to my face, and I slap his hand away. "James, I'm trying to look at the screen, not kiss it."

"Sorry, just thought I'd accommodate for your lack of vision." His finger pushes my glasses down to the tip of my nose, and I take his hand, twisting his wrist slightly. Pulling his hand away, he narrows his eyes at me, and I smile sarcastically.

I take the phone from his hand and look at the picture—a blond-haired girl and a guy walking down a busy street, holding hands. Cute. They're even wearing matching sunglasses.

"Why are you showing this to me? If you're trying to make me feel bad about being single, you're not exactly in a relationship either!"

"Look closely."

I squint at the photos. Wait a second. Is that? Oh *no*, it can't be . . . can it?

My eyes widen. Kiera Elizabeth Jones! With Daniel—I don't know his middle name—Samuels! No wonder the girl was too busy to answer my texts!

"I was surprised too," James says. "Daniel hates taking photos, let alone smiling in them! Now here he is doing a little photo shoot with his girl. Lara, what's that thing you always talk about again? Like, when I make fun of you for reading? Give me a second . . . ah, character development. Yeah, I think Daniel's going through that."

He takes his phone back and starts swiping through the post, which was uploaded last evening. In one photo, Logan is giving Jasmine a piggyback ride. James swipes to a candid shot of Carol and Mark talking. Did they all decide to become influencers or something? This is what I get for avoiding social media.

When I thought they were busy, I didn't think *this* was the business they were attending to. A part of me had a hunch that they were spending time with their boyfriends, so I wouldn't have been surprised about that. But they were together. Kiera, Jasmine, and Carol were together. Without me. I bite my lip, trying not to overanalyze the situation and failing drastically.

"Lara?"

Blinking away my invasive thoughts, I look up to see James with furrowed brows. I speak first, before he can ask me what's wrong. "Did you know that they were going out yesterday? I was texting the girls, and nobody replied."

He shakes his head. "No one said anything."

Our conversation ends when the bell rings, but the drama has yet to begin. And beginnings come simultaneously with first period and two of the three boyfriends.

"Logan Ford and Daniel Samuels!" I shout, entering the classroom and drawing the attention of the students who are filing in.

The two boys turn to me, wide eyed; they stand, holding their hands up defensively. "Kiera hasn't cried in the past forty-eight hours," Daniel says calmly. "I swear I've done no harm to your friend."

Not what I was wondering.

Stepping up to them, I stare them down. As you already know, being intimidating is tough when you're a foot shorter than the ones you're trying to intimidate. Though it seems to be working, as Logan avoids my intense gaze.

"Where were you last evening?"

"I was at home doing homework," Logan says. My eyes drift to the blank notebook sitting on his desk. *If he's going to lie, he might as well make it a reasonable one . . .*

Unlike Logan, who seems to sweat from guilt, Daniel sports a poker face. "I was at the gym."

Lies. All lies. "And you guys didn't see my friends after school yesterday?"

They shake their heads calmly.

"'Cause I haven't heard from them, and I thought you'd know where they were."

Logan presses his lips together before giving in. "We were with them! They didn't want you to know and I really didn't want to lie but they made us and please, please don't kill me I really want to live and I'm too young to die!" He drops to his knees right as Mr. Garcia enters the classroom.

Mr. Garcia looks at Logan, then Daniel, then me, his face resembling someone whose soul has been sucked out. "Is this how we're starting off our Thursday morning?"

I nod.

Our teacher sighs. "They don't pay me enough to deal with this," he says before going back to the hallway. "I need another coffee."

Once he leaves, my attention shifts back to Logan, who's still on the ground, begging for forgiveness. I didn't think I was that threatening but I suppose forwarding him screenshots of organ prices made a mark on his brain. "As much as I enjoy seeing you like this, can I ask why?"

Daniel shrugs. "Logan's pretty much an idiot and a lost cause so—"

"I meant why did they not want to tell me?"

"I don't know," he says. This time, I know it's the truth.

Only *my* friends would be dumb enough to go on a top-secret photo shoot and post it all over Instagram. Though I wonder if I would've found out if James hadn't ambushed me with the posts this morning.

Carol always says that the LKJC is unbreakable. One time, last year, I brought up the idea of us drifting apart after high school. I don't know why, but I figured that all friend groups do that. She shook her head and promised that we wouldn't. Jasmine said she'd text us every day and Kiera said that she would FaceTime us at every spare moment—even if she was paragliding in another country. But that was before they got boyfriends. Now, it seems like even the unbreakable can't avoid a few cracks.

Lunch arrives and I wiggle through the packed cafeteria, marching up to my friends, who are already seated at a table—their boyfriends have yet to land, which is good. They look up and smile innocently at me. I return the smile but feel a tinge of disgust inside.

"Hey, Lara!" Kiera greets me. It's almost concerning that they can act so normal after deliberately asking their boyfriends to lie to me. I take a seat beside Jasmine and plop my stuff on the bench.

"As I was saying," Kiera continues, "I have to pick between backpacking across Europe or backpacking across Asia. On one hand, I'll be able to save money with the Asia trip because things are generally less expensive with the currency exchange, but on the other hand I'd be able to stay with my aunt in Paris if I did Europe."

"Can't you do both?" Carol asks, biting the nail of her thumb as she thinks.

"I'm not rich!" Kiera exclaims, hands flying up in the air so that her array of bracelets shifts down her arm, and I hear faint metal clinks. "And I need to decide soon because my aunt's planning for some huge renovations and she said she'd postpone them if I visited. Plus, this decision would also impact whether or not I get a second job."

When I open my container of hot noodles, the nearby air goes warm, and my glasses fog up. Cleaning the lenses with the edge of my shirt, I wonder what the heck is going on. Europe? Asia? How much did I miss after one lunch? Or was it during the summer? Kiera always talked about leaving Toronto as soon as she got the chance. Whether it was choosing a university on the other side of the world or daydreaming about endless vacations—she wanted out of our city.

And I knew she was going to leave, we all knew. I just never expected it to come so soon.

"If you ask me," Jasmine says, "I think Asia sounds like a good choice. You've been obsessed with Japanese culture for the longest time and judging from your extensive pros and cons list yesterday, there are a lot of things you want to see. Plus, if you need to save money, I'm sure I can ask my relatives in Beijing to help you find a place to stay for cheap."

"Mine too," Carol adds. "If you're planning to take a route to India, my family would probably try to adopt you once I say you're one of my best friends."

I swirl a fork around my noodles, clueless as to how to contribute to the conversation. *What pros and cons list are they talking about?*

"What do you think, Lara?" asks Kiera. "Should I go to Europe or Asia? I can't remember what you said about it yesterday."

My gaze, which was fixated on my food, switches to Kiera. *Neither*, I want to say. *You could stay here. And you can't remember what I said about it yesterday because I wasn't there.* Carol and Jasmine look completely unfazed, meaning that they also didn't notice my absence. My heart sinks; it's probably done that too many times this week, but I choose to ignore the sound of it crashing in the pit of my stomach, focusing instead on the indistinguishable mix of conversation going on around us.

I already forgave them for not noticing my absence at lunch yesterday and deep down, I know I've already forgiven them for not answering my texts, regardless of the apology or lack thereof. It's easier that way, to avoid further conflict. In a few more months, everyone will be discussing their future plans and none of this petty stuff will matter. Maybe I won't remember how they forgot about me. I can already feel the world shifting, like how it was when Pangaea broke apart; and if I stayed mad about every little thing that happened, I'd be exactly like that saber-toothed squirrel in *Ice Age*, who catalyzed the continental drift.

Kiera's voice snaps me out of my daze. "Lara?"

I smile. "Asia. You'd like it there, and if you want to go to the Philippines, my family would love to let you stay for a bit."

Excitedly, she clasps her hands. "Perfect! It's set! This time next year, I'll be backpacking across Asia!"

We take a moment to clap for Kiera's decision but all I want to do is go back in time, when none of this mattered and nobody was getting ready to leave. I wish for it to be freshman year again, when Kiera's biggest problem was holding her drool in every time she saw a cute senior boy in the hallway.

Once the clapping fades away, I ask, "So, where were you guys this morning? I texted you."

"Ran a bit late," Carol says nonchalantly. "Were you guys not with Lara?"

"Kiera and I were finishing up an assignment," Jasmine answers. I can't tell if they're lying or not, but to avoid feeling worse, I convince myself that they're not.

"Okay, cool, but where were you guys yesterday? I was in the middle of a situation." *Are they going to lie to me now?*

"I had to take my brothers to karate practice and my phone ran out of battery," Carol says without hesitation. She's the best liar there is, but she's not supposed to use her skill on me!

I nod, pretending to believe her, then look at the other two.

"Me?" Kiera asks, pointing a perfectly manicured finger at her chest. "I had a dentist appointment. Ugh." *Of course, a dentist appointment on Bloor Street with cute sunglasses and matching outfits with Daniel.*

Next, my eyes go to Jasmine, who is looking for the nearest exit because she cannot lie for the sake of anything. It's the exact same face she had when they confessed their relationship status to me.

"I was—I was at the library," she manages to stutter.

"Carol was at a dojo, Kiera was at the dentist, and Jasmine was at the library? That's great. Who's ready to admit that they're lying? Unless, of course, you took those lovely Instagram photos at the dentist's office," I say, smiling sweetly.

They stare at me in disbelief.

"Quick tip, maybe don't post your date photos all over Instagram," I say and they all frown, knowing that I stay clear of any and all social media to protect my mental health. Before they can question me, I add, "I found out through my sources." By sources, I mean James.

"What? We never posted anything," Jasmine says.

I scoff. *Please don't tell me they're acting dumb about it too.*

Carol follows with, "I didn't post anything either." They narrow their eyes at Kiera, who is grinning nervously, her double chin as gorgeous as ever.

"I may have posted a couple . . . *dozen* pictures on my Instagram," she confesses.

Carol facepalms. "You're actually an idiot. I don't even want to look at you right now."

"The pictures matched my feed *so well!* How could I *not* post them?" Kiera justifies herself, pulling out her phone. "See? The pictures are so pretty!"

While the other two girls slap their foreheads, all I'm able to say is, "Why did you guys have to lie to me?" And it's a genuine question because there was honestly no point to it. I'm not a parent who can get mad about rules being broken, nor would I have convinced them not to go. I begin to wonder if this is really about their boyfriends.

What if it's about *me*? After all, a lot can change after one summer and if I'm not on the same wavelength as them, like how it's always been, where does that leave our friendship?

Jasmine opens her mouth as if to say something, but quickly closes it again at a loss of words.

Carol goes, "We didn't want you to feel like you were being left out, since we'd be, you know—"

How ironic that they're inclined to lie in order to protect my feelings. "Yeah, I get that. But you should've told me instead of lying."

"We're sorry. We didn't mean to hurt you." Kiera gives me her apologetic smile, the one that's usually reserved for mediocre casualties like spilling her coffee on my lab report or *accidentally* pushing me into a cute guy.

"I know," I say. But friends never mean to hurt their friends. *Sorry* was the word that came out of her mouth, but *don't make this a big deal* was the look that sat in her hazel eyes. Anxiety begins to bubble inside of me, and I don't know whether I'm overthinking her expressions or not.

Jasmine places a gentle hand on my shoulder. "We'll make it up to you. Next Friday is our day, remember? Mall and movie night, just like before."

"Of course." I refuse to acknowledge the lump forming in my throat. I'm not going to overreact. "Listen, I never want you guys to feel like you have to hide anything from me. We're best friends. We have to be there for each other, even if we're not going through the same things."

"Sisters before misters," Carol starts, trading glances with the other two.

"Fries over guys," Kiera continues.

"All foods before dudes," Jasmine finishes.

I glare at them. "Says the people who literally replaced me with guys on the freaking first day of school! Everyone says that until they actually get a guy and make me the third wheel!"

They laugh and for the moment, that's enough to lift the weight sitting on my chest. It almost feels normal. Despite the hurt, I tell myself that it's going to be okay. The pain is going to go away because it always goes away. That's how emotions work. I look around; the guys don't seem to be here yet—something I'm glad for.

"I don't understand what's so great about guys. They're so annoying," I add, thinking back to my recent encounters with James. Maybe it's bias, but James has tinted my view of guys ever since I was born into existence.

"Oh Lara, Lara, Lara, you will love someone one day and finally understand," Kiera says in a singsong voice.

"I've already loved a bunch of guys."

Jasmine raises an eyebrow. "Fictional characters don't count."

I click my tongue. "*Okay then*. I'll be that superrich single aunt who travels the world. Flying first class, of course."

"We'll go with you," Kiera says.

"I call throwing Jasmine off of the plane!" Carol yells a bit too loudly, raising her hand. The cafeteria monitor pushes her glasses down to give Carol a dirty look, while students from the other tables look like their eyeballs are about to pop out. And Jasmine's face is in her hands, absolutely mortified.

We all stare at each other for a moment or so before we burst out laughing so hard that I swear the whole cafeteria stops and looks at us like we're crazy. But this craziness is us and I'm beginning to realize how special these moments are, despite how limited they might become.

TIP SEVEN:
SEEK VENGEANCE

✸

The school day ends, and I continue my casual walk to James's place instead of my own. Now that we're doing the whole tutoring thing, Jasmine is free to walk home with Logan and I'm . . . I'm free to walk alone. It's a relaxing route, longer than going to my own house, but it gives me time to think. The city is undeniably noisy as usual, but it doesn't bother me. I've grown used to the constant humming of traffic from outside the neighborhood, the occasional honks and beeps, and the slight smell of gas from running engines. The chaos is a fitting soundtrack to everything that's happening.

In the midst of my thoughts, a pair of arms circle around my waist, pulling me back and setting me into panic mode. Instinctively, I jab my elbow backward, loosening the hold. I turn around quickly, my unruly hair whipping in front of my eyes, and push the attacker back. He falls onto the grass but drags me down with him.

I hold my fist up, ready to smack the living daylights out of him when I hear, "Lara, it's me!"

James?

My mind relaxes at the realization that my "attacker" is just an idiot, but my senses are still heightened. I can't believe I wasted my precious energy trying to beat up James.

I get up from my position, heaving from the unnecessary workout, and stand beside him. James is still lying on the grass, also breathing quickly. Feeling somewhat bad for him, I tap the side of his abdomen with my foot. "You okay?" Of course, he shouldn't have snuck up on me like that.

"What . . . the . . . hell!" James mutters between breaths.

"You're the one who attacked me! What was I supposed to do? If anything, you should be apologizing to *me*," I respond, crouching beside him, somewhat concerned for his state in a public area. Hopefully no one else witnessed that interaction.

"It was not a violent attack," he says, getting up and dusting the back of his jeans. "It was simply a poorly executed hug."

I raise an eyebrow. "You're joking, right?"

"Not a joke! Just a sign of peace and friendship," he says, making peace signs with both hands before converting them into Korean finger hearts and pursing his lips. *As if.* It's *James*. There had to be some malicious intent behind that gesture, especially since our relationship is not the "hugging" kind.

"A hug? Nobody goes behind someone's back and suddenly wraps their arms around them like a python and calls it a hug."

"Have you *never* seen those couples with the guy who goes behind the girl and rests his chin on her shoulder or, like, kisses her on the cheek?" he asks, as we begin walking in the direction of his house.

I've only seen those in various K-dramas, but the closest thing I've seen to that in *real life* would be a video of a research scientist almost getting choked to death by a boa constrictor on the animal channel.

"And you were going to kiss me on the cheek?" I ask jokingly. He doesn't respond. "Exactly. So that doesn't count."

"You were just looking sad, y'know? Whenever you're unhappy you have this pathetic little walk, like a sad penguin, with your head down and sulking—"

"And your point?"

"Usually, sad people need a hug." He shrugs, giving me a half smile and I hate to admit that it's kind of cute. "But I guess when you're sad you get a wave of superstrength so there's that."

His last sentence makes me laugh, and before I can reply James grabs my arm, pulling both of us behind a big oak tree.

"What are you—"

"Shhh." James cuts me off. *What the heck? Why are we hiding behind a tree?* I suddenly notice a police car on the other side of the street.

Holy. Freaking. Fishballs.

"Why are the cops after you? Are we going to jail? I knew you were conceited and stuff, but I didn't think you were a criminal! Are you a part of a gang? What am I saying, of course you are! I don't want to go to jail—"

"Can you be quiet! I'm not part of a gang and the cops are not after me!" he whisper-yells.

"Then why are we hiding at the sight of a police car!"

"What?" James says. I point to the car and confusion washes over his face. "There's not even an officer in there."

I look over at the car again. *Oh*. Yeah, it's empty.

"Then why are we behind a tree?" I whisper-yell back.

"Look." He points out the small café on the other side of the street, surrounded by an elaborate floral display. I scan over people drinking their afternoon coffee on the enclosed patio area, until finally I spot Kiera and Daniel talking and laughing. *Oh*.

"So what? Did you want to say hi?" I ask James. What's the big deal? "KIER—"

James places his hand over my mouth. "Shh! I don't want them to see me!"

I rip his hand away. "Why?"

He pauses for a moment, his jaw tensing for a split second but relaxing immediately after. He's frustrated. "I wanted to practice at the rink with the guys after school but Daniel said he had a dentist appointment."

I slap him on the arm. "You were gonna ditch me?"

"Yes, but that's not the point! I would've given you a heads-up. Anyway, I gave them a free pass for yesterday but here we are again today."

Suddenly I laugh, and he frowns at me, confused. "You'd think liars would be more creative. At lunch, Kiera gave me the same excuse for going MIA yesterday. Dentist appointment . . . that's bull."

"I'm going over there," he says, taking a step forward. Instinctively, I grab his hand, holding him back, and both of us spend a moment eyeing our clasped hands.

I quickly let go, suddenly feeling awkward. He returns his hand to his jacket pocket while I let out a cough. After a few seconds pass, I say, "Why do that, when we can have a bit of fun with this?"

From the conniving smirk tugging on his lips, I know he's undeniably intrigued.

Revenge of the Third Wheels is now playing in theaters worldwide.

The plan is simple, almost boring really. Part of the job description of being a third wheel is being able to handle uncomfortable situations. For example, when couples try to suck off each other's faces.

As a third wheel, of course I want to gouge my eyes out, but I suck it up and accept the discomfort. It's only fair that our friends feel the same distress as us, and this plan should make both Kiera and Daniel lightheaded.

We cross the street to the café; it isn't terribly busy so we're able to find a table near enough to the couple that once we start speaking louder than usual they should be able to hear our scripted conversation. When James and I catch the end of Daniel's lame joke and grimace at the same time, we're reassured that we're in good hearing range.

"What do you want to eat?" James asks suddenly.

I press my index finger against my lip, quickly glancing at the couple, making sure they haven't noticed us. "Shh!" We're supposed to be acting low-key so that the couple doesn't see us before they're supposed to.

James crosses his arms, leaning back in his chair. "Please, it's going to take a lot more to get their attention. At this point, I think they have a blind spot for anyone other than each other."

Gross but true.

"Now," James continues, pushing his cell phone across the table, toward me. On the screen is the café's afternoon menu. "Our first priority is ordering something to eat so we don't get kicked out for loitering. Tell me what you want so I can order it inside while you save our table."

Quickly scanning the menu, I get overwhelmed by the many, many options. "Uh . . . what are *you* getting?"

He stands up then leans forward, chest inches away from the table as he swipes through the menu pages until it lands on a decadent slice of cheesecake. "This. Their blueberry cheesecake is really good."

"All right, just get me the same thing and I'll pay—"

He interrupts before I can finish my sentence. "I'm paying, okay?"

"James, it's fine. I can pay for my—" I argue but James cuts me off again.

"Don't think I'm being nice to you for your own sake. I'm only doing this because of social constructs and my mom will scold me for being not gentlemanly." Before I can ask him when he's ever cared about social constructs, he turns to enter the building.

There has to be a ghost of a smile on my face, but I'll make sure it isn't there by the time he comes back. Sure, he's the exact opposite of a nice guy; he's annoying and teases me far more than any sensible person would approve of. However, despite our years of enemyship, I don't think I've ever had to pay for food when I was with him. Sure, he'd push me off of a tree branch or tackle me in a puddle of mud, but when it came to getting snacks right after, he'd always make sure to get something for me, and I thought that was kind of nice.

He returns after a few minutes with a plate of cake in each hand, extending one to me and then retracting the plate when I reach out. Then with a cocky grin, he puts the dessert in front of me and our preshow setup is complete.

Cue the lights.

"Lara, I need to tell you something," James begins, loud and clear, making sure that his speech is audible to Daniel and Kiera.

"What is it, *James*?" At that moment, Daniel's head shoots up and looks in our direction. Perfect. I can see his rounded eyes in my peripheral vision but pretend not to notice them.

"Please say good-bye to the guys for me. I can't face them," he continues, looking down at the table with a seriously troubled expression. I can hardly believe that he's able to keep a straight face. "I'm going to be a father."

"*What?*" I gasp, holding a hand to my chest like I'm in one of those over-the-top Filipino teleseryes. Daniel's jaw drops while Kiera's eyes widen. The people near our table sneak glances at us, too, their conversations coming to a halt so they can listen in.

"Please don't tell anyone, especially Luke," James says, grabbing my hand from across the table. The urge to pull away is strong, but it would ruin the act. "Ren and I, we've been seeing each other for some time now." Unfortunately, in our planning strategy, we had to sacrifice the names of one of the most popular couples from school in order to make it seem as realistic as possible.

After that sentence, Daniel starts to rise from his seat and Kiera tries to hold him back. See? This is what I was saying about being *uncomfortable.*

"She has a boyfriend, James!" I yell, drawing more attention to ourselves.

"I know. But we were drunk one night and then—"

"And then what? Huh? What kind of a person are you?" It feels so weird saying this to him because though he might date a lot, I know he'd never do anything like that. I tug on my right ear. Our signal for *Let's execute phase two.*

"Oh, and I'm moving to California. I didn't know how to deal with this, so I booked a flight."

Both Daniel and Kiera are walking over, and if Daniel was a cartoon, he would have steam coming out of his nose. Kiera's hand is raised to her mouth, and she's fighting back tears.

"You're just going to leave the baby!?" I yell angrily.

"Well—"

James's line is interrupted by Daniel, who pounds his fists on the table. "YOU GOT A GIRL PREGNANT! AND YOU'RE MOVING TO CALIFORNIA!"

"Daniel? What are you doing here?" I ask, innocently holding a hand to my chest, but he ignores me.

"How could you be so careless?" he shouts at James, hands now flying in all directions, gesturing frantically. "You got her pregnant! Luke is going to kick your a—"

James and I erupt in peals of laughter.

"What is so funny?" a clueless Daniel asks. "He got a girl pregnant for goodness' sake!"

James and I stop laughing, share a look of victory, then continue to laugh. He raises an eyebrow at Daniel. "So, how's the dentist appointment going? I didn't know that this café doubled as a dentist's office."

Daniel scratches the back of his neck, eyes darting from James to Kiera to me then back to James. "You see . . ."

James holds a hand up. "Save it. I already got my revenge. Just don't lie to me about these things. And warn the others, too, before they try to pull a fast one on me." The way he says it is the definition of relaxed; everything has blown over and no grudges are in sight.

Sometimes I wish I was like him; he doesn't dwell on things. He brushes problems off easily and it's like nothing affects him. Everything is resolved with three sentences and a good laugh—no hard feelings, no afterthoughts.

"Sure, man. You almost gave me a mini-heart attack when you said you got a girl pregnant. Thank God that was a joke," Daniel says with a sigh of relief.

"We're glad that isn't the case," Kiera adds, taking Daniel's hand in hers. They share a look and it's a bit less gross to witness. Instead, there's a moment in which his dark-brown eyes hold her hazel ones, and it almost feels magical.

James watches them too. For a second, I think that he looks

mesmerized or that he's longing for something like that. But then I realize that I must be overthinking again because the last time he truly cared for a girl was a long time ago, and I don't think anyone was able to replace her.

Daniel and Kiera go back to their table to continue their afternoon date, while James and I sit quietly at our own table, enjoying our cheesecakes. A refreshing wind passes by, sweeping his dark-brown hair to the side, and I can't help but notice how the sunlight turns his eyes into glossy caramel. Since our backpacks are with us, we end up staying for another hour, working on math homework.

As we begin to pack our bags he says, "Thank you for being such a great partner in crime today," before extending a hand to me.

"Pleasure doing business with you." I reach out to shake it. As much as I dislike James with all my heart and soul, I must say that he is a great partner for revenge. "I'll see you tomorrow?"

"Sure, but I'm not leaving yet. I still have to walk you home." I stare at his dorky grin for an unusually long time, but it's because dimples are naturally an aesthetically pleasing trait.

"Again, I'm perfectly capable of making it to my own home safely," I remind him, but he insists, leading me to the sidewalk and talking about social constructs again, using Tita Gia as the reason why he doesn't leave me to fend for myself.

As we walk, James complains about school and work while we trade insults between sentences. My house is finally within view when suddenly an uneven piece of sidewalk causes me to lose my balance and I fall front first onto the sidewalk. James laughs hysterically, not caring that I almost died in front of him, and I shift my body so that I'm sitting on my butt.

"Here, let me help you," he offers, offering an arm to me. I look at his hand, then his eyes, and my mind swims back to a warm summer day, when the lakeside breeze was about as cool as the one now.

Lakeshore of Lake Ontario, Toronto
July (Seven Years Ago)

"Let me help you!" the little boy insists as I hold on to a tree branch. James extends a small hand out to me, and I take it while keeping my other hand on the branch for support.

A few feet away from him, the lake is calm. There are hardly any waves and it's the perfect day to be outside; at least, the perfect day to get dragged to a family picnic. While James and I are maneuvering through overgrown shrubs and tree branches, our families sit peacefully in the nearby picnic area, probably thinking we are still at the playground. We are, in fact, not at the playground, but on an undesignated pathway to the beach because James thinks exploring is much less fun if you're not trekking through poison ivy.

I extend a foot onto the next rock but retract it immediately when the stone wiggles. The path is too steep. How is it possible that he jumped down from the top like it was nothing?

Gripping my hand tighter, he says, "Take your time," and I muster up the courage to let go of the branch. Finally, I get down and let the sand from the beach cover my toes.

"Thanks," I mutter stubbornly, letting go of his hand.

He walks to the water and picks up some tiny pebbles, tossing them one by one into the lake, the stones jumping on the water's surface.

"Wanna try?" he asks, holding a handful of pebbles out to me.

I shake my head. "I can't."

"Just try it," he insists, taking my hand and pouring the pebbles into it.

"Fine." I grunt, taking a pebble and throwing it into the lake. Instead of skipping, it sinks to the bottom. "I told you."

"It's okay," he says with an encouraging smile. "Try it again until it works."

We continue skipping (in my case, tossing) stones until we get bored. On our way back up to the park, I go in front of him and struggle to climb the big rocks. My foot slips, my ankle sliding against the rough surface, causing me to tear up. The scratch isn't what makes me tear up further, but the fact that I can't make it up. "I'm going to fall," I whisper to myself.

"No, you won't!" James reassures me. "And if you do, I'll catch you!"

"Yeah, right," I say in disbelief.

"Well, if you fall, I'll help you up."

He helps me up, this time, not letting go midway.

I dust the dirt off of my clothes and quickly pull out my cell phone to see if any damage was done. I exhale in relief when I see that the screen isn't cracked. Good thing the love of my life survived.

When I look back up, I catch him watching me—only for a moment, though. I don't think much of it, so I don't say anything. He walks ahead of me in the direction of my house. Sometimes I think it's weird when he's not loud or unruly; but it gives me space to really think about him, to see him. And at times I think, *Maybe he's a nice guy after all.*

TIP EIGHT:
DON'T BE SURPRISED

✱

It's three o'clock now and Jasmine still isn't at the bus stop. The bus comes in *five minutes*. She should be here by now. For her, punctuality is a personality trait, especially on our mall and movie nights. I pace back and forth at our beloved bus stop, holding a hand over my forehead to shield my face from the sunlight. It's warm today, and also a good body image day, which I'm grateful for. In celebration of that, I'm wearing my favorite plaid mini-skirt, despite my unshaven legs. Still, I am alone, and I don't see anyone coming. Taking my phone out, I flip to our recent messages. She never said anything about a change in plans, so I text her.

Me: *Jas, where are you? You're gonna miss the bus!!!*
Jasmine: *Don't worry, I'll meet you at the mall :)*
Me: *You're not coming with me?*
Jasmine: *Not today but I'll see you there!*

Shoving my cell phone into my purse, I pull out my Presto card when the bus greets me. I haven't taken the bus alone for a long time because when I go out, I'm almost always with friends. I guess venturing out alone might be another new affair.

There's never been a time where Jasmine has ditched me last

minute. Her agenda simply doesn't allow that. Unlike the disorganized mess of a human I am, she's the personification of the digital calendar; each minute of her day is blocked for maximum productivity.

As I enter the Eaton Centre, the sound of traffic is replaced by people talking and the noise of countless footsteps. Among the numerous people are hundreds of teenagers . . . a nightmare indeed.

The laws of magnetism pull me to the giant Indigo store with two stories and an escalator—literal book heaven. On the second floor of the store, in a vacant corner, I pull out my phone to diffuse the discomfort associated with being by yourself. Now, to the group chat.

Me: *Almost here?*

Unlike last week, they reply almost immediately, letting my diaphragm relax.

Kiera: *In a few minutes!*

Carol: *Yup, I'm on time today*

There is about an hour or so to kill before the movie starts, so I inform them that I'm at the bookstore again, an addiction that will ultimately cause me to go broke at some point. But at the end of the day, if I don't purchase as many books as possible, how am I supposed to tab stories with a rainbow of sticky notes? And if I don't tab books with notes, how else are people supposed to know what painfully funny quotes should be added to my eulogy? It would be selfish to leave my grieving community without guidance on how to honor my legacy.

There's a small table of books with interesting covers and I grab the first two that catch my eye, ending up with a double purchase after only being in the store for ten minutes.

"Lara!" My head snaps in the direction of Jasmine's voice.

Jasmine, Carol, and Kiera approach me. Carol waves excitedly and Kiera taps away at her phone, not bothering to look up. One day that girl is seriously going to run into a pole. Finally, she lifts her head and adjusts her turquoise headband, eyes darting from side to side.

"Are you okay?" Jasmine frowns, directing a judgmental stare at Kiera.

"She looks guilty," Carol says, crossing her arms. "I wonder what she did."

Kiera turns her body slightly, facing the extensive manga collection at the other end of the floor. "Carol, go get me volume seventy of Naruto."

Carol immediately raises both hands to her hips. "What? Why me?"

Kiera lets out a harsh breath, turning her back away from the section. "The anime club guys are here again and if they see me they'll try to recruit me into joining their club! I swear, it's gonna be another half hour conversation again."

My hand flies to my mouth as I fake a gasp. "Oh no! Joining a club with people who share your interests? What a *terrible* idea!"

She tilts her head to the side and gives my arm a little shove. "You know I don't have time for any more clubs, and I'll feel bad for saying no again."

"I still don't know why this involves me," Carol says with her arms crossed. Kiera gives her a little pout but Carol refuses to cave.

"Just do it." Kiera groans. Carol shakes her head again. There's a pause before Kiera finally says, "I'll pay for your movie snacks!"

My eyes widen and so does Carol's scheming smile. *Bad decision,* Kiera. Carol has no limits when it comes to eating at the movies. She usually buys popcorn, frozen yogurt, chicken wings, and nachos, and that's when she's *not* hungry.

"Hmm . . . that sounds *divine*. Let me find that book," Carol says before walking off to who knows where.

"The other way!" Kiera yells and she turns around.

Carol makes a one-eighty, passing us again. "I knew that." This time, Jasmine follows her, making sure she doesn't get lost.

Once they're gone, I turn to Kiera. "We're seeing that new action movie, right? I've been dying to see the Rock battle some intergalactic space creatures. I heard it was funny too."

She tilts her head from side to side. "I don't know . . . I thought that we could see something else . . . like a horror movie?"

I do not watch horror movies; I can't even watch trailers without freaking out. We never see horror movies for the reason of the "Great Paranoia of the Ninth Grade," when a cute guy dared me to watch *Insidious* for the first time at Kiera's Halloween party. And the only reason I even accepted that dare was because books have taught me that dares can lead to finding one's soul mate. You know what I got? I got two weeks of sleeping on my parents' bedroom floor in fear, and shampoo burning my eyeballs because I was scared that a demon would possess me if I closed my eyes while I was taking a shower.

My eyes almost bulge out of my head. "Don't you remember the trauma I went through!"

I refrain from attacking as she says, "*Please*, can we watch a horror movie?" Then she pops her bottom lip out.

I make that face that we all love from the memes—the one where the nostrils are flared and the double (or triple or quadruple) chin is present. "What spirit has possessed you?"

"C'mon, Lara, we haven't seen anything scary in forever and we thought it would be fun to watch with,"—she fiddles with her dangly earring—"popcorn."

"*We*?" It seems to me that Kiera is the only one who wants me to have a heart attack and die.

"Apparently, this new Paranormal Activity movie isn't *that* scary. It'll be great for you to overcome your fears!"

The only reason I don't strangle her is because my self-control is functioning at an optimal level today. "Again, not seeing what this does to repair my trauma."

"*Please.* I'll pay for your movie snacks too!"

I hate how my stomach grumbles in response to the offer of free food. "Fine."

The lunatic hugs me tightly and I squirm at the physical contact, already knowing that my decision will come with big regrets. I'm going to get zero sleep for the next two weeks. Again.

The Cineplex is a short walk from the mall, and immediately upon arrival the smell of melted butter on fresh popcorn fills the air. Kiera and Jasmine go to the ticket stand while Carol and I line up at concession. When placed in Carol's hand, Kiera's debit card becomes a nuclear weapon. There is no mercy as she purchases everything—hot wings, nachos, popcorn, candy . . . it never ends. By the time we're finished, we look like Shaggy and Scooby, holding piles of food in our arms.

Balancing the numerous meals, we make our way back to Kiera and Jasmine. I expect to see four tickets and to do a trade-off with the food. Instead, I am greeted with something more than four tickets—three boy-fries all standing in a line. *Don't drop your food, Lara.*

"Hey, Lara." Logan greets me, giving a friendly wave, paired with his regular charismatic smile.

I spin back around and hope that it is all an illusion, that maybe I'm imagining this horrific situation. I look back and they're still there, like *physically there.* I don't smile back; I don't even try to hide my disgust with their presence.

His cheerful expression quickly fades. "Okay, then . . . maybe I should . . . want some fries?" he stammers, holding out a large serving of french fries.

I glare at him, then stare at the fries, then back at him, then at the fries. I take a step forward and he winces, probably waiting for another grand lecture and a couple more threats. Surprisingly (even surprising myself), I drop the scowl and take a fry. Then, I take the whole cardboard container of fries from his hands, shocking everyone with my act of kindness.

"Told you the fries would work," Logan whispers loudly to Daniel.

Maybe the boys don't have my full vote, but they do know how to keep me from ripping their heads off, and I must say, I respect their tactics.

"What are you guys doing here?" I ask, chewing on a french fry.

"We wanted to see a movie," Logan answers, adjusting the cuffs of his jacket.

"What movie?"

"The new *Paranormal Activity*."

"What time?"

"Four thirty."

I narrow my eyes at the three boys, grimacing. I can't believe my friends had the audacity to pull this. "So, you're telling me that you three *coincidentally* came here at the exact same time to see the exact same movie as us?"

"Yeah?" Mark answers hesitantly. "It's not just us thr—"

"Guys! I just saw the best thing back there! They're giving away free popcorn—" Upon seeing me, his jaw gapes and I mirror the same expression.

"*You*?" we both yell at the same time, pointing at the other.

"What are *they* doing here?" James looks at his buddies who are smiling nervously. "I thought we were having a guys' night."

"And I thought we were having a girls' night, but I guess we were both wrong," I comment bitterly, but he simply shrugs. He's less infuriated than I am, or than he should be. How is he okay with his friends making him a seventh wheel? I don't get him—he's like a different breed of human, one who doesn't get annoyed as easily. It's always go with the flow for him.

Neither of us can do anything about the situation, so we follow the couples up the escalators and into the dimly lit theater. As we walk, he leans down to say, "Don't worry about them so much, sometimes people can be assholes without realizing it."

"Like you?" In most James-involving situations, I would've meant that—but here, for once, it isn't James's fault, and I shouldn't be so awful to him. "Sorry," I say, taking back the autonomic response.

In the theater, I sit between him and Carol. The ads take up fifteen minutes and by the time the actual movie starts, I've devoured more than half of my popcorn. Luckily, Carol has a whole buffet prepared, and we take turns holding the massive amount of food.

The movie starts off with the repetition of scary noises and sound effects. This isn't supposed to scare me; it's just the product of professional-grade equipment and makeup. As the scenes grow more frightening, everyone seeks comfort with their partner. Ex) Mark shrieks and Carol pats his head.

But then it gets more frightening and there's nothing I can do except shield my eyes with my hands. I am a logical, scientific thinker. *This is fake,* I repeat in my head. *There's no way that this could ever happen in real life. No way, no way, no—*

I scream along with everyone else in the theater, accidentally grabbing James's arm and letting go immediately because I'm not about to be embarrassed for doing two things. After a moment, I come to my senses and get up from my seat to leave. But before I go, Carol's eyes meet mine and they gleam with guilt.

But if they actually cared, they wouldn't have brought those guys with them. They were supposed to hang out with me.

I walk out of the theater.

It's five o'clock and the September breeze is a bit cooler than usual. I cross my arms in hopes of radiating some warmth, but that proves to be useless. It was stupid to go out and not even bring a sweater. Sure, it was warm earlier, but it's Canada—sunny one minute and threatening snow the next.

"That movie was boring." James walks up beside me and stretches, only for me to give him a dirty look. He laughs. "You got scared? Actually?" I punch him on the arm, not saying anything else. "Oh my gosh. You *actually* got scared." He stops laughing immediately.

Holding my hands to my chest and fighting a shiver, I start walking away from him, in the direction of the mall.

"Hey! Wait up!" He runs after me and for some reason I stop and wait. "Wow, it's chilly out here," he says, then starts to put on the black hoodie that was tied around his waist earlier. I enviously eye his sweater, wishing that I'd brought my own.

He notices my jealousy and a smirk tugs on his lips. "I feel so much better," he starts. "I feel so *warm* and *great*." I grit my teeth in response to stupid (but smart) James who actually brought a sweater.

Taking it off, he plops it on top of my head. "Here. You and I both know that my body's way too hot to be covered up with a thick sweater."

"And mine isn't?"

"*Well—*"

"Do you really want to finish that sentence?" I warn him. He doesn't. I pull the sweater over my T-shirt and finally stop shivering.

It's a bit large on me; the sleeves extend a couple of inches past my fingertips and the body goes past my torso, almost reaching the hem of my skirt. Most notable of all, it smells like oranges.

We hurry inside the mall, and I mumble a small, "Thanks," for the sweater.

"What did you say?" he asks, pretending that he didn't hear me. He cups an ear, waiting for me to repeat my words.

"I said *thank you*," I repeat, yelling it this time.

He winces and holds a hand to his right ear. "Wow. You really love to yell, don't you?"

"Yes, yes I do. What do you—," I start to ask but James interrupts me at the sight of an ice-cream shop, gesturing excitedly. For a guy who's considered cool, he acts like a little kid.

Grabbing my hand, he drags me to the shop. Okay, maybe he doesn't drag me because I go willingly. The store is decorated with light-up signs against the pastel-blue walls, and a couple of tables take up the floor space. There must be about two dozen ice-cream flavors arranged in two lines, and an overwhelmingly long menu of different combos.

James crouches, peering through the glass that separates us from the ice cream. "What flavor do you want?"

"A very complicated mix of ice-cream scoops and various toppings, so I'll order it myself." I know that James has a thing for ordering on my behalf, but before he can argue my phone rings. Pulling it out of my pocket, I look at the caller ID.

Mom.

I tell James to go ahead, then sit at a table to take the call. I answer before it has the chance to stop ringing because it is a commandment to answer the first call. I'd rather not have to dodge flying *tsinelas* when I arrive home.

"Hello?"

"*Ara! Nasaan ka na?*" (Ara! Where are you?) Mom asks, panicked.

"At the mall with my friends? I mean, I'm with James now but . . . I told you about this last week."

"*Magtatagal ba kayo? May ganap kasi dito sa bahay...*" (Are you guys going to take long? We have a situation here at home...)

"What—"

"Okay, okay, bye! *Kabayong buntis! Ano'ng nangyari sa halaman?*" (Oh my goodness! What happened to the plant?) There is a loud bark in the background and my mom hangs up. That concerns me because we don't have a dog.

I am about to go order my ice cream when the idiot walks toward me with two ice-cream cones in hand. Is he going to eat two ice creams? A normal person would think that the other one was for them, but knowing James, he could easily eat as many ice creams as he wanted (and still have the body of a model).

Shockingly, he hands one to me. "One scoop of chocolate chip cookie dough on the bottom. One scoop of cookies and cream on the top. Everything topped with crushed M&M's and sprinkles, all put together in a waffle cone."

Wow. Just wow.

I stare blankly at him. Half of me is wondering how he knew what my supercomplicated dessert was. The other half is paralyzed with happiness since I haven't had my favorite ice-cream combo in forever.

At the first taste of sweet chocolate pieces and cookies and cream, summer nostalgia overpowers my senses. The taste reminds me of bike rides and beaches, amusement parks and fast food, and road trips—oh, how I love road trips. I can't help but think forward to this summer, the last one before we're all thrust into college life and ultimately, adulthood. All I want is to feel this way forever, but if that's not possible, then I want this for one last summer.

"How did you know what my incredible ice-cream combo was?" I can't help but smile while admiring the most perfect concoction I've ever witnessed.

He shrugs. "It's you. How could I not?" Then he gives me a look—you know, the one where his eyes have a slight twinkle and you start to feel a bit fluttery inside and—*what the heck?* Perhaps I've become lactose intolerant within the past hour because whatever is going on in my stomach is *not* normal.

Ignoring the strange physiological symptoms, I say, "Because I didn't tell you?"

He rolls his eyes. "We've known each other since birth."

But for the most part, our relationship consisted of us almost sending each other to the emergency room every time we would meet. I still remember that day when he "accidentally" pushed me off of a tree branch that I was sitting on and my ankle broke. Then the next week, I "accidentally" spilled marbles on the ground while he was walking and his wrist broke. Little Lara and Little James sure kept the ER staff busy.

"I never told you anything other than the reasons that I don't like you, let alone how to build me the perfect dessert." I raise an eyebrow, an expression he copies.

"You've told me before. At the boardwalk? You called me stupid because I pushed you and then . . ."

Harbourfront, Toronto
July (Six Years Ago)

I pull myself out of the water, shaking my head to dislodge the water from my ears. "You're stupid, Jameson Bryer, and I hate you!"

"Sorry! It was a joke," he snickers.

"You're dead meat," I say angrily as I sprint toward him.

He runs away and I chase him, maneuvering through the adults on the boardwalk. I try my best to keep on his trail but he's too fast of a runner. Finally, he stops and raises his hands in defeat.

"Sorry, Lara," he pants.

"Sorry is not going to change the fact that I'm drenched!"

James bites his bottom lip before gesturing to a nearby ice-cream shop, a small one with pots of flowers decorating the exterior and circular picnic tables on the patio. "Do you want ice cream?"

After an eye roll, I give in to the offer. This is probably the third time this summer that he's done something dumb and offered me ice cream. Then again, this is my third time accepting the offer.

We enter the shop. I order my favorite ice-cream combo and he gapes at the heaping amount, which is almost falling off of the cone. He orders plain vanilla, and we sit at a table eating our ice creams together.

"What did you order again?" James asks, for the third time this summer.

I begrudgingly repeat my order as if he hasn't forgotten twice already. "One scoop of chocolate chip cookie dough on the bottom. One scoop of cookies and cream on the top. Everything topped with crushed M&M's and sprinkles, all put together in a waffle cone."

"You actually remembered," I say softly, mostly for myself because I need to verbally reaffirm that this is real. He gives me another look, like, *duh*, and I go back to eating and avoiding eye contact. When it finally sinks in that this is actually happening, my face grows warm. Thank God that ice cream is cold.

Who would've thought that my mortal enemy would be the one to remember a strangely complicated ice-cream combo?

TIP NINE:
CONSULT WITH A DOG

✱

When I get home, Mom is furious—this time, not at me. It's a nice change because she has a bad habit of getting mad at me for going out too often or staying home too much. Today, Illa and Dad are feeling her wrath. Unfortunately, they seek refuge at a local Jollibee, leaving me to deal with the root of the current family problem, which is currently sniffing my ankles. I wonder where the tiny toy poodle came from, but Mom shoos me out before I can even ask.

"*Alisin mo ang asong 'yan sa paningin ko*," (Get that dog out of my sight,) she yells dramatically before muttering, "*Nag-volunteer pa silang mag-alaga . . . e 'di naman pala sila mag-i-stay dito sa bahay.*" (They volunteered to look after the dog, but they wouldn't even stay at home . . .)

Hooking the puppy onto her leash, I read the name tag—*Milani*. We leave the house and she walks as fast as she possibly can along the sidewalk, something that I don't appreciate because my full stomach isn't built for speed walking. Despite our obvious barriers of communication, I assign Milani the role of my therapist and extend my life story as if she has the means to fix anything.

"Y'know, Milani, I never thought that my friends would be head over heels for a bunch of guys. Jasmine never had a crush on anyone. When we were seven we wanted to invent a chemical formula for boy repellent."

She barks at me, and I like to think it's her way of replying.

"And after Kiera's glo-up in eleventh, everyone was attracted to her like a magnet, but she never actually dated anyone. The rejections were amusing, though, I must admit. I remember that one kid she threw a pizza at because he overdid the flirting."

Milani looks up at me like she actually understands.

"I guess I predicted Carol and Mark would get together eventually. But I never thought I'd feel so left out because of it."

As if on cue, she barks once more.

"Then there's me," I say and Milani pauses. I draw my lower lip between my teeth, wondering, *Is she listening?* She stays in place, so I keep mine. "I don't even know where my friendships stand right now. One minute we're normal and everything is fine and how it should be. The next minute, they're ditching me and forgetting about my existence, and I have to pretend that I'm fine even when—"

Out of nowhere, my conversation (yes, I'll consider that a conversation) is interrupted by the loud barking of an energetic golden retriever that runs our way. The puppy stops at the sight of Milani, and they do that butt sniffing business. A couple of seconds later, the puppy's owner sprints over, holding the empty leash. His familiar face brings a smile to mine.

"Milo! How'd you get this far?" Xander says, slightly out of breath. He crouches to reattach the leash to the puppy, and his light-brown hair turns a dirty blond under the late afternoon sun. He looks up. "Lara? I didn't know you had a dog."

I sigh. "Today, I do."

"Dog sitting is always exciting." He gets up, folding his arms over his broad chest and exhaling. "By the way, I'm so glad I ran into you."

I tilt my head to the side. "Oh?"

"Do you remember Dr. Osei?"

I nod, though I haven't heard her name since the time we were volunteering at the hospital, when the elevator got jammed and the three of us were stuck for an hour. Dr. Eva Osei, Senior Scientist, Cell Biology, talked to us about her research while we waited for the elevator to start working, and I remembered how possibilities for the future flooded my mind.

"She's looking for summer research students," Xander says with bright eyes. Oh. Xander and I used to talk about research when we were volunteering together, and it became a shared dream of ours.

"How did you find out?" I ask.

"I saw on her website that they're working on a new project involving leukocytes and some other things that I can't remember off of the top of my head," he says excitedly. "I emailed her about it and how I thought it was really cool. She said they'd have student openings in the future and attached an application file. And get this, she remembered you!"

"She remembered me?"

"She referred to you as 'my friend,' but it obviously had to be you. She said she likes how we're ambitious and enthusiastic learners, so I feel like we might have a good chance of getting a spot."

I shift from one foot to the other, from both nervousness and intrigue. I've always dreamed of this opportunity, but I never thought it'd come *now*. I'd already planned to free up my last summer before university. I wanted time to volunteer, go on family road trips, get my driver's license, but most of all, I wanted to spend my last summer being a carefree kid with my friends.

For the past couple of years, my friends and I have been compiling a list of things we want to do before the inevitable next chapter of our lives. Most of them are simple, like bike riding at midnight. Others are borderline illegal, like sneaking into a celebrity's dressing room during a concert. But now I don't even know if they'll want to spend the summer with me. They all seem to be looking far into the future, a future that revolves more around their boyfriends than our group. Maybe I need to move on too.

Besides, if I have to reroute my summer, I might as well look at blood cells. "You had me at leukocytes, those are my favorite types of cells! But we have no experience. There's no way—"

He places a hand on my shoulder. "There's always a way. Everyone needs to start somewhere. Last year, Anannya got her first research opportunity too!"

"But your girlfriend is really smart—"

"And so are we," he finishes. "Don't stress about it. I'll email you the application file and we'll work on it together in the library at lunch. I'll even send both of our applications to Anannya, and she'll look over them."

The thought of going through with this makes my heart race even faster. "Okay."

"I'll see you," he says, leaving me with Milani and my own thoughts.

My hands feel clammy on the leash. Of course I want this position, and it's so lucky that Xander is back in my life, but my stomach does a little flip every time something new presents itself. The future is knocking on my door; it's here, but I don't know if I want to answer it.

I lie in my bed, staring at the ceiling with no energy to do anything. The sugar rush from the ice cream has subsided and all I'm left with are recurring thoughts plaguing my mind. My friends brought their boyfriends after saying they'd make up for their mistakes, James suddenly has a superspecific memory for my ice-cream combo, and I might be able to score a research position. I am the epitome of exhaustion. In the middle of my sulk session, Dad bursts into the room, a ringing phone in hand. The Messenger app ringtone. He definitely wants me to talk to someone, and surely doesn't care that my soul is deteriorating.

"Ara!"

I groan.

"*Tumatawag ang pinsan mo!*" (Your cousin is calling!)

I flip over on my stomach, taking a pillow and holding it over my ears, trying to drown out the painful and traumatic sound of that ringtone. Nothing good ever comes from these video calls.

"*Ara*," he warns, pulling the pillow from my hands and placing it on the foot of my bed.

"Fine."

I snatch the phone from his hand and answer the call as he disappears from the room, forgetting to close the door in the process. A teenage girl appears on the screen, and I force a smile. I've got no clue as to why our parents keep setting up these calls when we have absolutely nothing in common and all she does is assault me with subtle insults while reminding me that she has the perfect boyfriend and high school experience.

Exhibit A: Her first greeting.

"Hey, Lara! Look at you! You're still so cute with those chubby squirrel cheeks of yours!" An obvious anticompliment. Plus, she didn't even get the phrase right, it's *chipmunk*.

I continue to smile and nod, using the words of that one penguin in *Madagascar* as my mantra. There's no point in returning the negative energy because 1) I am tired and 2) respecting family is a huge thing here—even when they make you want to skydive off of a plane without a parachute.

I squeeze my eyes shut for a second, composing myself. "Hi, Eliza. What's up?"

She twirls a piece of her black hair around a dainty finger. "Nothing, really. My boyfriend and I just came back from a date. He was so sweet to buy us concert tickets to see The Weeknd." I raise an awkward thumbs-up, but my mouth is set in a hard line. "And how about you? Have you finally gotten around to getting a date?"

"Honestly—"

"It's okay if you're not *there* yet." She interrupts me. "A lot of people aren't and besides, who are you going to date if no one wants to date you?" She laughs before following with a pathetic, "Just kidding." People say that jokes are half-meant; knowing Eliza, she fully meant that.

I don't know why it's a thing to infiltrate the security of my private love(less) life. If Lola Nora was a detective—snooping through each nook and cranny, trying to figure out why nobody liked me—Eliza was the same, except she made her own assumptions as to why I remain unlikeable. Lola Nora does her excessive invasion for the reason of securing my future marriage before she dies (dark, but that's what she said). Meanwhile, Eliza pries out information in order to remind me of my flaws—though who ever said that chubby cheeks weren't cute?

"How's school?" I ask, trying to change the subject. I've calculated a set minimum time that I can talk to Eliza so that I don't get yelled at for not spending enough time with her.

"It's good," she says, eyes focused on something besides the camera. "I made the hockey team—again. I got captaincy for senior year, obviously. And my classes are good so far, probably good enough to get into my top nursing program next year."

Despite her condescending tone, Eliza's confidence astounds me. She's sure of herself and I admire that. But I wish she wouldn't try to blow me down every chance she gets.

"Nice."

Instead of relaying the same career question she goes, "How's James?"

Eliza lives in Swan River, Manitoba, a quiet town with a small population, too far from Toronto to see her regularly or even occasionally. She lived closer when she first came to Canada from the Philippines in the seventh grade. When we were younger and she still lived in the Niagara Region, Eliza found herself spending the summers with my family.

"He's fine," I say simply.

Back then Eliza was obsessed with monster trucks and skateboarding and WWE—the perfect match for James and the perfect antagonist to my lifestyle of reading in silence. Let's just say my eardrums were really happy that I only had to listen to flipping cars and screaming wrestlers on television for two months of the year, up until she moved for good before the ninth grade.

Her facial expression relaxes. Maybe she isn't totally rude or maybe her dad created a list of items to check off during our conversation, including looking remotely friendly.

"I'm glad to hear that." Tucking a loose lock of hair behind her ear, she cocks her head to the side. "By the way, I like your sweater. I've been trying to find one like it but they're always out of my size. Where'd you buy yours?"

My eyes widen and I look down at myself. *Fishballs.* I forgot to give the hoodie back to James and the idiot didn't even notice.

Warmth creeps up my face at the realization and suddenly the smell of oranges that lingers on the hoodie gets stronger by tenfold.

Eliza frowns. "Are you all right?"

I nod quickly. "Yeah, yeah, I'm great. I—I got the sweater from online, from the, the UK. They have a pretty big stock there."

She makes a note of the false information while I make a mental note to return the sweater tomorrow.

Eliza tilts her head to the side, squinting at her camera. "Is it personalized? There's embroidery on the sleeve. J.B. . . . is that—"

I cough. "Justin Bieber. Ha-ha, you know me, I'm obsessed with his music. I absolutely had to DIY his initials on the sleeve . . ."

Nodding, she goes, "You're seriously the same person you were when you were thirteen." My mind races back to when we were thirteen and my fists clench without warning. I release my fingers and try not to think so hard.

At the fifteen-minute time stamp, we end the call and I toss the phone to the foot of my bed, a sigh of relief escaping my lungs. The monthly Eliza conversation checks another box off of my mental to-do list, and at least one of my problems is over.

I contemplate taking off the sweater now, perhaps folding it into a little square and placing it in the corner of my room, by the door. I decide against that idea because it's too warm and too comfortable and it smells very nice. *I'll have to buy a sweater just like this one*, I think to myself, but even so, I don't think it would be the same as this one—it wouldn't smell like oranges.

TIP TEN:
BE A RELATIONSHIP COUNSELOR

*

Xander lies on his stomach, typing away at his application. We've claimed this spot in the library as ours; nobody ever ventures to the biology/medical section and if they do, they're usually gone within seconds of seeing us and our stuff sprawled on the floor.

"Did I tell you that I made the hockey team?" he asks cheerfully, after hearing me talk about Kiera's and Carol's sport success.

I haven't actually talked *to* my friends since their little antic on Friday. It's hard to make an effort when nobody seems to be reciprocating the gesture. A "sorry" text was received, but that was as half-assed as a text could get. I'm not heartless; I texted congrats in the group chat when Kiera made the volleyball team on Monday and when Carol reclaimed her position of captain on the soccer team yesterday.

I give him a round of applause. "That's great! Congratulations!" I also want to add a quick *Good luck*, because he'll have to deal with James.

He types quickly and my hands feel cold after being still for the past fifteen minutes. The library has a newly installed grandfather clock, one that's so loud that you hear the individual ticks for every second. My head struggles to distinguish between the rhythm of the clock and Xander's typing.

I stare at the blank application page before leaning my head against the bookshelf. I've done nothing of relevance to even have anything to say. What's Xander saying about himself? How did Anannya write her application? All my experiences sound so lame.

A breath creeps upon my neck and I jolt upward at Xander's close proximity beside me as he stares at my laptop screen. "Dude!" My heart races faster than usual, messing up the rhythm of the room entirely.

"Sorry, sorry," he says, before inching away. It wasn't his fault, but I've been more jumpy than usual after the few minutes I spent in that theater. You never know when some paranormal being is going to spring out and instigate your demise. "How's the application going?"

My eyes dart from the screen to him. "Obviously not well." Closing my laptop, I sigh and run a hand through my uncombed hair. I left my hair clip somewhere this morning, most likely in Ms. K's classroom. I was still wearing it during math class.

Xander waves his hand dismissively. "You've got a lot of time."

"I don't know what to write, though. I've done tutoring and volunteering and clubs, but how does any of that relate to this?" *And my body physically doesn't want to fill out this application*, I add in my head. It's not that I don't want to have this opportunity, I really do, but it feels like the opportunity is landing at a time that I should be doing other things, like spending the last summer before college with my friends, taking the time to hang out with Illa, and, I suppose, mentally preparing myself for the next leap in my life.

His green eyes gleam, amused. With a shrug, he goes, "I have no clue, but we're in the twelfth grade. What can they realistically expect from us? If anything, it's all about the last question, so fill in what you can and make sure to write something really good for the last part."

Why are you interested in this project and what skills can you bring to the team, I read in my head. *But that's where it gets even harder*, I think to myself.

I can think of a hundred reasons why I'm interested in the research, but the biggest flaw is that I'd be more interested if this was taking place in the summer after first year of university, or second. *And skills? What skills do I even have?* Yeah, I'm armed with the powers of binge-watching multiple seasons of a cartoon series in less than a week, I have the ability to read a six hundred–page novel in the span of a day, and I've probably broken the record for the number of mental breakdowns to be held in one hour, but other than that, I got nothing. I let my face fall into my hands before I let out an exasperated groan—sounding like a wild boar.

Xander gives me his regular lopsided smile that says *It's going to work out*, but I have a hard time believing that it will.

Unexpected footsteps grow louder, creating a steady beat with the ticking clock. *Tick*, step, *tick*, step. A shadow appears at the separation between two shelves and both of us look up to see Carol, disheveled but not in her usual way. Bags sit beneath her glossy eyes, and I swallow to get rid of the growing lump in my throat. Seeing other people cry almost always makes me cry too.

"Hey," she says, the corner of her mouth quirking up.

"Hi." I wave, but my hand's almost limp.

Xander gives my shoulder a squeeze before gathering his papers and laptop from the floor and shoving everything in his messy backpack. "I'll catch you later."

As he leaves, Carol sits beside me, bringing her knees to her chest and leaning on my shoulder. "I'm sorry," she croaks, before pressing her lips hard together.

"It's fine," I say, even though it really isn't. For the past two weeks and a half, my best friends have made no effort to fix our situation, but I haven't really done much to communicate my hurt, either, and I know that. Yet here I am doing it again, pushing down the yells and arguments that want to surface because her eyes are welling up, and they never do that.

"I broke up with Mark."

What?

Pulling away from her, I'm suddenly less worried about my own feelings and more concerned about what's going on with Carol. "What do you mean? But he really likes you. Don't you like him?"

"It's better this way," she says, her voice hoarse. "Better now than in the middle of my first semester in the States."

For some reason her words hit me harder than I expect them to. Like Kiera, who was set on her gap year of travel, Carol also had plans to leave. But Carol wanted to leave for university, attend a school in America for political science, and hopefully receive a scholarship for soccer. We all knew this was her plan since the beginning. Carol might not be the most organized when it comes to daily tasks like arriving on time or wearing matching socks, but when it comes to life, she knows what she's doing, where she's going, and how she'll get there.

I was worried about being excluded from her future plans, but I suppose it isn't just me.

I shake my head. "I don't understand. Things were going so well between both of you. Do you feel like he's holding you back?"

"I—" she starts but begins to sob. "No, no he isn't. He'd never . . ."

"Then why?"

My shoulder becomes a reservoir for her tears, and I know that by the time we walk out of the library, I'll look like I spilled water on half my upper body. She sniffles into my shoulder, and I silently pray that there isn't any snot—I am not equipped for this today.

Finally, she wipes away some of her tears with the sleeve of her shirt. Sniffling, she goes, "My older cousin went to college last year. She was dating someone in high school. They've been together for three years and . . ."

She has to take in a large breath before continuing. "They still didn't make it."

Stroking her arm, I try my best to give her a comforting smile. "I know most people would disregard my romantic expertise because I've never been in a relationship, but if you want, I can offer you my two cents on this."

She raises an eyebrow. "Bro, I know you well enough that you're gonna give it to me regardless of what I say."

"Valid point. Anyway, I think you should give it a shot before you call it quits. The strength of a relationship isn't measured in time. You could know someone for a lifetime and things could fall apart, the same way you can know someone for a day and they might be the one."

Carol presses her lips together while I ruminate on the words that came out of my mouth. Though the advice was directed to her relationship with Mark, it's difficult to ignore the pain that pierces me when I think about us—me and my friends. The argument of our friendship being unbreakable relied heavily on the fact that we've known each other for so long. But here we are, slowly falling apart and I'm the only one noticing.

Are these just intrusive thoughts again? I'm being so selfish. She has a problem right now and I'm thinking about myself again. Pull yourself together, Lara.

"I think you're right," Carol says. "I got nervous and freaked out."

"Does that mean you'll get back together with Mark?"

She winces. "He didn't get the same story I told you."

Apparently, the story Mark got was that Carol didn't like him anymore. When he wouldn't believe it, she proceeded to lie and say that she'd developed feelings for someone new. And now I go back to having a shoulder soaked in her tears. I realize that it's up to the third wheels to fix the problem and restore balance to the universe (which includes reverting Carol back to being the spirited and ferocious person that she is). James and I are the perfect pair for revenge plans, but perhaps it's time for us to transition into the roles of the heroes. I wrap my arms around Carol in a tight hug. "Things are going to be okay; we'll fix this."

I sit on my unmade bed with my legs crossed, waiting patiently for him to arrive. After some news that Seb's Little League team would be having a meeting at James's place, we decided to relocate our tutoring session to my house. Obviously, we both know that today's learning involves strategic planning for getting a couple back together rather than factoring polynomials using synthetic division.

My cell phone rings, and a very *strange* caller ID pops up on my screen: Most amazingly handsome and superhot model who is smarter than Lara. (Plus heart emojis and other various emojis that I do not wish to describe.)

"Hello? Who's this?" I ask, as if I know more than one overly confident guy who has my phone number.

"It's your amazingly handsome and superhot model who is smarter than you, of course." His smirk transfers via audio waves now; what an impressive technological revolution.

I swallow a laugh because I don't want to provoke a cascading event of more egotistical statements. "Are you almost here?"

"Almost. I'll be there in five more minutes."

"Perfect."

After hanging up the phone, five minutes turns into ten minutes and when the doorbell rings, my petty self doesn't answer it and instead I stay sitting cross-legged on my bedroom floor with my back against the side of my bed. Lucky for him, Lola Nora opens the door and lets him inside. When James arrives at my bedroom door, I shoot foam bullets at him using a Nerf gun—payback for the five extra minutes he kept me waiting. He raises his arms to cover his face, approaching me quickly before ripping the toy gun from my hands and flinging it onto the bed.

"Really, Lara?"

I stick my nose in the air, holding my chin high. "You were late, it's a legal form of punishment, and I wanted to. I probably would've decided against it, had you been here earlier. Where were you?"

He sets his backpack on the floor and sits down, resting his back against the wall opposite my bed. Since my room is small and his legs are long, they almost reach the bed frame. "Ms. K kept me for a long conversation." He sighs. "She can talk forever."

"Were you asking about math? Or was she rambling?"

"Well, I wanted to ask about the last test we got back, and we went over that. She actually marked one thing wrong, so I scored a little higher than expected and got a B," he says sheepishly.

I clap for the good news. "That's great!"

His face brightens and I swear he turns a little pink. "Thanks. I mean, I guess I have to thank you for *some* of it but"—he sports a cocky grin—"I am kind of smart."

I give his leg a little kick, but my own smile doesn't fade.

"Afterward, while she was complaining about her no-good nephew who took her car without asking, I saw *this* on her desk," he says as he pulls a large, sparkly white butterfly-shaped hair clip out of his backpack and holds it up. "I said I'd return it to you." He slides the clip across the floor in my direction.

"Thanks." My stupid stomach does that thing again and I tell it to stop.

"Your hair's practically a bird's nest without it, so it would be a crime to humanity if I didn't step forward and solve the problem."

And just like that, my usual facial expression returns, eyes glaring at him as his face twists into the most annoying smirk you've ever seen. "*Wow*, you solved a humanitarian crisis today, good for you. Should we nominate you for a Nobel Peace Prize now?"

He clicks his tongue then looks away from me, biting down on a smile and shaking his head.

Across from me is James's hoodie, folded perfectly by the door. It's stayed in my room longer than anticipated only because I never remember to give it back and he seemed to forget about it. It's so close to him but he hasn't noticed it. I slide my butt across the floor, reach for the sweater then hold it in front of him.

"You forgot to take your sweater back last Friday."

Rather than making an effort to reach for it, he pushes it back to me. "I didn't forget about it. You would've been cold on your way home, and it looked good on you."

I blink. "Oh."

Oh.

It finally registers in my brain that James has given me a compliment, and the rest of my body doesn't know how to process it. Neural impulses suddenly get transmitted a gazillion times faster than normal and my body temperature rises way too fast for my liking. We sit in awkward silence for a moment, both our cheeks reddening. I know why this is happening: my room's much warmer than usual and the humidity is terrible. Too bad Dad's too cheap to let me turn on the AC.

Finally, James breaks the awkward silence with an even more awkward cough. "You can keep it, I have a lot more at home and you could use some new wardrobe pieces," he says, judgmentally eyeing my current loungewear.

I throw the sweater at his face. "Excuse me, but I have great taste! It just so happens that you're blind."

"Says the one with the glasses."

"Just take it back. I don't want your sweater. It's too big and too warm and it smells too much like oranges." I cross my arms over my chest and move over to the other side of the room.

He follows and plops it back in my arms. "The secret to smelling like oranges is the orange scented shower gel from the Body Shop," he says with a wink. I scoff even though that was a question I had. If anything, I liked how comfortable he was with himself. When we first started high school, he got teased for his preference of fruit over the regular men's cologne or dare I say, Axe (which infused the hallways). He couldn't have cared less, and for a short amount of time after, the trend carried on and guys started to smell like fruit punch.

I climb onto the bed, folding the sweater back into a square and placing it near a couple of throw pillows. "I'm guessing you heard about the breakup?"

He joins me, sitting at the edge of the mattress and causing it to sink beneath me. Chewing on the nail of his thumb, he says, "Yeah, that your best friend broke Mark's heart?"

"She lied," I argue. "Carol only broke up with him because she was scared that they'd eventually break up when she goes away for university. She knew Mark wouldn't accept that reason, so she lied and said she didn't like him anymore. Is he talking to you? Because he's ignoring me, and we have to do something to get them to communicate."

James scrolls through some messages on his phone. "Yeah, he is. The man's depressed, not to mention his hygiene—*that* went downhill quick. But why do we have to do all this work? Can't Carol talk to him herself?"

"First of all, she's convinced that Mark won't give her the chance. Second of all, considering his reaction, she's probably right."

James agrees. Apparently, Mark has only spoken to him after the breakup, and even their communication is infrequent. The question is, how do we get them to talk to each other?

His eyes light up with a wild flicker, the same one Carol usually gets. "Let's kidnap them, tie them up in your basement with their backs together, then leave. It's like an intense version of an escape room and those always bring people together."

Ignoring the fact that his plan is borderline illegal, actually, *fully* illegal, I say, "James, I'm not locking them up in my basement. My house is chaotic enough."

He raises both hands behind his head before lying down. "Fine. What do you suggest we do?"

My plan is equally unethical, but involves a lower chance of us getting arrested, so it'll have to do. "Since they'll both be at school regardless, we could lock them up in a classroom. It'll force them to talk to each other and we'll be ready to let them out once they've sorted through their problems."

He springs up from the mattress. "*At school? Really?* Do you want to get caught?"

"Think about it," I continue, "the only place that those two will be at, at the same time, is school. They're both way too upset to actually go anywhere else. We'll easily be able to lure them into a classroom."

"That's great and all but how about the, I don't know, *teachers*?"

I laugh and shake my head. "Jameson Bryer, leave that part to me."

He massages his temples, probably wondering what I'm getting us into. But if we're going to get those hormonal teenagers back together, this is the only route we can take. Equipped with the powers that come with being third wheels, James and I must succeed at this mission.

TIP ELEVEN:
REUNITE THE HORMONAL TEENAGERS

✸

James and I sit at our desks in the middle of second period biology as Ms. Perez explains yet another concept regarding homeostasis. He stares blankly into space, hooking and unhooking his foot around the metal leg of the chair, while I prop my chin on my hand, trying my very best to look interested. He pulls a hair tie from my wrist, stretching it out to create a star shape, before proudly showing it off to me and the girls behind us. I hold out my palm for him to return it, but he ties up his own wavy hair—the top half of it—into a short ponytail so that it looks like a palm tree. And I guess that's fitting because his green army jacket reminds me of a forest.

Half the class is dazed or dozed off, and I think Ms. Perez is getting tired of choosing me to answer every single question. The worst part is, I didn't volunteer! I raised my hand for one question and now she's expecting me to answer everything. But she did yell at me on day one, so I need to revive Lara 2.0 from the grave, in hopes of securing a shiny grade for my transcript.

Suddenly, Ms. Perez stops teaching, and her eyes light up. Scurrying over to her organized desk, she pulls out a pile of papers. "Class, I almost forgot to tell you, we have a field trip next Friday!"

At the words *field* and *trip* everyone comes back to life: eyes focus to the front, backs straighten, and people start talking. She says we're headed to Ripley's Aquarium but that hardly matters. We're jumpy teenagers who constantly complain about school—the field trip could be to the recycling center, and we'd get excited.

James and I shove the permission forms into our backpacks as the bell rings and we move onto our math class, ready to ask for Ms. K's help. By help, I mean asking to use her classroom after school. Upon entering, we see Ms. K writing at her desk, while our classmates sit quietly at theirs, flipping through their binders. What is normal for some teachers is bizarre for Ms. K. Where are the daily memes? Where is the generic pop music? Why is there nobody dancing or debating or drawing on the SMART Board?

"Hey, Ms. K, did someone die?" James calls.

"Not yet, James," she answers. *That escalated quickly.*

"Yet? What does she mean by yet?" he whispers to me. He isn't the best whisperer because Ms. K answers before I do. I had Ms. K before and whenever she was acting bizarre it was because—

The bell rings and she walks over to the door, slamming it shut. "James, by yet, I mean one thing." She rubs her hands together and a wicked grin forms on her face. "I hope you've all prayed for your grades because today we will be writing a pop assignment!"

"Who the hell gives pop assignments? Pop quizzes, yeah, but pop assignments?" Two lines appear between James's brows. Perhaps we shouldn't have skipped yesterday's study session. Oops.

"All teachers have to torture their students sometimes," Ms. K jokes. "It's the only fun part of our job."

A student named Joe (who never really speaks) mutters, "That sounds . . . cruel."

She waves his comment off with a flick of her wrist. "Of course not, dear, cruelty is only a requirement for mathematics *professors*, not high-school teachers. My job description only requires me to have a *tinge* of ruthlessness."

Everyone stares at her with unreadable expressions, maybe something between bewildered and afraid.

She breaks the concerning silence. "You guys have the whole period to do this assignment. You can start once you get it."

When the two pages of problems hit my desk, I already know that this is going to take me the entire period and perhaps more brainpower than I currently have. Our plan instantly sinks, and I only hope it can resurface later.

At the end of the day, James and I find ourselves staring at a steel door, waiting for the last of Ms. K's fourth period students to get out, ready to continue with our plan. I give James a mischievous grin as he frowns at me in question. "So, how exactly are you planning to convince her to let us 'borrow' her classroom?"

I whisper, "Just let me do the talking."

Finally, the last student leaves and I knock on the open door. Ms. K turns around and walks over to us, arms crossed, with a puzzled look across her face. "What are you two doing here? *Again*. Have you guys finally decided to get along and stop fighting? While I do enjoy your company in the morning, it would be nice if I could listen to something other than both of you arguing over a *muffin* at eight a.m."

James shoots me a wink before wrapping an arm around me. "Actually, yes. We're getting along *so* well. We're together now."

I glare at James. Why does he never listen! *I'm* doing the talking!

Her eyes widen and before she has the chance to go into cardiac arrest, I jump in to control the situation. "By together, he means that we're conducting an *experiment* together. Which is the subject that we came to discuss." I jab James's side with my elbow, and he grunts.

"So, you guys *aren't* together?" she asks, probably disappointed that our morning bickering is not coming to a halt anytime soon.

"Not at all," I confirm.

She looks at James for his statement.

"Yeah, she's not my type." He shrugs casually.

That was blunt and a bit unnecessary, but okay. I catch him eyeing me up and down. "Why are you scanning me?"

"I'm looking at you to confirm that you are definitely *not* my type."

There's a small pang in my chest that I believe can be categorized as anger. James shouldn't be the one doing this! *I'm* supposed to be saying that *he's* not *my* type. Not the other way around! I'll consider it a compliment that I'm not his type. I'm so *glad* that I'm not in the category of his "type."

"It's too bad that you're not into smart, confident, and opinionated girls then," I huff. Maybe the confident part was a lie, but nobody has to know that.

"Why? Do you *want* me to like you?" He raises an eyebrow and a smirk forms on his annoying face.

My brows furrow. "No, actually. I find this works well. For the record, you're not my type either."

Suddenly, fingers snap in front of our faces, causing us both to blink in Ms. K's direction. "Wonderful that you've both established that you're not each other's cup of tea, but I have a staff meeting in five minutes so . . ."

We apologize at the same time.

"Can you guys tell me what you need?" She smiles sweetly though she must want to kick us out for her own sanity.

"Do you think we could borrow your classroom for our psychological experiment?" I ask hopefully.

"This school doesn't have a psychology course."

"I'm planning to major in it next year," I lie. "My aunt's a professor and I asked if I could try out one of the assignments to see what I would be going into." *I am not planning to go into psychology, and my aunt actually sells pirated CDs.*

Ms. K gives me a look of approval. "That sounds very much like the bright Lara I know. I'm looking forward to seeing what you end up doing in the future." Even though everything I'm saying is part of a scam, it feels weird pretending that I know where I'm going. There's a type of pressure now, knowing that even my favorite teacher has those expectations at the back of her mind. Thankfully, she shifts her focus to James. "What about you?"

"We're doing this project together. She convinced me to be her partner since she clearly can't find anyone better." He winks at me again and I roll my eyes.

"James, stop teasing the girl! She already has two classes too many with you," she jokes, and James acts with mock offense. "Could I ask, what exactly is the experiment?"

"We are going to be examining the reaction of two people within a confined space over various time stamps," I explain. "Our participants will not be expecting to be trapped in the room, so we hypothesize that they'll react negatively. On top of that, we will be seeing if they can get along for an hour and without the use of any personal devices."

"Have you considered the ethics behind your study?"

James and I share a look before responding, "Nope."

She doesn't seem to care about our answer anyway, eager to get to her meeting. "Okay, then! That's very interesting!" She hands me a lanyard with the key to the classroom. “I’ll be in the school until five in the conference room so return this to me when you guys are done. Lara, watch that James of yours and make sure he doesn’t set anything on fire.”

Before James can defend himself (with little to no evidence for his side), I say, “Don’t worry, I’ll keep an eye on him.”

“Tell me how the experiment plays out!” She strides away, high heels loudly tapping the floor.

When she gets far enough away, out of hearing range, I dangle the lanyard in front of James, who stares at me in shock.

“How did you do that?”

“You’d be surprised with the things you can get away with when you talk about academia.” I shrug. “Now, you get Mark and I’ll get Carol.”

He salutes me and we part ways, ready to conduct our “experiment” with our participants. I get back first, having convinced Carol that I lost a bracelet in the classroom and need help finding it. She crawls under the desks while I step out, saying that I need to use the washroom.

While keeping Carol in the room is easy enough, Mark puts up a larger fight when he sees her crawling underneath the desks. “She’s the one who broke up with me. If she doesn’t like me anymore, I’m not going to make myself get hurt all over again.”

James holds him in an effort to prevent his escape. “Sorry, buddy, but I have to do this.”

“Do wha—” Mark starts but unfortunately, James is bigger and stronger than him (plus he has the advantage of surprise). He forcefully pushes Mark into the classroom, and I rush to lock the door. Once he realizes what just happened, Mark pounds on the door with a balled fist, shouting profanities muffled by the barrier between us.

In reply, James makes a heart with his hands. Carol crawls out from under the desk and asks, "What are you doing here?"

Mark removes himself from the window to acknowledge her. "I should be asking you the same thing," he says with a frustrated look on his face. Ah, young love, so *expressive*. James and I shove each other in an attempt to get the best view from the tiny window.

As they yell, I ponder aloud, "How long do you think it'll take for them to make up or make out for that matter?"

James tilts his head from side to side a few times. "Fifteen minutes. Tops."

"Fifteen? I feel like they won't talk to each other for, maybe, the first twenty minutes. It's probably going to take more than forty-five minutes to reach reconciliation."

"Are you sure?"

"Confident."

"You want to bet on that, Dela Cruz?" He inches his arrogant face to mine, eyes shifting down for a split second before locking with mine.

I keep my stance because even though his close proximity is inducing strange physiological responses, I will never let myself back off from a bet. Especially if it's against him. "Why not? I'm going to win anyway. How much do you want to bet? Ten bucks if I'm right."

"Sure," he agrees seriously. "And if I win?"

"If you win, then I'll give you ten bucks."

"I don't want ten bucks. If I win the bet, you have to . . ."

I tap my foot impatiently and glance at my nonexistent watch. "I have to do what? Go on a date with you?" I tease, as if he would actually say that.

"Ew. *No*. There's no need for me to expose myself to more trauma. If I win the bet you have to save me a wish because I'm indecisive and don't know what to ask for," he says, a small sparkle forming in his eyes.

"That's not fair. That wish could be anything, and anything could be something disgusting or illegal."

"No, the wish will be something appropriate and not disgusting or illegal. I promise." After receiving a skeptical glance, he raises a hand to his chest. "I swear on my life."

"Whatever. But you have to win the bet first, and frankly, I think I know much more about hypotheses and probabilities, so that ten bucks is mine."

"If you say so . . ." He walks to the classroom door and peeks through the glass window. "Hey, how much time has passed since we locked them in there?"

I look at my phone. "Ten minutes."

"I think I need to start thinking about that wish . . ."

I run to the window to see what the idiot is looking at. The sight of Carol and Mark hugging greets me, taking the potential of ten extra bucks from me in the process. They pull away, and he cups her face. She closes her eyes as Mark leans in to—

"STOP! THIS IS A CLASSROOM FOR GOODNESS' SAKE!" I burst through the door and yell so loudly that they jump away from each other. "AND THANKS TO YOU I'M NOT GOING TO GET MY TEN BUCKS!"

I realize my loudness and regain some composure. "I—I mean, I'm so glad you guys are okay again!"

Before I have the chance to say anything else, James butts in, "Oh thank God. I could *not* handle Mark's endless sobbing."

"Thank you," they say before walking out of the classroom and engulfing me in a group hug. I squirm, looking for a way out of this death grip. As much as I like seeing people happy, I really wanted ten extra dollars and bragging rights. Couldn't they have been mad at each other for another five minutes? I finally escape their grasp, only for James to tug on my arm.

"Ah, the endless possibilities of my wish," James starts with a cocky grin. I turn around with a huff, ignoring him. "Lara—"

"Let me grieve my ten dollars in peace!"

In reply, he picks me up and throws me over his shoulder, giving me the regretful view of his rear end. I slap his back multiple times, but he doesn't put me down and instead starts to walk away from Mark and Carol.

Carol and Mark chuckle and James carries me across the hallway. "Put me down!" I yell and he gently places me on the ground.

He wiggles his eyebrows. "I wonder what I should wish for . . ."

Mark and Carol leave the school first, thanking us again for our service. We lock up Ms. K's classroom then head to the conference room to return the keys. She asks us how the experiment went, and I answer with some big words that I don't fully understand but Google uses them a lot when describing social experiments. Finally, we can say "mission accomplished" but there's an awful feeling of regret that sits heavily on my chest, a selfish regret about getting them back together. I wish it wasn't there, but a part of me wonders if they had stayed broken up, would my old friend come back to me? Would I have solved my third-wheel dilemma?

The questions continue to circle around my mind as we walk back to James's place. Despite the unusual quietness of our surroundings, James talks for as long as he doesn't need to breathe. Most of it is about hockey, which I don't get, but I try to listen. The team drama (for him at least) is that someone is "out to take his spot," which seems like an overexaggeration considering he's been able to beat out the upperclassmen since the tenth grade. Nonetheless, I can't even be sure if I understood that correctly because I'm still thinking about Carol and Mark getting back together and what that means for us and our friendships.

"Can I ask you something stupid?" I look up at James, hoping to be met by a reassuring glance or sympathetic smile, but it's merely his cocky grin.

"Lara, I've known you since diaper days. Personally, I think most things you say are pretty stupid."

"Just because you know that everything you say is stupid doesn't mean you have to project your insecurities onto me," I say, narrowing my eyes.

"Aw, look at little miss psychologist and her long sentences," he coos, pinching my cheek, and I slap his hand away. "Am I getting a romantic gesture? Several girls have asked me to prom already but go ahead, take your shot and I'll add your name to the raffle."

"Whatever," I grunt, walking away.

He runs up to me, grabs my hand, and pulls me to a halt. "Okay, okay, I'm sorry. What's wrong?"

I take in a sharp breath. "Do you think we should've done that? Helped them get back together?"

I chew on my inner cheek, feeling my breathing grow heavier. Saying the question out loud leaves a distasteful flavor on my tongue, one that extends into my body, and thinking about it makes me feel worse, like I'm repulsive.

"What? Why would you ask that?"

"Never mind, I told you it was stupid." I turn to walk away again but his grip on my hand tightens, keeping me in the same position.

"You can tell me," he says gently, a sharp contrast to his usual loudness.

"They're always forgetting about us, don't you see it? The only time they came back to talk to us was when they were mad at each other! When was the last time you hung out with your friends alone?" My throat starts to dry up right after and I feel my heart racing and that *stupid* lump forming in my throat again, the one I *always* have to swallow.

And besides that, there's so much guilt; it's like a tsunami that washes over the shore and when it recedes, you're left with nothing at all. *It's not fair,* I want to shout. It's not fair that I have to feel so horrible and I can't even feel horrible because my brain tells me that it's wrong and I'm selfish and I feel disgusting. Noticing that my hands are shaking, I break from his grasp and shove them in my jacket pockets.

Then he hugs me. My breath hitches when he does. The hug is tight and comforting, but it's also awkward—somewhat. And although we receive a couple of judgmental stares from bystanders, I stay for as long as he doesn't let go. Luckily by then, the rising and falling of my chest is steady; the waves are calmer and it's like the storm never happened.

For the rest of the way, we don't say anything to each other. He doesn't try to crack any jokes or initiate any playful arguments. I can't tell if he's uncomfortable or not and I hope I didn't accidentally do something wrong. I don't remember the last time he's seen me like that.

We finally get to his house and there is a deep laugh coming from the kitchen. It sounds superfamiliar. I look at James but he's already running to the kitchen with me chasing him. We enter and see Lola Edna laughing with—

"Dad? Dad, you're back!" James exclaims and runs to Tito Danny. His dad gets up from his seat and takes James in his arms, engulfing him in a tight hug as he laughs. It's almost as if time rewinds as I see

James as the small, vulnerable boy who was at his father's side at all times. Now, he's a bit taller than his dad, but I don't think they've ever looked so similar.

Tito Danny is tall, with the same broad shoulders as James; his hair is a bit lighter and more curly than wavy, but it's obvious that James shares many features with his father. They share the same light skin and dimpled, charismatic smile; and although James's eyes are dark like Tita Gia's instead of light green like his father's, they both have the same mischievous sparkle—the unpredictable kind that intrigues you.

"Weren't you coming back in December?" James asks, mouth still hanging open from the surprise.

"Yeah, but we landed a few deals early so here I am! When's your mother getting home? I have a reservation for a family dinner tonight." He adjusts the cuffs of his well-tailored navy blazer before going, "Plus, I kind of missed you all."

James laughs, his eyes lighting up with childlike happiness. I haven't seen those eyes in a while. "She's coming soon," he says.

James seems to remember that I'm standing awkwardly at the door, observing their interaction in silence. Tito Danny follows his gaze, and his eyes go round when he sees me. "Lara? How's my daughter that I never had?" He pulls James and me into another tight hug. I always found it a bit funny that Tita Gia and Tito Danny always brought up how they desperately wanted a daughter but ended up with three sons. The opposite was true in my household, in which everyone would question my parents for not trying a third time in hopes of a son.

Tito Danny's like a second father, just like how Tita Gia's like my second mom. Before his business exploded in Europe, he'd spend a lot of time with us. But that was a long time ago, even before Gabe and

Illa were born. Tita Gia was the breadwinner for their family when his business was merely seeds planted in the ground. During those times, I vaguely remember how he'd take us to the park and the zoo and McDonald's.

"I'm great," I say with a big smile.

James glances at me for a second before looking away, and I assume he's thinking about the mini–anxiety attack I had earlier.

"Wait, what *are* you doing here?" Tito Danny asks, but before I get the chance to answer, he turns to James with widened eyes. "Are you guys finally dating?" Before James can respond to that, Tito Danny turns to me. "You're going to be our daughter-in-law. You're literally going to be a part of this family!" He almost starts clapping but we both interrupt him.

"We're not dating," James and I say in unison then look at each other.

"Oh." A wave of disappointment washes over his face. "But you guys are the perfect match! Just think about the stories you'll be able to tell your kids because you've known each other for so long—"

James laughs awkwardly, cheeks turning the slightest shade of pink, stopping his dad from saying anything more. "Dad, always making *great* jokes. How about we talk about your trip? How was it?"

Tito Danny rambles on about the business trip and tells us about the beauty of Paris. After a while, he leaves James and me to our studies, which we finish in the upstairs library this time.

Their library is massive and gorgeous; it's everything I'd want for my future study. It's calm and quiet except for the ticking of the old clock that hangs above the door. Dark wooden bookshelves line one of the walls, while the opposing one has glass cabinets against large gray stones in an irregular pattern. At the end of the room is a single window, curved at the top and extending inches from the ceiling to a long seat created by the recessed wall. We don't turn on the chandelier lights and instead let the sun illuminate the large space in the best way it can. James and I sit beside each other at the wide desk in the middle of the room. Out of nowhere, he looks up from his work and smiles at me.

My brows furrow but I can't suppress my own lips from curving up. "What?"

"Nothing. I'm just happy," he says softly. His hair falls against his forehead, and I catch a glimpse of his old self, the boyish James I haven't seen in a while.

The James that I missed. So much.

Without thinking, I inch closer to him and brush the hair from his face. He looks at me in surprise and I pull away, my heart beating a mile a minute. There's a scientific explanation: heart problems run in the family. There's no way that . . . he can't be the reason that I can't catch my breath.

"Sorry. Your hair was bugging me. It looked so horrible that I had to fix it." *Stupid ugly hairstyle.*

He points at his ruffled hair. "And *this* looks better?" I scrunch my nose. He's right, it looks even worse.

I ruffle his hair and it becomes so messy that it looks almost good. "There. That's better."

James presses his lips together and looks at me with eyes so gentle and soft, like how they were when we were little. They're the same eyes that would make me feel like everything was going to be okay. Right here, in the dimly lit library with my annoying childhood enemy, I realize that even though my best friends seem to be fading away by the day, he seems to be returning. Little by little, I see pieces of the James I used to know.

TIP TWELVE:
BECOME A COUPLE'S PHOTOGRAPHER

✱

Ripley's Aquarium is fascinating because for a few hours you can pretend that you're exploring the deep seas instead of a concrete jungle in a province with no seaside. I have no clue as to why the biology department chose this place when marine organisms have close to nothing to do with our current unit of study. Perhaps it's for the visual appeal—which I wish I could enjoy.

I shift around, trying to get a good angle to take a picture of a shark, but Jasmine and Logan block the view with a *disgusting display* of public affection. "I'm trying to take pictures of the fish and you're scaring them away!"

James grips my shoulders, getting ready to pry me off of the couple in the event that I physically jump on them. Luckily, they break from the kiss before I have a complete meltdown.

"Lara," Jasmine starts, walking toward me and extending a hand with her cell phone. "Can you take a picture of us, *please*?"

"Do I *look* like a photographer?" If anything, I only like to photograph not-vomit-inducing subjects.

"Yes," Logan answers and he receives the death glare. "No, I mean no. I'm sorry."

"Please, Lara?" Jasmine repeats with a pout, and I gesture for Logan to stand with his girlfriend.

They pose in front of the display of tropical fish, making silly faces and googly eyes at each other as I snap pictures of them on Jasmine's phone. On the bright side, she's less picky about photos than Kiera, so there's only one adjustment period during which she fixes the barrettes in her hair. "Now can you guys move so I can take a picture of this shark?" Fortunately, they listen and walk away, finding another place to traumatize fish.

I snap a couple of pictures of the shark before continuing onto the moving sidewalk, excited to get to the Dangerous Lagoon—the best exhibit because the glass tunnel allows you to see the sharks swimming right above you.

James pokes my arm and I turn to face him. He points to two red fish with their lips pressed together. "Look, it's Jasmine and Logan," he says, and I snort. "I didn't know that fish kiss."

I pull my phone up to take a picture. "They don't. At least, not romantically. It's a form of aggression."

"Interesting. We'd be kissing all the time." His words come out as a statement rather than a flirtatious joke, but it doesn't minimize the flush that slowly creeps up my neck. "I mean, if we were fish," he finishes.

Attempting to hide my face, I walk past him. "Well, thank God we're not fish."

As we make our way through the Dangerous Lagoon, my cell phone stays tucked inside my pocket because there's absolutely no way I can admire the animals swimming gracefully around us if I don't give them all my attention. A tiger shark swims right above our heads, and its shadow moves along the floor. The colors of the fish create a swirling rainbow around the tank, and it feels like magic.

James and I reach the end of the path, where there's a little pool with horseshoe crabs and stingrays. Becoming little kids again, we push past each other to touch the stingrays. Even the elementary school kids watch us with raised eyebrows, but neither of us minds. For the first time in a long time, I feel airy and light, like I'm floating.

The field trip finally ends, and students file out of the aquarium. Outside, we wait for the bus, sitting on nearby benches. I lean the back of my head against the bench, staring at the sky. The CN Tower, situated right beside the aquarium, looms over us. Having looked up at it for our entire lives, it isn't really interesting anymore; it's simply a tall, gray tower that casts its shadow over the city, catching the attention of tourists and photographers. Sometimes I wonder why we start to lose interest in things. After too long is it inevitable? Do we simply get tired of the old and move on?

Jasmine and Logan sit a couple of benches down, laughing at something again. I wonder if it's the same thing they laughed about that day on her porch when I walked home behind them. My left thumb traces circles on the back of my other hand as I think about my friends losing interest in our friendship. Why is it so hard for us to spend time together now? Are they simply tired of our group? Do they laugh more with their boyfriends than they do when we're together? Is our friendship not interesting enough for them?

But most of all, and it makes my heart ache when I wonder, *Do they miss our group like I do?* Even sometimes?

I am pulled out of my daze when I turn my head to the side and see James with his chin propped on his hand, staring.

Looking over my shoulder, I make sure that he's looking at me and not some other rando on the street, before saying, "Would you care to tell me what is so interesting about my face that you have to stare, my mortal enemy?"

He sits up straight, frowning the way he does when he thinks.

"Do you still think we're enemies?" he asks, catching me off guard. "Quite a bit has changed between us, don't you think? For one thing, we can hang out without one of us ending up with a bruise."

And sometimes we're the opposite of enemies, I want to add, thinking about the way he held me last week, how he delivered my hair clip and gave me his sweater and never ditched me like my friends. Instead, I go, "My punches and kicks don't give bruises? I need to start working out."

"Oh they do." He laughs. "But my point is, I think we're actually *friends* now," he says, cringing at the word friends.

I let out an overdramatic gasp. "James, it's been only a few weeks since we were full-on mortal enemies! Don't you think this is going too fast?" *Everything's going too fast. I'm supposed to despise you and now I don't.*

"So, we *can't* be friends?"

"How about frenemies?" I extend a hand, and it takes a second for him to take it.

"Frenemies." That word is enough to make me feel at ease. It's not that big of a jump, enemies to frenemies. It just means that we're equal parts nice and mean to each other and whatever we have now is going to continue smoothly. Frenemies.

Unexpectedly, a figure appears over us, blocking the light, and we both look up to see Xander, smiling. "Can I join you guys?"

"Sure!" I say, and at the same time, James says, "No." I give him a pointed look. *Don't be rude,* I say with my eyes.

Xander seems unfazed by James's response, probably thinking that he's joking, but I know he isn't. Nobody talks for a few beats, so I pray that James stops frowning at Xander and clear my own throat. "So . . . uh . . . Xander, this is James, and James, this is my friend Xander."

"Lara, we—" Xander starts.

"We know each other," James finishes firmly.

There's a tension between the two of them, but it mostly radiates from James.

Xander sits beside me on the bench, and I ask, "Do you have bio? I didn't know that you're in Jasmine's class." There are only two biology classes this semester, so if he isn't in ours, he has to be in Jasmine's.

He shakes his head. "I have it next semester. Actually, I'm here with the grade ten science class. I'm doing the teaching co-op program. I thought it was too good of an opportunity to pass up." The co-op program at our school has senior students act as mini-teachers for a junior course and in return, they receive a credit.

"That's cool! I'm going to be doing that next semester with Ms. K," I say excitedly. I'm nervous about helping out with grade nine math but doing anything with Ms. K has to be some type of fun.

"You'll be great at it," Xander assures me.

"I didn't know you were planning on doing that next semester. Why didn't you tell me?" James asks, leaning forward in his seat and butting into the conversation. His brows are furrowed, and he looks almost offended that Xander knew before him.

I shrug before uncapping my water bottle and taking a sip of water. "You never asked."

Changing the topic, Xander says, "Lara, have you finished the application yet?"

As I say "No," James inquires, "Application?"

Xander nods. "We're trying to get a summer spot in a lab at the children's hospital. It's with this doctor we met while volunteering and it would be a great opportunity for both of us—"

"Like the whole summer?" James interrupts rudely.

I shoot him a glare. Yes, James can be rude, but it's usually never directed at people he hardly knows. *What's up with him?*

"It's like a regular job," Xander explains. "Eight to four on weekdays." His voice is the opposite of James's right now; it's patient and calm, which I'm grateful for, otherwise the levels of aggression around us would be too much to deal with. Xander continues, "But there are also presentations, seminars, and training days besides that, so it's going to be busy. Good thing you're not doing anything, right?"

Pressing my lips together, I nod. "Yeah . . . nothing." I guess that part isn't a lie, right? As each day passes, the further my friends seem to drift. They're moving ahead with their lives, with their boyfriends. Everyone's taking the next step and maybe I need to do the same. I focus on the tips of my shoes to avoid James's gaze burning through me. "But I guess that's something to think about if I get accepted." I shrug.

Xander gives me a reassuring squeeze on the shoulder while James shifts uncomfortably in his seat. "Trust me, you will." The statement makes me feel worse rather than better because deep down, I kind of want that rejection letter.

A younger kid pops up beside our bench, tapping Xander on the shoulder. I assume it's one of his students. "Xander, I think two kids are about to start a fight."

His eyes widen. "Where?"

"Around the corner."

Xander gets up quickly. "It was nice talking to you again," he says. "I'll see you both on Monday!"

I wave good-bye and the minute Xander leaves, James suddenly springs back to life. "I'm confused," he says.

"Aren't you always?" I walk away from the bench to stretch my legs before we board the bus.

He follows. "*I mean*, you're spending your entire summer, the last one before university, *in a lab?* Didn't you have something planned with your friends? That list thing? It doesn't sound right to switch it up." *How does he even know about that?*

"Your attitude back there also didn't sound right." I cross my arms, ignoring the remark about the list. "Why were you acting like such a jerk? Xander's a great guy."

James has the audacity to narrow his eyes at me. "I admit, maybe I wasn't as welcoming as I could've been, but how do you even know the guy who almost made me lose my captaincy?"

An exasperated groan escapes me. *Is this why he's being erratic? Because Xander's a good hockey player? Holy freaking fishballs.* "Did you not listen to anything he said? We volunteered together at the hospital. *Volunteering*? It's something people do when they care about other people. Besides, you have no reason to be angry about someone else playing on your team."

James opens his mouth then closes it again, unable to counter my point. He inhales deeply, eyes shut, composing himself. "You're right. I'm sorry."

Even though he says that, his tensed jaw fails to relax. I can't tell if he's still frustrated about Xander or if there's something else on his mind. My gut tells me it's the latter, but I can't be sure, I don't have any evidence. The tips of my fingers and toes feel hot and cold at the same time; they curl and uncurl as if that'll make the temperature return to normal. It doesn't. All I can think about is that this wasn't one of our regular arguments.

The ride going back to school is shorter than the one there—not that it's short at all. Getting anywhere in Toronto takes double the time because of how congested the roads are. I don't even notice that I doze off, only that I'm jolted awake by a flick on the forehead.

"We're back," James says. "You were drooling on my shoulder."

My eyes open and I wipe some saliva from the corner of my mouth with the sleeve of my sweater. "Sorry."

We arrive at school after the last bell has rung, so most of the students are gone. Heading straight to his house, neither of us initiates a conversation. I don't know what to say and he clearly doesn't want to talk to me, so I don't push it.

At his house, we study in the upstairs library again, sitting across from each other in the dimly lit space. It's quiet and Lola Edna doesn't bombard us with questions like she does when we're in the kitchen. I go over the notes first before teaching them to James, who is still awfully quiet. Toward the end he gives up on half the work and glues his eyes on his phone screen.

I snap a finger in front of his face. "Earth to James?"

He finally looks up. "Sorry, what?"

"You stopped on question forty-nine and we still have ten more to go. Don't forget, Monday's test is supposed to be brutal."

"I know. I really can't focus right now. Do you think we could schedule a session for Sunday?"

"Fine, but what are you even looking at?"

He places his phone, screen up, on the table, before slumping lazily in his chair. I glance at the phone screen to see an application site for Oxford. The page is filled with information about their business program and as I scroll through, the list of requirements starts to blur together. Suddenly, my mouth feels dry.

"You're applying to universities outside of the country?"

He nods. "I don't want to, but Dad wants me to think about every single option there is. There's no way I can get into Oxford with my grades, but he might murder me if I avoid applying completely."

"Why does he want you there so badly? It's just a school and it's kind of far."

"Kind of?" He laughs. "I think it's because he went there, and my grandparents went there. I'm assuming he wants it to become some sort of family tradition. He's making me apply to all the major universities in England."

I rest a cheek on my hand, imagining what it would be like if he went. Even though we didn't get along at times (fine, most of the time), I don't remember a time that he wasn't here. Even when I didn't want him near, he was always there. I try to ignore the pain that accompanies the thought of him leaving. He gets up from his seat and walks to the massive bookshelf at the side of the room, pulling books out halfway before pushing them back in.

Rising from my own seat, I walk over to where he stands. "Would you go if you got in?"

He does something that's a cross between a head shake and a nod. "Yes? I think so. I'm not sure. Over the past few years I haven't been able to spend much time with my dad, and he does most of his business things in Europe so . . ."

I bite the inside of my cheek and look down because I get this weird feeling when he talks about leaving and I don't want him to notice. All we do is bicker and we have almost nothing in common. Shouldn't I be okay with this?

"I don't care for university in general," he continues, "but if I have to go, I want to at least be near him. And I don't want him to be alone. Granddad's dementia has gotten worse, and he probably won't make it another year. Someone needs to be there for my dad, and it just so happens that university is an easy excuse to leave."

I don't know how to reply to that, so we stand in silence, leaning against the shelves and staring into the distance. I never met either of my grandfathers because they died before I was born, but James lost his *Lolo* a few years ago and it feels unfair for him to lose another grandparent so soon.

He returns to what he was doing before, pulling books out and pushing them back in over and over again. On the outside, James makes it seem like he doesn't have a care in the world. He flirts easily, dates on and off, and never lingers on a problem for too long. Sometimes I catch glimpses of the parts of him that he doesn't want to show, the moments when he's vulnerable and cares more than I'd expect him to. It's like invading a private moment no one should be watching. However, in those moments, I feel that he secretly wants to be seen; he wants to be caught in the act so that he isn't alone. But if he leaves, how can I do that?

Suddenly, James asks, "And you? You were right back there. I never actually asked you about your life."

I shake my head. "You're not obligated to."

"But I want to know," he says so seriously that I want to go ahead and give him all of my concerns and complaints about the uncertainties of my future.

"I don't know," I answer honestly. "I'm okay with going anywhere near here. I think I'll go into some type of life science."

"Have you thought about medicine?" he asks, and I fight the urge to say, *Yes, a thousand times*. It's always easy to think about a career but hard to pursue one, and harder to tell people in case you don't make it. "Then again, I've always seen you causing injuries instead of fixing them."

I laugh, punching his shoulder. "Just to you."

"Seriously, though, I could see you as a doctor," he says and my heart flutters. Someone really needs to hook me up to an ECG and have me checked.

"Really?"

"Really."

His confidence brings those strange symptoms back again, the same symptoms that had me thinking I was lactose intolerant. We've never talked about our futures like this—actually, we never had any serious conversations until this year. Yet here he is, reading my mind without knowing it and acknowledging my secrets without permission.

He rests his back against the shelf, dark hair blending into the umber-colored wood. There's no trace of a smile on his face, no hint of a joke, nothing. Light comes in through the one large Victorian style window of the study, illuminating his face. My chest aches slightly; he'll definitely see more windows like that in England.

"Would you miss me?" he asks, and my brows furrow at the unexpected question. His questions are supposed to be nonsensical, or funny and sometimes annoyingly flirty, not ones that put me on the spot and make my pulse increase.

"What do you mean?"

"If I left, would you miss me?" His dark-brown eyes pierce mine as we hold each other's gazes.

I press my lips together and nod slowly. "I think I would," I whisper.

"Good."

I don't know why, but my stomach does a quick somersault and I kind of like the feeling.

"I'm sorry about earlier," he says; this time his body relaxes. "I just thought this summer would look a bit different to you. You and your friends have been making your after grad list since forever and I thought it was something important."

My voice refuses to pick up strength when I say, "Me too." Again, my eyes travel anywhere but his face, though I know he can still read me like an open book.

"Don't give up on your friends so easily."

"I'm not the one letting go!" I snap. The words feel like fire against the walls of my throat. I'm the one holding on for dear life. Can't he see that?

He takes a step toward me, and his close proximity is comforting. His familiarity is safe.

Softly I say, "I don't know if things will be different with them by the time summer comes, and this is a great opportunity."

James nods understandingly but I can't help but notice the way his face falls slightly. He chews on his fingernail and stares right past me.

"Are you okay?" I ask.

His eyes focus back on me. "Yeah. You were talking about summer, and I started thinking about summer."

"And what about it?"

A half smile forms on his face but nothing reaches his eyes. Even in the light, they refuse to sparkle. "That it might be my last one here, before I leave."

I run a thumb over the knuckles of my other hand. There are airplanes, he's rich, of course this won't be his last summer here. But even if it isn't, is it going to be the same? The family road trips and swimming in the lake, the pranks and teasing . . . how long does that last?

"Don't think about that, it's hardly October. You're thinking too far ahead." Words that I never thought I'd say to the most careless and spontaneous boy I know come out of my mouth tart, like an expired sour candy.

TIP THIRTEEN:
TRY TO FIT IN WITH THE *PAMILYA*

✱

The beginning of a new month brings a particular type of chaos into my house, known as the Official Dela Cruz Decontamination Session—a dreadful name patented by Illa, suggesting that there's some type of contamination to begin with.

On hands and knees, I wipe the wooden floor of the living room—Cinderella-style because my dad doesn't believe in a Swiffer—with a rag soaked in some type of bubbly concoction that he's whipped up.

Loud laughter comes from the family room, and I frown. *What on earth could be so amusing in the middle of this horrendous event?* Curious, I walk over to the noise to see Lola Nora and Illa almost falling off of the brown leather couch while staring at Illa's cell phone.

"*Akalain mo . . . napili rin si Jade! Hindi na ako masusurpresa kung mag-divorce din sila pagkatapos ng isang linggo!*" (Who knew he'd pick Jade! I wouldn't be surprised if they got divorced after a week!) Lola Nora manages to say between chuckles.

"*Lola naman! Paabutin n'yo naman po kahit dalawang linggo man lang!*" (Lola! Make it at least two weeks!) Illa says.

"*Kontrabida talaga ang dating niya, e,*" (She really seems like an antagonist though,) Lola Nora replies, playfully slapping Illa's arm.

I stand, confused and holding a dirty rag in one hand. "*Ano na naman ang pinag-uusapan n'yo?*" (What are you guys talking about again?)

Illa and Lola Nora direct the same judgmental look toward me.

For some odd reason, the oldest and youngest members of our household are carbon copies of each other. And both of them are overdressed for the occasion. Illa's pink hair is tied up in a messy bun, but I don't think that she'll ever fully sacrifice fashion—even when we're in the middle of a deep clean. A purple satin slip dress sits over a white floral patterned T-shirt, and if I was wearing an outfit as nice, I'd probably accidentally spill some sort of chemical on it.

If Lola Nora was a thirteen-year-old today, I bet she'd look the same. But since she isn't, her black hair stays in its pixie cut, but accessorized by an array of jeweled hair clips. It just so happens that her *pambahay* (house) dress is also a light shade of lavender.

"Ate," Illa starts, "you don't get it. We're talking about the season finale of *The Bachelor*. It was the biggest fail we've ever seen. Like, ever."

I hold an arm out just in case there's some sort of attack coming. Occasionally, they get so worked up about a show that they express their emotions through intense (and sometimes dangerous) physical gesturing. "You guys are not going to do anything about it . . . right?"

Illa shakes her head again. "Why would we do anything? The ending was great."

"You just said it was a failure."

Lola Nora nudges Illa, saying, "*Hindi niya mage-gets*." (She won't get it.)

"*Alam mo . . .*" (You know . . .) Lola Nora starts and there are only two possibilities for what she'll say next:

A.) She is going to insult my lack of social knowledge.

B.) She is going to rant about my lack of social life.

"*Baka hindi mo kami maintindihan kasi hindi ka naman pamilyar sa mundo ng social media. Sinabi ko naman sa 'yo na mag-install ka ng Instagram para mai-send ko yung mga pinag-uusapan namin ni Illa. At isa pa, wala ka rin namang alam sa usaping pag-ibig so . . .*" (You might not understand us because you're not familiar with the world of social media. I told you to install Instagram so I can send you what Illa and I are talking about. Besides, you don't even know anything about love so . . .)

Hold the phone. *Excuse me?* "*Walang alam?*" (Don't know anything?) I say, hands on hips. "Actually, I know a lot about love, which is the reason why I'm trying to avoid it. I'd rather not turn out like Jasmine and Logan, who keep sucking each other's faces off."

Illa laughs. "Is that the real reason?"

"Yes. It's disgusting and it makes me uncomfortable. Enough about my lack of love life, you guys should be cleaning and not rewatching *The Bachelor*."

Lola Nora reclines her seat and puts her hands behind her head, relaxing. "*Retired na ako so . . .*" (I'm already retired so . . .)

"Illa?"

She starts to wipe down the blinds. "I can multitask perfectly," she says, holding her phone in one hand and cleaning with the other. Meanwhile, it looks like she's about to knock over some of the potted plants.

In the driveway, our parents are working together to wash the cars. Mom has the weekend off, which is great since she's been working weekends for the past two weeks. I approach them, hoping to get permission to go out with my friends. *Maybe the KJC is finally free for once . . .* I feel stupid that I keep trying, but friendships have obstacles, and James was right when he said not to give up on them.

"Mom?" I call.

There's loud laughter and shrieking coming from the front. When I get there, water is splashing all around and the elderly couple next door is staring at my parents. My mother chases my dad with a hose in hand. He runs around the cars, avoiding getting sprayed. Speechless, I turn to our neighbors, who gave me a concerned look. I wave and hold an awkward smile. This is one of the reasons why we're never invited to any block parties.

"Sorry, *na*!" Dad shouts, his hands up in surrender.

Mom doesn't budge and continues to run after him. He gives up and ends up getting sprayed with the hose. It isn't long until he runs up to her and engulfs her in a big hug, lifting her from the ground and transferring water onto her clothes as well.

And as amusing as my parents' relationship can be, all I want to do is ask if I can see my friends and run out of here. Romance in itself is a cringey thing, and although I'm thankful to have parents who obviously love each other, having parents who've never left the honeymoon phase can get kind of weird.

"Mom! Dad!" I yell, and they both stop what they're doing.

"*Anak, sabihin mo nga sa mom mo na hindi tama na i-spray-an ng tubig ang asawa!*" (Tell your mom that it's not right to spray water on one's husband!) Dad jokes, putting her down.

"*Ineng, pakisabi rin sa dad mo na pag day-off ko, mas gusto kong gumala kaysa maglinis nang buong araw*," (Dear, tell your dad, too, that I'd rather go out on my day off than clean the house the entire day,) she says, throwing him a little glare.

They're acting like they're not enjoying themselves.

The weirdest thing I've noticed about our family dynamic is that everyone seems to have their pair—except me. Illa and Lola Nora go wild over social media scandals and celebrity crushes, and my parents, well, they're married, so I'd hope they got along.

"Anyway, could I go hang out with my friends? I finished all my chores."

Surprisingly, Dad agrees right away. Mom has that disapproving look on her face that says, *You're going out with friends again?* Seriously, that woman has no problem kicking me out of the house to tutor her best friend's son, but the moment I want to go out with friends, she goes strict Filipino *nanay* mode. I pull out my phone immediately, before her facial expression becomes concrete words.

Me: *Anyone down to hang out today? Maybe this can be our rain check for the M&M night*

Carol: *Man, I would so love to, but I'm at the skate park with Mark and my brothers rn. We're having a skateboarding lesson!*

Me: *Is he teaching them how to skate?*

Carol: *Nah, we're teaching him to skate and it's kind of hilarious. I just hope he can still walk by the end of this. I'll send vids*

Jasmine: *LOL. Ok but me too. Logan and I are watching a musical tonight. I think we have an extra ticket, wanna come with us, Lara?*

I'll admit, it was nice of her to ask, but after trailing home behind them and becoming their aquarium photographer, there's no need to barge in on an actual date.

Me: *I'll pass. Kiera, you available? I could take those IG pics you wanted of the outfit you sent the other day*

Kiera: *Okayyyy so actually, that's very ironic. LMAO we're on Queen St. rn taking my photos. Didn't think I'd convince Daniel that easily LOL. Thanks tho!*

Me: *Have fun :)*

Another day, another fake smiley face text message.

Pacing around the kitchen with phone in hand, I wonder what I'm doing wrong. Am I the obsessive one? Overdramatic at times, for sure. But *obsessive*? Is it wrong for me to want to hang out with my friends and not have three make-out initiators in the way!

I return to Lola Nora and Illa, who are chatting in the family room. Hardly any of the blinds have been fully wiped off. Out of the four windows, Illa's only halfway through her second one and even still, she scrolls on her phone. I give her an unimpressed look. "I thought you said you were good at multitasking."

Instead of arguing, she waves her screen in my direction and swipes through a sea of posts on Instagram. "Whoa, look at Ate Eliza's photos! Our family in the Phils was right, she could totally be an *artista*," she says with a sigh.

Looking over her shoulder, I find myself admiring the latest posts from our Philippines vacation, in which Eliza's family met up with ours. The photos are variations of her standing in front of palm trees and the ocean, and another one where she holds her hands up in front of Taal Lake. She's beautiful in the way that everyone can see—tall, toned, with absolutely clear skin. Although I know her beauty doesn't diminish mine, it's so hard not to be jealous when she's the obvious family goddess. She gets showered with compliments while I get showered with face soap recommendations from our relatives in an attempt to get rid of my pimples. Not that my skin is necessarily bad, but the stress of being around Eliza literally gives me breakouts.

Lola Nora joins us in scrolling through her recent posts and mimics Illa's sigh. "*Ang tangos ng ilong! Parang morenang Liza Soberano*!" (Her nose is so sharp! She's like a tanned version of Liza Soberano!) She proceeds to pinch my own nose and frowns.

"Lola!" I groan. "*Hindi nga gumana 'yan no'ng baby ako! Ganito talaga ang hugis ng ilong ko*!" (That didn't even work when I was a baby! My nose shape is really like this!)

She releases my nose and I inhale sharply. I seriously wish Eurocentric beauty standards would fall off the face of the earth. I mean, it's great for the people who have them, but then there are people like me who get lolas and titas pinching their round noses since birth because apparently, it'll make them smaller—which doesn't work. While my nose isn't sharp like Eliza's, it isn't as flat as Mom's and Illa's. It's the middle-ground product of both my parents' genes, but somehow it still isn't good enough for cultural "artista standards."

Speaking of "artista standards," my life definitely became more manageable when Eliza moved away before high school. Since we're the same age, it was constant comparison from relatives about our physical appearances.

Luckily, the topic changes with a loud ding on Illa's phone. "*Lola! Lola! Nag-text si Kaden!*" (Lola! Lola! Kaden texted me!)

Lola Nora springs out of her reclined chair as if she isn't on meds for her arthritis and muscle pain. She looks over Illa's shoulder, "*Ano'ng sabi niya?*" (What did he say?)

Illa lets out a deafening screech, holding the phone in front of Lola Nora's face. Before I can ask about what's going on, Lola Nora makes the same sound and I instantly regret not putting my noise canceling headphones to good use.

Still, I lean over to participate in the drama. "*Ang OA n'yo—ano'ng balita kay Kaden?*" (You guys are so over the top—what's new with Kaden?)

Illa twirls ungracefully in the middle of the living room, hardly noticing her leg skimming against the edge of a side table. "Kaden asked me out!"

Lola Nora: "AHHH!"

Illa: "AHHH!"

Me: "Huh?"

The screaming fest comes to a halt when the two stare at me, wide eyed. I take a step backward. Did I give the wrong reaction? Ignoring my confusion, Illa and Lola Nora link hands, jumping and continuing their scream duet. Meanwhile, I scratch the back of my head thinking about what I should be doing right now.

"*Ano'ng susuotin mo?*" (What are you going to wear?) asks Lola Nora, pausing to breathe. I think she forgets that she's a seventy-year-old with medical conditions.

"*Hindi ko rin alam!*" (I don't even know!) says Illa.

"*Hija, bukas na bukas, mag-shopping tayo!*" (Dear, we're going shopping tomorrow!)

I clap my hands. "Congratulations!" (I promise, there's no hint of sarcasm in my voice; it's my go-to reaction when people are happy, and I'm confused.)

Illa places a hand on my shoulder, giving me the look that a big sister should be giving to her little sister—not the other way around. "Ate, you don't have to pretend you're excited. It's okay if you don't get it."

I really don't. "What do you even like about this boy? You haven't mentioned him until this year. What do you know about him?"

She starts to stare longingly at the blinds that she hasn't finished cleaning. I snap my fingers in front of her face. "Hello? Illa?"

She blinks, returning from a daydream. "Yeah? Sorry, I was thinking about his dreamy dark eyes and pretty hair and his smile is just—"

"*Ay naku! Perfect match nga kayo!*" (Oh my! You guys really are a perfect match!) Lola Nora exclaims.

I cough into my fist. *Are they serious right now?* "But what do you like about him? Like about his personality?"

She shrugs. "A lot of things. He's nice and he smells good."

"Smell isn't a personality trait."

Ignoring my last statement, she continues to converse with Lola Nora, discussing their shopping plans and how Illa is going to escape to her date without our parents knowing. Obviously, my mom, who barely trusts me to go out, would never let Illa go on a date. The rule is simple: no dating until you turn sixteen. Illa isn't even in high school, so we're not hitting the target on that one. Regardless, Lola Nora couldn't care less about my mother's rules, and I don't feel like snitching, so it looks like Illa's going to have her date.

I stay for a bit longer listening to the conversation, but quickly grow bored. "You still have to finish wiping the blinds," I remind her before leaving for my room. My heavy feet step up the slightly creaky staircase. There are times when I feel okay about myself but then there are times like this, when I don't fit in anywhere. It's like, you love so many people but you're just in a completely different room, peering through a glass window and observing. Sometimes I'm merely a spectator of the show, and I wish I could be okay with that.

TIP FOURTEEN:
BRUSH IT OFF

*

Illa and Lola Nora head to the mall right when it opens on Sunday morning, which happens to be right after mass. An hour of praise and worship followed by a couple more hours of Lola Nora maxing out her pension money. They don't ask me if I want to come but it doesn't matter because I have to go to James's house for our last-minute study session before tomorrow's math test.

When James opens the front door, the striking silence of the house surprises me. Although it's usually quiet, it's never silent, and on the weekend everyone's usually home. A quick glance around—nobody.

Sensing my confusion, he says, "They'll be back in the evening. They're attending a symphony concert."

"Without you?" I ask, following him up the stairs to the study, setting my bag on the floor. The only light in the room comes from one large chandelier that's clearly in need of a couple of bulb replacements. Although the large window lets some light in, dark clouds congregate in the sky, so it's not much help.

He shrugs, unfazed. "They all seem to like it—even Seb. Not my thing, though."

This reminds me of my own family, how Lola Nora and Illa bond over reality TV and dating and it's just not my thing. The difference between James and me is that I can't shrug things off. I really wish I could.

Avoiding the desk that we usually work at, I plop myself in the window nook, taking one of the throw pillows and holding it tightly against my chest. James sits beside me, close enough that his knee touches mine, and I wonder why he's so close when there's clearly enough space at the other end. The lack of space between us causes my heart to race faster than what should be physically possible. If he'd sat this close to me a couple of weeks ago, I would've shoved him away, no doubt. But it's different now. *Fishballs.*

It's different now.

"You know," he says, "your face does this thing where you look like a distressed ogre, and if I know you well enough, it's either because you're sad or because someone ate the last slice of pizza."

I manage a weak smile. "You said the same reason twice and I'm not sad, I'm just tired."

"Don't lie," he says, moving an arm to my back, his hand resting and rubbing circles with his thumb. The motion is steady and constant, like the hands of the ticking clock on the wall, no awkward pauses or sudden stops. *You're okay*, he means to say.

"If it's about last time, I'm sorry I brought it up. Dad and I've been talking about the move for a while, and it's not an easy decision to make." The circles on my back come to a sudden stop when he leans forward and clasps his hands.

My chest starts to rise and fall, like a rapidly oscillating wave, but I try to keep myself steady with a breath in through the nostrils and out through the mouth. From summer plans to our entire future, it seems like every single decision is a hard one nowadays. "We can talk about it."

His eyes focus on the other side of the room, perhaps on the carvings of the large wooden door. "He still wants me to help with the business."

"Do you want to?" My voice is soft, almost inaudible, not because I'm trying to make it like that but simply because there isn't much left in me to make it any louder.

"I don't know." His eyes look glossy, and I wonder if it's because of the lighting or if he's actually about to cry. He said that he never asked about my future, but I never asked about his either. To make things worse, his future never even crossed my mind.

The gray clouds, growing darker, start to release their rain all at once. It doesn't start with a trickle or a drop but more like one of those buckets at the water park that fills and tips over every quarter hour. But just because you know it's going to tip, it doesn't make it less of a shock when the water hits your skin at full force, driven by the inevitable force of gravity.

The only thing I can do is take his hand in mine and squeeze it tightly. *You're okay.*

"I think it would've been easier if I had something I was obsessed about, if I liked something the same the way you like your science and research and all that. But I don't. I just go to school, interested in nothing at all." His nostrils flare and he starts to take deeper breaths. His eyes start to glisten, and tears well up.

"I don't really know where I'm going, either, and I get you, it's scary—"

He stands up quickly, unexpectedly removing his hand from mine, and I jolt back. "But you do, Lara! You do know where you're going, even when you say that you don't! You have a field of study you love so much that you're willing to sacrifice your last nonadult summer for it!"

But James is wrong. I feel like an imposter, pretending that I know what I want all the time. Of course, the smart girl who volunteers has to have a plan, has to be taking steps toward her future. The worst part is, I don't have the heart to tell anyone that I'm not ready for it. Not even a little bit. If I say I can't handle it, I'll look weak. So instead, I sit with my hands in my lap and swallow any words forming in my mouth.

He runs a hand through his hair and for once, I notice the bags under his eyes. Even his usually bright eyes are duller now. Quietly he says, "And I'm happy that you have those passions, but I don't. Whatever I study won't mean that much to me, at least, not in the same way it does to you. What I do today, the grades I get or how hard I try in class, it doesn't lead to some big, dreamy tomorrow like how your decisions do. *My today is just today.*"

My chest hurts at the sight of his clenched jaw and teary eyes. *Please don't cry.*

"We're just kids," he whispers. "How the hell does everyone expect us to know what we want to do for the rest of our lives?"

The rain doesn't stop—not in the afternoon nor in the evening. The air around us is heavy with tension and the study is quiet aside from my voice explaining various lessons and James's repetitive "Mhm." The material proves to be more difficult than initially expected, which pushes my shoulders into a slouch. I don't know if I'd bet on James passing.

James's family comes back in the early evening, and we have dinner together. Tito Danny and James sit at either end of the rectangular table; Tita Gia and I take one side, while Seb, Gabe, and Lola Edna take the other. Besides the lack of conversation, there is a slight strain, particularly between James and Tito Danny—one that wasn't there before. Tita Gia senses it, too, eyes darting between her husband and her eldest son. The wrinkles of her forehead look deeper, and dark circles sit beneath her eyes.

She offers me a smile, not forced but definitely tired. "How did the studying go?"

I wet my lips before saying, "It went all right."

James moves pieces of pasta around his plate, refusing to look up. "Lara, you don't have to lie to her. It's better that we're prepared for the fact that I'm not passing tomorrow."

Tita Gia and Tito Danny look at me, probably waiting for a contradiction. All I can give is a hesitant, "He's right," which is met by disappointed looks on both parents' faces.

"Is there anything we can do now?" asks Tita Gia, twisting the wedding ring on her finger.

I sigh. "If we had more time, I bet we could get somewhere, but I have to be home in the next hour before Mom takes my head. You know how she can be."

Tita Gia lets out a small laugh, one that nobody expects, leaving everyone staring at her. "I'll never understand how such a disorganized woman became a strict mother." She laughs again before continuing, "Your mom would probably never tell you this, but in college we were horrible procrastinators, and we would only study one or two days before exams and had to pull a bunch of all-nighters, too many to even count."

My heart flutters the slightest bit when Mom and Tita Gia talk about their past. Their memories are stories, so clear that you're able to imagine them in your head, in full detail. I always thought I'd grow up and the LKJC would be the same way.

Then she grins, the same grin that James has right before he does something shocking. "Speaking of . . . your mom might understand if you guys need to pull an all-nighter," she says with a wink.

James and I make eye contact underneath furrowed brows. I scratch the back of my hand and he does a half-shoulder shrug. *What's happening,* we ask with our eyes.

After dinner, Seb and I lie on the living room floor, setting up some dominoes while James shouts out pattern ideas. Tito Danny and Gabe are scheduled for dish washing duty and stay in the kitchen while Tita Gia ventures into the next room to make a phone call. After a couple of minutes, she pops her head around the door, ponytail hanging in front of her shoulder. "Hon, do you mind joining me for a sec?"

The boys share a confused look, not knowing which one of them she's calling.

She rolls her eyes. "Not you guys, I mean Lara."

Getting up, I join her in the other room. There's a simple white couch with a long coffee table in front of it, decorated with a couple of fake flowers sitting in tall vases. Behind, raindrops trickle down a row of narrow rectangular windows.

She motions for me to sit beside her on the couch, and I do. "I talked to your mom, and she said she's okay with you staying."

"Are you sure you were talking to *my* mom?"

She chuckles before going, "Yes, *your* mom . . . but I wanted to ask if *you're* okay with this. I could tell that you weren't ecstatic about helping James, but you still did it. I've never seen his grades this high before, so thank you. I know this favor is stretching it a bit far, and if you don't want to, I'll get him to drive you home or I'll bring you home myself."

"I'd like to stay if that's all right."

This favor isn't for Tita Gia anymore; it's not even a favor for

James because I'm doing this for myself as much as I'm doing it for him. I want him to do well, as well as he possibly can, but I also want to stay for the selfish reason of not wanting to be alone. If I go home, I know I'll lock myself up in my room. Then I'll inevitably start to think about everything—the LKJC, how I can't fit in with Illa and Lola Nora and . . . James. I'd rather read an entire textbook to him than be stuck listening to the voice in my head, reminding me that he's leaving, that he's unhappy, and I can't do anything about it.

The corners of Tita Gia's mouth quirk up, eyes revealing a small twinkle in the midst of the tiredness. "Then I'll get the guest room ready."

She rises from her spot, ready to leave when I blurt out, "Tita? Can I ask you something?"

Sitting back down, she gives a slow nod.

"Is—is everything all right? James seems *distracted*."

Another smile that doesn't reach the eyes. "There's been a little turmoil about his plans after high school, but everything is going to be okay," she tells me, patting my hand before turning to leave. At the doorway, her back faces me but she pauses. There's a soft, "Thank you for caring about him," before she walks out completely.

James and I spend our night in the study, preparing and practicing for tomorrow's test. Eyes are glued to the books and the only topic of conversation is math—something I'm grateful for because I don't think I can handle any more exhausting conversations about the future.

Surprisingly enough, by 1:30 a.m., James isn't panicking about the test, and neither am I. Problem sets have been solved, and I expect him to pass tomorrow. The last thing I need to do is print out some notes, so I connect my laptop to the wireless printer in the study and wait for the papers to come out.

But they don't. Instead, there's a sound of grinding followed by a concerning beep.

I watch in horror as the machine shakes. "Is that normal?"

James bites his bottom lip. "I don't think so." Grabbing my laptop, he goes, "I'll connect you to the printer in Mom's office. You can collect your papers from there."

"Sure."

I walk down the hallway, reaching the door to the office. I swear my hand was on the office doorknob first, but the streak of light coming from the next room pulls me and I find myself quietly slipping inside. Three large windows fill the wall opposite the bed. Light from the full moon illuminates the room, not in its entirety, but enough so that I can see what I need to. While different than before, everything from the photo frames and the jar of guitar picks in the corner make it obvious that it's James's.

The last time I was in his room, we were kids. There was a big TV with a bunch of controllers, some arcade games, and toys lying around the floor. His acoustic guitar sat in the corner, like a prized possession. The walls are now painted a navy blue, with the exception of one wall, which is lined with stone. His bed is nice and neat, with nightstands on each side, with identical lamps. The arcade games and toys are gone, now replaced with an organized desk and a bookshelf; sports trophies and medals are displayed in a large case. I don't turn on the light switch—it's already bright enough.

Forgetting about the printed papers, I look around and stare at the pictures in the frames atop the shelves. The biggest picture of all is a framed one of his family. I feel sad when I see the old photo; his Lolo is still there, with an arm wrapped around James. It sends me back to a time when James was quieter and loved guitar as much as he loved hockey.

There's a photo of him, Daniel, Logan, and Mark. Then there's one of his first pet, Sam the turtle. As I look at each photo, a specific one on his desk catches my eye—I'm here too. I pick up the framed photograph of him and me dancing together. No, not slow dancing or anything. We were dancing side by side when we were little. I remember that the photo was taken during our first ballet recital.

We were five years old, and we both hated it, but James looked great in a tutu. He wasn't supposed to wear one, but I hated wearing it so he wore one, too, probably thinking he could lessen my suffering by doing the same thing. As I said, we hated it. So we ruined our first recital by jumping around and doing dances that were not close to ballet. Unfortunately, the little girl who played Cinderella did not get to dance with mini–Prince Charming because he was dancing horribly with the mini–evil stepsister (*moi*).

Long story short, we never did ballet ever again.

I almost drop the frame when the door suddenly opens. "What are you doing in my room?"

"I'm directionally challenged?" I give him an innocent smile and slowly place the frame back down on the desk.

He raises an eyebrow. "Really now? You're not sneaking into my bedroom and messing with my stuff?" He picks up the frame. "This is supposed to go over . . ." When he sees the picture, there is a moment of silence between us, and he chews on his lower lip. "I haven't done my room in a while."

"I can see," I reply sarcastically.

There's a short pause before he asks, "Do you remember this day?"

"Like it was yesterday."

Out of nowhere, he starts laughing. For the amount of laughing and smiling he does, I should be used to his dimples by now, but I'm not. And I'm glad for it.

"You were the best evil stepsister."

"I know."

His phone is in his hand, and he presses things on the screen, ruining whatever moment we were having. I turn to the door, but he takes my hand before I can leave. "Wait," he says, and I stay.

He grabs the earphone case from the nightstand and places one of the Bluetooth earphones in my right ear and the other in his left. With a click of a button, the song from our ruined recital starts to play and I can't contain my laugh. It's the song from the scene where Cinderella dances at the ball—"So This Is Love"—except the instrumental version. Part of me wants to cringe but the other part adores the overwhelming wave of nostalgia.

He holds a handout. "Don't you think it's time for a redo?"

"You do know that the prince isn't supposed to be dancing with the evil stepsister at all, right?" Despite this, I still put my hand in his.

He shrugs. "I don't see Madame Beaumont yelling at us this time."

Pulling me closer, he rests the other hand on my waist. I place one of mine on his shoulder. Then, we dance. It's awkward. It really is. There are no fireworks or sudden expressions of emotion—it's just an awkward waltz. However, something about it still seems the slightest bit magical.

"I understand why she cried afterward," I say with a smile.

"Me too."

Our attempt at a slow dance is tragic. He steps on my toes multiple times and after the first few minutes, we start bickering (in the quietest way possible because everyone else is sleeping).

"I think you're doing it on purpose!" I move to the other side of the room and grab a pillow from his bed, chucking it at him.

"You're the one who can't dance!" he whisper-yells, throwing another pillow at me. Luckily, I do a swift duck and it misses my head.

At the same time, we climb onto the bed to grab more pillows for our battle. I throw the first hit, giving him a good whack to the face. He retaliates with a blow on my torso, and we go back and forth, running around the room, jumping on the bed, and fighting like we're ten again.

Unfortunately, our stamina is not that of ten-year-olds anymore and within minutes, we fall onto the bed, exhausted. My chest quickly rises and falls from the cardio and so does his. Everything is quiet and the music has stopped.

"That was fun," he says. "Tiring, but fun." His close proximity doesn't help my racing heart return to normal and I lie there, staring at the ceiling and wondering when my breathing will return to its normal pace. His arm rests on mine and I can feel his racing pulse. I kind of want to insult him. What a shameful resting heart rate for an all-star athlete. The rain still crashes onto the roof and blurs the view outside his window.

Everything seems to be like it was before—normal. We're just us, with our stupid arguments that never last more than a minute and the knowledge that all problems have to go away at some point. Thinking about the picture and the dance makes my heart ache, and I desperately wish to cling to the days when there was no talk about labs or degrees or universities.

We both lie so that we're facing each other. "Are you really leaving after the summer?" Right after the words come out of my mouth there's instant regret. Whatever barrier was keeping everything in the air, I just broke it.

"It's nothing certain. Don't worry about that right now," he says, but we both know that I'll keep thinking about it.

"All right." I push my body up, ready to leave for the guest bedroom, but his hand tugs at the back of my shirt and I pause.

"Could you stay?"

His voice is low and gentle. There's a hint of hesitation but he can't take it back, so he waits for my reply. My heart crawls up my throat, blocking my airway. It takes all my energy to keep myself grounded, to not run or hit him with a sarcastic line that I don't mean. I focus on the pitter-patter of the rain that hits the roof, asking my heart to beat slower than the pace of the rain. And finally, I say it. It's quiet and slow, probably hesitant, and maybe even inaudible. I don't know, but it's there.

"Yes."

TIP FIFTEEN:
UNDERSTAND THE APPEAL OF COUPLE INTERACTION

✱

I used to argue that the best part about being single is the fact that you get the bed all to yourself. Couples who sleep together have it the worst; they have to endure people snoring like bulldozers beside them, they have limited space, *and* they have to share a blanket.

Sure, they can tell you things like it's great to cuddle or whatever—but in the summer, when there's a heat wave? It's excess body heat in one place, putting them at a risk for heatstroke or something. Do you know what's ten times better than cuddling? Being able to sleep in starfish position, climbing salamander position, or any way you want because nobody is in your way.

Then again, I had never experienced sharing a bed.

The sound of soft, rhythmic breathing greets my ears. I let out a yawn and try to shift my body but find myself unable to move freely.

Something is wrapped around my waist.

My eyelids fly open.

An arm. *An arm is wrapped around my waist.*

His grip loosens and I turn to face his chest, rising and falling like a soft wave. His eyes are still closed, with long lashes grazing his skin.

A lock of hair curls perfectly in the middle of his forehead, looking lighter in the morning sunlight. Still mesmerized by his features, I can't help but be frozen.

Finally, he wakes up, dark-brown eyes catching the sunlight and becoming a mixture of honey and chocolate. "Hey," he croaks, voice still rough, giving me a small smile. *Those dimples are going to kill me.*

"H-hi."

Holy crab apples and sauce. He's just staring at me. And smiling. And not letting go. Maybe I'm not fully awake yet, but I don't think I want him to. I don't know what to do. I can't move or smile back or blink or do anything.

He pushes a strand of my hair behind my ear, and the feel of his fingertips brushing against my neck sends something akin to an electrical shock down my body. The taserless electrocution invokes panic and I fall off of the bed, landing with a big thump. Through the pain, I manage to hear loud, obnoxious laughter. *And* . . . I want to kill him again.

I get up and he's almost crying through chuckles. Heat rises from my neck to my cheeks. It's too early to be this humiliated. "Stop laughing, you idiot!"

Sitting up, he extends both arms in my direction. "Why don't you just come back here and we can get back to cuddling? Aren't you cold?" he teases, as my face flushes red and I so obviously look like I'm about to burn.

Before he can get a chance to make fun of me again, I hop onto the bed, grab a pillow, and whack him with it as if my life depends on it.

"Okay! I'll stop laughing!" Ironically, he tells me this while wheezing from laughter.

The pillow slams against his arm. "I'll"—hit—"kill"—hit—"you"—hit.

He hurriedly wraps his arms around me, trying to stop me from murdering him via pillow. Pushing his weight on me, he pins me to the bed. "You can try your best, but I don't plan on dying today, sweetheart."

"My original plan was to dump your body in Lake Ontario, to let you become a useful food source for the fish, but maybe even that's too merciful."

He gives me a smug look. "Really? You'd dump me in a lake?" He inches his face closer to mine and I go silent. His gaze burns right through me. "Maybe the tables have turned and I'm going to kill you."

If you keep looking at me like that, you just might.

His grip on my arms loosens, then releases entirely. His hands slowly go up to my face, cupping my cheeks ever so lightly, as if I might shatter into a million pieces—and I might well. I should've dumped his body in the lake while he was asleep. If I'd done that, I wouldn't be in this situation right now, begging my hands to stop clamming up and breathing so heavily that my lungs hurt. I wouldn't be wondering why James is looking at me like that, in a way that could change everything between us. He leans in, closer, and closer, shutting his eyes and I think a hundred butterflies are migrating from my stomach to my bloodstream, trying to kill my cardiovascular system.

Without thinking, my hands shoot up to his right arm, my right leg wraps around his left, and using full force, I push him down, his back crashing onto the bed.

He opens his eyes and a pained expression flashes across, but only for a second until he blinks it away and I second guess if it was even there. Surely, it didn't hurt since we're on the bed. Finally, I realize, *I might've messed up.*

I get up and run to his washroom, but not before flinging a pillow that lands beautifully on his face. Shutting the bathroom door, I press my back against it, realizing that my entire body is shaking. Was he actually going to . . . *No, of course not, he was just teasing you.*

Holding a hand against my chest, I count my breaths, praying they slow. *Would I have kissed him back*? I splash some water on my face, trying to get some sense into myself.

I've been spending way too much time with him.

By the time I get out of the washroom, his bed is fixed neatly and James is nowhere to be seen. Following the sound of rustling, I make my way to the kitchen.

"Good morning, Lara!" Tita Gia greets me before taking a sip of coffee.

The entire family is in the kitchen, with the exception of James. Seb is still half-asleep, his face about to hit the scrambled eggs on his plate. Gabe's immersed in a novel, hardly touching his food. Lola Edna places some dirty pans in the sink while Ate Kelly prepares Seb's lunch.

Tito Danny looks up from his plate and asks, "Any requests for breakfast? We have scrambled eggs, some fruit, bacon, and muffins, but we weren't sure if you wanted anything else."

"I'm good. I'm just going to get myself a drink." *Maybe I need something to help me cool down.* I continue to the fridge and pull out a carton of orange juice. I pour it into a tall glass, then turn around, crashing into James. The juice spills all over his white shirt and I try to apologize but end up only mouthing, "Sorry."

I rush to get some napkins but he holds a hand up.

"Don't worry about it. It's just a shirt," he says, giving me a small smile, but it seems forced. "I'll be back in two minutes," he tells the family. "I'm just going to change."

When he gets back to the room, he's wearing a navy-blue pullover with our school's logo and gray sweatpants. Once everyone is seated at the table, the room goes silent again. Tito Danny clears his throat, and we divert our attention to him. "I wanted to let everyone know that our business has been successful in acquiring the investors from Cambridge and we'll be proceeding with the deal within the coming months."

"That's wonderful, honey," says Tita Gia, but she seems more interested in the eggs than the news.

"Congratulations," I follow.

"Awesome," James grumbles and Tito Danny has a stern look in his eyes.

I brace myself for an argument or a serious conversation, but Tito Danny's expression relaxes quickly, and he gives a dejected sigh before continuing with more information that nobody pays attention to. James and Tita Gia wear the same tired expression, repeating nods, while everyone else looks bored. Seb probably doesn't understand any of it. All *I* can think about is the almost-kiss and if it would've happened if I'd let it. *Would I have enjoyed it?*

Tita Gia drops us at school on her way to work, and for the entire car ride we avoid each other's gazes, leaning against opposite windows in the backseat. Usually, he doesn't take these things so seriously; acting unnecessarily aggressive is how we are with each other. When did things change between us?

All I want to do is text my friends and ask for advice. I need someone to tell me what to do and that it's going to be all right. I need Jasmine to point out the logic and keep me from catastrophizing, I need Kiera to tell me that she feels my pain, and I need Carol to make a joke that's slightly inappropriate for the situation but funny enough to distract me. Part of me wants to reach out to them again, but the other part of me doesn't want to get my hopes up in the likely case that they won't have time for me.

It's early when we get to school; the hallways are deserted relative to how they usually are. There are a couple of people sitting against their lockers and a few teachers setting up in their classrooms, but the extreme quiet around us is suffocating.

James walks in front of me, faster than usual, like he's trying to get away. I try my best to keep up because I tell myself that this morning's events will soon blow over and we'll be back to normal again soon.

"How do you feel about the math test?" I ask, hoping that we can have a normal conversation.

"We should be fine," he says bluntly, not bothering to look back at me. I stop in my tracks, stunned by his coldness. "I have to talk to Coach Dawson real quick, but I'll catch you later." With that, he throws his backpack over his shoulder and walks down the hallway, leaving me behind.

"Sure, I'll be in the library!" I call, but he disappears into the adjacent hall without turning around, not even the slightest bit.

The only lights that are on when I get to the library are the ones at the back. Other than that, it's dark and nobody's inside except me and the pregnant librarian snoozing at the checkout counter. Making my way to my usual spot, I pace my footsteps to match the familiar ticking of the grandfather clock. It used to annoy me but now the steady rhythm keeps me sane. It's one of the only things that doesn't change as the days pass by.

As I get nearer to the back, a soft voice meets my ear—Xander. Perhaps I can talk to him, ask him for advice. Maybe he can give me some reassurance that James is simply being strange, that hockey players always act cold in the early mornings, and he'll return to normal. However, when I see Xander, his face is illuminated by phone-screen light and he's laughing at something. It takes him a moment to notice my presence and when he does, he shoots me a smile.

He says, "Hold on" to the person he's FaceTiming. Removing his earphones, he waves. "Hey, Lara! I'm just talking to Anannya." He looks at the screen and back at me. "She says hi."

I smile. "Tell her hi back."

Xander is a different type of bright when he talks to his girlfriend or about her. Sometimes I wonder what it's like to have that. They continue their conversation while I awkwardly sit in the corner. It's funny that I now feel out of place *here*—the one place where I can hide from the feeling of being left out. While waiting, I send a couple of text messages to James. We need to talk about whatever happened earlier.

Me: *Hey, could you meet me in the library before first period? We need to talk*

Me: *It's important*

Finally, Xander and Anannya say their good-byes and I finally have a chance to talk to him about things other than research. He drags his stuff near mine and we sit together, side by side, on the floor. "All right, what's going on?"

"I—How did you know that you liked Anannya?"

He laughs. "Why do you ask? Plus, weren't *you* the one who kept annoying me for half of the summer, saying that I liked her and I should ask her out?"

I pull my knees in, resting my chin on one of them and letting out a groan. "It's different. I can tell when other people have a crush, but I can't tell with myself."

"I don't know." He shrugs. "You just *feel* it."

"Feel what? *Nausea*? I've been feeling a lot of that lately if that's what you mean."

"Listen." He shifts so that he sits in front of me now, leaning forward so that I can't avoid staring into his green eyes, never lying. "If you're asking me about crushes, chances are you have one. Is it the captain of the hockey team?"

Maybe this is the time when I should admit to myself that I don't hate James, nor do I dislike him. But that's what scares the shizballs out of me to the point where I feel like someone just punched me in the gut and I'm about to violently vomit. It's not realistic for me to develop feelings like this in such a short period of time. Anything that I'm feeling is probably a mere infatuation. You know, stupid hormones and stuff.

I do, however, believe that feelings can come back, *crushes come back.*

But I refuse to be in love with him. Again.

Before we were enemies, James and I were actually friends. Great friends who occasionally played pranks on each other. When my anxiety got really bad in the later years of elementary school, he was the one who'd rub circles across my back to distract me. He was the one who'd make everything better with a calming song on the guitar, who'd annoy me when I'd tell him to leave me alone. Being his friend was great, until it wasn't. The fatal flaw in our relationship? I was kind of, sort of, hopelessly in love with him for a huge portion of my life.

James was my first crush and I tried so hard to lie to myself that I was over him because there was absolutely no way he'd feel the same way about me. He wasn't attracted to me, at least not in the way he was attracted to other girls. And because of that, he broke my heart countless times without knowing it. I silently shattered behind the words of:

You know, I really like her.

I'm gonna make her my girlfriend.

Hey, tell me her favorite color. I'm going to buy . . .

But I was his friend. Listening to stuff like that was kind of in the job requirement for friendship. No matter how many times he dated other people, I could never tell him how I felt, and instead tried to accept that it would never be me with him. Now I'm here with my only available friend, the guy he hates, asking for direction because what if this time, it *is* me. I don't want to accidentally see something that isn't there.

Xander whispers and his voice is soothing. "Between you and me, I think he really likes you. He's always mentioning you. Don't tell him I said anything, though; I don't think he likes me that much." Then he winks, which brings a smile to my face even though I still have a hard time believing that James could see me in that way.

"By the way," he continues, "why are you here so early? The library isn't your usual morning hangout place."

"I got dropped off today, so I'm a bit earlier than usual. And I used to hang out with my friends in the mornings, but they've been a little . . . preoccupied lately," I say, looking away. "Then I started spending the mornings with James but he's busy today too."

"You know what might make you feel better?"

"What?"

"There's a new sci-fi movie coming out on Saturday, based on this novel that I recently read. I'm sure you'd love it. It's like the love child of Star Wars and The Hunger Games. We should see it together."

I gesture to his outfit, consisting of a black, long sleeve, buttoned halfway, and black and white checkered jeans held up by a leather belt. "I didn't think you were into that stuff anymore after you switched your entire wardrobe," I joke.

"Just because I don't wear Star Wars shirts at every waking moment doesn't mean that I'm not a geek at heart. Do we have a deal for Saturday?"

He sticks his hand out and I shake it. "Deal."

On the third floor, Kiera and Jasmine sit at our spot near the art department, Kiera on her phone and Jasmine reading a chemistry textbook. Strangely enough, Daniel and Logan are nowhere to be seen. Carol's gone until Wednesday, attending campus tours in the States. She's probably at UPenn right now, scoping the soccer field and itching to stay. With her athletic ability and stellar grades, she'll get in for sure. I already miss her. It's too quiet without her.

"Hey, guys," I say, approaching the two girls.

Kiera smiles brightly, standing up from her spot. Her light hair is in two braided pigtails today and, despite the cold weather, she has fishnet tights beneath her flouncy pink skirt. "Hey, Lara!"

Jasmine stops studying her textbook to stand and greet me. "Haven't seen you in a while. What's up?" I'm taken aback for a small second when I notice her new look. Instead of her usual jeans and plain sweater, she wears black dress pants and a formal blouse, a nice shade of light blue. Her short hair is curled and she's even wearing a bit of makeup.

Everything, I want to say. *James, research, school, Illa's first relationship, missing you, and everyone's getting ready to leave.* "You know, the usual . . . I don't know, there's a lot. We really need to catch up soon. You look different, Jas. Is there something going on today?"

She fixes a piece of hair into her black barrette. "Yeah, actually, representatives from the different music schools are visiting the school today. They'll be listening to us playing but it's always nice to look professional, right?"

"You look very pretty," Kiera tells her.

"You do," I repeat.

Jasmine blushes at the compliments. "Thanks, guys."

"You're applying to the Royal Conservatory of Music, right?" I ask. Her eyes have been set on that place since we were eight.

She nods, pressing her lips together. "I'm still deciding but . . ."

Kiera and I share confused glances. Kiera says, "Isn't that your dream school?"

Jasmine lets out a heavy sigh. "I don't know anymore. The Victoria Conservatory of Music seems like a good option too. I've always wanted to live in BC, and my cousins are there too."

Out of everyone, Jasmine said she'd stay. It was just her and her mother, and she promised not to leave her. A selfish thought emerges immediately: *I don't want to be left here alone either.* She doesn't need to hear that, so I smile and say, "Wherever you go, you'll be great."

Daniel and Logan walk over, and I take that as my cue to leave. My friends say that we'll talk again later but for them, later is never a definite time.

James gets to second period biology before I do and I walk in to see him looking over his math binder with earbuds in, getting ready for next period's test. I've never seen him so focused, like I could wave a hand in front of his face and he wouldn't budge.

"Hey." I greet him, taking my spot beside him.

No response.

I pull out one of his earbuds and he looks at me as if I took his dying body off of life support. "I said hey."

"Hi, Lara," he says, with a raised eyebrow. He sticks out his hand and I return the earbud.

"I texted you this morning. I wanted to talk about something important. Did you get the message?" My heart races out of my chest and I feel another wave of nausea from wondering why he never responded.

"No, I didn't see it."

"Oh okay." *At least that buys me some time to think about what exactly to say.* "How did your talk with Coach Dawson go this morning?" I ask, trying hard to start a conversation with him again—trying too hard.

He seems dazed, thinking about something else. "Sorry, what did you say?"

"I was wondering how your talk with Coach Dawson went."

"Good," he says, still not looking at me.

"I was thinking that maybe before we go back to your place today we could stop by the new pizza place across the street? I heard it's really good and—"

"About that . . ." James interrupts me. "Coach wants to add another evening practice besides our two regular morning ones, so I won't be able to make it today. And with the games starting up, it's going to be busier in general, so I don't think we can continue our sessions."

I don't understand where this is coming from. It's so sudden and my brows furrow in confusion. "You're joking, right? It's only October! The hard stuff hasn't even come yet! And just so you know, that doesn't mean you'll be busy *every* evening."

He forces another smile before looking back at his notes. "Don't worry, if I really have trouble, I'll just ask Mom to hire a professional tutor again."

I nod and attempt to conceal the sadness that fills my chest. "Are you free this Saturday at least? I was hoping that you could help me bake practice cookies for a charity fundraiser on Sunday."

"Sure, I guess." His eyes never leave his binder when he replies and I lie to myself, saying that he's really worried about our test.

"Thanks."

The bell rings and I don't push the conversation any further. Clearly, he isn't going to interact with me today and I'm not going to force him to. A hundred different thoughts create an endless hurricane in my mind. Part of me is reassuring, saying that James is just being weird and will be back to normal soon. But another part is a chilling voice that vibrates throughout, telling me that he's ditched me for good.

TIP SIXTEEN:
KEEP YOUR FRIENDS CLOSE

✸

Saturday morning arrives and as I walk down the stairs, the soles of my feet feel like they might freeze. It's horribly cold but the sunlight outside is another form of cruel trickery that makes it seem like it's warm. October's like that, but I still appreciate the sun's presence before it almost entirely goes away in the winter. Lola Nora sits at the round kitchen table, glasses resting just above the tip of her nose, eyes glued to her tablet. The rays of light peer through the vertical blinds, creating a lined pattern on the ground.

James hasn't talked to me for the whole week. I mean, he has, but in sentences with word counts of under five words. I tried talking to him for the first couple of days, but it's hard when all your attempts are unsuccessful. So I've let him be and have kept my distance.

"*Apo, parini ka,*" (My grandchild, come here,) Lola Nora says, waving me over. She points to the screen, showing a website for Sport Chek and an array of brightly patterned leggings. "*Ano ang maganda sa mga ito?*" (Which of these looks nice?)

My eyes widen. "*Lola, saan naman kayo pupunta?*" (Lola, where are you going again?)

"*Zumba! Nag-sign up kami ni Edna sa Zumba class doon sa*

community center," (Zumba! Edna and I signed up for a class at the community center,) she says with a proud smile.

"*Online? 'Di ba, sabi ng doctor, bawal sa inyo ang sobrang mapagod?*" (Online? Didn't the doctor say that you shouldn't tire yourself out?)

She holds a finger to her lips. For Lola Nora, the resting order doesn't apply to things she wants to do. "*Shhhh . . . Hindi naman nakakapagod 'yon kasi pangkatuwaan lang.' Pag may tinanong ang mama mo tungkol sa $200 sa credit card bill niya, quiet lang tayo, okay?*" (Shhh . . . It won't be tiring since it's just for fun. If your mom asks about the two hundred dollars on her credit card bill, let's stay quiet, okay?)

"Um . . ."

She glances over my outfit, an orange knit sweater and baggy overalls, with a surprised eye. "*May lakad ka? Hindi ka nakapambahay . . .*" (Are you heading out? You're not wearing your casual clothes . . .)

Shaking my head, I walk over to the pantry, reaching for some flour and other ingredients, preparing for my and James's bake session. "Hindi po. Gagawa lang kami ng cookies para sa bake sale bukas." (No. We're going to bake cookies for tomorrow's bake sale.)

"*Kami?*" (We?) A fold forms between her brows.

I nod, going over to the sink now and pouring myself a glass of water. "*Opo, kami ni James.*" (Yes, James and me.)

A high-pitched shriek escapes her lips and she springs out of her chair, running toward me. God, this woman scares the shizballs out of me. "*Kayo na ba? Ang pogi ng batang 'yon, mestizo, matangkad . . .*" (Are you guys together? That kid's so handsome, fair-skinned, tall . . .) I roll my eyes at the *mestizo* part, but I know she won't let go of our culture's beauty standards overnight, especially after being raised with the notion that having a lighter skin color granted greater opportunity.

She holds her hands together, sighing dreamily. "*Cute ng magiging anak n'yo*!" (Your kids are going to be so cute!)

The statement causes water to squirt out of my nose and I cough up liquid into the sink. Lola Nora pats my back. "*Okay ka lang*?" (Are you okay?)

It takes me a couple of moments to stop coughing and not feel like I'm on death's door. "*No, Lola, mali po ang iniisip n'yo.*" (No, Lola, you have the wrong idea.)

She sighs. "*Ah, pasensiya na. Nakalimutan ko na naman ang sinabi n'yo sa 'kin. Na hindi porke't maputi ang isang tao, ibig sabihin mas maganda na.*" (Ah, sorry. I forgot what you told me again. That just because someone's fair-skinned, it doesn't automatically make them more beautiful.) Though that's not what I meant by her having the wrong idea, I feel happy that she remembered something we taught her. I nod approvingly.

Lola Nora goes upstairs to ask for Illa's opinion on the leggings, leaving me alone to wait for James to show up. Staring at the clock, I wonder where he is. I asked him to come over at ten to help me with the practice cookie batch, but it's already ten thirty and he isn't here yet. We must be good now, right? It's been a couple of days; this tension should be over.

I give him a call and his cell rings for a while before he finally answers. "Hello?"

"Hey, idiot. It's me, where are you? You said you'd help me bake today." I try to sound as typical as possible, hoping that it'll trigger our relationship to go back to normal.

He coughs. "I'm sorry. I have a cold right now so I can't come over. I don't wanna get you sick too. Maybe Jasmine can help you? Doesn't she bake?" *She does*, I think in my head, *but I wanted you specifically to help me.*

"Oh. Yeah, for sure. I'll ask her . . . I hope you feel better soon!" I try to put some enthusiasm in my voice but I don't think that I'm hiding my sadness all too well.

"Thanks. See you on Monday."

A bright idea pops into my mind. The perfect way to get James to act normal again is through food! I mean, everything can be solved with food, right? The remedy to a cough is hot soup and Vicks VapoRub, but I'm not about to get him the latter, so I make him my specialty—instant cup noodles. Poured into a glass container, of course, so it looks extrahomemade.

After the painstaking task of boiling hot water, pouring it onto the actual noodles and soup mix, then transferring everything to a fancy container, I make my way over to James's house. I ring the doorbell, clutching the plastic bag holding the noodles in one hand, thinking, *That idiot better appreciate my effort in making this!* Ate Kelly opens the door and lets me in. "*May tutoring ba kayo today?*" (Do you guys have a tutoring session today?) she asks.

I shake my head, holding up the plastic bag. "*May ibibigay lang po ako kay James.*" (I just have something to give to James.)

"*Nasa kwarto siya,*" (He's in his room,) she says, and I head upstairs.

At his door, I inhale sharply, remembering the last time I was here and the last time we were still okay. I knock twice but there's no reply. Assuming he's asleep, I slowly open the door, and it lets out a small creak. I step inside and see his back facing the door, hunched over and—

Kissing a girl.

My jaw doesn't drop, I don't fume angrily, nor do I feel any heat overpowering my body. Instead, my mind goes numb as James breaks the kiss. He slowly turns around. When our eyes meet, my breath hitches, my heart sinks to my stomach, and my breathing becomes heavy again, fast, so fast but I somehow can't get enough air.

I break the stare, instead finding the photo of the young dancers, which sits in its original position on his desk, and my fingers slowly begin to curl into a fist, realizing that the James who danced with me is never coming back and I was stupid to think I saw him again. Reality slaps me in the face once again. *James isn't your best friend anymore. He hasn't been since that summer, and he'll never be.* My hands grip the plastic bag tightly and I try to keep myself steady even though the room is spinning and everything looks like a compilation of distorted shapes.

I've seen him kiss and flirt before, all while rolling my eyes to hide any hurt. Why can't I do it again?

The girl on his bed is pretty, with soft brown hair that reaches her waist and big blue eyes, but she's staring like she wants me to burn. James bites his bottom lip before looking to the floor, probably embarrassed from having an audience. Part of me wants to kick both of them out of the freaking window, but the other part of me wishes that James was with me instead of her.

"James, I—" I force a fake smile and hold out the plastic bag. "I brought you some soup for your . . . cold. I'm *so* glad to see that you're doing better." I walk in with my back straight and head up. Placing the soup on the desk I say, "You know that you're probably still contagious, right?"

Then I turn to the girl. "I hope you don't catch any bugs."

I slam the bedroom door shut when I exit. My foot is already on the first step of the staircase when a hand grips my wrist, holding me back. When he turns me to face him, my eyes start to glisten unwillingly. *Don't cry, don't cry.*

"Lara, I can explain—"

As I push his arm away harshly, an estranged laugh escapes my lips. "You don't have to explain anything. What am I? Your girlfriend? We're not even friends!" The reality breaks everything inside of me. A teardrop escapes from my eye and I hastily wipe it off with my jacket sleeve.

"I—"

"Just be glad that as an aspiring doctor, I have the heart to care for people who are sick." I don't even have the energy to hide my shaking hands in my pockets.

"I'm sorry," he whispers, his voice hoarse. He leans forward, brushing his hand on mine but I pull away instantly, like touching a hot stove.

"*Don't.*" My breath hitches again. *You're okay, Lara, you're okay.* "Don't touch me."

He takes a step backward.

"You know what? Flirt with whoever the hell you want but we scheduled something, and I needed your help. I don't understand why you would just blow me off like this! You could've said no, but you didn't!" I shout, though trying hard not to. Seb and Gabe are somewhere in this house for sure, and I hope to God they don't hear me yelling. I think about the time James said his decisions today don't lead to tomorrow. I don't know why I thought I was an exception, that I would be in his future.

I wait for him to say something else. When he doesn't, I turn around with tears beginning to fall. I run down the stairs and out of the house. *Why am I even crying?* I'm used to this. I'm not supposed to cry. I'm supposed to be the funny one, the strong one, the problem solver.

My heart beats fast as I sprint down the sidewalk. My lungs feel like they're being torn apart, pieces crumpling into a ball. Still, I don't stop. I run as if the ground is on fire. My brain feels like it's about to explode with every thought pushing the walls, trying to escape.

Escape.

Escape.

Escape.

My legs can't take it anymore, giving up and letting me fall into a crouch on the sidewalk, even though my mind tells me to run faster, to get as far away as possible. I can't. The tears fall without remorse, and I stop trying to wipe them away. The crying morphs into uncontrollable sobs, taking away any air that's left in my lungs.

I stop sobbing when a familiar golden retriever licks the back of my hand. Xander, who towers over me, stares down at me with furrowed brows. "Need a friend?" He sticks his hand out and helps me to my feet.

I shrug. "Maybe."

"Why are you crying?" he asks softly, digging into his pocket and handing me a handkerchief.

Taking it, I wipe the tear streaks on my cheeks. "I wasn't. I was exercising so hard that I started sweating through my eyes. I can't believe you've never seen this, you're an athlete for goodness' sake."

He laughs a small laugh before saying. "All right, track star, let me walk you home. I don't want to see you sweating through your eyes anymore."

I nod and let him be a friend to me.

We walk side by side and I fold my arms, holding myself so I don't expose my violent shaking. The chilly air brushes through my tangled hair, past the tips of my ears. I bet they're colored red.

Xander has his hands in the pockets of his long brown coat and walks steadily, in a perfect straight line, talking about *something*. I'm thankful he is filling the silence because it gives me something to listen to other than my own uneven breaths. His footsteps are as calming as his voice, pace never drifting away from the constant rhythm. It blends smoothly with the soft background noise of the wind. I don't know how much time passes before I can breathe normally again.

"You don't have to explain anything to me," he says, and I hear that clearly. "I can tell it's been rough for you."

I sigh and nod. "Maybe I'm overreacting but sometimes I feel like everyone around me is walking away. They're all leaving this place after high school, and it feels like we're already starting to fall apart."

"Your friends?"

"Friends, frenemies, *everyone*." I change the topic before I start crying again. "Are you still up for that movie later?"

"I am, but you look like you need a break," he says.

I shake my head. "I need a pick-me-up to distract me from all of this nonsense."

"All right."

"You know what's funny?" I start. "If this movie came out last year, I'm a hundred percent sure that my friends would've preordered tickets by now, especially Carol. Ever since we were kids, we've been obsessed with fantasy movies and novels." Gravity ceases to exist when I think about the past; everything becomes light and airy, like I'm back in the clouds.

"Why did you guys stop?" he asks, bringing me back to the present.

"I went on vacation and when I came back, they were all in relationships. It's not the same anymore." I wish I had a better answer but that's exactly what happened.

I don't even notice, but we're already in front of my house. Xander stops me and sticks a hand in the back of his pocket. He pulls out a rectangular piece of paper. "Here," he says, handing it to me, "this is your ticket. Ask your friends if they can see the movie with you later. If they say no, call me and I'll sit with you. It might not be the same, but they're still your friends. The spark might still be there."

He gives me a reassuring squeeze on my arm, and I thank him for walking with me. *The spark might still be there* plays over in my head and it's more scary than comforting. I've been waiting for my friendships to return to how it was before, holding my hands together and praying that the present circumstances change the next day—but they never do.

When Xander leaves, I linger at my front door, allowing myself to float one more time.

Lakeside Elementary School, Toronto

May (Six Years Ago)

Ms. Silvera writes equations on the whiteboard and we scribble down the notes in our binders. Not all of us. Carol sits in front of me with a novel tucked in the little hollow space of the desk. Her eyes don't peel away from the book for a second. It's usually at this time, right before lunch, that she gets caught by the teacher.

The boy sitting in front of her coughs, an alert that our teacher will look our way. At that, Carol shoves the open book into Kiera's desk, which is right beside hers. Kiera narrows her eyes at Carol but proceeds to take the book out and hides it between her back and the chair she sits on.

Ms. Silvera walks over to us. "Carol, please hand over the book. It's the fifth time this week that you've been reading in class."

Carol's brows scrunch together. "What book? I don't have a book. See?" She slides her chair back to show that there is no book on or in her desk.

While Ms. Silvera continues to interrogate Carol, Kiera sneakily extends the book behind her, through the hole in the seat backing and under the sweater that rests on her chair. Jas pretends to lay her head on the desk, only to reach her arm under and grab the novel from Kiera's hand.

Then Jas hands it to me, and I slide the open book in the binder inside of my desk. The crumpled-up pieces of paper at the front make it impossible to detect anything. We are clear.

"Kiera, I hope you're not conspiring with your friend here," Ms. Silvera says, and Kiera shakes her head.

She also slides her chair back and shows off her clean desk. Ms. Silvera goes to Jas, who does the same. When the teacher gets to me, the sight of my desk interior repels her instantly.

"Lara, you need to clean your desk," she says. "It's a pigsty."

We all giggle and she rolls her eyes.

Lunch arrives and Ms. Silvera's tyranny is replaced by the lunch monitor. I take out the book from my desk and hand it over to Carol. "Was this your page?"

She scans over the two pages of the open book. "Yes, exactly where I left off."

"You should really invest in a bookmark," Kiera scoffs.

Carol laughs. "When we have a system that's this good? No way."

TIP SEVENTEEN:
KNOW WHEN TO END THE GAME

✱

I open the group chat and convince myself to reach out to my friends one more time. One more try before I consider it game over. It's frustrating how I can't bring myself to stop completely, even when the outcome is always the same and they choose to prioritize their boyfriends instead of our friendship.

One last time.

Me: *There's a new movie coming out tonight, based on a YA sci-fi. Anyone free?*

I brace myself for a series of rejections and excuses while waiting for their responses.

Jasmine: *I think so :)*

Kiera: *Yeah, I'd be down*

Carol: *Yup!*

Huh?

There aren't many things that could bring my mood up after the events of this morning, but this is a start. Sometimes it amazes me how life works. When James and I are on good terms, my friends and I aren't. The moment he's gone, they're finally available. It's like

I can't have both. Nevertheless, this evening means forgetting James, that girl, and the kiss. Not only that, but tonight I'll forget about our almost-kiss too. Maybe I'll even forget that I liked him in the first place. My friends and I plan to meet at six, and by then, things should fall back into place—the LKJC being my source of a social life and hating James while he goes about his never-ending dates.

When I get to the theater, I wait by the concession because surely, if Carol arrives first, this is the first place she'll go. Ten minutes later, when nobody arrives, I walk around, thinking that maybe I'll see them in the crowd of people. Five minutes after that, and I am back at the concession stand.

I look like a complete idiot for half an hour before finally making my way into a packed theater. Taking my seat at the back, I pull out my cell phone to switch it to silent mode, but when I open the screen, I have three new messages, none of them from the group chat.

> **Jasmine**: *I'm so sorry, Lara, Logan has a flat tire, so I have to pick him up. Let's hang soon tho. Have fun with Kiera and Carol*
>
> **Kiera**: *Hey girl! Daniel's family from out of town suddenly came over so we need to have dinner with them. Gotta take a rain check but please tell Carol not to raid the concession stand*
>
> **Carol**: *Hey, man, Mark was supposed to watch my brothers tonight, but their cooking session didn't go too well. Unfortunately, I'm stuck repairing a few wounds. . . sorry :(*

Stood up again, and somehow, it's even worse than the last time. Maybe this is what life is when you're the side character; you need to wholeheartedly accept the role of being the comic relief that people can forget about.

I look around the dark theater at all the grouped figures. Some people are here with dates, others are with their friends, some with families. It takes a second for my stomach to drop at the painful realization that I am not a third wheel anymore.

I am completely and utterly alone.

And nobody is coming.

With heavy steps, I lead myself out of the theater. The last thing I do is leave one voice message before taking myself out of the group chat. "I always thought it'd be an asshole who stood me up on a date. I never thought it would be my best friends."

I take the long way home, a two-hour walk. It's darker now, the air is fresh and it's kind of relaxing, but being alone in the city is always scary. Though my thoughts are anything but nice to me, I keep walking in the direction of my house. When I check my cell, there are numerous messages and missed calls from Kiera, Jasmine, Carol, and James.

I delete all of them.

All I wanted was a frenemyship with James, to hang out with my friends once in a while, and not feel like a piece of garbage that's been discarded multiple times. Was that too much to ask for?

When I get to my house, it's dark. The first person I see is Illa, but she hardly looks like she's alive, hanging off of the living room couch and wearing sweatpants. Sweatpants! Ever since she could dress herself, she's vowed to never touch loungewear.

I tiptoe to her lifeless body and poke her back, only to receive a threatening grunt.

Taking a step back, I ask, "What happened to you?"

"I hate everyone," she groans. "I hate boys and couples, and nothing matters because we're all going to die."

She's not wrong but that sounds like something I would say, which is concerning. "Since when are you the bitter one?"

She flips herself over so that she's lying on her back. "Since I met a boy named Kaden stupid Lee." *Oh damn. Her date . . .* I guess we're both not having the best luck with guys today.

"I thought you liked him?"

"Not anymore. He's such a jerk. On our date today I left him for a few minutes to use the washroom and I came back to see him talking to another girl—but in a way that was more than friendly. I don't think he ever liked me at all." She holds a pillow to her face, screaming into it.

I wrinkle my nose in disgust but also at the painful relatability. Not knowing how to comfort her, I awkwardly pat her on the back. "I'm sorry."

I try to think of something encouraging to say but then I notice a strong scent in the air, something burning. Lola Nora walks into the room, holding a smoking stick of incense and chanting something so quickly in Tagalog that I don't have enough time to process it.

I tilt my head to the side. "*Lola? Ano po'ng ginagawa n'yo?*" (Lola? What are you doing?)

"*Tinatanggal ko ang mga masasamang espiritu,*" (I'm getting rid of the evil spirits,) she says in the most normal way possible. "*Siguro ito ang rason kung bakit kayo may masamang kapalaran sa mga lalaki.*" (Maybe this is the reason why you guys have such bad luck with men.)

She proceeds to wave the stick over us, and we cough.

"Lola, you can stop," Illa says, and I notice her eyes watering. "*Walang spirits dito. Ako yung problema.*" (There are no spirits here. I'm the problem.) Her lip quivers but before I can hug her, Lola Nora shoves the stick of incense in my hand, and I start coughing again.

She takes Illa's face in both her hands, cupping her cheeks until she looks like a blowfish. "*No! Makinig ka sa 'kin! Nagmana ka sa 'kin at never akong naging problema! Malamang possessed si Kaden o may mga espiritu rito. Iyon lang ang malinaw na dahilan.*" (No! Listen to me! You take after me and I've never been a problem! Either Kaden's probably possessed or there are spirits here. That's the only reasonable explanation.)

And Lola Nora probably believes that in its entirety.

Next, she turns to me, taking my hand. "*Alam kong parang apo ko na si James, pero p'wedeng-p'wede kong gawan ng paraan para sumakit nang kaunti ang tiyan niya.*" (I know that James is like a grandson to me, but I can totally find a way to make his stomach ache a little.)

My eyes widen. I just got here and didn't tell anybody about what happened earlier. "*Paano n'yo—*" (How did you—)

She winks. "*Alam ko ang lahat, ineng.*" (I know everything, dear.)

Sometimes I think that Lola Nora and Illa have the stronger relationship because they're so similar. But I always forget how well my grandmother knows me too—so well that she can know what's happening in my life without me saying it. Taking the stick of incense back from my hand, she continues to wave it over us. I personally don't believe in evil spirits roaming my house and causing misfortune, but the fact that our grandmother knew about our heartbreak and decided to cast out demons, speaks volumes about her love.

I'm lucky to have her.

I remind Illa and Lola Nora about tomorrow's bake sale, and they get on their feet instantly. If there's anybody who can pull off a project within a couple of hours and without practice, it's them. I should've asked them in the first place. Lola Nora refuses to let me touch the ingredients, instead putting me on dish duty because I cannot bake for my life. Because she's bossy, she basically said, "Screw cookies" and that we would make *ensaymada* instead—a type of sweet bread roll. Illa has a natural knack for most things, so she's the main helper. The only thing I'm allowed to do with the food is slather the ensaymada bread with butter and sugar and sprinkle loads of grated cheese on top.

It's midnight when the task is finally complete. Lola Nora, Illa, and I slump onto the couch at the same time, finally able to bask in the quiet of the house. With the mixer put away and the oven shut off, we can finally catch the dialogue of the movie that was playing all along on the television. As I admire the rare occasion of the two of them watching in silence, I realize that even if I don't always fit in with my family, I can always count on them for last-minute baking.

TIP EIGHTEEN:
BE A VETERAN THIRD WHEEL

✸

The church we attend Sunday mass at always holds charity fundraisers once a month. Last month they had a sale of handmade jewelry, rosaries, and other crafts to raise money to aid refugees coming into the country. This time, it's for the local children's hospital Xander and I volunteered at.

"It's quarter to ten," I tell my dad, who comes down the staircase. Everyone is already dressed up. Illa is in the living room, while Mom and Lola Nora powder their faces upstairs.

"Ready, *na*!" He grins, the skin beside his eyes wrinkling. I smile back, but I know it doesn't reach my eyes when he frowns. I'm still sad about what happened yesterday with James and my friends. Dad lays a hand on my shoulder. "*Okay ka lang, Ara*?" (Are you okay, Ara?)

Shaking my head, I decide to be honest for once and tell him the truth. "Not really."

He pulls me in for a hug, which is weird. My parents have never been the kind to really talk about feelings. They don't bud in on social problems or ask about your crushes or say "I love you" too often. Instead, they make your favorite soup when you're sick, and they never let you skip a meal.

"*Si James ba?*" (Is it James?) he asks. He must've picked up that we were hanging around each other much more often.

I nod slowly. I did not think I would ever have to talk to my dad about boy problems but here we are.

He sighs. "*Hindi ko alam kung ano'ng nangyari sa inyo, pero alam kong mabait siyang bata. Babalik din siya.*" (I don't know what happened between you guys, but I know that he's a good kid. He'll come back.)

"*Paano kung hindi siya bumalik?*" (What if he doesn't come back?)

"Ara, *ang mga taong naglalakbay sa buhay nang mag-isa ay magpapatuloy pa rin ano man ang mangyari. Kahit na mag-isa ka, iikot pa rin ang mundo at magiging okay ka.*" (Ara, people who journey through life alone will still go on no matter what happens. Even if you're alone, the world will still turn, and you'll be okay.) Patting my shoulder, he says, "*Maliwanag*?" (Clear?)

"*Maliwanag.*" (Clear.)

Dad loads the boxes of food into the car and the family heads off to church. When we get there, we carry the boxes into the hall where people are setting up their tables. By noon, the preparations for the bake sale are long over and people crowd around, lining up at various stands to buy treats for a good cause.

Illa is the face of our booth, selling to people with a huge grin. Being herself, peppy and cheerful is kind of her thing, which is attracting everyone. She's recovering well from the Kaden drama; I think our baking session really helped, unless it was the incense doing its magic. Lola Nora is behind the register, taking the money and handing out change.

The ensaymada proves to be a hit, with the full table of sweets being ransacked in only twenty minutes. Luckily, there are a couple of extra boxes beneath the table, and as I set the bread on the stand, a deep voice says, "Hey, *p'wed-eng bum-i-li nang ti-na-pay?*" (Can I buy some bread?) in the most Canadian accent I've ever heard, so strong that I can hardly understand.

I don't look up as I say, "Sure! Just go to the pink-haired girl and she'll give you one," answering in English in case the customer assumed I *couldn't* speak it.

"Can I have the one that *you're* holding?" he asks, and I recognize him immediately. I spring up and James snatches the bread from my gloved hand, not bothering to pause for a moment (or even pay for it) before taking a bite.

"Hm, this actually tastes good. You didn't bake this, did you?" he says, and this time I fight back the sass creeping up my throat, wanting to spit fire at him. *You're at a church, Lara; holy thoughts, holy thoughts.*

"Lara," he says, his dark eyes guilty. "Can we talk?"

I want to tell him to stop looking at me, to stop making my heart beat so fast only to break it in a millisecond. But no matter what I do or try, he'll always be the one who gives me butterflies. As much as I care about living creatures, I need to get insect repellent.

Looking him in the eye, I give him the harshest glare that I can possibly give. "That's funny, I needed to tell you something, too, but it's a bit late for that."

"Please. I didn't mean to—"

"I don't need to hear anything."

But James has a track record of doing what he wants, so he continues. "There are a lot of words I'd use to describe myself," he starts, and I wonder where this is going. "I'm arrogant, loud, annoying, and many times I've been a downright idiot. But this arrogant, loud, annoying idiot is really sorry for hurting you, Lara. I'm sorry."

"Why'd you do it?" As the words come out, I hold in tears

threatening to spill. "Why did you ignore me? Why did you detach from me? Did you realize that you were tired of being my friend, so you left? Was it because of what happened that morning?"

He doesn't answer, and instead his eyes drift to the ground, just like mine.

"I want to forgive you." My voice cracks. "Just tell me why you did it. I'll understand."

"I can't," he says, and I freeze up. It was so easy to do. He could just give me an excuse and I'd get over it.

"Just tell me your excuse," I plead, hoping that he'll give me something, anything.

"I can't."

Those two words send a paralyzing feeling through my spine, leaving me standing in front of him, frozen and beginning to suffocate.

"Then I can't forgive you."

As I turn around and speed walk to the washroom, I try to control my breathing, which is so uneven that to the normal eye it looks like I'm having an asthma attack. *I will not cry. Not this time, not me. He should be the one crying, not me.* Then a memory floods back to me; it's uncalled for, but clear as day, and no matter how much I try to wave it away, bright red-orange fire replaces the washroom ceiling. The sun is setting again and I'm back.

Sunshine Park, Toronto
August (Three Years Ago)

What did I get myself into this time?

After a ketchup packet exploded on my white shirt, I'd run off to the washroom, leaving James with Eliza, who's spending yet another summer with us. I make my way back with my newly formed stain.

As I walk, I admire the beauty of the soon-to-be setting sun and its reflection on the water. A few little kids play on the big playground, and I recall how we were like them not too long ago.

Lara, Eliza, and James. The remarkable trio.

I finally see them sitting in the area hidden in a circle of trees, which has been mine and James's place since we were little, even before Eliza joined us. We went from organizing rocks in the dirt to sitting on the same bench under the willow tree, listening to the calming sound of the breeze and the faded crashes of the waves onto the shore.

When Eliza came we shared our secret hangout with her. Only the three of us knew about this place.

I push past the pine tree branches, ready to complain about my nonremovable ketchup stain to them.

That's when I see it.

Him.

Her.

They're sitting on our bench. His fingers are in her hair. His lips are on hers. It looks like a scene from a movie, with a blazing sunset accompanying their kiss. They look . . . perfect. But the only thing I can think of is . . .

Why isn't it me?

Then it hits me.

I don't belong here.

TIP NINETEEN:
BEFRIEND THE BOY-FRIES

*

By the next Monday, nothing has changed with my friends or James. I've had to reroute my entire school life in an attempt to avoid them. Of course, it's still mandatory for me to attend classes even when James is there, but I don't think I've spoken a word to him since I ran away from that bake sale. The only person I have now is Xander, and even then, I can only talk about science and university so much until I lose it. This is painfully ironic, and I hate to say this but the only other people I interact with are the boy-fries.

We have a silent work period in English class, but the memo doesn't reach Logan, whose wide blue eyes stare at me with concern as he bombards me with questions. "Are you sick? Or are you just not wearing makeup today?"

Oh God.

"I'm fine," I reply, but his brows furrow farther, unconvinced. I give him a reassuring smile, trying to prove that I am indeed fine, but he seems to panic even more.

"There's something wrong with Lara!" he yells, shaking Daniel by the shoulder.

"Logan, you're wrinkling my shirt." Daniel sighs, not looking up from his work.

Logan's hands shoot up. Daniel flattens the fabric of his shirt where Logan's hands ruined the perfect iron. Then he looks at me like I'm on the verge of death. "You're acting strange. Why haven't you snapped at or threatened Logan yet? This is the time of day when you usually try to kill him, and Mr. Garcia doesn't notice."

Mr. Garcia looks up from his laptop. "Oh, I notice."

"And you do nothing to help your favorite student?" Logan lifts a hand to his chest.

Mr. Garcia opens his mouth to say something but closes it again and goes back to his laptop.

"Guys, can't it just be that I'm trying to be a nice person?" I sigh, dropping my pen onto my notebook.

Unable to process my words, they blink before exchanging worried glances. Daniel doesn't seem to buy anything I say. "You might not like us, but you don't need to lie. I'd rather see you blackmailing Logan on a Monday morning than whatever the hell you're doing now."

"And I'd rather get blackmailed by you than have a silent seat partner," Logan adds. "Plus, your being distracted is not helping us at all. How am I supposed to understand the literary devices used in *Hamlet* if you're not writing them down?"

At that, Mr. Garcia nods in our direction again. "Logan, you do understand the concept of an academic offense, right?"

Logan tries to reason his way out of a cheating scandal, saying that learning Shakespeare is useless anyway, that I must be a reincarnation of the English playwright because I understand it so well, etc. It's amusing and takes my mind off of my problems for a few minutes. But what helps the most—even bringing an actual half smile to my face—is knowing that there are people who care enough to notice when I'm sad and miss the person I am when I'm happy.

None of my problems were their fault; they never were, and I wish I'd seen that earlier. Out of all the people in the world, I never thought I'd be thankful for my former best friends' boyfriends.

At home, Lola Nora and I sit comfortably on the couch in the family room with the leather seats reclined, focusing 100 percent of our attention on our K-drama. When God created the world, he decided that *Boys Over Flowers* and Lee Min-ho would be the cure for emotional pain, and I stand by that.

It's been two and a half hours since we started. Although I pride myself on being an avid television consumer, even my body can't take this anymore. I retire from my position, earning a scoff from Lola Nora. "Weak," she jokes, continuing with the show.

The house is hardly chaotic nowadays. In fact, it's awfully quiet. Everyone seems to have their own thing going on; Illa shifted her focus onto her big French project with Gabe, Mom does night shifts more than usual, and Dad constantly has a new house project to work on. Usually, I'd be a fan of the quiet, but the overwhelming silence is a perfect setting for my annoyingly intrusive thoughts to emerge. And I don't want to overthink anymore.

There's something about living in the city and growing up with a full house that makes you despise silence. Silence becomes deafening at some point; it swirls around the room and annoyingly displaces everything. Unfortunately, the only solution is to search for noise, yet even in the loudest of cities, sometimes you can't find it.

I head out the door, zipping up my jacket as the cold October air reaches the bottom of my lungs before floating out slowly like a balloon deflating through a single prick. It's dark out even though it's hardly six o'clock, and the wooden bench on the porch feels like a block of ice beneath me. Our porch lights are dimmed; one of the lightbulbs has burned out while the other flickers, inevitably reaching the end of its life.

Funny how I'm outside searching for noise but finding nothing. *Give me something, anything,* I silently pray, shutting my eyes tightly. Suddenly, I can hear Daughtry's "Feels Like Tonight" playing faintly in the distance, and I close my eyes, transported back to the floor of my old, pink-painted bedroom, where I'd spend hours listening to the local radio stations. Suddenly, a blaring car alarm disrupts the song, and my eyes fly open to see a black Jeep parked in a slant in front of my house, front tire eating the curb and blocking my driveway. The alarm finally stops, but the song continues. An old boom box sits on the roof, duct-taped tightly, and I wonder if driving like that is even legal. Immediately, the doors open and three girls—all wearing neon pink and covered with glow sticks—hop out of the car, holding plastic microphones and singing (very dramatically) along with the song. Even Carol.

I'm supposed to be mad, really. But it's so hard when they look like illuminated highlighters under the streetlight and are singing songs from 2007. How can you not laugh? Kiera's winged eyeliner matches the shirt perfectly, both the brightest neon pink I've ever seen. Meanwhile, Carol sways from side to side, missing every beat while Jasmine does each step perfectly.

"What is all this?" I ask, fighting the corners of my mouth, which are trying to curl upward.

Kiera climbs to the top of the Jeep, feet never faltering, and pauses the music.

"We're really sorry," Jasmine starts. "We all stood you up on Saturday . . . and all those other days."

"We haven't been good friends lately," Carol continues. "It's terrible how it took a voice message to make us realize it."

"So we wanted to serenade you and beg for your forgiveness." Kiera pulls out a large Sharpie and places it in my hand. "You can also write Really Bad Friends on our foreheads if it makes you feel better."

I look at them, then the Sharpie, then back at them. A tired laugh escapes my lips, and my eyes begin to water at the painfully ridiculous offer.

"I told you the idea was bad!" Carol shouts. "You're making her feel worse!"

"At least I *had* an idea!" Kiera argues.

"Please don't be mad at us anymore," Jasmine says, reaching for my hands. "We were horrible to you but we're back now, and we're not going to leave your side."

I chew on my bottom lip, having a hard time believing it. Words threaded in a pretty sentence can be as easily broken as a bracelet held by a single string. But I know it's sincere; their eyes meet mine this time and there are no barriers between us. Though probably meant metaphorically, the leaving part is a lie, of course. They're headed for their dreams while I'm here, still figuring out mine.

"Lara?" Kiera takes my hand and squeezes it.

Softly, I say, "Don't lie to me. Don't say things like that and get my hopes up and not follow through."

"We mean it."

My face heats up before I have the chance to control it, before I can even count to ten in my head and breathe deep breaths. "Do you? Last time you lied to me, you apologized and told me we would spend time together, just us. What's the difference between that time and this time? You didn't even notice when I stopped sitting with you at lunch or when I stopped meeting you every morning."

Everyone looks at their feet and the silence rushes in like water through a broken dam. All I wanted was noise, and now I'm letting out everything I've bottled up since the first day of school.

"And don't talk about not leaving. All of us know that's a lie. Kiera, you're off to travel the world, and I know you bought a one-way ticket to who knows where and God knows when or if you'll come back. Carol, you're going to get in to UPenn and become a superstar soccer player while working for that law degree because you want to defend yourself in court. Jasmine, you look like you'll pick Victoria over your old dream school, and I get that dreams change. But guys, I really don't want you to leave."

I start to sob but force myself to continue.

"More than that, I don't want you to stay. I want you to chase the life you want and not feel held back by anyone, not me, not your boyfriends. But please don't leave earlier, *please*." I hate the sound of my voice when I cry, it's embarrassing. Still, I allow my breaking voice to continue. "We were supposed to have our best summer before you all . . ." I pause to catch my breath. "This is the last full year we'll have together, and I don't want us to break before we're supposed to."

By now Kiera's crying, and it sounds like the wails of a sad ghost. Jasmine sniffles a bit too. Carol keeps her stone face, jaw clenched, breathing heavily through her nose.

"No one's breaking," Carol manages to spit out. She turns, then grips my shoulders tightly. "And nobody is leaving. We're here for you, okay? From now on, we're at your doorstep when you need us. Even if I have to commit multiple crimes to get there, I will be at your side."

"You don't have to forgive us just yet," Kiera says, "but as Carol said, we'll always be on your doorstep."

"Minus the crimes," Jasmine adds.

Kiera wipes the tears off my cheeks before wiping her own. She embraces me once more, whispering, "Sorry." I rest my head in the familiar curve of her shoulder, letting out a deep sigh of relief because I know we'll be okay. Soon enough, all three of them are around me and things finally feel like they are where they should be. Even their bickering is like music to my ears.

However, as one issue fades away, another always has to resurface. I want someone to hear me. Maybe it's time that I give them the chance to listen.

"There's been a lot going on actually . . ." I start and am instantly greeted by looks of confusion. Perhaps it's a thing to assume that I never have anything going on in my life. ". . . with James."

"*James*?" they all exclaim at the same time, releasing from the group hug and staring at me with widened eyes.

Kiera runs her fingers through the tangled curls of her hair. "We've missed *a lot*."

"I think we need to have an LKJC meeting," Jasmine says.

And that is exactly what we do—after I write Really on Kiera's forehead, Bad on Jasmine's, and Friends on Carol's. They stand in a line with black Sharpie on their foreheads, smiling for a poor-quality picture that will later be stored for blackmail/embarrassment purposes.

Honestly, maybe they're not that bad.

In my bedroom, Carol lies on the bed, flat on her stomach and resting her head on a huge pink stuffed whale, while Jasmine sits crossed-legged on the floor beside me.

Kiera paces back and forth, and I pull a large bowl of popcorn toward us so that she doesn't accidentally step on it. "So you're telling us that you think you might like James? The guy who literally tripped you on the first day of school?" she repeats for the third time.

"The guy you've hated since . . . *forever*?" Jasmine continues.

I stand up and fall onto the bed, my body bouncing slightly from the springs. "I don't know. He's so annoying and says dumb things and does stupid stuff all the time."

Carol raises an eyebrow. "*But?*"

There's an awkward pause before I answer. When I think about him, memories blur like a tangled tape. But the James who bought me ice cream after every mishap is the same James who held me on the street; he's the person who causes my heart to flutter and ache, stomach to turn and drop, my breath to come quickly and not at all.

"But he does those things because he's *there*. He's always been looking out for me, and when life gets serious, he'll do things like squeeze my hand or hold me, and sometimes he'll just look at me and I—"

Their jaws are wide open and so are their eyes. *I've said too much.* This sap-fest is *not* me. I slap myself across the face in an effort to knock some sense into myself and it doesn't help relieve their shock. I purposely don't mention my past crush on him because I don't want to induce any myocardial infarctions this early on.

"You're in love with him," Kiera states and I grimace.

Immediately, I sit up. "No way." Love is a strong word for a complicated series of emotions. "And even if I was—and I'm not saying that I am—what do I do? I'm supposed to be bitter and single! Frankly, I kind of like being bitter and single!"

Jasmine says, "You have two options. You can either tell him how you feel or—"

"Forget about him by taking a nice vacation to Mexico!" Carol finishes, tossing the pink whale to the side before wrapping an arm around me. "Think about it! White sand beaches, dolphins, palm trees . . ."

I would be lying if I said I wouldn't consider it. "And warm weather. Oh! We could go swimming in those underwater cenotes! I heard those were really refreshing."

"Guys!" Kiera yells and we shut up. "Lara, you need to be straight up about it. Say 'James, I like you' and get it over with."

"I don't know if I can physically do that."

"I know it's hard to put yourself out there when you don't know if the person likes you back, but it's the only way to find out. And if he doesn't like you for you, then he's missing out because you're amazing and anybody would be lucky to have you."

A comforting warmth engulfs me when she says that. I missed her reassuring words. However, they do nothing to relieve my anxiety.

"Lara's literally a terror!" Carol chuckles while devouring a handful of popcorn. "We're going to have to supply James with a helmet if they ever go on a date."

I throw a piece of popcorn at her, which she simply catches in her mouth.

"Besides," I continue, "I don't think that me liking him is going to change anything. He didn't seem to like me back when his tongue was down another girl's throat."

"That was a graphic that I did not need to picture," Kiera says, gagging.

Carol frowns. "Personally, I think we should kill him."

All of our heads turn.

"*Carol—*" Jasmine throws her a warning look that she ignores. Carol smiles evilly. She clasps her hands and her eyes light up. *Shizballs*, that's her "idea" face. Whatever comes after that face is never good. "You remember when I redecorated my room last month?"

Jasmine gulps. "Uh-huh."

"I still have the drill, hammer, and some nails!" Carol gets up and makes a beeline to the door.

As if I were a professional football player, I sprint and tackle her. We tumble to the floor, one of my body parts accidentally cracking in the process. "I may be mad at him, but you can't kill him!"

Carol groans from beneath me. "Ugh, why?"

"You'll have no friends in prison," Kiera says.

"So?"

"You'll be lonely," Jasmine adds.

"And?"

"The food in jail sucks," I say and she gasps.

Carol shakes her head. "Sorry, but I don't think I can sacrifice all-you-can-eat buffets for you, kid. James is such a lucky asshole."

"Yeah, because who cares about legal and moral transgressions," Jasmine comments sarcastically.

It's quite ironic how Carol aims to pursue a profession that upholds laws while almost all of her instincts are toward actions that break them. Nonetheless, as long as her love for food is stronger than her drive for murder, we're all good.

"But seriously," Kiera continues, "we want the best for you, but your situation is pretty different from any of ours. You guys have known each other since the beginning of time, and honestly, there's no avoiding him."

She's right. Mom and Tita Gia probably hold the record for the world's strongest friendship, and our families have been merged ever since they met.

"You guys need to talk, and that's final," Jasmine says and the thought of approaching him again makes my stomach churn.

Seeing James is already an emotional roller coaster; it's a mix of liking and hating and being annoyed and angry and sad but at the same time, all I want is for him to be beside me, hand on my back and rubbing circles with his thumb. I want to be close enough so that

I can find it funny that he smells like his favorite fruit. But more than anything, I want to understand why he did the things he did.

"Excuse me!" Carol yells, disrupting the silence. "Are you going to get off of me or am I just going to be your new mattress?"

After being released from my weight, she pushes herself up and holds both arms above her head, stretching. "So what I'm hearing is that Plan A is to talk to him and Plan B is to kill him? And if so, Plan B is basically Plan A because there is no way Lara's going to talk to him out of the blue. I should start preparing for the lawsuit."

Jasmine brushes her dark hair back with her fingers before holding both of Carol's arms and looking into her eyes. Slowly, she goes, "There will be no murder and no lawsuits because Lara's going to be mature and communicate her feelings."

Carol huffs in disbelief and I can't blame her. There might be murders and lawsuits.

TIP TWENTY:
BE MATURE

✱

I am not mature. I like kids' shows and cartoons; I have a strong belief that our world will end with zombies or aliens; and I would gladly live in a ball pit. Most of all, I don't like feelings and if I can avoid talking about them, I will.

And I do. Our mornings slowly return to normal—hallway conversations with the girls are like how they were before, with the exception of the added boyfriends. Now I don't mind it. Logan and Daniel have grown on me; the dynamic duo never fails to make me smile. Mark has always been a good guy, and it's much better now that he and Carol don't have their secluded conversations while in the group. It's the end of an era—both friend groups have merged into a happy one and everyone gets along.

With one exception.

I must admit I have not made an effort to talk to James. My days consist of one-word answers, deleting text messages, and avoiding eye contact. He's resilient, I'll give him that, but I can't bring myself to tell him the truth.

Because of this, Carol goes around holding large black (strangely body-sized) bags in the hallway, making sure to hold them up and glare at James whenever he passes by. Of course, he hardly understands the threat, but the rest of us know she'll attack him when given any kind of Go signal.

Now, the smell of pumpkin spice hangs in the air, suffocating all who despise the season but bringing pleasure to those who live for it. We're deep in infinity scarves and green military-style jackets, combat boots and beanies, and costumes that will leave you freezing, wipe out your bank account, or do both. Even Kiera can't battle the season. Her usual flowy dress or cropped top is replaced with a pair of black leggings and a brown crew neck sweatshirt paired with her brand new Doc Martens. Unfortunately, by the time we get out of school and make our way to the shopping district, she's limping from the blisters that have formed on her feet. Funny enough, she doesn't even grimace while shuffling through the clothing racks.

Our local thrift shop has been ravaged by a natural disaster in the form of inconsiderate humans. Kids run loose, throwing Halloween decor into their parents' carts, only for the parents to remove the items and place them back on the closest racks. Groups of teenagers float by, holding up costumes as they check their reflections in the mirror before tossing them on whatever hanger is beside them. Clothes are scattered on the floor, and the scariest thing is the look of disdain on the employees' faces. I bet they could use a pumpkin spice latte . . . with two shots of espresso.

Kiera hangs a costume back on the rack before releasing a frustrated sigh. After hours of searching for the perfect costume, we've got nothing. She wanted something different, but I hardly know what category she's going for.

"We could do a group costume?" I suggest.

Her face lights up like a kid seeing free candy. "We should be Disney Princesses!"

My face twists into a wince before I can think. "That's an . . . *idea*. But it also involves looking nice, so . . ."

She folds her arms before standing up. "What were *you* thinking of then?"

"What if I was Darth Vader and you guys were stormtroopers? We don't even have to do anything since our faces will be covered." Can you go wrong with Star Wars?

"I want something cute, though." She sighs. "Plus, can we really trust Carol with a lightsaber? Sure it's fake, and plastic, but she'll be jabbing people with it all day."

"Stormtroopers don't have lightsabers."

"She'll take yours."

"Point made."

Her phone beeps and she immediately cringes at the screen. When she shows me the text message, I laugh so loudly that I snort. "I can't believe Daniel wants to do a couple's costume. This is too hilarious," I say, wiping an escaping tear from my eye.

Kiera groans. "We're not doing this." She begins to text him back, but I snatch her cell phone from her hand and run through the messy aisle.

"Hey!" she yells, limping after me in her Docs, but I'm already halfway out of the store, running and sending a message to Daniel about how much "I *love* the idea of a couple's costume."

She catches up to me by the sliding entrance doors but it's too late. The message has already been sent and Daniel isn't a slow texter by a long run.

Daniel: *I knew you'd love it! So excited! :)*

I smirk at Kiera as I hand her back the phone.

"You didn't," she says through her teeth.

"I'm your best friend, of course I did. You wouldn't want to break your darling's heart now, would you?" I coo, and she rolls her eyes. "Ah, I can't wait till Halloween. What an amusing day that'll be."

She grunts. "Please, all you're going to do is make fun of us until you lose your voice."

I hold my right hand to my heart. "As your best friend, that is my obligation."

We walk out of the store without having bought anything. A swift gust of wind reaches my face and I zip up my black leather jacket. It's fully autumn now and the leaves are a lovely shade of auburn, half of them still on the trees and the other half on the ground.

She checks her phone again. "I've gotta go. My mom's waiting around the corner. She's been nagging me to get ready for some mother-daughter social or whatever. See you, Lara." She gives me a quick hug before walking to the end of the street.

A few minutes later, I find myself waiting at the bus stop, the chilly fall breeze running through my hair and making me shiver although I'm wrapped up in layers. I check my phone, looking at the time. The bus should've been here ten minutes ago, and to make things worse, it looks like it's about to rain.

I look up at the gray sky and groan, as if my plea would change the unreasonable ways of the universe. Then, across the street, my eyes land upon the guy with those unmistakable dark-brown eyes half-covered by the messy hair hanging over them. His presence alone is enough to make the butterflies in my stomach grab their rifles and start a chaotic war. The discomfort isn't even the worst part. The worst part is that he's eating fries.

Here I am, trying to get over him, but he just has to go and eat a bunch of freaking french fries as he strolls along the freaking sidewalk like the annoying douche bag he is! If we were on good terms right now, I'd go right over there, attack him, and run away with those fries.

But the thing is, we're not. So I'm not going to run up to James; I'm not going to steal his fries; and I'm sure as hell not going to talk to him just to get those fries.

Public transportation, please don't fail me. Your arrival would be greatly appreciated.

Instead of a lovely bus sweeping me off my feet and saving me, I find myself in a horrible situation. His eyes meet mine, and I immediately crouch behind the nearest traffic box. *Maybe he didn't see me.* I sneak a quick look and confirm that he indeed saw me and is now reaching a crosswalk and walking in my direction.

My mind switches to panic mode, activating all internal system alarms, and the red lights flicker uncontrollably. Adrenaline courses through my veins and I run into the nearest building like my feet are on fire. Suddenly, mannequins fall on the floor like dominoes, displacing a basket of panties on sale for five dollars each and knocking a couple of bras from the display table.

The dimly lit store does nothing to hide my embarrassment. Several older ladies share concerned looks, eyes shifting from the mess to my disheveled shelf. A Victoria's Secret employee doesn't hesitate before approaching me, hands on her hips and an unamused expression like this is her absolute last straw and she'll be filing her two weeks' notice after her shift.

"*Yeah* . . . I'll fix that." I grin awkwardly, lifting the fallen mannequins back up before getting on my knees to pick up all the brightly colored bras and panties scattered on the floor.

She forces a smile then heads off to assist another customer with her handy dandy measuring tape, which will probably add a couple of inches to someone's bust in an attempt to increase customer self-esteem.

Just as I drop a lace thong into the woven basket, the door opens. James looks down at me and stares. *Rude.* I glare at him. Telling by his empty hands, he must've finished the fries. Now I've got absolutely no reason to talk to him.

Because he knows that I'm still angry, he manages to press his lips together, trying to hide a smile. "Nice bra you got there," he says, gesturing to the black lace bra in my hand. "Bet you could pull it off if you actually had boobs," he jokes, as if nothing has happened within the past few weeks and everything's the same.

"First of all, your concern with my boobs is worrisome. Second of all, I told you to stop talking to me."

He crouches so that our eyes are level. "You've gotta understand that I can't do that."

"You've done it before so I'm sure that's not a problem," I scoff, remembering how he literally ignored me for days prior to when I saw him kiss that other girl. He looks at the ground. I've struck a raw nerve, but he fails to realize that it hurts me just as much, if not more.

Still, he continues, "Lara, I never want to stop talking to you or seeing you or being with you."

I roll my eyes. "Save that crap for Britney, or Sydney, or Cindy, or Lindy, or say that to a girl named *Kidney* for all I care!"

"Lara, please—"

"Just go away!" I shout, throwing the black bra at him, which catches him off guard.

He responds by using said bra as a catapult, launching a pair of underwear into my territory. "I refuse!"

The offender is met with a series of attacks in the form of a pair of red panties, a polka-dot bra, a lace bralette, and everything else on the floor. He flicks the flying lingerie away like he's playing a game of

Fruit Ninja. Much like the result of rapidly sliced fruit, we're left with a mess that covers more area than expected.

Footsteps grow nearer and an inevitably annoyed voice joins the conversation. "What is going on?" The angry store lady glares at me yet again.

"I know this looks bad, but it's his fault this time." I point a finger at James, throwing him under the bus without hesitation. "He doesn't even have a reason to be here! He doesn't even wear or need a freaking bra!"

James gasps and stares at me like he's incredibly offended. "And you need one? Last time I checked, this isn't a battery shop, and nobody stocks the size quadruple A."

"*Excuse you*, I'm at least an A cup and sometimes even a B." Right after the words pour out of my mouth, I think, *God, I sound stupid.*

The frustrated employee snorts. "Let's not get ahead of ourselves, hon."

James stands up and crosses his arms. "Hey! I'm the only one who makes fun of her!"

My eyelids slam shut and I massage my temples with my index and middle fingers. "Why can't you just leave me alone?" I yell before striding out of the store, leaving the mess for the snobby store lady.

In an instant, cold raindrops hit my face and begin to drench my hair without remorse. I don't make a mental plea because no matter what I negotiate with the universe, I know that the water will keep falling. I let out a frustrated scream that draws stares from bystanders, particularly from an old man with a long white beard, leaning against a nearby brick wall. He takes a joint out of his mouth and a puff of smoke escapes his lips. "When the going gets tough, stay groovy."

Before I can even wonder what the stoned man means, the rain stops around me. I tilt my head up to see a black umbrella held above my head by the bra size bully.

"Just go," I whisper, too drained to yell.

"I'm not going anywhere. I don't care how long it takes, but I'll be here until we're ready to, y'know, not be like this anymore."

Moved by frustration, I turn around. His face goes serious, and his voice becomes softer.

"I'm really sorry," he says, eyes not drifting from mine. "For everything. I'm sorry for ignoring you and kissing that other girl. I'm sorry for taking your friendship for granted. And, God, I'm so sorry for trying to kiss you out of the blue. That was—"

"I know! *I know* that you're sorry, but I want to know *why*. Just *one* reason. That's all you had to—"

"I like you," he says and I start to choke, either on his words or by inhaling some raindrops.

I stare at him, wide eyed like a deer in the headlights. I can physically feel my neurons malfunctioning; the messages are not getting passed on as they should. My brain throws out everything I know about language. *Like?* As in, I *like* pomegranates?

He scratches the back of his neck then exhales deeply. "I—you, you make me feel all weird, and it took me a while to realize that I actually liked you. When I figured it out, I didn't want to accept it. More than that, I didn't want to face the possibility of you not feeling the same way, so I tried to ignore it and moved on in the worst way possible.

"I know what you're going to say, and I agree, I'm such an idiot." He sighs, giving me a crooked smile. "Was my excuse too late?"

What do I even say to that? Chewing on my inner cheek, I make an effort to concentrate. Someone help me because I don't know how to respond to a confession coming from a boy I've been hopelessly in love with since elementary school.

"I like pomegranates too," comes out of my mouth before anything else that makes the slightest bit of sense.

My first instinct is to run, but that brain signal doesn't reach my limbs, so I stand there, frozen. My gaze shifts to my feet, then to the old, stoned man, then to James. To my surprise, he's not making fun of my response.

"You like me?" I repeat to make sure. Perhaps I'm hallucinating.

"I mean, that's what I just said. I get it if you don't feel the same way. I saw you that morning when you were with Xander at the library, and if he's who you like, then—"

Eyes focused on my feet, I mutter, "I don't like him that way."

"What do you mean?"

I groan into my hands. This is way more embarrassing than I thought it would be. "For goodness' sake, I like you!" I yell in his face. *God, I hate confessions.*

That one statement alone is enough to get him to grin like an idiot, showing off his dimples—something I haven't seen in a long time. I missed them so much. His laugh is like sunshine amid the rain. He gives my hand a tight squeeze and I finally feel like I'm home.

I point a finger at him. "Don't start getting cocky about it! I only like you a little bit."

"You like me a lot, don't you, sweetheart?" He hits me with a flirty wink and I roll my eyes.

The rain continues to fall onto the umbrella and the surrounding pavement. He looks from one end of the street to the other. "The bus probably isn't coming for a while. I'll bring you home. And we can stop by the grocery store to get you some pomegranates."

I nod slowly and walk alongside him as we make our way to the car. Our steps are in sync and water ripples beneath our feet. He opens the door and I take a seat in the passenger's side. I try to fight the smile that tugs on my lips but I can't.

And when he slips into the driver's side, sparing a few seconds to look at me before starting the car, I wonder if I'll ever stop smiling.

TIP TWENTY-ONE:
DON'T LAUGH AT COUPLES COSTUMES

✱

We drive to the nearest Walmart and get six pomegranates in total.

"I'm sure Seb misses you," James mentions when we get back to the car. "After all, he hasn't seen you in a while." Leaning close, he tucks a loose lock of hair behind my ear. "Wanna come over?"

My answer is obviously yes.

The house is quiet when we enter, except for a television humming in the background with the sound of two lightsabers smashing together. In the living room, Seb sits on the couch, half falling asleep in the middle of some new Star Wars show on Disney Channel. Gabe bops his head to music from his earbuds, shuffling through papers scattered on top of the coffee table, not noticing when we walk into the room.

James crouches down beside Seb, sweeping the kid's hair back to reveal sleepy eyes. "Hey, bud."

"I'm not sleepy, Kuya," he says, shaking his head, but his eyes are already closing.

"Hm, I don't know . . . you look pretty sleepy to me. I guess I'll bring Ate Lara home."

"Ate Lara?" His eyes light up when he sees me and he proceeds to run over.

I lean down to pick him up and he goes, "I'm so glad you're back. I made a cube out of marshmallows and toothpicks at school, and I learned how to add numbers, and I'm going to show you my new Lego set."

"Very impressive, little dude."

He cups his hand over his mouth and whispers, "But I think Kuya missed you more. He's less grumpy today." We exchange smiles while James frowns, excluded from the conversation.

"What are you guys whispering about?" He attacks Seb at the side with tickles that make the kid squirm in my arms until I eventually have to set him back on the floor.

Gabe removes one of his earbuds and glares at us. "Do you guys mind? I'm trying to study for my science test." When he sees me, he raises a hand in a wave. "Oh hey, Ate Lara. Good to see you back."

I wave back but soon after he goes back to an intense study session. Seb tugs on my arm, leading me to the staircase. "Someone always has to be grumpy here," he mutters. "My Legos are in my room. Let's go! Let's go!"

The three of us are about to go up when Tito Danny emerges from the downstairs office, dark shadows looming beneath his eyes and hair tousled in a way I've never seen. "James, can we discuss something?" he asks, removing the square-framed glasses from his face and wiping them with a corner of his untucked button-up. When he sees me, the corners of his lips turn up—more of a polite smile than a happy one. "Hey, Lara."

"Hi, Tito."

He gestures for James to follow him to the office. "James?"

"Right behind you," James replies. My Seb-free hand grips the staircase and James pats it twice. "You guys go ahead. I'll be up in a bit." With that, they vanish into a dark office.

Seb continues to pull me. "You heard him! *Vamanos!*"

We walk and the sound of ghostlike weeping echoes through the hallway. Both of us peek into an open room where Ate Kelly sits on the floor, holding an iPad in her lap. She grabs a tissue and blows her nose so violently that I wonder if the bones might break from the vibration.

"K-drama?" I ask.

She looks up. "*Coffee Prince*."

Iconic. A rush of good memories floods my mind. Her confirmation is enough for us to leave her alone and be on our way.

Seb's room is smaller than James's, and much smaller than the study. Somehow, it's still bigger than mine. A twin-sized bed covered by an olive-green comforter and stuffed animals sits beside a large window. At the foot is a wooden toy chest, and shelves with books and Lego models line the walls. The ceiling is covered with glow in the dark star stickers, reminding me of my old bedroom.

I sit on the spherical chair that hangs from the ceiling, planting my feet on the ground so I don't accidentally launch myself into a swing. Seb excitedly pulls out everything he meant to show me, starting with the cube model. Holding the toothpick-marshmallow architectural piece in his hand, he explains how a cube is composed of six squares for the sides. I nod enthusiastically, pretending everything is new information and drowning in adorable.

He dumps a container of Lego onto the floor and begins to construct what seems to be a unique high-rise building. *Mini-architect*, I think to myself. We build his city, but he grows more tired with each passing minute, rubbing his eyes.

There's a knock on the open door and Tita Gia leans against the door frame. Her eyes go round when she sees me. "Oh! Hi, ineng. James didn't tell me you were coming over. You want something to eat or—"

I wave my hands. "No need. Thank you, though!"

With an eyebrow raised, she looks at Seb. "Anak, you're supposed to be taking a nap. We still have somewhere to go later. Where's Ate Kelly? She was supposed to put you to sleep."

Ate Kelly and I share a spiritual connection now that I've seen her dedication to her show, prioritizing the rom-com over her actual job. It's admirable. With that being said, everyone can use a cover sometimes.

"Seb and I were just hanging out, but I can stay until he falls asleep," I offer before turning to him. "What do you think, bud?"

He gives his mom two thumbs up.

"*Salamat ineng*," (Thanks, dear,) she says. "Now it's time for me to check on my other boys—except Gabe, of course. You'd think I'd actually get to rest on my day off but James and Danny . . . they're something, all right." With an exhausted huff, she leaves.

Seb slips into his bed and I tuck him in. Almost immediately, the exhausted boy falls asleep. He looks so much like James when he was younger—so innocent, unproblematic.

I quietly step out of the room, closing the door slowly enough that there isn't even a creak. Then I go down the stairs, following the noise coming from Tito Danny's office. The walls of the downstairs office struggle to keep the noise inside the room. The yelling is muffled but the words are important enough that they become clear as day.

"There's no other way," Tito Danny says, not exactly a yell, but his voice is firm—which is somehow worse. "Your grandfather's sick and you need to start helping with the business. Your mother and I need you."

I expect James to yell right away, to shout that he doesn't want to go and that he belongs here. But the outburst never comes. Instead, he says, "I understand."

Tito Danny sighs, exasperated. "Then why are we talking about this again?"

"Because you're not understanding me and you're not trying," James says. "I told you I'd go after graduation. I'm only asking for a few more months."

"I'm sorry but we don't have a few more months. Your mother and I need to make sure you'll be a capable successor!" He grows more desperate with each sentence, and the strain in his voice gets tighter.

James speaks softly now, lower. "What if I don't want to be?"

A fist slams against a wooden surface; maybe it's his desk or the walls, but it causes me to jolt either way. I've never heard Tito Danny like this, not this stressed and not this angry. He was the parent who made jokes at the dinner table, played card games, taught James and me silly magic tricks to perform at family gatherings. Was he always like this?

"Danny!" Tita Gia scolds.

He ignores her attempt to calm him. "Fine! Then tell me what you want to do! Do you even know what you want to do with your life, James?"

I imagine Tita Gia clinging to her husband's arm, pleading for them to quit it. "You're going too far—"

"No! If he wants to do something with his life, then he better speak up about it! Go ahead!"

There is silence before the last explosion.

"Exactly! So don't argue with me unless you have some other great plan yourself!"

Footsteps sound behind the door and I run back up the stairs before they can reach the office door. I slip into the closest room, James's room. The footsteps continue from downstairs, up into the hallway until they're at his bedroom door. He opens it only enough so that he can get through. Despite the obviously exhausting argument, he smiles at me like he knew I would be here right after.

"Hey," he says.

"Hey."

He sits on the bed, elbows resting on his knees and chin propped on his clasped hands. It's a different comforter than the one that was here last time. I'm grateful for that, at least. I link my arm with his, plopping down beside him and he sits up straight. He rests his head on my shoulder and we stay like that for a while.

"Do you want to talk about it?" I ask. "It's never good to keep anger inside."

One of his hands shifts over to my knee and he taps his fingers in a steady rhythm, *one, two, three.* Shaking his head, he goes, "I'm not angry with him. He's not only worried about the business. We're all frustrated, but there aren't any other options. And he's right, I don't know what to do with my life."

"It's okay if you don't. It's not a reason for your dad to force you into doing something you don't want to do."

He takes a deep breath. "I was never close to my grandad, but my dad loves his father, who at this point hardly remembers him." He stares at me intently. "I can't even imagine how hard that is. He needs someone there for him, too, even when he doesn't say it." Without saying it, I know he's thinking about his Lolo—the person who was there for him unconditionally.

When we were in elementary school, Tito Danny was starting out with the business, opening up local hotel branches and working day and night to achieve success. He made sure to spend as much time as possible with his kids, but even then, it wasn't a lot of time. Lolo Andres became James's best friend. They shared the same humor, and despite the obvious language barrier, they understood each other. It's not surprising that the only Tagalog James knows by heart are song lyrics.

"I've been keeping something from you," he admits. "There was another reason why I didn't tell you how I felt."

My face falls, knowing exactly what it is. It's the same reason why he was begging Tito Danny for a few more months. "When?"

"December."

Though I expected it, my heart still shatters, as if it was never mended in the first place, as if the *I like you*s were a distant dream and they never existed. Everything aches, and I want him to take it back. I needed more time to process this, not less of it. *You said August; you said the end of summer, not—*

December.

I tune out the rest. I don't mean to, but I can't help myself. I've heard the important part, and my mind doesn't know what to do with that piece of information. He doesn't go on for too long, probably because he notices my unfocused stare. Instead of saying anything else, he takes my hand and brushes his thumb over my knuckles, again and again like a song on replay. *It's going to be okay*, he means to say. I don't think I can believe that.

"I used to tell people that I don't care about my future that much," James says with a sad smile, "but I think I was lying."

He grips my hand tighter, like I'm the only thing anchoring him. "The truth is, it scares me so much that I try not to think about it at all. I don't know what I'm doing with my life. I don't know if I'll love or hate this whole business thing. I don't know *anything*, really."

Me too. *Me too, me too, me too*. All this time was he overthinking and stressing as much as I was? Was he holding it in like me?

"But there's one thing I'm sure of," he continues. "I love my family.

Dad needs me right now, and I'll be there for him. If I have to sacrifice some time doing something I don't like, I think it'll still be worth it."

Some people see the selfless choice as the wrong option. We're told to follow our own dreams and not let anyone hold us back. But we tend to forget the beauty of sacrifice, the beauty of a love that lets go of our own wishes for the sake of someone else. Selflessness and sacrifice don't have to be weaknesses. Sometimes they're our greatest strengths.

"I know that at the end of the day it's my decision and I—I'm choosing to leave."

Usually, my stomach would turn like there's no tomorrow, a wave of nausea would creep up my throat, but now . . . there's nothing. He looks at me with a crooked half smile and I know we're going to be okay. It isn't exactly making peace with reality but knowing that we can't escape it. I feel okay knowing that it's *his* choice.

He whispers, "I'm sorry."

"Don't be. I'm proud of you."

Pulling his head away from my shoulder, he brushes the flyaway hairs from my face. "I should've liked you earlier—I mean, told you I liked you earlier. I could've held your books and your hand in the hallway. I would've looked forward to telling everyone that you're mine, cuddling when it's cold, and hugging you whenever, without being afraid that you'll shove me and snap my neck."

"If we dated, I'd still shove you, but I would not mind having someone trail behind me in the hallway with all my stuff."

We both laugh.

He stands up. "I don't know how you can twist anything romantic into something *like that*. But if we were together, I'd lift you up and kiss you in front of everyone when I just can't help myself."

I tilt my head to the side before getting up so that we stand toe to toe. A sudden burst of confidence surges through me. "Then do it. All of it. You're still here."

His smile falls. "I'm afraid that if I do, I'll like it so much that I won't know how to live without it. It's too bad time isn't on our side."

"I don't think time cares if we try or not."

He pulls me in close then, locking us in a safe embrace. My arms wrap around his neck, his around my waist. His chest rises and falls against mine—the familiarity keeping my heart steady. "I guess not," he whispers and I think, *This is where I'm supposed to be. This is where I belong.*

Being with James is a big step, a scary one that I am not adequately prepared for. The closer we get, the harder it is to accept that we'll eventually be pulled apart again. But right now, it's bliss. Today, I'll let myself float on cloud nine, and if that means falling on hard pavement tomorrow, then so be it.

Halloween rolls around the following Monday and that means trying to contain the excitement of knowing James likes me, in an effort to remain as scary as possible. Do you know how hard it is to act dead when three days ago your frenemy you low-key liked since forever confessed their romantic feelings for you? It's hard!

People stare as I start down the hallway, looking for my friends. I take it as a compliment. My zombie makeup, complete with the outfit and fake blood, is good enough that I could be an extra on *The Walking Dead*. Our school takes the holiday seriously, and that means a plethora of black and orange streamers hanging around the halls and decorated doors in the spirit of classroom competition. Fake spiders are plastered on the walls while carved pumpkins are arranged on the usually dusty shelves.

Finally, I see my target: the guy who's dressed up as some off-brand Disney prince, surrounded by Kiera, Jasmine, Carol, and Mark, who are laughing at something. Kiera's dressed as a packet of mustard, which I can only assume was Daniel's idea, and I fully expect to see a giant ketchup packet walking toward us in a couple of minutes. Carol and Mark are pirates, but she has two plastic swords while he has none. And Jasmine's dressed as a sorceress for the third year in a row.

I tap James's shoulder and he turns around, letting out a high-pitched shriek that pierces my ears. Immediately, I start laughing my head off, pointing at him. "You're so adorable. What are you supposed to be? Prince Charming?"

He sticks his nose in the air. "Yes, I *am* supposed to be Prince Charming, but that's because I thought we were all doing couples costumes!"

"But we're not a couple—"

"Yet." James throws an arm around my shoulder and winks.

There is a loud, simultaneous "YET?!?" from our friends.

Mark's the first one who waves a hand in the air, shaking his head. "Hold up, hold up. I know both of you and this has to be a prank, right? Watch, Lara's going to slap his arm off any second."

In response to that, James pulls me even closer, and I willingly snuggle into his side.

"Holy crap," Mark whispers with widened eyes and a hand over his mouth.

Kiera squeals as she grabs my arm, pulling me away from James in order to do an excited jump (in which *she* jumps and I lazily stay put). Jasmine and Carol stand with gaping mouths.

Ignoring them, I turn to James. "Where on earth did you get the idea that I was going to be a part of your couples costume?"

"You love Disney! I texted you a few days ago and you said that it would be really funny. You also said that you would borrow your mom's heels or something."

"What? I never got a text message!" I open up my phone and show him our message history. "See? Nothing!" He returns the confused look that I wear.

"Then who did I—"

"Guys, I'm here!" Logan's loud voice announces. I look at Logan and think, *He can become a great meme.*

Daniel (yes, dressed as a ketchup packet) walks alongside him, fingers massaging his temples. "I tried talking him out of it, but he insisted. I swear."

"What do you guys think?" Logan asks with an amused look on his face. He gives a little twirl and shows off the bright-pink dress that might rip any second. Lifting the skirt a little, he points at the nude heels on his feet, on the verge of falling apart. I can only imagine him stuffing his giant feet into his mother's poor heels.

James exhales deeply. "So it was Logan I texted, not you."

"I guess it's understandable, I mean, our names were probably right beside each other in your contacts," I say, patting him on the back.

"Are you trying to tell me that you wanted Lara as your princess, and not me? I feel so hurt, bro," Logan says, shaking his head disappointedly, and I bite my tongue, trying not to laugh at his attempt to tease James. Jasmine stares blankly, still trying to comprehend the reason for her boyfriend looking like Pinkalicious.

"I thought you were going to match with me and be a warlock," Jasmine says, more confused than anything else.

With a flip of a pink wig, Logan says, "Sorry, honey, bros before—"

Jasmine raises an eyebrow.

"—incredibly hot girlfriends," he finishes, saving himself. "But that rule only applies for costumes, of course."

Jasmine grunts while James sighs, coming to terms with his error. Logan wraps an arm around James, laughing. "C'mon, bro, just admit that I can pull off anything. We're going to win the couples costume contest for sure."

James groans but begrudgingly says, "I swear to God, we better."

James inches closer to me and wraps an arm around my waist. Logan watches with furrowed brows, before looking at his girlfriend as if to say, *What just happened?* Jasmine shrugs, still trying to process the resolution between James and me.

Daniel is still in the beginning stages of confusion. "I missed something," he states.

Carol nods in agreement. "All I understand is that I don't need to carry around that body bag anymore."

James takes a step away from me. "Body bag?!"

"It's nothing," I say, awkwardly waving a hand.

"Are you guys dating or what?" Kiera blurts out. Everyone stares at us, faces obviously still wondering the same thing.

My cheeks burn under their stares and, mostly, *his* stare. Yes, I was pretty forward when I implied the whole maybe we should try to date while he's still here thing, but *holy fishballs*, this is real life now.

I shake my head no. For the past sixteen years of my life, I have not been on a date, nor have I been asked out on one. "We're not dating. I've never even been on a date."

"Let's change that," James says. "You free on Saturday?"

When am I ever not free is the question. "Yes?"

He grabs my hand and looks me straight in the eye. "Lara Emelina Dela Cruz, will you go on a date with me?" *God, he's the only person who'd make this into a mock proposal.*

Our friends squeal, with Logan leading the corny cheer. "Say yes! Say yes!" he shouts, drawing more attention to our group than necessary.

So. Painfully. Cringe.

Instead of a yes, what comes out of my mouth is, "Eh . . . I guess so."

"She said yes!" James exclaims, lifting me off the ground and leaving me hanging over his shoulder.

"James, put me down!"

Our friends clap happily, as if we just got engaged, while Logan raises an arm, twirling his wig as a celebratory gesture. The chaos is contagious and random students start to clap, too, even though they have no clue what's happening.

Despite the mayhem, I find myself laughing so hard that my face hurts. Over the past weeks, I've noticed that many things in life don't work in our favor. Fog hits when we ask the universe for a guiding light, silence swallows us when we beg for noise, and we're met with solitude even during our most desperate searches for companionship. Still, the least favorable of all would be giving up completely because sometimes, just sometimes, things work out and it's absolutely perfect.

TIP TWENTY-TWO:
DON'T TAG ALONG ON DATES, ACTUALLY GO ON ONE!

✸

It's Saturday afternoon and my furry purple blanket wraps around the entire length of my body in an effort to combat the frigid November temperature nibbling at my bare feet. I lie down on the sofa like a giant sushi roll, eyes closed and listening to an audiobook through earbuds and imagining a realm of magic and kingdoms—

Lola Nora pulls out an earbud, which causes my eyelids to fly open. "Lola." I groan. Her upside-down face hovers over mine and she proceeds to pull out the other one. I'm forced to retire from my relaxed position and sit up.

I hold a hand out for the return of my earbuds. She gives them back but not before she says, "*May date ka ngayon,' di ba?*" (You have a date today, right?)

To avoid an eternal discussion about my recently activated love life, I shake my head from side to side rapidly. Her life's goal is for me to not be single forever and achieving it would fuel her craziness. It's like giving gasoline to an arsonist and staying to see the light show.

"*Sinungaling*," (Liar,) she says, smirking. With two loud claps, Illa rushes down the stairs with six different dresses, three hangers in each hand. Her thin arms look like they're about to snap.

"*Bakit po ako lang ang nagbubuhat nito?*" (Why am I the only one carrying these?) Illa whines before dropping the clothes on the couch.

Lola Nora raises her hand dramatically. "*Apo, alam mo naman na bawal sa 'kin ang mapagod. Wala akong magagawa d'yan. Sabi ng doctor, e,*" (Granddaughter, you know that I can't tire myself out. I can't do anything about that. It's the doctor's orders) she says as if she wasn't dancing at the community center this morning.

Lola Nora raises each option in front of me, and I conclude that my family wants me to freeze to death. "First of all, it's *November*! And second of all, why are these all party dresses? I don't even know where we're going for our date!"

Illa sighs. "The rest of your closet was atrocious. At least if you freeze, you'll die cute. You'll thank us later when your ghost looks pretty."

"Excuse me?"

The bicker fest is on the verge of commencement when my cell phone rings. Everyone makes a dash for it but Illa's the first one to grab it. Her eyes light up in amusement. "Most amazingly handsome and superhot model—"

Before she can finish reading the cringy caller ID that I never changed, I swipe the phone away from her and hold it against my chest. Unfortunately, Lola Nora claws it right out of my grasp and answers it. "Hello?"

Illa scrunches her nose. "What was the deal with all those emojis? Y'all are freaky."

Lola Nora puts the call on speaker. "Hello, *hijo*!" (Hello, dear!)

"Hey, Kuya James!" Illa greets him.

James isn't weirded out at all. If anything, he sounds excited to speak to them. "Hi, Lola Nora! Hi, Illa! Is Lara there?"

"Hi—" I start but Lola Nora interrupts me.

"Yes, *pero* what should she wear?" she asks in a thick Filipino accent before she and Illa hold their breaths, awaiting a response.

James says, "Umm . . ." before saying, "something warm, definitely."

That answer immediately crushes their dreams and they let out exaggerated sighs, along with Lola Nora muttering something in Tagalog that we don't understand. Illa hauls the clothes away, heaving up the stairs, while Lola Nora shoves the cell phone back at me. I smile victoriously.

"What just happened?" he asks.

I laugh. "Don't worry about it."

I'm nervous.

Like, actually nervous.

I don't know why. There's no logic behind it. James and I see each other almost every single day. We talk, we eat, and aren't those the two main components of dates? We'll be doing the exact same thing tonight so why are my hands suddenly so clammy? Ugh.

The doorbell rings and I grab my coat. *Let's do this.* Complete with a maroon hoodie and gray sweatpants, my look screams broke chic, but at least I'll be warm. I open the door, expecting James (and perhaps a giant bouquet) but instead, my dad rushes in with grocery bags lined up on each arm, which he transfers to me without notice. My body slouches under the weight of the bags, but I trudge to the kitchen, nonetheless.

I go back to the door and sit on the ottoman close by. Dad returns with fewer grocery bags and raises an eyebrow at me. "*Ano'ng ginagawa mo?*" (What are you doing?)

My eyes shift from left to right. "Uh . . . sitting?"

"*Dito*?" (Here?)

"I'm waiting to go out. Remember? I told you guys I have a . . . *date* . . . with James."

His face falls. "Right." Dropping the groceries, he takes a seat beside me, silent for a moment. My dad doesn't get emotional, not really, and I admit that it still feels bizarre when his care becomes more apparent. He once said that he thought James was a nice kid, and now I'm waiting for him to pull up in a metaphorical white horse. But Dad looks less than happy; he looks almost sad. I guess it's different when you see your daughter dressed up (or down, in this case) for an actual date.

Still, he gives me a soft smile, gently placing a hand on my shoulder. "*Sigurado ka na ba sa date na 'to? Ready ka na ba?*" (Are you sure about this date? Are you ready?)

As I press my lips together and nod, he squeezes my shoulder reassuringly. My dad likes to hide behind his goofiness and jokes. I guess that's where I get it from. Even so, he's transparent today. I give him a big hug to remind him that his little girl is still here and that a part of me will never grow up. As he hugs me back tightly, I know that the message has been received.

The doorbell rings again and I let my dad open the door. James stands at the front, dressed in gray sweatpants, a black hoodie, and a puffy jacket layered on top. Even in casual clothes he still looks good.

James is beaming, despite my dad's serious face. His eyes scream confusion though. "Good evening, Tito." He greets my dad, extending his hand—a gesture that he never does.

Dad shakes his hand firmly, brows furrowed, something that catches James off guard because Dad's the opposite of serious. "I've seen you grow up to be a good guy but I'm still her dad and I won't think twice about revealing my bad side. You take care of my daughter, okay? You respect her, eh?"

James nods quickly. "Of course, Tito."

With a curt nod, Dad lets go of James's hand and gestures for me to go. "You told me that you'd be late but try not to stay out past midnight." *Midnight*? I was not expecting that late of a curfew, and I pray for Dad's soul once Mom realizes he gave us that amount of freedom. At least she and Tita Gia are out together; Tita can help keep her calm.

"Noted," James says.

Dad waves good-bye before closing the door. Outside, there's an unusual pickup truck. James opens the door to the passenger's seat and bows his head like a prince asking for a dance, while I roll my eyes at the exaggerated courtesy.

"What am I, the royal princess of Genovia?" I say, stepping in.

He chuckles at the *Princess Diaries* reference as he closes the door. He walks around the vehicle and hops into the driver's seat.

"You couldn't pass for a princess even if you tried," he starts right when he enters the driver's side. "You have unbelievably uncoordinated feet, a passion for hugging the floor, and you sort of eat like an animal."

I look at him with my mouth hanging wide open, trying to keep my face looking as shocked/angry as possible, but my lips end up curving into a smile since all of that is true. "I think you're doing this romance thing wrong. I'm almost a hundred percent sure that you're supposed to compliment a girl on the first date."

He leans in, close enough that I can feel his breath on my skin and smell his orange scent. "So how would you advise me to do this romance thing right?"

Leaning closer, I place my hand lightly on his cheek, "I think you should start driving or else we're going to have our first date in the comfort of my house," I finish, pulling away from him and reaching for my seat belt.

"Even if we got stuck in the middle of nowhere, it would still be the perfect date because I'd be with you and being with you puts the brightness of the sun to shame." He gives me another crooked smile, reminding me of the ones he used to give me when we were growing up.

The corniness causes my nose to scrunch up before I erupt in a peal of laughter. "Hallmark wants their card back." I snort without second thought.

He sighs. "Of course."

The drive is relaxing and quiet; not because it's awkward but because we let ourselves appreciate the beauty of silence. The sun disappears in a blur of reds and oranges although it's only half past five. As winter approaches quickly, there's less and less daylight with every passing day. Usually it's depressing, but I couldn't imagine having this drive at any other time.

James is focused on the road, and I get lost in observation, noticing the difference in his hair today, styled so that none of it covers his forehead. His eyes seem brighter even though the sky gets duller with the sunset fading and finally, his jaw is relaxed; for now his worries are released with each frosty breath out.

He grins, not bothering to look at me. "I know I'm pretty, but if you stare any longer, I'm going to have to stop in the middle of the road just to beat you in a staring contest."

I roll my eyes before asking, "Where'd you get the pickup truck?"

"It's my cousin's."

"Why did you have to borrow it? You have your own car."

"Ah, so I do. The answer is that my car will not work for this occasion."

Why wouldn't his car work for our date? The curiosity is killing me. "Can you just tell me where we're going? For all I know, you could be taking revenge on me for all of my threats!"

"Not at all," he assures me. "Actually, I'm taking you to the Taylor Swift concert at the Scotiabank Arena."

I scream. My smile reaches from ear to ear as I turn in my seat and lunge toward him, wrapping both arms around him and hugging him tightly. Have you ever just wanted to ki—

"Just kidding," he says.

—kill someone in the harshest way possible, letting every inch of their body suffer before taking their life? There is silence as a scowl replaces my smile.

"Lara? Ha-ha . . . was that not a good joke?" He chuckles nervously, probably regretting not having written a will. Meanwhile, I'm regretting not having taken advantage of Kiera's Netflix account, because I'm not getting that luxury in jail.

"James. Why don't you pull over for a moment?" I still have some sanity left in me and safety is always a priority.

Without uttering a single word, we pull over and he stops the car. "So, sweetheart—" he starts, but I respond with a slap on his arm. Afterward, I permit him to continue the safe drive.

Two and a half hours of bickering in the car ends in blushes and hand holding. It's so dark out that you can only read the sign if you walk right up to it, which is what I do once he parks the truck. TORRANCE BARRENS DARK SKY PRESERVE, the sign reads, and I grin like an idiot. James is crouched at the back of the truck, laying a dozen pillows and blankets over the whole platform. He holds up a little picnic basket, and I can't believe this is real.

"You always said you wanted to see the stars, didn't you?" he calls, sticking out a hand to help me get onto the back platform.

"I did. You remembered because you always remember everything, don't you?"

He wears a proud grin. "In seventh grade, we were learning about the planets and the stars, and you said that you never saw a sky full of stars in your life. People asked you if you've ever been camping and you said no. I called you out and said that you would never camp because your face would scare the animals out of the forest."

I laugh. "Do you remember what happened next?"

He sighs. "Yup. Your fist kissed my face ever so romantically."

We sit down on the layers of blankets, which provide a soft cushion against the hard metal. He pulls some food from inside the picnic basket and arranges the containers before us. "For the main course I made some lasagna, some garlic bread, and wait for it . . . fried chicken."

"You didn't."

"I did." He holds the container of fried chicken and I grab it from his hands, opening it and admiring the pieces, fried to golden perfection. "It's Lola's Edna's recipe."

I start eating right away because spending almost three hours in a vehicle can work up quite the appetite. Everything tastes so good that I forget any nervousness I felt about our date.

"If you cooked for me every day, I would be the happiest girl in the entire universe," I say with my mouth full because I forgot my table manners in my other jacket at home.

"I could do that." He nods. "There's a catch, though."

"What is it?"

"You'll have to wake up beside me every morning without trying to injure me."

"If I wake up to your face every morning, that might be a hard task to fulfill," I joke. The nervousness returns and I try my best to keep it at bay by stuffing my mouth with as much food as possible. I know we're not being completely serious about anything, but even these small phrases remind me that *this is real.* I'm on a date with James, and we might just find ourselves in a relationship soon.

Even if we do start dating, I don't think we could change our dynamic fully.

He narrows his eyes at the half-eaten drumstick in my hand. "How does one eat fried chicken so aggressively?"

"It's called talent."

He's still him and I'm still me.

Soon enough, the sky clears up, revealing the universe. It takes me a moment to register a sky full of thousands of stars. When you live in one of the brightest cities, gazing at the night sky becomes something miraculous.

Holding a blanket closer to myself, I try to keep warm since it's gotten a bit colder. When it doesn't work, I subtly inch closer to James and he not-so-subtly wraps both his arms around me, pressing my head on his chest. I continue to nervously chew on a piece of mint gum, and he's so close that I can smell the mint from his mouth too. So there we lie, in the back of a pickup truck, snuggled up in blankets and a dozen pillows and looking in awe at the stars, each handcrafted by God Himself.

"Lara?" James whispers in a low voice, sending a shiver down my spine.

I gulp nervously, accidentally swallowing the gum in the process. "Hm?"

"I don't want to rush or force you into anything. So if you're not ready to be my girlfriend, it's okay. I respect that and I respect you."

Smiling against his chest, I say, "Thank you. I appreciate that."

"But," he continues hesitantly, "if *perhaps*, a guy were to ask you out, could you, maybe, tell a little lie and say that you have a boyfriend?"

I push away from his chest, only to go even closer, our faces separated by a mere few inches. I don't know where my confidence is coming from, but it's there. My chest against his, I wonder if he feels my heart racing. "I'm not a liar. If I'm going to say I have a boyfriend, it better be true."

He exhales. "Will you be my girlfriend?"

"Why not? You made me fried chicken after all." I shrug. My answer makes him laugh.

Trying to hide my uncontrollable blushing, I roll over quickly. It doesn't last long before he grabs my arm and shifts my body so that I'm facing him again. We're so close, just like how we were when he almost kissed me. My heart starts to beat quickly again, but this time I'm not scared or confused or second guessing if he likes me. I know how he feels about me now, and I think I'm ready.

He takes both hands, lifting them to my face, cupping my cheeks lightly. "Can I kiss you?" he asks, and I laugh, nodding. "Please don't flip me over," he whispers.

I place my hands on the base of his neck as he leans forward. His lips brush against mine, not aggressively or possessively, but soft and slow. It's the kind of kiss that doesn't come with exploding fireworks or a big spark. Instead, it's the kind of kiss that could linger on your lips forever, that makes you a bit dizzy, and a bit crazy, but you still end up loving every second of it.

I kiss him back with the same intensity. It's a kiss that seems to stop time; it's so magical that you could forget how to breathe and not even care. It's a kiss that makes you believe that fairy tales come true sometimes. It's a kiss that could never grow old. We part, and I take a deep breath.

He smiles that dorky smile of his. "Lara, what's one plus one?" he whispers against my lips, his forehead pressed against mine.

"James," I say softly, as I exhale, not remembering any words except that one name. I plant my lips on his again and his hands find their way to my waist as he pulls me in closer, kissing me back.

Our kiss is the kind of kiss that makes you forget what numbers are and what adding is and even what your own name is. And frankly, I don't need to remember my name anyway.

TIP TWENTY-THREE:
ACT NORMAL

✱

November passes like a swift breeze and December finds itself nipping at our fingertips. Snow falls lightly outside, piling up on the window ledge of the study. James's house is empty, and we sit in the window nook; he has one hand on my knee and the other beneath my jaw. He leans in for another kiss, which I block with the palm of my hand.

"We need to study," I say with a smile, but he ignores the reminder, gently kissing my hand before setting it down and attacking my lips.

The past month has been almost perfect. Nobody (not even the boy-fries) ever mentions James leaving, and I'm grateful for it. It's almost like if nobody says anything, we can avoid the problem altogether. My friends and I have adjusted to our new normal, consisting of numerous girls' nights and the occasional quadruple date. We're on the same page again. James is busier with additional hockey practices on some evenings, but it isn't too bad. Sometimes I stop by the rink to say hi and it's amusing to see the flurry of boys shove my boyfriend against the glass when they see me. And of course, we can't forget that Ms. K was overjoyed with our newfound relationship. Sure, the joy was from not having our arguments destroy her eardrums, but it's joy, nonetheless.

Our lips part for a second so that James can claim it's illegal to study today because it's my birthday, then he continues to trail kisses from my cheek down to the side of my neck.

Ah yes, the big seventeen. Having a birthday so late in the year is both good and bad. Good because you're younger than everyone and bad because you're younger than everyone.

I laugh so hard when his lips get to the middle of my neck. As a ticklish person, this never goes to plan, and I end up squirming like a fish out of water before ultimately falling off of the seat. "It's not illegal when you have a biology test tomorrow," I groan, rubbing my sore tailbone.

James helps me up from the floor, not letting go this time. "You know you'll ace it," he says, pulling me close into a hug before placing a gentle kiss on my forehead. "Happy birthday, sweetheart."

My own family sucks at remembering birthdays, so I don't expect much when December third hits. They'll probably remember sometime before tonight and run to Walmart for one of those five-dollar chocolate cakes. I won't complain; those taste good.

Fortunately, my friends are human calendars. Jasmine has a birthday planner for each of us, noting everything and anything we've done on our birthdays since we started celebrating them together. This year's birthday celebration was brunch at a Japanese pancake shop, where we stuffed ourselves with the fluffiest pancakes on earth before heading off to freeze in the snow for Kiera's annual *Happy Birthday, Lara* Instagram photos. They handed me a small envelope with their joint birthday gift of a Kindle gift card. It was awkward for me to bring up that I didn't own a Kindle, but they shrugged and told me to keep it for the future.

And now I'm here, in James's study, wondering how it's humanly possible to feel so happy. James pulls away and a twinkle in his eye reveals yet another surprise. "Do you want your gift now?"

I raise an eyebrow, while taking a seat. "Another one? You already gave me flowers," I say, gesturing to the potted orchid sitting in the corner of the room.

"That's my pre-gift, but I still haven't given you your *gift*."

"A *gift* . . ."

James rushes out of the room, leaving me alone and confused. A part of me is still afraid of his presents, because the past years have revolved around us giving each other things that would induce slight trauma to the other. He returns with a pink paper bag, colorful tissue paper emerging from the top. Setting it on my lap, he goes, "Hope you like it."

Hesitantly, I pull out the pieces of tissue paper. "I swear to God, James, if this is another insect terrarium, I am going to—"

He laughs. "I promise it's not. I must say, I was very creative that year."

"Very," I grumble.

I finally get past the paper and take out the white box at the bottom. A Kindle e-reader. The last piece of their elaborate plan. I stand up and kiss him on the cheek, right where his dimple caves. "Thank you, James." I want to say something else, but I don't know what. It's so thoughtful and sweet, and I'd never imagine getting an e-reader from someone who loved to make fun of me for reading.

"Better than the terrarium?"

"Way better."

Suddenly, his cell phone chimes, and he pulls away to answer the call. The only thing he says is, "Okay . . . we'll leave now . . . bye," before grabbing my gifted plant and rushing out of the room. "Let's go back to your house!"

"What?" He doesn't give me enough time to grab my stuff, let alone ask questions. By the time I step foot on the first floor, he's already out the door and starting the car. "Hey!" I call out. "Are you gonna lock your front door?"

I walk over to his car and he steps out, throwing the keys up in the air and catching them in the same hand. "Right."

The drive to my house is quick but the piling snow makes it more difficult than usual. Familiar cars are crammed in the driveway and on the side of the small road—even Tita Gia's car sits close to the curb. Maybe my family did remember my birthday.

"What a perfect night to have a *casual family dinner*," James says unnaturally and I roll my eyes. On the other side of the door are loud whispers and people shushing even louder than the talking. I almost laugh.

Grabbing my keys from my jacket pocket, I open the front door to reveal a large crowd of people jumping out of horrible hiding spots and screaming "HAPPY BIRTHDAY, LARA!" followed by a huge round of applause.

I place my stuff on the table, along with the other gifts, before making rounds to thank everyone. I hug numerous relatives before they all return to the chaotic scene composed of tubs of food, half-drunk uncles, gossiping aunts, and blaring karaoke—the best of parties.

Illa emerges from the crowd with crossed arms, wearing a long teal dress over a white blouse. "How was your study session?" she asks, then gives James the side-eye, which looks more threatening because of her winged eyeliner. "I thought you'd be done by four *not* four thirty."

James scratches the back of his head and glances at me then Illa. "Well, we had a really productive study session with math."

"Biology," I correct.

"Yeah, *that*. Um . . . it was so good that we got a little sidetracked."

I remove my winter jacket and begin to unwrap the scarf sitting around my neck when Illa starts to giggle. I frown. "What?"

She points to the side of my neck and my eyes widen, cheeks burning up. I throw the scarf back over my shoulder, covering the apparent mark. "The only thing you need to learn is to invest in a trusty concealer," she comments, walking away. Someone really needs to put back the parental controls on our Netflix account—she's learning a lot from those reality TV shows.

James wears an amused smile as he pulls up my scarf and reveals what I assume is a purple bruise-looking thing. "Hey, I think it's cute."

I glare at him. "I don't think you'll be saying that when my dad sees it."

His Adam's apple bobs with a nervous gulp and he drops the scarf back on my neck. "Actually, I think *that scarf* is really cute." He steps a few feet away and hangs his jacket in the closet.

I am about to launch another remark when a bubbly, high-pitched voice greets me. "Happy birthday, 'cuz!"

A tall, slim figure walks toward us wearing tight-fitted yoga pants showing off her perfect curves. As if it couldn't get worse, she smiles, revealing an array of white teeth in perfect alignment.

Eliza.

She's back.

My House, Toronto
August (Three Years Ago)

"So, you and Eliza now, huh?" I ask awkwardly, while hanging upside down on my living room couch.

James lies on the couch adjacent to the one that I hang on, looking like he won the lottery. He stares up at the ceiling with a carefree smile and a twinkle in his eye. After what seems to be an endless daydream, he finally comes to terms with reality as I snap my fingers.

"Hello?" I say to a distracted James.

"What were you saying?" he asks, turning his head to look at me.

"You and Eliza are a thing now, right?"

His smile doesn't falter for a second. "Are we that obvious?"

"Well, you guys have been more . . . friendly lately." I hesitate. "But you do make quite the cute couple."

He doesn't see through my fib and laughs instead. "I can't believe she's finally my girlfriend. I've had a crush on her since last year. Insane, huh?"

"Insane," I repeat, trying to mask the immature jealousy in my tone with that of an uninterested one.

"She's amazing. For real. It's just—"

"Something about her?"

"Yeah. She's got it all. She's kind, athletic, smart, beautiful, not to mention she can play hockey."

There it is. Hockey. Eliza loved hockey and he loved hockey and I simply can't stand hockey, so I'm going to die alone.

"She's quite the package," I whisper softly.

"Have you ever heard of those stories where people who were friends as kids grow up and end up together?" he asks seriously.

That was supposed to be us.

"Yeah, I have."

He pauses for a second.

"I think that's what me and Eliza might have."

She pulls me into an embrace, and it's suffocating; her arms wrap loosely around me but I still have trouble breathing. My mind races with images of James and her, and my heart sinks again. But that's not even the worst part. The memories of our once unbreakable friendship come flooding back, breaking the dam holding them back, the dam that I thought was concrete. And it hurts because I miss her so much. I hate myself for missing her so much.

I pull away first, holding her an arm's distance away. "Thanks, Eliza."

She hands me a box wrapped in white wrapping paper, tied with a gold ribbon. "Here's your gift but this isn't the only gift," she says, and my lungs have a harder time holding air. I hold the box with one hand and the other stays in the pocket of my jacket, nails pressing against my palm. "We're moving back!"

The noise of the party suddenly disappears, and I feel like I'm the only one in the room. I beg my mind not to go back to the past, but it does, memories running through my mind at 2X speed. The only words I can remember right now are the six that clogged my mind back then.

That was supposed to be us.

And now that it *is* us, a whisper in Eliza's voice seeps into the back of my head, saying, *But what if it isn't.*

"Isn't that exciting?" Eliza exclaims, snapping me back to reality.

"Like, moving into a house? Here?" I try to smile but I think I look as if someone hit me with a bus.

"Yeah! Our neighborhood is a five-minute drive from here! *But* there were some minor problems with the house once we got here. The renos got delayed for a few weeks. So guess who your temporary roommate is," she says excitedly. Am I supposed to be as enthusiastic about this?

My breath hitches. "Cool."

"So what's up with—" she starts but stops immediately when her eyes draw upon the person returning to my side. I turn around to see James standing there, semiconfused like me.

"*No*. You've got to be kidding me." Her jaw is wide open. I expect her to ask him how he's doing or something of that sort, but instead she freaking attacks him! Like, girl, he ain't Harry Styles.

She jumps into his arms for an overexaggerated hug. *No one told me we were re-creating the pivotal K-drama scene*. They hug for a few seconds before she finally stops hanging from his shoulders like an orangutan and releases. I contemplate running upstairs and grabbing the bear repellant.

"Hey, Eliza." He greets her, awkwardly prying her fingers off of his shoulder.

"You got so . . . so . . ." She turns back, looking at me like I'm some sort of dictionary.

She rolls her eyes when she doesn't remember what she's going to say. "I'm just gonna say it. You got really hot."

He opens his mouth, then closes it again, not knowing what an appropriate response would be. Instead of saying anything, he gives a little smile and nods.

"This is so great! It's so awesome to see that you guys are still *best friends* after all these years." She sighs, happily clapping her hands together.

Instantly, he wraps an arm around my waist. We exchange glances before he states, "*Girlfriend*. Actually, Eliza, Lara's my girlfriend."

"Oh." Her smile falters for a second as she tries to process the new information. "Wow. I mean, I never expected that but that's amazing." She then turns to James, still beaming. "You *have* to spill the details of how this relationship was founded."

We trail behind her as she makes her way to the living room. She props herself on the couch and I position myself between her and James, thinking of how to explain our partnership. The explanation of our relationship dynamic is quite complicated. The events leading to our union each have a complex—

"I like her, she doesn't hate me, I think that's how marriage works," James blurts out. Or that. He could just say that.

"I see you're still quite the joker," she says.

"Some things stay the same."

Turning to Eliza, I ask, "Anyway, what's up with you? How were things in Manitoba?"

She shrugs. "To be honest, coming back here was the best thing that happened to me in a long time." Her confident expression is replaced with a sad smile—I wonder what happened. "It'll be fun going to a school where I can hang out with you guys."

"I know you love it here, but wasn't it hard for you to leave your whole other life back there?" I mean, she's Eliza. She's the popular and gorgeous Eliza. She must've had a bunch of friends in her old town.

Her gaze shifts to the floor and she shakes her head slowly. "There wasn't much keeping me there. I was always planning on moving back here for uni. Plus . . . my boyfriend and I just broke up."

Honestly, I am so threatened by Eliza. I always have been. I won't lie and say I'm ecstatic about her presence and having her as a roommate, but I will say that I feel sad on her behalf. She looked like she really liked him, at least that's what it seemed like on her Instagram.

"Guys are . . . ugh." She sighs.

"Tell me about it. On the first day of school, I got tripped by this guy and he held out his hand to help me up and then purposely let me go and humiliated me in the middle of the hallway." I shake my head, then raise my eyebrows at James.

"What a jerk!" she exclaims.

She looks over at James, who is subtly trying to avoid any type of eye contact and hiding his flushed cheeks. “Did you make that guy pay for what he did to her?” she asks.

“Yeah, James, did you?” I repeat, smiling innocently and enjoying the way he shifts uncomfortably in his seat. It’s the least I can do when I feel myself overheating in this scarf.

He scratches the back of his neck. “Lara did a good enough job defending herself. But I do recall this other time when I was walking on the sidewalk, trying to greet this girl, but then she almost beat me up instead,” he says dramatically, making it seem like I almost killed him.

“Okay, now that chick sounds awful. I bet that’s Lara’s worst enemy, huh?” She laughs, nudging my arm.

I shrug. “I didn’t care too much. He didn’t get hurt so no harm, no foul, right?”

Eliza gets up from her spot and stretches her arms. “You guys are too cute. I guess I shouldn’t keep you from enjoying your birthday party, so I’ll be in the kitchen if you need me.”

Eliza leaves the room and James leans over so that I can hear him over the noise. “I can tell that you’re mostly unhappy about sharing your bed.”

“Don’t remind me about that.”

He nudges my side. “You and I both know that you’d much rather share a bed with me so why don’t I sneak you into my room for a while to fix your problem?”

My eyes narrow at him. “I’d rather share my bed with *no one*.”

“You *say* that”—he nods, placing a hand on my shoulder, acting like some sort of therapist—“but you love cuddling with me.”

I leave with a grunt, heading to where the food is. James follows, and because most of the relatives are unaware that we’re dating, he has to explain that *I’m* his girlfriend whenever people ask if he has one. They ask the same question of Eliza, jaws dropping when she says she's single because apparently there's no way someone as beautiful as her can *possibly* be single. Nobody asks me if I'm dating anyone, but that question gets answered when they ask James.

The party continues and the atmosphere is saturated with background noise; the same three Tagalog songs are sung on the Magic Sing karaoke machine, and conversations buzz in every corner. No matter how hard I try to submerge myself in the chaos, it seems like an impossible feat. The same sentence repeats over and over in my mind.

I think that's what me and Eliza might have.

TIP TWENTY-FOUR:
SIT IN THE BACKSEAT

✱

The morning after the party, I wake up to loud chatter coming from the kitchen as the direct sunlight from the window burns my corneas. My head throbs like a drum because apparently that's what happens when you go to sleep at two in the morning after having to relocate to the living room couch. Let's just say if you recorded Eliza sleeping, you could mistake her for a boar. I grab my glasses from the coffee table and as my bare feet meet the chilly hardwood floor, I have the urge to crawl back onto the couch with my blanket.

When I step into the kitchen, the family, erm, *families*, are scrambling. Illa's dressed in a thick knit sweater and mom jeans, waiting impatiently for her toast to pop out of the toaster. It's weird because she never eats before me. Confused, I turn to my mom, who sits at the round table, sipping her morning cup of coffee and looking relaxed as ever since it's her day off.

When she sees me, all that relaxation disappears. "*Ara! Bakit hindi ka pa bihis? Nakalimutan mo ba na may pasok? Mag 7:50 na*!" (Ara! Why aren't you dressed yet? Have you forgotten that you have school today? It's almost 7:50!)

What? I squint at the microwave clock. It says *7:48 a.m.* "I slept on the couch last night! I had no alarm! Didn't you guys notice me sleeping? I have an in-class essay in first period!"

"*Hay, Maria,*" my mother sighs. "*Sabi ni Eliza, nakatulog ka sa sofa, pero ginising ka raw niya*!" (Eliza said that you fell asleep on the couch, but she also said she woke you up!)

"That's so not true! She did not *gising* me!"

Instead of arguing further, I run upstairs, only to find Eliza in my room, long nails tapping away at her cell phone. She looks up at me, glossed lips forming a smile. Her back is perfectly straight, shoulders perfectly squared, probably priding herself for looking like she's got it all together. She wears her normal wardrobe of athleisure—black leggings and a black quarter zip—looking like Kendall Jenner for an ad campaign.

"Apparently you woke me up this morning?" I mention, while hurriedly rummaging through drawers.

She nods slowly, eyebrows furrowing. "Yeah I did, at seven. You told me to leave you alone and that you'd get up in five minutes."

Though that does sound like something I'd do, I feel like I'd remember if that happened. Still, I lack the time to delve deeper into the situation. With a huff, I say, "All right."

Eliza makes her way for the door but pauses. "I never got to mention this yesterday, but I wanted to say that I'm happy for you."

I stop rummaging for a moment. "What? I don't—"

"You're lucky," she says with a small smile. "James looks at you like you're his world."

My brows furrow. I'm lost. *Where is this coming from?* We're going to be late for school! I don't have time to think about how James looks at me!

"You're lucky to have him," she repeats, before walking away completely.

When she leaves, I wonder if I was wrong to feel threatened by her. Maybe she *is* happy for me. Maybe we could be different this time, friends again. Yet, no matter what angle I look at us from, all I can think about is their history.

I quickly change into a regular pair of baggy light-wash jeans and an undershirt, ready to slip my shirt on, when . . .

"It's eight o'clock!" Eliza calls from downstairs. "James is here with his car!"

"Coming!" I yell back, loud and panicked and on the edge of insanity. *Since when does James pick me up in the morning?* It really doesn't matter because it's saving my butt at the moment. I hastily shove my books, cell phone, and the remainder of my clothing into my backpack and run down the stairs. The heavy winter jacket is loose around my body since I'm used to having more layers underneath, but I'm warm enough.

Running to the parked car in the driveway, I realize that Eliza's sitting up front, already deep in a conversation with James. Instead of analyzing the situation, I throw my stuff into the backseat.

"Good morning—" James starts, as he backs out of the driveway.

"Don't."

Dismissing my simple request, he teases, "I love your hair today. Trying a new look?"

Ignoring his comment on my unbrushed hair, I say, "I'm going to be changing back here so don't mind me." I take off my jacket to slip on a T-shirt, then the sweater. "Why'd you come pick us up?"

Eliza smiles at him. "Actually, I called him. Thought it would be easier since I didn't know the way to school."

"I could've shown you." I sigh. *If you'd actually woken me up*, I want to add.

She shrugs in reply, not bothering to look back at me. "But now that we're here, don't you think that carpooling is a great idea?"

There it is again—Eliza calling the shots. When we were younger, Eliza was a "natural leader" as the adults called it. I don't think that's what it was. She made decisions the fastest, so naturally, people followed. And when she joined James and me for the summers, we always did *everything* on her command. She's like that, coming around like a storm, and everyone pauses for her. I don't know how she does it.

James laughs, going along with it. "Sure, I can pick you guys up if you want. I was actually going to re-suggest for Lara to ride with me in the mornings," he says as he pulls into the school parking lot.

"*Re*-suggest?" I inquire.

James turns off the ignition. "Weeks ago you were walking to school with that huge cell model for bio and I thought you were going to topple over."

"Why didn't you offer to help me then?" I ask.

"I did, and you flipped me off."

Eliza outright laughs and says, "That *does* sound like her."

We all step out of the car and walk through the parking lot, making our way to the door. At first, Eliza walks between James and me, but he manages to switch spots and puts his arm around my shoulder.

James pokes my side. "You've gotta smile now. I got you here on time." He does that funny thing with his eyebrows, wiggling them quickly, which always makes me laugh. As we enter the school, he whispers, "So, care to explain why you look like you got run over by a truck and why you look like you absolutely want to murder Eliza?"

Once past the side entrance, the warm air from the heater blows in our faces and I can physically feel my skin drying out. "Did you just say I look like I got run over by a truck?"

"I didn't mean that you look necessarily *super*–run over, but you look . . . I was just using a hyperbole? I mean, have I told you how *radiant* you look lately? Sweetheart?"

"*Sure*. Anyway, today is *not* the best day for anyone to get on my bad side," I say, increasing my pace. Eliza shrugs and says that I'll be fine. It's supposed to be reassuring but from her, it sounds like a dismissal. "There's way too much I have to do."

I run up the yellow staircase, maneuvering through kids trying to get to their first period. Though the warning bell still hasn't rung, I feel like I'm late because I'm not early. In reality, we probably have a good fifteen minutes before class.

James follows, grabbing my hand and pulling me to a halt. "You are seriously going to face-plant if you keep sprinting up the stairs."

I hate that he's probably right.

We walk the rest of the way with Eliza behind us. When we get to the third-floor hallway, I catch some students staring at her, gawking like she's a celebrity. Perhaps they recognize her from her fitness blog. She doesn't notice, instead squinting at her schedule, printed on a piece of blue paper. "Do you know where room 208B is? Why does your school have letters along with classroom numbers? That's weird."

"I don't know, that's just how it is around here." I shrug. "But it's downstairs in the math hallway."

"Math hallway?"

"It's the hallway that smells like despair. You can't miss it."

Suddenly, Ms. K walks by with her high heels, flipping her blond hair. "Thank you, darling! I try my best," she jokes, making her way to the staircase.

"Who do you have for math?" James asks, looking over Eliza's shoulder to catch a peek of her schedule.

"Roberts." She looks at both of us to get a reassuring review that neither of us can provide.

"Mr. Roberts . . ." James starts.

". . . is something," I finish.

She stares at us in horror. I pity anyone who has to spend a morning with Mr. Roberts, including Eliza.

Before she can ask us any follow-up questions, Xander appears, wearing a brown button-up, half-tucked into baggy jeans. "Morning, Lara!" he calls. He greets us with his usual bright smile, holding about a dozen pamphlets in his arms.

Eliza leans closer to me, whispering, "Who's that?", eyes not leaving his face.

"Xander. He has a wonderful *girlfriend*."

"Here," Xander continues, dumping the pamphlets in my arms. "I thought these might help you out since you haven't figured out which programs you're applying for."

"Thanks." Truthfully, the problem isn't that I don't have enough information about the programs; all of the programs I'm considering are more or less similar to each other. But I think I'm afraid of the application site itself, about life after high school. That's why I've been procrastinating.

James fishes one of the pamphlets from my arms and skims it before raising an eyebrow. "You still haven't decided?"

I shake my head slowly. "I've been a little preoccupied. Especially with that lab application. There's so much to think about—maybe I shouldn't do the summer lab thing." Even talking about it makes my heartbeat quicken in a way that it shouldn't.

Xander frowns. "Lara, you're one of the smartest people I know. This is a big decision, but I know you can do this. It's important for your future, y'know?"

I feel my chest tighten. Maybe Xander is right, maybe I just need to get myself together and dive right in like everyone else. I love science,

I know I love science, but I'm so tired. I'm tired of people expecting me to be passionate and hardworking and motivated *all the time.* Is it so bad that I want to rest and not question if a decision I make when I'm seventeen will lead to the rest of my life? I inhale sharply, trying to compose myself before I inevitably succumb to the overwhelming pressures. If I stop trying, does that make me lazy? Will that mean I don't deserve a career as much as people like Xander, who don't feel the pressure or at least don't show that they do?

"Okay," I say, but not too convincingly.

The tension in my voice is noticeable enough that Xander, who never passes on the opportunity to carry on the conversation, passes on this one—probably also because of my eye bags. The conversation quickly shifts to the world of hockey and thankfully, I don't have to contribute to James and Xander's game plans.

When the rest of our friends approach us, Jasmine's, Kiera's, and Carol's jaws hang at the sight of Eliza. I guess they do remember my cousin from the few times we all hung out. Though Eliza and I spent a fair amount of time together when she was visiting, I kept her in a separate world from my friends. They were two circles that never formed a Venn diagram. My friends tried to hang out with Eliza, especially Kiera, who wants everyone to be her friend, but they never really clicked.

But I know why Eliza didn't like them. We were the group of unapologetic "losers" who geeked out about things that we liked and hardly cared what other kids thought of our brace-faced, acne-prone, frizzy-haired vibe.

Now Eliza's eyes are wide, observing the ways the girls have changed. She's probably too stunned by the ugly duckling to swan transformations to see that we're the same weirdos.

After a few moments, their gapes turn into friendly smiles and they all exchange pleasantries. Just like that, it's seventh grade all over again, when Eliza first arrived from the Philippines and my friends were all over her, trying their best to include her. I love them for that, but I wonder if they ever figured out why Eliza didn't want to hang out with us. Perhaps they did and moved on.

Eliza was my best friend when it was only the two of us. She listened to my jokes and could read me like an open book. We went to our first concert together and I helped pick out her outfit when David Kim took her out on her first date. Back then I thought it was an honor just to be related to the golden girl.

But Eliza was and still is an F5 tornado materializing on a warm summer day. She's destructive, but storm chasers follow her, nonetheless. This time, I'm not a storm chaser, but I doubt I can escape her path of destruction.

TIP TWENTY-FIVE:
TRUST DURING THE CHRISTMAS RUSH

✱

The Eaton Centre is ten times busier than usual, if that's even possible. I frustratingly sip my matcha flavored boba while trailing behind James and Eliza, who are laughing at some stupid joke. I have already swallowed 50 percent of the tapioca pearls, forgetting to chew them (and almost choking) because I'm laser focused on the pair in front of me. It's a safety hazard.

They walk past the hundred-foot red Christmas tree and against a current of people rushing in the opposite direction. While they easily navigate the crowd of people and oversized shopping bags, I get bumped around like a ball in a pinball game. One man shoves me so hard with his shoulder that I wonder if he did it on purpose.

"Lara, could you hurry up a bit? You're walking a bit slow today and we need to get Seb that Lego set before they run out," James says, glancing back at me.

"C'mon, 'cuz, we don't have all day, and the people here are getting crankier by the second," Eliza adds.

Dodging another onslaught of bulky bags coming my way, I mutter, "I'm one of them," beneath my breath.

James shakes his head before spinning around and marching

to me. He grabs my right arm and links it with his left, then speeds forward again, dragging me in the process.

"My arm is gonna break off!" I complain.

"If this is what it takes to get you to walk faster, then this is what I'll do!"

"You guys can't hold it against me! I have short legs! It's not my fault that God chose to make you two into freaking giraffes!" I wiggle my arm out from his and take his hand instead, which is warm against my cold one.

Ariana Grande's version of "Last Christmas" plays in the background. At this rate, the excessive physical activity is making it seem like this will actually be my last Christmas. And if these two keep annoying me, it might be theirs too.

The plan was for Eliza and me to do our Christmas shopping together this weekend. To be perfectly honest, we've been getting along better than expected. She's officially taken over my room, but the basement hasn't been that bad. I thought she'd run off to assimilate into another friend group at school but she stuck with our little crew and surprisingly, she tries to spend as much time with me as possible . . . except when James comes around.

Not that I'm blaming the fella, but when he's around, I practically turn into dust.

Even though she hasn't done anything outright mean, I can't help but feel uncomfortable whenever they take part in friendly conversations. When they do talk, I notice that what they have is nothing like what James and I have. I'm not jealous, but as the end of December approaches, bringing his inevitable departure, I want to hold on to him as tightly as possible. And right now, it feels like a chase to even grab his hand.

James is confident about how our long-distance relationship is going to work. He says he'll FaceTime me every day and text me all the time, that we'll hang out the same amount as we do now, except virtually. He says that he'll fly back on holidays and bring me as much European chocolate as he can possibly fit in his suitcase. He says we can make it. I agree with him, mostly because I don't want to face the possibility of the opposite. He's been beside me my whole life and I can't lose him. As long as he doesn't let go, I'll hang on for dear life.

Still, the logistics of our situation sow seeds of doubt inside my head. We'll see the sun rise and set at different times, go to school at different hours, but most different of all, he won't be a walk away.

And how the hell are you supposed to prank someone virtually?

We rush past the Indigo store and I suddenly remember that I still need to buy a book set for Kiera, who has specifically requested some volumes of a new manga that she has gotten sucked into.

"Wait, guys! I need to buy something here." I heave, and James stops, dropping my hand. My lungs are expanding and collapsing like I ran a marathon. They both look back at me. Neither of them is panting because of their freaking flamingo legs. James lets out a heavy sigh and that alone is enough to make me feel guilty for slowing them down.

So I say, "You guys go ahead. Let's just text each other later to meet up."

He frowns, confused. "It's okay, I'll go with you."

I know he would, but I doubt he wants to. "I'll be fine."

"Are you sure?" Eliza asks.

I nod and give her an awkward thumbs-up.

James hesitates but says, "Text me, okay?"

"I shall."

The enticing scents of paper and Starbucks fill the air as I enter the store. *How wonderful.* My hand trails along book spines, and I long to purchase an entire case of novels for myself, but I'm here for Kiera and Christmas is the season of giving. *And empty bank accounts.*

It doesn't take me long to find Kiera's manga set and pay for it. The last of my gifts is bought. Jasmine gets a new set of stationery from our favorite Japanese shop, Carol gets a giant stuffed fish that she'll probably name something weird (for example, her banana plush is named Mr. Mango), and James gets a vintage acoustic guitar. And because I'm somewhat of a good person, Eliza gets a gift card to the Korean beauty store since skin care is a universal thing.

Outside of the store, I pull out my phone to text James when a pair of arms wrap around my waist and a loud voice shouts, "BOO!" I jump up before turning around and slapping the culprit on the side of his arm.

"Ow!" James winces.

"Dude! You can't just sneak up on me like that!"

James rubs his arm while Eliza stands there shaking her head and laughing. A large plastic bag hangs from James's arm and I can imagine giddy Seb on Christmas morning.

Done with our shopping, we make our way out of the mall. James walks at a reasonable pace beside me and holds my hand tightly.

"James, did you see what happened last night . . ." Eliza starts to asks him, and a heavy weight sits on my chest because I have a feeling this conversation will not include me.

"Yeah! Did you see the way they . . ." James responds excitedly, and my brain fails to comprehend what topic must be so exciting. *I think he said something about a penalty . . .*

"But he's really improved this year, hasn't he?" Eliza says.

"I know, right. It's crazy."

Then it hits me like a ton of bricks. They're talking about hockey. Of course.

When we were kids, that was their thing. They'd talk about their favorite teams and players, who was their role model, what calls were unfair, and I'd be left confused on the sidelines. You'd think after hanging out with two hockey freaks, I'd be converted to some sort of ice sport worshipper, but I'm ashamed to say that I know absolutely nothing about hockey. I've watched countless games because others were watching them, but sadly have retained zero information.

Eliza's interest in the sport was one of the big reasons why James liked her so much. Watching them like this again makes me feel displaced and suddenly questioning why I haven't gained even the slightest sports knowledge though I'm around athletes all the time.

I decide to take a shot and try to contribute to the conversation. "He's skating better, am I right?"

There's a moment of silence before laughter erupts from the both of them.

"You're still the same, 'cuz, so cute with your limited knowledge of hockey," Eliza coos.

James puts his arm around my shoulder and kisses the side of my head. "Oh sweetheart, you're absolutely adorable."

I never thought being called adorable would ever make me feel bad about myself, but I guess it just did.

Whoever thought that Christmas spirit week would somehow lift the spirits of the burdened students was absolutely mistaken. The school fails to understand that playing Christmas songs on the PA and having fun little decorating events doesn't balance out the amount of first semester work that piles up at the end. Not only are there the usual assignments, reports, and presentations, but exams are absolute hell. To top it all off, there's the added stress of filling out university applications and convincing myself that applying for a lab position will not make me lose my sanity. Because of that, I'm running on three hours of sleep and an extralarge coffee.

I've become such a venomous monster that my friends and my boyfriend are aware that being in my line of sight can lead to possible doom. At least they've known me long enough to give me my space. On the other hand, some people have yet to experience me at crunch week.

"'Cuz!" Eliza shouts from down the hallway, flailing her arms like one of those inflatable tube men at the car dealerships. Her coat folds over her arm and her matching two-piece light-gray sweatsuit shows off her athletic physique. I don't think I've ever seen anyone look so perfect in sweats. I walk over to her and raise my eyebrows, giving the *what do you want* face. It still doesn't faze her as she continues to smile.

"Guess what?" she says.

"What," I reply, my tone seeming uninterested because I *am* uninterested. I know I'm grouchy, but when you haven't had a full cycle of sleep-in days, it really does a number on you.

Before Eliza can continue her story, James, my friends, and their boyfriends approach us, all grouped together. Kiera waves and I acknowledge her with a salute. James shuffles near me, plucking the coffee cup from my hand and taking a sip. I'm too tired to yell at him for not asking.

Eliza takes a look at our tiny crowd before asking, "Okay, guys, are you ready?"

"I'm at the edge of my seat," I say sarcastically.

"I just scored two front-row tickets to a game at the Scotiabank Arena!"

A confused look appears on my face at the same time that all three of the guys (and Carol) start screaming in the middle of our school hallway, and suddenly I understand what they're talking about.

"That's awesome!" Logan yells loudly, causing me to shift another foot away from him.

Daniel lunges forward, his braids swinging over his shoulders. "Who's playing?"

Carol quickly pushes Daniel to the side, wrapping an arm around Eliza. "So, Lara's cousin. You must realize that any family of my best friend is my family. Therefore *you* are basically my family. And it would be a shame if you didn't take your own cousin—"

Eliza almost laughs at the thought of taking *me* to a game. "Lara?"

"No, *me*," Carol confirms. "It would be a shame if you didn't take *me* to the game. Unlike these idiots,"—she gestures to the guys—"I already know who's playing. Bruins against the Leafs?"

"I didn't even say the date!"

"Correct me if I'm wrong." Carol smirks.

"I can't. You're right. How'd you do that?"

"She's a sports psychic," Kiera answers.

"Right. Anyway," Eliza starts, "I'm really sorry that I can't take you, Carol, but I already decided who I'm taking." *Oh no. Please don't say what I think you're going to say.*

"You're going with your dad?" I ask, hopeful.

"Nah."

"Uncle?"

"Not exactly."

"Cute college guy?"

"Lara—"

"Your favorite cousin?" I attempt, pointing to myself.

She laughs at that one, before turning to James. "Surprise! Your Christmas gift!"

James is stunned. It takes a lot to shock him, but there he is, speechless, breathless, maybe on the verge of collapsing. Eliza pulls a ticket from her back pocket, takes his hand, and places the ticket in his palm. His fingers don't close around it and he smiles awkwardly. Carol lunges forward at the sight of the ticket, but Mark holds his girlfriend back, tightly wrapping his arms around her waist.

"But . . . but . . . hockey . . ." Carol whines in tortured athlete agony.

"Shh, babe, it's okay. We'll watch the game on TV," Mark says.

Right before they leave the group, Carol points at Eliza and yells, "We are *not* cousins anymore!" Mark hauls her away, mouthing an apology.

Eliza continues. "What do you think, James?"

My brain wants to convince Eliza to take Carol instead of my boyfriend, to tell James to reject the offer, and to purchase another cup of coffee for myself. However, I can't tell if I'm thinking rationally or if I'm under some electrolyte imbalance from all of the caffeine I'm on. I do know that James loves hockey and really wants to go, but I do not love the fact that he's going to be with Eliza. Alone.

"This is great . . ." he says, and I involuntarily give him the death glare, which comes to me like unexpected muscle spasms.

". . . but I probably shouldn't." he finishes, extending his hand to Eliza in an attempt to return the ticket.

I start to feel bad. Hockey is not my thing, but it's his. Before, when we thought he'd stay until summer, I know he was upset about my research thing with Xander, but I also know he wouldn't stop me from doing it. I guess it's my turn to be a good person and all that bull crap. He deserves that at least.

"You guys go ahead. It'll be fun," I say, trying to smile.

"*Really*?" James asks hesitantly, taking my hand in his.

I have to trust him. "Of course."

Eliza and James start another round of sports talk, which still sounds a lot like an attendance list. It's less awkward for me now, since the others are here. Logan joins in on their conversation but Daniel refocuses his attention on his cue cards, practicing for today's English presentation. At least this time I have Kiera and Jas to keep me company—which means a distraction from the green-eyed monster trying to get into my head.

Finally, the warning bell rings and we all disperse. "I have to finish my math seminar lab." I yawn, before turning into the next hallway.

"You mean your English seminar?" James corrects, walking beside me.

"Uh-huh."

"You are going in the complete opposite direction of your class." He laughs and grabs my waist, spinning me around. He takes my hand and my head slumps on his arm as we walk.

"I really think you should get some sleep, Dela Cruz."

"And I really think that humans should do something about global warming, but we don't see it happening, do we?"

He kisses my forehead, chuckling. "Please get some sleep. You are a monster."

"Sorry, I know that I'm a bit of a mess right now, but the week before break always kills me." But it isn't just the week before the break. I've *been* stressed and I know it. I seriously want time to stop so I can rest, even for a minute.

"I know, sweetheart. Thanks for being cool about the hockey thing, by the way," he says, squeezing my hand a little tighter.

I hate that I'm counting down the number of days left until I won't have his hand holding mine and his kisses sprinkled throughout my day. I wish I didn't have to count, and we could stay like this forever. I'm going to miss this so much.

TIP TWENTY-SIX:
COMMUNICATE YOUR THOUGHTS

✱

My house is dark and empty when I get home. My mom texted to say she, Dad, and Eliza's parents went to visit Tita Gia, which means that they will probably get home sometime close to midnight. Lola Nora and Illa went to watch two new Filipino movies at the local Cineplex, which will keep them occupied for a few hours. James is getting in extra practice at the rink and Eliza's there, too, probably trying to convince Coach to start a girls hockey team. I pick up the phone and dial the only number I have memorized. Looks like Pizza is my friend tonight.

Everyone hanging out without me was a concern that I thought I'd left in the past, once the LKJC returned to a normal state. I guess I was wrong.

Xander FaceTimes me on my laptop and it works out that I'm home alone. We start off working on my lab application, but I'm still not in the right headspace.

"I feel like I'm rushing into this," I admit with a sigh. "My friends and I had this whole last summer planned out—"

His face looks fuzzy due to a bad connection, but I assume he's frowning. "But what do you want?"

What *do* I want? The question catches me off guard, though if I'm being honest, it's been at the back of my mind forever. I want James to stay and my memories of Eliza to go away. I want to be her friend and not worry about what her past relationship with James might still mean to her. I want to be able to think about my future and see it through clear water, not mud.

But that's the problem. I don't know what I want anymore. Do I want to savor the last summer of simplicity—watching marathons of *Stranger Things* with Illa and going out as much as possible with my friends—or should I focus on building a future that I'm not ready for? Now that I have both choices available, I don't know what to do.

God, more than anything, I want a break.

Before I can answer him, he continues, "Lara, if your end goal is med school, this is a really great opportunity to get early research experience. We're really lucky that Dr. Osei remembers us, and a lot of undergrads run into trouble finding a lab placement."

If my end goal is med school? I never told anyone about that besides James, and even then, it wasn't a creed set in stone. I just turned seventeen. Why is everything about an end goal? Why can't I want something and not treat it like a constitution for how to live my life?

Xander continues to talk like this is the be-all and end-all, and I don't blame him. The road to medicine is always an uphill battle, and this opportunity we've been given is lucky. He's not wrong but it doesn't make my decision any easier.

There's always been a part of me that knew I'd be a doctor one day. It's something that I can't shake off, no matter how strenuous the future looks. The gut feeling is what propels me forward, no matter how exhausted I am. But I'm also still a kid who isn't ready for the next step yet. I don't want to make decisions where I have to hesitate.

I try not to linger on it for too long once we get to studying for exams. We stay on the call but neither of us talks because solving math equations gets more difficult if you try to multitask. A part of me wishes I was studying with James instead. Definitely less productive, but more fun.

The doorbell rings and I bring my laptop to the door since Xander is in the middle of a math-related rant. Instead of the pizza delivery guy, James holds a pizza box, with Eliza right beside him.

"Hope you don't mind that I covered the pizza for you," James says, before frowning. "Who's on the phone?"

"Hey, man!" Xander greets him. James gives him a friendly wave. I'm glad he isn't being a douche to him anymore. "Looks like your pizza delivery's here," Xander says to me. "Want to study again tomorrow?" I tell him of course and say a quick good-bye before shutting my laptop.

Eliza gestures to the large pizza in James's hands. "I guess you were expecting our company, huh?" She grabs the box and pushes past us, taking it to the kitchen.

When she's out of sight, James leans over to me. "You were planning on eating that all by yourself, right?"

I give him a dejected sigh. "Then y'all had to come along."

"Oh sweetheart, you don't have to pretend you're not ecstatic to see me." He gives me a quick kiss on the lips, and I roll my eyes. "Admit it."

"In your dreams," I say, but fail to hide the smile creeping onto my face.

Honestly, I *am* excited whenever I see James. His smile's contagious, he gives warm hugs and addictive kisses, and, well, he makes me happy. It's all of those things plus the fact that he's leaving at the end of the month that makes me want to see him as much as I can.

Three of us, with our equally large appetites, devour the pizza in the family room while watching *Full House*. I sit on the couch directly in front of the television while Eliza drags James beside her on the other couch, pointing at hockey-related things on her cell phone. Could he not push her away and sit beside *me*?

". . . so if the game starts at seven, do you wanna pick me up at five thirty?" Eliza asks James.

He nods. "Sure, that'll give us a bit of time to get there and settled."

"I'm so excited. What are the odds of me winning that radio contest?"

"You're a lucky person, I guess." James shrugs.

"You're a lucky person, I guess," I mumble to myself, mocking his tone. Still, he doesn't seem to notice me.

They continue their hockey talk on the couch, which annoys the hell out of me. First of all, how close does Eliza have to position herself beside someone else's boyfriend? Whatever they're saying goes over my head entirely because I'm too busy steaming from watching them together. The way they're acting right now reminds me of how they acted when they were thirteen. I feel burning vomit rising up my throat.

"So, guys." I interrupt in an attempt to change the subject. "What are our plans for the winter break?" The awkward level increases by tenfold but at least I'm in the conversation.

"Well . . ." Eliza begins, and my mind tries to think of the best possible outcome.

Oh Lara, I'm going to be moving out on Christmas Eve, so you get the whole room back to yourself! Better yet, I'll stop leeching on your boyfriend!

I smile at the thought.

"Lara?" Eliza calls, snapping her fingers and dragging me out of the best daydream I've had in days.

"Huh? What were you saying?"

"We're obviously spending Christmas together, silly. But the family should do something fun. How about your folks, James?" How is it that whenever she starts talking to me, she finishes with James? I don't get her.

"Our families usually spend Christmas together," he says. "It's the same thing every year. We have a Christmas Eve party at my house where Lara gets a good present from my mother and a *fun* one from me."

This is the point where he shoots me a smirk and I respond with a glare. "What makes you think that fake cockroaches are fun?"

"It's fun for me to see the terror on your face," he says, face clearly amused by the memory. When I don't reply, he immediately backtracks. "*But* I got you an actual good present this year, I promise. No more cockroaches, worms, or empty boxes."

I roll my eyes. "What a *great* boyfriend."

He winks. "You know it, sweetheart."

"I think we should shake things up this Christmas," Eliza says. *There is enough shaking going on here*, I want to tell her. Y*ou arriving was very much the equivalent of a 7.5 magnitude earthquake.*

James prods the bear to demonstrate her attack, with one word. "How?"

"Let's go ice skating in the afternoon! It'll be a fun change from Coach yelling at your ass during practice." She laughs.

"I don't know—" I start, but James interrupts me.

"I haven't skated for fun in a while. Doesn't that sound fun, Lara?"

I purse my lips and nod, suddenly embarrassed that I can't skate. I live in Canada and can't skate! I didn't know this could translate into such a big insecurity. Plus, it's obvious that they're both excited about skating, so I keep my inability to skate to myself. I can learn while we're there. But I can't believe James doesn't remember this about me.

They continue to exchange ideas while I sit there like I'm invisible, mindlessly staring at the television. I glance back and forth at them, scoffing at the sight and trying to focus on my show but the jealousy I feel leaves me restless. *Perfect*, I think. *I'm the third wheel in my own relationship, and in my own house.*

I see James off at the door at about seven o'clock. He looks cute in his puffy coat and with his scarf rising past his chin. The snow outside falls softly, and through the door opening, I catch the glimmer of the streetlights lighting up the dark evening.

"Thanks again for the pizza," I say. "I hope you and Eliza were able to figure out whatever it is you came here for." I shrug. At that, he knits his brow.

His lips brush over his scarf slightly when he says, "I guess we did, but the real reason I came over was to spend a little more time with you. You've been cramming like crazy and I always have practice after school. I wanted to see you."

That's not what it looked like.

I can't help it and explode. "*Me*? I could've sworn I wasn't the one you were talking to for the past couple of hours." After I say it, my face flushes red. I sound like a clingy girlfriend but why should I care? All of it is true! Is he forgetting that in a few weeks he'll be gone? Is he forgetting that we won't be seeing each other like this anymore? All I want to do is scream into the abyss.

His cold hands fly up to my face, squeezing my cheeks. Instead of arguing, he grins and kisses me lightly on the nose. "Am I seeing my girlfriend *jealous* for the first time?"

Seriously?

Eliza eats away at our last moments together and *that's* what he says? I used to be jealous of the way he could brush off problems easily and not dwell on them, but this shouldn't be cute at all. He shouldn't be grinning at me like that when we both know he's going to leave. I've prepared myself for that. But when I knew he had little time, I thought most of it would be mine. Not hers.

I scoff and swat his hands away from my face. "Of course not," I say, not bothering to hide my frustration. "Whatever, I'm going to sleep. *Good night.*"

I attempt to close the front door but he holds it open.

"Seriously, James? I'm not in the mood for your games! Spend your last few weeks here with whoever you want!"

The amusement in his face vanishes immediately and he takes my hand. "Is that what's bothering you?"

My gaze shifts to my feet. The only sound is the wind rustling through bare tree branches outside.

"I guess we've been avoiding the subject, haven't we?" he continues. "Lara, I know I'm leaving but I'll still be here for you. Always. There's text and call and FaceTime and Zoom and—"

"Are you going to name communication methods until midnight?"

He laughs a little then shakes his head. "No, but my point is I'll always find a way to annoy you. Plus, I'll visit you on your school breaks."

He grabs my waist with both of his hands and pulls me toward him, looking at me like he's solved the problem. In reality, we haven't solved anything at all. We haven't even touched the Eliza part. The closer we get to his departure, the more restless I get. I don't want to see his caller ID. I want him beside me in biology. I want him to rub circles on my back when I'm anxious, and I want to be the one to reassure him with a tight hug. I think he senses the same thing because his smile falls and he holds me a little tighter.

"I'll still miss you," I whisper.

With Eliza upstairs and the two of us alone at the door, he sweeps the strands of my hair from my face, leans over, and places his lips on mine.

His kiss doesn't falter, not even for a second.

For a few moments, we are alone again, and things feel like the way they should be. I kiss him back, unwilling to let go of him just yet, not ready to step back into reality. My heart sinks, knowing that I might be the third wheel until the day he leaves. The only difference this time is that I get the occasional kiss.

When I finally break the kiss, he keeps me close, arms tightly wrapped around me. And we stand, both of us silent, breathless as though the air has suddenly got thin.

"Lara, please don't be mad at me."

I'm mad because he didn't remember that I don't skate, and he doesn't see me trying to understand his sport. More than that, I'm mad at myself for expecting him to know those things. I'm mad at myself for not telling him how I felt when Eliza was here or what happened between us. I don't want to revisit any of it. But no matter how angry I am, the dryness of my mouth doesn't let me talk, let alone talk about that. Again, I lie to him. It makes me feel sick but it makes things easier for the both of us.

"I'm not angry at you," I say softly. "If I was, a measly kiss wouldn't solve the problem. I guess I was a bit . . . a bit . . ." I start, but I can't possibly say the next word.

"A bit?"

"Please don't make me say it."

He shakes his head. "I won't, but don't be. We're just friends."

"You're just friends *now*. It doesn't change the fact that you guys were together before," I grumble.

This time, he actually does laugh. "We were thirteen! Puppy love. It's barely significant."

Barely significant my ass, I think in my head.

"You're mine and nobody could ever change that," he says, giving my hand a reassuring squeeze.

But I never questioned if I was his.

The question was if he was mine.

TIP TWENTY-SEVEN:
GIVE UP ON ADVICE

✱

Lugaw, also known as *arroz caldo*, is one of my favorite dishes. Lola Nora empties the bowl of diced onion, garlic, and ginger into the pot with sizzling oil, followed by the sliced chicken. The comforting aroma of her home cooking diffuses into the air until the whole kitchen almost smells like her old *karinderya* back in the Philippines.

I wash the dishes while swaying along to her playlist of OPM (Original Pinoy Music) love songs from the 70s. When I was younger, I complained about her old Tagalog songs and pleaded for us to listen to my One Direction playlist instead. Being Lola Nora, she never caved in, and now I have her go-to playlist basically memorized. I'm thankful for it. She sings along to the song while stirring her ingredients and I finally feel relaxed after a stressful last day of school and of course, thinking about tonight's hockey game.

She continues to cook until everything's added—the rice, fish sauce, and water—and all that's left to do is stir. "*Ara, tikman mo nga 'to! Dadagdagan ko pa ba 'to ng asin?*" (Ara, taste this! Should I add more salt?) Lola Nora says, raising the ladle to my mouth.

I turn off the running tap, taste it, and nod. "*Tama na yung asin.*"

(The salt is good enough.) Sometimes Lola Nora overdoes it with the salt, and we have to restrain her because of her blood pressure.

She shrugs before turning the burner off.

The last dish in the sink is the large knife used to cut the chicken. She warns me to be careful and I roll my eyes, reminding her that I've washed dishes for half my life. But then Eliza walks into the kitchen and at her presence the knife drops into the metal sink, clanking twice before lying flat.

"*Susmariosep! Sinabi ko nang mag-ingat.*" (Jesus Mary Joseph! I told you to be careful.) Lola Nora reprimands me but trails off when she sees what I see.

"*Okay lang kayo?*" (Are you guys okay?) Eliza asks, catching our stares.

Lola Nora does an incredibly horrible fake laugh. "*Oo naman, ineng.*" (Of course, dear.) Then turns back to her pot, continuing to mix with the ladle even though the lugaw's already finished cooking. Her widened eyes do not plan to blink.

Eliza's dressed like she's about to sneak into some sort of nightclub—a plunging V-neck black bodysuit sits over what I believe is (a very effective) push-up bra and is paired with a skin-tight skirt. She holds a pair of black, heeled boots dangling from her fingers.

My initial thought is, *Where can I get a good push-up bra like that?* My second thought is, *Can't this girl wear a jersey to a hockey game like everyone else?*

"Have you seen my phone?" Eliza asks, moving into the family room and digging into the crevices of the couches. She finds her cell phone at the last seat, and says, "Never mind," before tapping away.

Of course, girls dress up for themselves and just because she looks good doesn't necessarily mean she's going after a guy. However, in this case, I'm actually quite certain she's going after James regardless of what she wears. And Eliza *never* dresses up like this. She always looks good, but I've never seen her in anything but leggings, a sweater, or some other type of athleisure. Combine this information with her clinginess toward James and I think my conclusion seems plausible.

The doorbell rings and Eliza immediately runs to the door. Quickly, I place two fingers on my wrist, checking my pulse to make sure I'm still alive.

Yup, still here. *Unfortunately*.

I follow her to the door, where James stands, dressed in possibly a million layers because it's literally below freezing tonight.

"Hey." He waves awkwardly at her before looking at me.

"I'm almost ready," Eliza says. "I just have to grab a sweater." Then she proceeds to run upstairs.

I know that I'm getting jealous again, and I also know that James literally told me that I have nothing to worry about a few days ago. However, it is not a few days ago anymore. Maybe I'm not actually jealous anymore. Maybe I'm angry.

"I'll catch you in a bit," I say to James before rushing upstairs.

I throw open the door to my own bedroom, where Eliza rummages through our shared closet. She can't seem to make up her mind about what to wear over her night club attire. I lean against the door frame, waiting for her to notice my presence, but she's way too absorbed in her fashion choices. I clear my throat and she turns around.

"Oh! 'Cuz, I didn't notice you here!"

"I know what you're doing," I say, crossing my arms and attempting to stare her down.

She frowns, faking innocence. "I don't understand."

I walk into the room and stand directly in front of her, which proves to be much less intimidating than planned, considering her tall, lean build. I'm starting to think that what I've imagined in my head won't actually play out the same way. "Eliza, stop trying to steal my boyfriend."

She blinks. "How could you even say that? I can't believe you don't trust me."

I groan in frustration. "Stop doing that! You say things like this and somehow try to make me feel bad about it!"

She lets out a large exhale. "I'm not trying to do anything. Listen, we can talk again later, but I still need to grab a sweater." She sighs then heads back to the closet. She picks up the large, black hoodie from the hanger at the back and I feel my body tense. I'm frozen and I've lost all ability to say anything.

She slips James's sweater on and looks like one of those perfect Pinterest girls in those cute photos of couples. My fists ball at my sides and I don't have the control to unclench them. I *am* angry. She's doing this on purpose, smiling like she's won whatever game she's playing. I watch her pull the sleeves up so they don't slip past her fingers and my mind easily spins into comparisons.

She's beautiful.

But so are you, I tell myself, hoping that I'll believe it this time. *Please believe it this time.*

It's hard to see myself after looking at Eliza. She was always the beautiful one, praised by our family members. She did beauty pageants and went on runs and was a great athlete. She got good grades and said the right things. It's so wrong to be jealous, but I am.

But no matter how jealous I get, I'd never want to take anything from her. I don't know why it's so easy for her to take from me. Does she reason that it's hers to have?

She then removes the sweater and hangs it on her arm. "This is cute. Could I borrow it?"

A lump in my dry throat forms and I try to swallow. I finally find my voice. "No. Take a different one."

Her voice is soft and gentle, smooth and sweet; I don't know why she's still pretending. "Now, 'cuz, don't be dramatic about this. It's just a sweater—"

"Eliza," I warn, taking a step forward. "*Please*, give it back."

Her mask falls away completely; she smiles so cynically. "No."

"I said, give it back!" I repeat, surprising myself with my volume. I walk toward her and grab the wrist of the hand holding the sweater.

Suddenly her smile disappears, and she winces like she's in pain. Oh please, I didn't even hold her that tightly.

"Lara!" James shouts, grabbing my hand and pulling me away from Eliza, who massages her wrist. *That's* why she made that face. "What are you doing?" he asks, but by his furrowed brows and darkened gaze, I know that he already has his answer. I don't think I've ever seen him like this.

Eliza gives him a pitiful look, acting like I just slapped her. "I just wanted to borrow a sweater."

"I told you not that one, you—" I start, attempting to grab the sweater from her arms, but James beats me to it.

"Lara! Enough!" he shouts, taking it from both of us.

My mouth starts to dry up. Why is it only me that he's yelling at? I've never seen him this angry before, especially at me.

He tries to compose himself, but his voice is still louder than usual. "How many times do I have to reassure you that you have nothing to worry about?"

"I—"

"I'll take my sweater now, thank you," he continues, staring right at me with his dark-brown eyes. Let me rephrase, *angry* dark-brown eyes. "This is the stupidest thing to be fighting over." He only stops staring at me when he walks out the door. Eliza follows closely behind him, leaving me alone in my room which has somehow become dead silent.

If only he realized what I was really fighting for.

I rest my head on the kitchen table, sulking. Lola Nora hands me a bowl of steaming lugaw, along with a large spoon. She heard the fight. As I begin to eat, Lola Nora stands behind me, braiding my hair and humming the tune to an old Filipino lullaby, "Sa Ugoy ng Duyan," which she sang to Illa and me growing up.

Illa enters the room quietly and smiles when she hears the song. She sings the lyrics and surprises us with her voice. Though we rarely hear her singing voice, it is angelic. I join her and Lola Nora goes teary eyed.

For a moment, my problems cease to exist, and we go back to a simpler time when Lola Nora was able to protect us from everything bad. When she was around, there was no such thing as heartbreak or jealousy or guilt. I wish we could stay like this.

But we can't.

Lola Nora retreats to her room shortly after to video chat with our family in the Philippines. She'll probably be gossiping until the late hours of night.

Illa and I sit on the couch, ready to zone out to some TV. She turns on the television, automatically set on the Sportsnet channel, courtesy of our dad.

It's the hockey game at the Scotiabank Arena.

Knowing that James and Eliza are there together is enough to make me squirm in my seat. Illa's only interested in the score, and I wait for her to change the channel. She doesn't.

We both watch as the camera pans to the audience, shifting from faces with temporary tattoos and waving flags. The announcer begins to talk but my body is already paralyzed when the screen shows two familiar faces.

". . . lovely couples we see! Look at that! I don't know what's better than taking your significant other to tonight's game . . ."

I never thought I'd witness anything worse than their kiss at the park all those years ago, but a split-second camera pan of her lips on his is enough to shatter my heart into a million little pieces.

TIP TWENTY-EIGHT:
PRIORITIZE YOURSELF

✱

I once told Carol that the strength of a relationship isn't measured in time. Saying that was a punch in the gut because I thought the LKJC relied so much on our long history. When I said that things could fall apart, despite knowing someone for a lifetime, I only thought about losing my best friends. Losing James never crossed my mind. It wasn't even a possibility.

Until now.

Illa turns the television off before rushing over to hug me, saying something reassuring that I can't fully process. Something about him recoiling and getting up right after, being taken aback by Eliza's sudden kiss, but it doesn't matter. It doesn't make anything better. She squeezes my arm and keeps talking and talking and talking and I really wish I could hear her voice. Instead, it echoes in my mind, which somehow feels empty and full at the same time.

My eyes don't leave the television screen, even after it's turned black. My breathing stays regular, perhaps slower than usual. No tears stream down my face and my eyes don't well up. Slowly, my body releases its tension and I reciprocate her hug, relying on the transfer of her warmth.

I should be comforting Illa for her first heartbreak, I should've been stronger, set a better example, I should have confronted Eliza from the start, told James the truth about my feelings.

But one thing I shouldn't have done was let fear and my self-guilt control everything I did. I was always scared of people leaving so I held on too tightly, allowing myself to suffer through pains that I never deserved instead of standing up for my own feelings. I wanted so badly for my relationships to work out that I let people hurt me. Over and over again. Love at the expense of losing myself. Losing my own voice.

My subconscious would once guilt me into silence. Now, I tell my subconscious to shut up, hoping that choosing myself gets easier after this.

My eyes close shut and I let her warmth guide my thoughts. Tonight, my little sister is my strength and when she needs it, I'll be hers.

The sudden sound of the doorbell ringing forces my heavy eyelids to open. Illa and I must have fallen asleep on the couch. Illa's still asleep, snoring peacefully like a mini-bulldozer. Not even a fire alarm could wake her. Lifting her body from mine, I stand up before carefully setting her head on a pile of pillows. I dig out my cell phone from my pocket and see that despite the powerful nap, only an hour has passed. There are about a dozen calls from James and double that in text messages. I press Clear Notifications without hesitation.

The doorbell ringing gets crazier. They've already broken my trust and dignity; can't they leave my freaking doorbell alone?

I get to the door and my heartbeat quickens. My breathing speeds up as my hand reaches for the doorknob. It's cold to the touch and the chill spreads through my entire body, causing my fingers to tremble.

Pull yourself together, I think, and my fingers immediately straighten. I won't grant them the satisfaction of seeing my shaky hands.

The last deep breath is shaky and so is the rest of my body. As the door opens, I am relieved to see that I don't have to go all Karate Kid on the visitors.

"Lara!" the three girls shout at the same time as they wrap their arms around me. They pull me back into my own house and I try to reach my arm out of our tangled bodies in an attempt to shut the door. *Goodness, suffocation is real.*

The door slams shut, and they finally let me out of the tight embrace. All three of them take a step backward and I take a moment to admire their questionable fashion choices as they remove their snow boots.

"What are you guys doing here?"

Kiera's gray parka is half-zipped but contributes nothing to hiding her pink pajamas, decorated with little bunnies. Gel under-eye masks are peeling off her face, but she doesn't seem to notice. Jasmine's puffy coat is fully zipped but her flannel pajama pants stand out with their bright purple. Her short hair is twisted into the smallest messy bun ever, strands falling out of the back. And Carol . . .

"I brought a bat," Carol blurts randomly, not answering my question at all. She goes on to twirl the baseball bat in her fingers, eyes glowing like she inhaled a can of Red Bull. Still, she looks the most put together of the three of them, with her dark-wash jeans and regular hoodie under her army-green parka. It's surprising, considering she's usually the disheveled one. Then again, her face screams premeditated murder, and I suppose she had a premeditated outfit to go with that.

Kiera approaches me and sticks her hands on my face, wiping away nonexistent tears. Her sudden contact causes me to retreat into double chin stature. "I'm so, so sorry, Lara," she sobs, the under-eye masks peeling off completely and falling onto the floor. "We saw what happened on TV."

I grab her shoulders and hold her at a safe distance away from me. She continues to cry, and I look at Jasmine, who simply shrugs.

Carol slaps Kiera's arm with the back of her hand. "Kiera, why are *you* crying? Lara was the one who got cheated on!"

"I just—she just," she stammers between sobs, "I feel so sad for you!" She throws herself at me and continues to unleash a waterfall on my shoulder, staining my top with her tears. I think their intention was to comfort me, but here I am, comforting her for the pain of my relationship.

"Thanks? Your concern astounds me, really." I push her over to Jasmine, who heartily accepts the disastrous Kiera. She continues to cry on Jasmine's shoulder and Jasmine pats her back.

"We thought you'd look more, I don't know, angry? Frustrated? Sad?" Jasmine says as we walk over to the staircase.

I lead them up the stairs. "I am, but once this happens to you over and over again, heartbreak becomes more of a heart-crack." Their faces fall and I leave it there.

We get up to my room and nobody says a word as I plop down on my bed. Carol stands by the door, still twirling her baseball bat. "You haven't said much," I mention, raising my eyebrows at her.

"I have a bat," she repeats, this time, smiling evilly.

"I can see . . ."

"This is my lucky baseball bat." Carol laughs so crazily that I shift closer to Jasmine and Kiera.

"I'm scared," Kiera whispers, holding on to Jasmine's arm for dear life. Jasmine and I nod in agreement at the same time.

"Carol's the one who organized this! She suggested that all of us should come over together to comfort you!" Jasmine tells our little huddle.

"Actually, I just wanted to have an audience," Carol responds, smirking.

Kiera's eyes widen. "Audience?"

Carol takes a seat on my desk chair and spins around in it. "The worst part is waiting," she starts. "I can't wait till James and Eliza get back. Then the fun will truly begin." She holds the bat under her arm and rubs her hands together, and I swear Kiera shivers beside me.

"Carol!" Jasmine exclaims. "This is not the time for your violent antics!"

"Jasmine, do you hear yourself? Because I think this is a very appropriate time," Carol argues.

Jasmine looks at me, probably waiting for me to back her up.

I give her an apologetic look. "Sorry, Jas, most of the time I'd agree with you, knowing Carol's destructive potential—"

"But what? Sure, we're all mad here, but do we really want to end up in jail!"

"The only people who end up in jail are the people who get caught, dummy," Carol says, flicking her on the forehead.

They continue their little bicker while Kiera's head darts back and forth between the two arguing girls. I slap my own forehead. *We are getting absolutely nowhere.*

"YOU ARE NOT GOING TO HIT THEM WITH A BASEBALL BAT, CAROL!"

"THEN WHO'S GOING TO BEAT THEM UP, JASMINE? YOU?"

"STOP!" Kiera finally yells, standing between them and holding them apart with her arms. "How is this going to solve our problem? At this rate, you guys are going to kill each other before James and Eliza even get here!"

Not even I know what to do when they come back. Am I going to open that door and start firing off every bad thing I can think of? Am I going to slap Eliza and yell at them both? I don't know if I can do that. Can I do any of this without bursting into tears?

The answer to all of my questions spurs out when tears start to trickle down my cheeks. I *can't* confront them. I can't handle James and Eliza right now. Maybe I'm being a coward, but I can't do any of this right now.

Kiera comes over to hug me first, followed by Jasmine, and even Carol drops her bat to join the group hug. "It's so unfair," I whisper, trying to wipe the never-ending teardrops on my cheek. "He was going to leave and *that's* when I was supposed to feel sad. It wasn't supposed to be like this."

I had been preparing myself for the wrong type of heartbreak. I was bracing for the feeling of getting left behind, of saying good-byes at the airport. I wasn't getting ready to watch them kiss for a second time, to feel exactly the same way I felt the first time I saw his lips on hers. I wasn't expecting to be their third wheel. Again.

Jasmine strokes my hair back as I continue to sob. Kiera squeezes my hand and Carol wipes the tears from my cheeks while holding in her own. "We love you, okay?" she says, with a trembling smile. "Don't forget that."

As I look at the three girls around me, I realize that even though we've hurt each other and made many mistakes, we will always have each other. Our friendship hasn't always been easy, but we've learned to stand by each other through the tough times. Like real sisters, we've learned to be each other's strength.

The doorbell rings again. This time, I know it's them. Without me saying anything, Kiera gestures for me to stay put. They all get up.

Carol picks up her baseball bat. "It's my time, ladies." She gets a little laugh out of me, and we all smile at each other.

"We got this." Jasmine winks, then they exit my bedroom.

Footsteps trail down the stairs, getting softer as they get closer to the first floor. When I am sure that they've reached the bottom, I quietly open my door and sneak over to the top of the staircase. The doorbell rings again and Kiera opens the door. Behold, Jameson Bryer and Eliza, whom I wish to perform an exorcism on.

Carol goes full force, holding her bat in the air, about to bring it down toward them, but Jasmine grabs her arm in enough time to avoid any damage. James's and Eliza's arms shoot up, protecting their faces.

"LET ME HAVE AT THESE JACKASSES!" Carol yells, trying to break through Jasmine's strong grip.

"NOT YET, CAROL!" she shouts back.

"If it isn't Mr. Destroy my best friend without remorse and might soon get a black eye and Eliza the extremely evil eyesore who so has a terrible sense of style. *What* do you want?" Kiera crosses her arms, eyes shooting daggers at them.

He takes a step inside. "Please let me talk to her," James pleads, so desperately that I feel my heart ache a bit.

"She doesn't want to talk to you," Jasmine snaps back.

"This was all a mistake. I didn't want any of this to happen. Please let me talk to her," he begs again. "I need to explain."

"Explain what?" Eliza mutters from behind James, squeezing herself inside. "She saw everything."

James turns and points at Eliza. "YOU! HOW DID YOU GET HERE?"

"I took the bus, no thanks to you."

He looks up at the ceiling, then presses his fingers between his brows. "This is your fault. You're the one who kissed me."

She frowns at the accusation. "It takes two, babe," she says, and I wish I didn't agree.

I bite my thumb, holding a scream inside. If only I could walk down there and confront them, but my body is truly paralyzed.

"Can I smack them now?" Carol asks Jasmine, holding her bat up.

Kiera holds an arm in front of Carol, signaling for her to wait. "I think both of you should leave," she says calmly.

Eliza clicks her tongue. "I *live* here. So, if you don't mind, I think I'll just—"

Carol immediately blocks her. "And if you want to *continue living*, I suggest you take a hike, Eliza."

"You can't do this—"

"I'm the one with the bat."

Carol lifts up the bat for a swing and Eliza lets out a little yelp before running in the opposite direction, out of the house. Finally, she's out of sight.

"I'm not going to leave until I see her," James repeats, and Carol proceeds to lift up her bat again. "You can beat me up if you want, I clearly deserve it, but I'm not leaving this house until I see Lara."

"We're sorry but—" Jasmine starts but I slowly step down the stairs.

"Lara!"

When my eyes meet his, I remember his anger from earlier, the way his gaze burned. I try to think back to the ways he looked at me before, but the pain blocks any incoming nostalgia. Each footstep toward the front door feels like I'm walking on a never-ending pathway of hot coals.

"Lara."

I pause for a moment before saying, "You said you wanted to see me. Well, here I am. I've been seen."

"Yes, I—"

"I would rather not speak to you right now, James. I need some time to let everything sink in. I'm not asking for much, just that you give me space," I manage to say, sticking my hands in my back pockets.

His eyes start to well up but I refuse to cave. "Please let me explain. Please. I'm so sorry. I didn't mean—"

I inhale sharply, fighting tears that might spring out any second. "Stop."

"Please, Lara."

I'm done.

He takes another step forward, but my friends hold him back, specifically Carol, who holds the bat horizontally against his abdomen. A tear escapes his eye, then another one, and another. He cries softly, not bothering to wipe his face. His eyes, once vibrant and comforting, safe, are now glossy and unsteady. I think he knows that I'm long gone from his grasp.

"I love you."

Everything stops, and I feel sick to my stomach. Words that are supposed to comfort and mend instead rip my heart out completely. When are people going to realize that those three words aren't magic? Saying them doesn't restore anything.

"I think you should go." I take another breath and hold my eyes shut for an extra moment. "We can talk tomorrow."

He nods disappointedly before exiting through the front door. Kiera shuts it. I let out a large exhale, and Carol gives my shoulder a reassuring squeeze. I do not allow myself to feel an ounce of guilt because sometimes I need to prioritize myself.

TIP TWENTY-NINE:
BEGIN YOUR JOURNEY

✱

For the next few days, everyone is too nice. Mom holds me when I cry, Lola Nora keeps me in her prayers (though I don't think Jesus answers vengeful prayers), Illa takes over my house duties, and Dad cooks all of my favorite foods. He attempted go to Tito Danny's house that night "for a relaxing drink," but we knew that wasn't the reason. Needless to say, James is still alive because we had Dad tied to the foot of his bed until he calmed down. They all want the heartbreak to end, maybe even more than I do—and that support makes the mending process a little bearable.

Eliza and her family are leaving sooner than expected. Their house finished a week earlier than anticipated, pulling them out of our hair. I hibernate in the basement while she stays. I don't want to see her face. Still, I can't help it when I need things from my room.

I don't say a word when I enter. I only need to grab my favorite YA romance trilogy to help boost my serotonin levels (duh). She sits on the floor, folding her newly washed laundry. Half of her clothes are scattered on the floor and the other half are stacked in one of the three cardboard boxes lined against the wall. Dark circles sit under her eyes, which are red, probably from crying.

I don't understand why she's crying so much. Sometimes, at night, I can hear her through the vents. When you hear people crying, you feel sad, sympathetic. Yet when I hear her muffled sniffles, I feel angry. She wanted to hurt me, and she succeeded. What more could she possibly want?

Eliza doesn't seem to understand the concept of don't talk to me you're literally evil because she opens her mouth immediately. "Lara," she says gently, unable to look me in the eye. "I'm sorry." Her eyes are glued to the floor. I'm standing above her and she's sitting like she's asking for forgiveness.

Eliza is family and each time I let her hurt me, I keep reminding myself that we share the same blood. I can never hurt her back. But not forgiving her is not me trying to inflict pain. My not forgiving her is not criminal.

I'm hurting. Isn't that enough of a reason?

I can't bring myself to ask for an explanation, like I did with James the first time. Stories are important to me. I like knowing other people's sides so that I can create my own best judgment. Yet some people's stories have a twisted way of distorting my own. Sometimes I see too much of one side and forget my own. I get guilty and forgive, thinking that I've solved the problem when I haven't.

Eliza talks about her heartbreak, trying to answer the questions she assumes I have. I don't listen.

I suppose it's selfish of me to close myself off because of that. But I so desperately want to be selfish. And maybe it's not even selfishness. Right now, I can't take her story and keep my own. Maybe one day, but not today.

She finishes, tears welling in her eyes. She wipes them away on her sleeve and I know she's in pain, maybe in as much pain as I am, but I guess I'll never know for sure. Maybe at one point she wanted the same thing as me—to be friends again. Maybe she wanted it as much as I did. But she also wanted to be loved more than she wanted to fix our relationship, and that's out of my control.

"I'm sorry," she repeats, closing the final cardboard box before standing up.

I can't offer her forgiveness today, but I need to close this for myself. "I hope you find what you're looking for."

And I truly hope she does.

The weather today is the definition of gloomy, not a ray of sunshine in sight. The snow has melted into piles of brown slush, coating the gutters and puddling the sidewalks. Now it drips off my winter boots and onto the wooden floor. Clearly, I didn't wipe them hard enough on the floor mat at the entrance. I shoot an apologetic smile to the worker who mops the trail of slush leading to my table.

One of my legs is crossed over the other as I wait in the almost empty coffee shop, the scent of gingerbread and peppermint swirling around. Red stockings hang on the fireplace, and a few feet away is a small Christmas tree. A piano rendition of "Have Yourself a Merry Little Christmas" plays softly in the background, and I tap my heel on the floor to whatever beat seems to fit. An elderly couple sits on a green sofa in the corner of the room. One person rests their head on the other's shoulder; the other kisses their partner's forehead, and my heart melts a little. I hate that my first thought is, *Would James and I be doing that if the incident hadn't happened?*

It's impossible to stop loving him.

He was all my firsts—first best friend, first enemy, first boyfriend, and first kiss. Deep down, I always loved him. It was the type of love that kept evolving, but love, nonetheless.

I try not to shake my leg too much, especially with a steaming cup of peppermint hot chocolate perched on the table. The problem with letting go of James is that he was always there. Even when we hated each other, he stuck around and saw parts of me that I never let anyone else see. He saw the messy hair and panic attacks. In eighth grade, when my anxiety got so bad that I didn't step foot into school for a month, he was the only one who knew.

I mean, he only knew because Mom told Tita Gia who told him . . . but still. He never told anyone about it and kept my secret without me having to ask.

The bell chimes as the door opens. James steps in, dressed in a long gray coat and gloves, holding a white potted orchid in his hands. The first thing he does is set the plant on the table and I fight the urge to grab it and run. He removes his coat and hangs it on the chair, revealing a fully monochromatic outfit—a black turtleneck tucked into black pants. I mentally scold myself for making him watch all my favorite K-dramas. This leading-man fashion sense is making this way harder than it needs to be. A freaking turtleneck, come on!

"Are you trying to make me look like a sewer rat," I say, before gesturing to my outfit, composed of a thick school sweater and baggy jeans that are poorly stuffed into snow boots. The fit really says *Goodbye, dignity!*

He leans back in his chair, blinking. His face is duller now and when he shakes his head, there isn't a hint of a smile. "I—"

"You come here with your nice shirt and pants, a freaking orchid in a freaking pot, your little fancy watch, and you don't even send a freaking text that you were gonna see me like this?"

One of the baristas glances at us, concerned, but gets back to pouring a drink almost immediately.

James's voice is low. "You said you didn't want me to say anything else to you."

"I know what I said! But maybe a little heads-up would have been nice, so that I could look somewhat socially acceptable!" I whisper-yell this time. "And a potted plant? People who apologize get freaking *roses,* James, roses! In like, a *bouquet*? Have you even memorized the rom-coms I told you to?"

Now he looks more confused than sad. Arms flying up, he goes, "You hate roses!"

"I know what I hate and I . . . I do hate roses. But that's not the point!"

What was the point again? Ah yes, breaking up with James.

James taps his foot on the floor, and I can feel his nervousness. "Lara, I'm sorry," he starts. "I should have never gone with Eliza in the first place. I was so stupid. I should have had better judgment."

The aura around us changes, and everything starts to tense up again.

"Yeah, you were more stupid than usual. But do you know what really hurt the most, James?" I ask, relieving my tension by cracking my knuckles underneath the table.

He doesn't flinch.

"When Eliza and I were fighting, you took her side and I relived *everything*. All the pain I felt from before just came rushing back. You and Eliza. Again. Me being the third wheel. Again. You guys kissing. Again."

He presses his lips together, breathing heavily through his nose. He looks at the ceiling instead of my eyes, in an attempt to keep tears from spilling.

In a softer voice, I say, "I was just waiting for you to leave me again."

James and Eliza got together and broke up the summer before high school. She was moving away for good; we knew she wouldn't be able to visit in the summer like she did when she lived a few hours' drive away. After Eliza left, he drifted and we became less than friends with each passing day. The only time I was able to get his attention was when we'd trade insults and pranks. Even then, I never felt he was truly back—until our third-wheeling situation forced us back together. Maybe I should've known that things were too good to be true.

I think losing James that summer was part of the reason why I couldn't fathom my best friends getting into relationships. Somehow, it felt like I would end up alone again. When you become the third wheel once and it causes you to lose your best friend, it's pretty difficult to recover from. I still don't think I have, at least not fully.

My eyes begin to well up so I get up from my spot and head to the door. No way am I going to cry in a coffee shop and have people judge me while they wait for their lattes. The cold air bites my skin as I start down the sidewalk. I know he followed me out. I search for his car until I find it parked along the street.

He unlocks it and both of us step inside. I let a tear slip down my cheek but immediately wipe it away on my sleeve. The confession comes out bluntly and every atom in my body wishes I had told him earlier. "Did you realize that I was kind of in love with you for our whole childhood?"

"I didn't," he whispers, and I nod.

"We stopped being friends after you and Eliza broke up."

"I—" he starts but can't seem to find the words to finish his sentence.

The next part is harder because I'm so angry with him. "I can't blame you for all of this, though. I wasn't upfront about my feelings then, and I wasn't upfront about them recently. It's just—I just, I wanted to hide. I should have told you. Then maybe,"—I begin to cry—"maybe this wouldn't have happened." Again, I wipe the tears from my face, taking big breaths and wondering if my lungs have simply reached their capacity.

When he reaches for my hand, I pull away and clasp both my hands in my lap. He lets out a large exhale like he doesn't know how we got here. "I know my apologies won't change anything," he says, "but you mean the world to me. You're the first person who comes to mind when I think about my future. You're the only person I'd ever want to spend my life with."

I can't breathe.

"I'm begging you, give me a second chance. I promise that I'll be smarter, I'll work harder, I'll do anything for you. I'll do anything to be with you."

His eyes are so sincere, and it almost makes me want to lean over and kiss him and tell him it's going to be all right.

But I can't.

"I'm sorry, James."

Tears start to fall down his cheeks, even as he tries to keep his composure. He swallows before saying, "I'm sorry, Lara, but whether you like it or not, I'm in love with you and I always will be. I know you won't admit it because I've hurt you too many times to count, but I know that you love me too."

"You're right. I love you."

And I mean it. A part of me hates myself for still meaning it, after all he's done. But it's still James. It's not logical, I know, to still love a boy who makes you cry too hard and question yourself until you lose your mind. But those tears came with laughs so hard that my chest ached, smiles so big that I couldn't frown if I tried, and kisses so sweet that for moments, I forgot how to breathe. He was the boy who betrayed me but also believed in me.

"Please give me another chance."

But he's just a boy.

He saw all of me, and I saw more of him than most people, which is why it's so hard to leave. For the past seventeen years I've watched him grow, fail, succeed, make mistakes, and fix them, because like me, he's not perfect. Not even close. I know his heart, and that it's good and true and he never means to hurt anyone. I know he'll love me with all of it but break me just as easily. People say that love takes risks, but I can't keep risking myself while I wait for him to learn, for me to learn. I can't let people take pieces of me for the sake of training. It doesn't work like that.

So, yes. I love him. But I love myself enough to let him go.

My breathing is slower now and my heart doesn't feel like it'll jump out of my chest. "Just because we love each other doesn't mean that we should be together." I give him a half smile. "A relationship can't rely solely on love alone. You need trust, communication, understanding . . . and I think we both have to work on those things."

He presses his lips together, still looking unconvinced.

I continue. "And working on them as a couple would be difficult here together, let alone on opposite sides of the world. We'll be apart for the next while and maybe that's how it's supposed to be."

He nods, disappointed but accepting. A dried streak of tears paints his cheeks and when he goes to wipe his face, there's nothing. "I'm yours when I get back," he says, mirroring my half smile and the dimple reappears.

"The 2.0 version I presume?"

"The 2.0 version."

And so we start the journey. I tell him as much as I can—how I feel now, how I felt before—and slowly, I know the pain will subside. It doesn't disappear with our smiles; it lingers as you'd expect it to. He sits there, dark hair messed up like he hasn't brushed it in days. Beside him, a girl who looks like she rolled out of bed and started her day like that. It's a gruesome scene, but this is us. We were never perfect and a lot of times, we are far from it. We're just two teenagers, trying and failing, hoping to eventually find what's ours.

TIP THIRTY:
BE YOUR OWN UNICYCLE

✱

I lie down on my bed, taking a breath and wondering if this is really it. Xander and Anannya are on the right side of my laptop screen, watching with widened eyes as I attach the lab application to the email. The email is composed, professional, and Anannya says it's almost perfect. Xander jokes that I'll get in before him. It's fully loaded now and the only thing I need to do is press the Send button. The mouse is there already, just a tap on the trackpad and it'll be off to Dr. Osei.

I don't send it.

Guilt overcomes me, and I try so hard to fight it; my chest rises and falls uncontrollably as I sob into my hands, apologizing over and over and over again. "*I wasted your time, I'm sorry, I'm sorry.*"

My glasses are blurred with tear streaks, and I can hardly see through them. I can make out Anannya with her hands over her mouth. "No, honey, it's okay, it's okay." I wanted so much to be like her; she's achieved so much and done everything right. Xander shakes his head but still smiles. I wanted to be like him too; he knew exactly where he was going and how to get there.

But it's difficult to run a race on the wrong track. Their finish line looked so much like mine at the start that I thought we could run the same race, that we could go together. Yet while they took another excited step forward, I kept looking back. Everyone says it's wrong to hold yourself back, to prevent yourself from moving forward, but if moving ahead quickly means sacrificing your mind, it isn't worth it. Not jumping at every opportunity doesn't make me any less deserving of success. It's useless to feel burned out and pressured to the point of questioning everything I do. It's exhausting to compare myself to people who can handle more than I can. Maybe I'll be able to do more in the future, but right now, I need to take that break.

I reach for the box of tissues on my bedside table and wipe my tears. My face is all splotchy and I look even worse on the FaceTime camera. Still, I release a large breath, feeling lighter than I've felt in weeks.

"Are you okay?" Xander asks.

I give him a small smile. "I will be."

At James's house, downstairs is loud—Christmas music, chatter, clinking wine glasses, and cheers. I escaped the actual party a while ago but people, including my parents, are congratulating Tito Danny for his business successes and praising him for continuing through the tough plateau. Excited faces bid him and his son bon voyage, unaware it took days for Seb to stop holding on to James's leg like his life depended on it. Upstairs, it's quieter, but not silent. The Christmas lights outside illuminate part of the study, hitting the window nook just right. Fresh snow on the window ledge reflects the colors of the lights as I hold the vintage guitar in my lap—James's gift—wondering if he'll even play it. I handed it to him, and it looked as if he could barely touch it, though his smile was so genuine.

The door creaks open, a streak of light on the ground expanding as James walks in with two steaming mugs in hand. Despite the dim lighting, he looks as perfect as he always does. The usual jeans are replaced with black dress pants and a black button-up—which isn't even buttoned up all the way.

"Still can't find your tie?" I tease.

He quirks an eyebrow. "Oh, you didn't catch me throwing it in the fireplace?"

I gently drop the guitar to the floor. "You always have the best gifts," he says, handing one of the mugs to me, and I inhale the wonderful aroma of chocolate and peppermint. We sit silently beside each other in the window nook, sipping our drinks slowly and admiring the neighbor's decorations. Across the street is a house that looks like a Christmas carnival with dozens of inflated characters lining the grass.

"Is that a snail with a Santa hat?" he asks.

I nod. "They come up with all sorts of things nowadays."

He finishes his drink first, setting it on a nearby coffee table before heading over to the bookshelf. He opens a book—an obviously fake one—and pulls out a long rectangular box. "Your gift," he says, simply handing it to me. "Keep in mind that I bought this a while ago, so don't get freaked out or anything."

I laugh but take the box anyway. "Can I have that fake book too?"

"All yours."

I open the box and almost gasp at the shiny piece of jewelry—a beautiful silver bracelet, adorned with charms.

"May I?" he asks, before unclasping it and reaching for my hand. The bracelet sits on my left wrist and every charm has me one step closer to tears. *Ice cream, book, fish, star, and car.*

He takes my hand in his and starts pointing out the charms. "Ice cream, because I'll always remember your ultimate ice-cream order of one scoop of chocolate chip cookie dough on the bottom, one scoop of cookies and cream on the top. Everything topped with crushed M&M's and sprinkles, all put together in a waffle cone."

The book is for studying and the fish is for the aquarium, he tells me. "A star," he says next, "because we went stargazing for our first date. You passed out after eating all that fried chicken, but they didn't have a chicken leg charm so . . ."

I playfully slap his arm and he laughs.

"Lastly, a car, because you're my favorite person to have in my passenger's seat and I'll miss driving with you the most."

I give him a tight hug, a hug that I never want to part from—a sad hug, because I know that he'll be gone from my arms soon. "I promise I wasn't trying to hit on you," he says, voice breaking, "but I'm *really* gonna miss doing these kinds of things with you."

"Me too."

He doesn't let go of me. I don't want him to leave, and it isn't long until he begins to tremble. "Why can't we be happy together?"

A sad laugh escapes my lips. "We just happen to be the perfect third wheels?"

He holds me tighter. "You know I love you, right? You're my best friend. Promise me that you won't forget that."

I pause for a second, letting tears roll down my cheeks. "I'd never forget. Promise me that you'll find something you love? That you'll pursue the goals you have."

He starts to cry, too, and I feel his hands shaking against my back. "I promise. And promise me that you'll visit the house to play with Seb and hang out with Gabe?"

I nod against his chest, hesitating on my last one, but proceed to say it, though it makes me sob. "Now promise me that you won't, *you won't*, wait for me."

"Lara—"

"If you find that you fall in love with someone else, don't think about me. Please." I cry, tears falling on his nice shirt.

He strokes my hair back, placing his lips to my temple. "I won't promise you that."

The hug lasts forever, like we've finally discovered the secret to defying the laws of time. Still, sorrow rings in the air; it doesn't go away quickly, and I wonder if it'll ever go away at all. His thumb rubs tiny circles on my back, the familiar rhythm of his touch, though becoming infrequent, always stays the same.

We part and a mischievous smile forms on his face, as if we weren't crying two seconds ago. "You owe me." Arms folded, he raises an eyebrow.

I wipe tears from my cheek before patting my nonexistent pockets. "No wallet, no cash. Sorry."

He shakes his head. "I meant that you owe me a wish. Remember? When we gambled on Carol and Mark?"

I am never gambling again.

"How about we go on one last adventure?"

There's no one at Allan Gardens when we get there. The snow is lighter now, a few snowflakes landing on our jackets but melting instantly. James carries his guitar in one hand as we walk along the cobblestone pathway, lit by a long row of lampposts. I wish it was summer and the flowers were alive. James is the only one who would have the idea to go to a garden this late at night during the *winter*. I don't think I'll ever find someone as strange.

James tells me that this was his second option for our first date, in case it rained that night we went stargazing. I know why he would choose this. Mom and Tita Gia tell our story like it's Genesis in the bible. "You were three months old and crying," Tita Gia would say to James, getting teary eyed. "It was spring, and we were here in this greenhouse." Then Mom would go, "And I told Gia I was pregnant." They would hold hands while James and I stared at each other, confused. In the corner, Dad would grumble, "She told her before me," before adding that my mother ran out of the house with a pregnancy test, leaving him to finish the chores.

Neither of us thought too much about it, but I suppose our story really started here.

The only living plants are found in the greenhouse at this time of year, and the fairy lights inside are turned on. James tries to pull on the door, one hand on the handle and the other on the guitar, but it fails to open. It's closed, obviously. The only person inside is a blue-uniformed janitor, probably close to finishing his job. I guess we were expecting some sort of Christmas miracle.

I link an arm around his. "It's okay. Let's do something else."

He shrugs and we start to walk back, only to see an elderly couple sitting on a nearby bench. The woman has her head on a man's shoulder. Blue eyeshadow shines on her eyelids, complementing her bright blue eyes, which occasionally look up at her partner. Her pale skin is dull beneath the fluorescent lighting, but she's still beautiful. Unlike her, the man's skin is a deep brown, and his eyes are dark as night. He sits calmly, caressing her wrinkled hand. He wears a newsboy cap on his gray hair, despite the cold.

We pass, overhearing their conversation. "I wish we could've celebrated in the greenhouse," the woman says in a distinct French accent. "After all, we did get married here."

"I know, I know." The man sighs. "But you heard the cleaner, we can't go in."

James stands in place, holding my arm back. "Please don't say what I think you're going to say," I plead.

The glimmer in his dark eyes is unmistakable. "We're going to break into the greenhouse, Dela Cruz style. From what I learned from you, a little fib isn't illegal . . ." Then he makes a run toward the couple, not letting go of my wrist.

We stand before the pair, like a tandem of creeps. Looking up, though, they seem anything but terrified. A fogged breath escapes James's lips before he announces, "The ultimate third wheels are here for service."

The old man furrows his brows, concerned. "Excuse me?"

I shove James to the side before they call the cops on us for harassment. "What he means to say is that we accidentally overheard your conversation, and we want to help you get into the greenhouse."

The lady's eyes light up as she clasps her hands. "Yes! Thank you!"

The man is less convinced. "How are you kids going to do that?"

The lady hits him with her purse and politely tells him to shut up. Her frailty disappears when she stands up and speed walks to the greenhouse door. Even I don't know what James's plan is until he asks the woman to knock on the door while he hands the man his guitar. Suddenly, he lifts me up, bridal style.

"Play dead," he whisper-yells.

I scramble to get out of his hold. "*What?!?*"

"At least play *almost* dead!"

The door swooshes open and I'm left with no choice but to go limp in his arms, closing my eyes and praying that this works and that he doesn't drop me on the pavement.

The janitor has a deeper voice than I expected. His body through the glass said praying mantis but his voice says John Cena. "Didn't I tell you folks that we're closed for tonight."

"Good evening, kind sir," James starts. *Kind sir?* "Apologies for the misunderstanding but *my wife* and I just got here. You see, *my wife* has a *condition*, and her dying wish is to see her grandparents reenact their wedding dance at the place they got married." I turn my head and sniffle for added pity.

The janitor doesn't seem to care about our story, instead looking from the tall Black man to the thin white woman to their dying Asian granddaughter in some guy's arms. Luckily, he doesn't say anything about it and moves on to a new question. "Aren't you guys a little young to be married?"

James chuckles. "Why, thank you. It's all in the SPF. We run a family sunscreen business . . . right, grandfather-in-law?"

The old man hesitates before saying, "Yes . . . we do."

His wife jumps in as well. "It's called Miraculous Melanin! But it's only sold in—"

"New Zealand," James finishes. "*So*, can we come in?"

When he begins to say no, James keeps going. "My poor sweetheart, suffering from a cardio . . . photo . . . neuro . . ."

I turn my head, still looking drowsy. "Blastoma." I cough and the cleaner backs away like I'm contagious.

"Cardiophotoneuroblastoma," James finishes confidently.

The cleaner groans in defeat. "Fine. Just—You get twenty minutes before I lock up." He walks in before us but quickly disappears to another section of the greenhouse, probably to yell at some plants.

James places me on the ground and holds a hand up for a high five. I roll my eyes before smacking my hand against his. The old man laughs deeply, shaking his head. "You kids are funny. In my forty-four years of being a neurosurgeon, never have I heard of a *cardiophotoneuroblastoma*."

"You guys are golden," the woman adds, before taking her husband's hand. "Thank you both so much."

"You deserve a memorable anniversary." I smile.

The man hands the guitar back to James. "Do you play, boy? Maybe you could give us a little something to dance to."

James holds the guitar and examines it for a minute before nodding. He takes a deep breath and starts to play "Sana Ngayong Pasko," his grandfather's go-to song at every Christmas Eve party since the beginning of time.

They walk to the center of the circular pavilion, surrounded by luscious green leaves and tropical flowers. Big Christmas ornaments hang from the ceiling, adding more color to the already vibrant room. I feel like I'm watching a fairy tale. The old lady places both of her hands around the back of her husband's neck and he rests his on her waist, both figures melting together as if they never existed in separate pieces. Their eyes meet and it's like they share a secret that nobody knows. They dance slowly, elegantly—nothing like mine and James's horrific waltz. Still, I wonder if we could be like that one day. I catch him staring at me and maybe he wonders the same thing.

Lolo Andres said his mom played the song every Christmas after his father died because she missed him so much. Eventually, she grew old and frail and couldn't play it. From then, it was his song to learn and play for her. Now, James strums the guitar, hitting all the right chords, and it's almost like his grandfather is here with us. The song is peaceful and sad, but looking at the elderly couple, it's also romantic and hopeful.

Alas, the song ends and the couple parts. They give James a round of applause and the old man gives him a pat on the back. The woman holds her hand out, gesturing for James to give her the guitar. "Dance with her," she orders. "You have ten minutes left."

He frowns. "But—"

"Go!" The annoyance and desperation in her voice, plus the French accent reminds me of the dance practices James and I were forced to attend.

I take his stubborn hand to the middle of the garden, and it doesn't take long for him to pull me to his chest. She plays "So This Is Love," and I wonder how this night is even real.

The world is full of people, all of them different; James and I are only two of the seven billion on this planet. We grow up among married people, single people, friends, enemies, and family. There are so many people around us that it can't be helped to be a third wheel, to feel out of place sometimes. Yet there are people out there who welcome us with open arms, accept us despite our flaws, and remind us that we're more than what we are to others.

The waltz has yet to improve from our old recital, but it's our dance now. Nobody can tell us it's wrong because it's ours. It was always ours from the moment we stepped on that stage and ruined that recital. Foreheads pressed together and breaths shaky, we take a moment to grieve the memories of our childhood together, holding each other tightly in one another's arms, as if we might as well vanish at any moment. But that's the reality of growing up.

Sometimes, growing up can mean growing apart.

And sometimes growing apart can mean growing closer to yourself.

He kisses me; it's gentle but different. Our kiss isn't needy or passionate; it's caring and hopeful. This kiss says good-bye. As we hold each other under the array of lights, our breaths even out. We find our air. It is calm.

I let go first when the music ends, giving his hand one last reassuring squeeze. I always knew why I loved James but wondered what *exactly* it was that he saw in me. Perhaps I'll never figure out what anyone thinks of me. I suppose that doesn't matter. Whether my life functions as a unicycle, bicycle, or tricycle, I'm always capable of completing myself. Besides, one day my completed self will ditch the bikes for a Lambo anyway.

Moving forward is difficult but it's something we must do. For some, it's a fast sprint; for others, it's slow and steady. But we're all chasing the same thing—ourselves. Sometimes we find ourselves when we're alone and other times we need another pair of eyes to help us in our search. Still, we search for who we are, the version of us that changes, that gets lost, and that has to be looked for again. Over and over.

James offers one last song on the guitar before our time is up and the woman asks if he knows their wedding song—"Unchained Melody." James laughs and says, "Who doesn't know that song?" before playing it happily, doing them one better by singing the lyrics.

They sway to the music and so do I. The couple is lost in their joyful dance, barely noticing that James is dramatically singing their wedding song to me as I stifle a laugh. The sight is so beautiful that you could cry, but enough tears have been shed for tonight. Tomorrow again, we can cry. But tonight, we laugh.

As we look at the couple, deep in each other's gaze—dancing in a greenhouse because of my fake illness and our pseudosunscreen business—I realize, *we'll always be the best third wheels.*

THE FRICKIN' END

ACKNOWLEDGMENTS

First and foremost, I thank God. Not only has He given me such a romance-deprived life that I resorted to writing as a coping mechanism, but I've been blessed with an amazing support system that has allowed me to bring this little publishing dream of mine to life. If someone had told me I'd be given a publishing deal at eighteen, for a story I started in my first year of high school, I'd probably laugh in their face. But God works mysteriously and here we are, holding this in our hands and occasionally wanting to hurl it against a wall.

This would not have been made possible without the incredible team at Wattpad and Wattpad Books, so thank you to everyone who worked behind the scenes to make this dream work. Deanna McFadden, I'll always remember my first call with you and how kind you were, even though I accidentally never saw your emails and you literally had to message me via Wattpad, and my internet was cutting out for, like, half the call. Thank you for believing in this story. Now for our team of Rebeccas. There's a 2:1 ratio of Rebeccas to Loridees, so maybe this story is more Rebecca (jazz hands) than Loridee (smaller jazz hands) . . . Rebecca Sands, I was so scared/embarrassed to get that first edit letter from you because that first draft was *wild*. But I never felt discouraged with your notes; you pushed this story to be the best version it could be, while reassuring me with each step. Thank you for always giving me extensions during my disgusting midterms/finals seasons and never saying anything when I submitted my edits at four a.m. Rebecca Mills, thank you for catching all those pesky (and very embarrassing) mistakes with grammar and continuity. A big thanks to Delaney, for giving me grammar lessons I very much needed (ha-ha but also ahhh). Mitch, thank you for making sure the Tagalog in this book looks right and preventing me from getting bullied by my relatives in the Philippines. But if anyone asks, tell everyone *fluent ako.* Amanda, my talent manager, thank you for being so excited about this, for hopping on calls, listening to rants, and advocating for my visions. You're a Taylor stan, so I knew you'd be awesome, but you've surpassed the awesomeness scale.

Now for my family. I know I hid this from you for a solid four(ish) years, but thank you for being proud of me despite Dad asking me, "*Anong ibig sabihin niyan?*" (What does that mean?) every time I talk about publishing. To Mom, thank you for reminding me that I'm worthy of good things. Shortly after receiving my publishing deal, I had a panic attack because I felt so inadequate, that I had robbed someone else of a dream opportunity. But you held me while I cried and told me I deserved it. And you never get tired of saying it again and again when I don't believe you. Dad, thank you for telling *everyone* I wrote a book, even relatives I've never spoken to. To my little sister, Neridee, thanks for simultaneously being my top hater/marketer and giving me such cruel editorial notes. For someone who picks up one book per year (or less), you have strangely good and valid criticisms. Ninang Charisse, thank you for shifting your attention away from *90 Day Fiancé* to listen to my book rants. Ninang Ejane, thank you for being one of my biggest promoters. Ate Marianne, thank you for also checking my Tagalog. And to my (not-so) baby cousin Elise, thank you for loving books, excitedly telling people at your school that I'm a writer, for sharing your own stories with me, and for being intrigued enough to take and read my rough notebook. When you're old enough to read this story, I hope you'll like it.

To my chaotic and funny and loveable best friends. Thank you for inspiring the LKJC. Quiana, you had something to complain about every time I released a new chapter but always continued to beg for the next update. Janine, thank you for being as obsessed with this story as I am. Janelle, thank you for listening to me complain and plot for hours on end, for talking all about books, and even driving with me to a sketchy warehouse to get books. And Caroline, sweet Caroline, though we're "grown-ups" now, I know you'd still dig up a baseball bat *si nécessaire*. All of you, thank you for being with me at my lowest points and cheering for me at my highest.

Sawsan, thank you for introducing me to this app in the eighth grade and being my first ever reader and supporter. Julianne, thank you for dating that one guy (also in the eighth grade) and giving me my first third-wheeling experience.

And to all my writer friends. Philline, thank you for the amazing memes to boost my mood during editing and being my bookish big sister. Brianna, thank you for offering to read my draft and complaining with me when we were at the peak of exhaustion. Also for the countless, "IT'S GOOD!!!"s during the times I needed it the most.

Of course, I thank my readers. Thank you for your funny (and extensive) comment chains, your encouraging "UPDATE!!!" and the little messages here and there about how my story has impacted you. I wouldn't have finished this without those (sometimes aggressive) reminders. Thank you for sliding into my private messages and Instagram DMs to tell me how much you loved this, resonated with the characters, how you were inspired to write.

Last but not least, thank you for picking this book up and bearing with me through this cringey imperfect confusing but somehow still came together roller coaster ride of a story. You all deserve pizza. And cupcakes. And unlimited ensaymada.

ABOUT THE AUTHOR

*

Loridee De Villa is the author of the Watty Award–winning *How to Be the Best Third Wheel,* which has accumulated 2.5 million reads on Wattpad. She also wrote *The Infinite Worlds of Ella Jane,* which won the Shaw Rocket Prize Teen Writing Contest in 2020 and is being turned into a theatrical podcast. When she's not typing up a new chapter, Loridee spends her days drawing, sewing, and watching cartoons, all while balancing courses at the University of Toronto. Loridee currently resides in Ontario, Canada, and is pursuing a career in health sciences.

AUTHOR Q & A

*

A Conversation with Loridee De Villa

When did you first want to become a writer?

I don't think there was ever a specific moment when I realized I wanted to become a writer. Growing up, I wanted to be so many different things, and I would picture myself doing absolutely *everything* in the future (now I realize that the days only span twenty-four hours, and one cannot be a baker-doctor-biologist-writer-painter all at once). But I knew I wanted to write a book when I started to read YA fiction at around twelve years old. I loved it so much and figured that I had to have my own book in my elementary school library one day. Once I started to plan/write my own novels (and simultaneously do fake interviews in front of my mirror), I fell in love with it even more and thought, *I don't mind writing. Not a bit.*

What do you need to have/eat/drink while you're writing?

There's nothing specific that I need to have. It's more like, what shouldn't I have? And I should not have my phone. I get distracted way too easily and will succumb under the ruthless and hypnotizing forces of Instagram and TikTok. Again, I'm cheating on this next one, but I also cannot actually "eat" while writing. I always chew gum—and only one specific type. Excel White Bubblemint. It's the only gum I will chew. Ever. As for drink? Water all the way. I can chug 750mL in under a minute. Stay hydrated, folks.

Where did you get your inspiration for *How to Be the Best Third Wheel?*

I've been a third wheel for my entire life. In the fifth grade, a guy friend of mine tried to win over one of my best friends with little success, so I got to eat her gifted chocolates. In the eighth grade, one of my friends got her first boyfriend. I became the ultimate third wheel to their relationship. Not only did I tag along with them at recess before they shooed me away, but I also gave her boyfriend a stern "talking-to." I loved reading romances and this story began when I was fourteen, when I was ambushed by the reality that YA books and movies had no place in an actual high school. There was no sight of a cute relationship brewing anywhere, well at least not for me. Meanwhile, a bunch of people began to date—since that was around the age that everyone started dating. For some reason, looking at the real teenage couples around me made me slightly nauseous. I felt a bit odd, knowing that I would not be ready for a romantic relationship while kids around me started to pair up. I'd listen to classmates talk about their relationship drama and give advice as if I knew what I was talking about. Although my close friends weren't romantically involved with anyone, I based the LKJC group on their personalities. Ultimately, the book was supposed to be a tribute to those who've felt like third wheels in relationships, friendships . . . etc. I find that a lot of stories revolve around that one couple that we want to end up together, and although my book has that element, the main theme is about being left out and how to cope with that.

If *How to Be the Best Third Wheel* were a movie, who would you cast to play the main characters?

This question always stumps me, haha. I think Lara is particularly difficult to "cast" if we're thinking Hollywood, because I haven't really seen a full Filipina teenager represented in North American media. And for James . . . you don't really see half-Filipino teen boys either! There's a lot of room for rising Filipino stars to make it into the acting industry, and I hope that one day, I'll be able to name many Fil-Can or Fil-Am actors from the top of my head.

But for Lara's friends, I'd go Maitreyi Ramakrishnan for Carol (because she's *hilarious* and bonus points since we're from the same city), Ashley Liao for Jasmine (because I have a thing for Full House and Fuller House), and Sadie Sink for Kiera (because I'm a firm believer in a Sadie Sink supremacy).

What's your favorite thing to do when you're not writing?

When I'm not writing, I'm usually doing the basics for survival—sleeping, eating, and *homework*. The last one takes up, like, 50 percent of my time. But if we subtract my horrendous school life from the equation, my favorite things to do would be drawing and hiking. Drawing because I love art and hiking because I love nature (as well as grappling onto rocks occasionally).

ENSAYMADA RECIPE

*

Lara's lola makes this soft, cloud-like, creamy dessert pastry in *How to Be the Best Third Wheel.* You can even pretend she's making it for you, which will make it taste better, and it's accessible even if you're not an expert baker.

Serve it with tea or coffee for the ultimate boost to your discussion.

PASTRY INGREDIENTS:

1 cup milk

⅓ cup sugar

½ cup shortening - softened to room temperature

1 envelope active dry yeast (about 7-9 grams—¼ oz—or 1 tablespoon) - proofed in ¼ cup warm water (See Note 1 for alternative)
Note 1: You may also use instant yeast, which requires no proofing and can be added directly to the flour before kneading. Using instant yeast will also cut the rising time. Add the ¼ cup of water for proofing ADY to the liquids instead. I recommend using Saf-Instant Gold, which is made for sweet dough.

3 ½ cup flour

3 egg yolks

¼ tablespoon salt

¼ cup butter - softened to room temperature (for brushing)

TOPPING INGREDIENTS:

½ cup butter - softened to room temperature

½ cup powdered sugar

1 cup Kraft cheese or other grated cheese

INSTRUCTIONS:

1. In a mixing bowl, mix together milk, shortening, sugar, and salt.

2. Add half of the flour and the bloomed yeast and mix for 3-5 minutes at medium speed until a paste-like consistency is achieved.

3. Add the egg yolks and the rest of the flour and mix for another 3 minutes.

Add more flour if the mixture is too liquidy or too sticky, but not too much. The dough is supposed to be sticky.

4. Scrape the sides while folding the dough in the middle of the bowl and then cover with a kitchen towel. Let it rest and rise in a warm place for 2-3 hours or until it doubled its size.

5. Scrape the sides of the bowl while tipping the sticky dough over to the thinly floured working surface.

6. Roll the dough into a log and cut into 2. Roll each log again and cut into 2. Repeat this process until you end up with 16 slices.

7. Using a rolling pin, roll a slice into a rectangle (about 8x4 inches) and brush the surface with softened butter. Roll it from one end of the long side to the other end, creating a long, thin log, then shape it into a coil (spiral) with the end tucked under.

8. Place each coiled dough in a greased mold and let it rest in a warm place for about 30 minutes to 1 hour, until it has risen to almost double its size.

9. Bake them in a preheated oven at 300°F/150°C for 20-25 minutes. Once baked, let them cool down for a few minutes before removing from molds. Then let them cool completely.

10. Meanwhile, prepare the buttercream by creaming ½ cup of softened butter and ½ cup powdered sugar.

11. Using a knife or spoon, cover the top of the ensaymadas with buttercream, and lastly, with a generous amount of grated cheese.

Source for ensaymada recipe:
https://www.foxyfolksy.com/ensaymada-recipe/

Turn the page for a preview of

Available wherever books are sold

1

Leonardo da Vinci once said that when you looked at your work in a mirror and saw it reversed, it would look like some other painter's work, and then you'd be a better judge of its faults.

I stood, feet anchored to the ground like they were sprouting roots into the carpet beneath me, and glared at the mirror in front of me. It glared back. Flat, shiny, and unrelenting. So utterly bloody unrelenting that I wanted to toss something at it just to break its icy stare. Shatter it, like it was so fond of shattering me.

When I couldn't take it a second longer, I turned my back on the thing, pulled yet another T-shirt off, and tossed it to the floor. My previous school was easy; I'd wake up each morning and slip on our black and white uniform, no mirror needed. But everything was different now, and it wasn't just the lack of a school uniform that made it that way. In fact, it couldn't be more different if my mother had decided to uproot the family and move us to one of Jupiter's far-flung moons.

I'm a city girl. Born and bred. And up until seven days ago, we'd lived in a penthouse in one of Johannesburg's cool, newly renovated downtown areas. My school, the Art School, where I was studying fine art, was only a few blocks away. After class, my friends and I would walk the streets lined with coffee shops, art galleries, and vintage clothing and record stores, and hang out in our favorite place, the smoky, laid-back jazz café, Maggie's.

At night, I'd sit at my window and watch the city below spring to life. I loved listening to the frantic symphony of the city. A soundscape of honking taxis, shrieking police sirens, rushing, shouting, pushing people. Everything so alive. Everything pounding, blaring, screaming, and growling at you.

I'd gaze at the brightly colored lights of the Nelson Mandela Bridge that took you right into the thumping heart of the city. Johannesburg. Joburg. Jozi. It's called many things. But my favorite name is its isiZulu one: Egoli, Place of Gold. Which is exactly what it is when the sun dips down and the city lights flicker on, casting that warm, molten glow across the tops and sides of the skyscrapers.

Gold's my favorite color, by the way. But there's no gold here. Looking out of my bedroom window all I could see now was blue, the massive sea stretching to the horizon, reaching up into a never-ending cloudless sky. An infinity of it.

Blue . . . it's such a simple color, really. A primary color.

Gold, however, well, that's another story. It's complex. Layered. Much harder to create, and it's also so much more than *just* a color. Gold contains a certain magic, an extravagance, a mystique.

I tried to sigh but the breath got caught in my esophagus. I turned my back on the window now too. I've never liked the sea. Too much water. Too much sand. Besides, I'm not exactly a bikini kinda gal. I haven't been beach-body ready since, well, forever. How ironic then that I've landed here, in the middle of bikini-Barbie, thigh-chafing hell.

Clifton, Cape Town. A place where you're either wearing activewear because you've just left your early morning gym sesh—green smoothie in hand—or you're in swimwear 'cause you're headed to the beach, green smoothie in hand. And don't even get me started on what it's like when the sun goes down. Let's just say you won't find a moody jazz club on these streets. It's more upscale eateries, shucked oysters, and cham-bloody-pagne.

Currently, I'm staging a silent protest against my mother for uprooting my life and dragging me here. But what's new? My mother and I have been locked in a kind of protest for the last four years now.

I do, however, understand *why* we came here. I just can't help feeling that I wasn't consulted. Which I wasn't. The closest thing to a consultation came when she'd walked into my bedroom three weeks ago and declared, *We're moving to Cape Town.* She might as well have detonated an atomic bomb—that's how it felt as I sat on my bed and saw my entire life explode into a million pieces.

We came here for my brother, Zac. I'm not blaming him for this, how could I—I love him more than I can probably describe. He's nine. He's also *specially abled*, as my mother prefers to say. She enjoys upbeat euphemisms, but between you and me, he's on the autism spectrum.

Over the last few years, his symptoms had gotten worse, until his school had finally "suggested" that he attend a facility "better aligned with his unique needs." (Everyone likes euphemisms, it seems.) So, after a quick google search by my mother, the best assisted learning school in the country was located, and now here we are. Sunny, beachy, activewear central—*with green smoothie in hand.*

"Crap!" I pulled yet another outfit off and tossed it to the floor, adding to the massive patchwork of clothes that lay twisted at my feet. My floor was starting to look like a Hannah Höch artwork, my favorite collage artist, and I swear, if you looked hard enough, you could see a galloping horse desperately trying to break free of the tangled mess.

But nothing I owned seemed right. And you need to wear the right thing on your first day. Something that gives off the vibe that you didn't try *too* hard, but that you tried *just* hard enough.

"Hurry." My mother's voice raced up the stairs and burst into my room like an unwanted guest. I'd already told her she didn't need to take me to school—I had my own car—but she was insistent. "I'm going to be late for my meeting!" She sounded rushed and angry, which had been her general vibe for a while now, certainly since that fateful day four years ago—the day the doves cried, as I've come to call it in my head.

"Late, late, late," my brother echoed. Zac often repeats words. I try not to swear in front of him, not since the unfortunate *crap, crap, crap* incident.

I forced myself to face the mirror again. On some days, I can look at myself for longer than a few seconds; today was *not* one of those days. My pale, flabby thighs that touched, my stomach that oozed over the top of my very unsexy panties, and worse, my "hellos and good-byes"—those flappy bits of fat on your arms that jiggle when you wave at people. I try not to wave.

"Aaargh." I covered my face and turned away from the evil

thing again. I've long suspected that mirrors were invented by some gorgeous, stick-thin, yet completely sinister, creature for the sole purpose of tormenting girls like me.

I reached for the nearest outfit I could find: my most comfortable pair of worn jeans and a cute, vintage, button-up blouse I'd found at a little secondhand shop with the boys—my BFFs—Andile and Guy. At art school there were four distinct groups: art kids, drama kids, music kids, and dance kids. For some reason, I'd made friends with the ballet guys pretty early on. We'd just found each other, like attracting magnets, and since then we'd moved around school like a little impenetrable team. I missed them so much . . . and we'd been separated for only seven days.

I tugged my jeans on. They felt a little tighter than usual, probably from all the stress eating I'd been doing lately: *carbs really are from the devil* (perhaps also invented by the same person who gave us mirrors?). I pulled them up, trying to cover the muffin top, but not pulling them so high that I was now sporting a gigantic camel toe. The black, collared blouse also felt like it was straining across my bust. I adjusted my bra, trying to flatten the ladies, but clearly they were also protesting today, because they weren't going anywhere.

And then there was my hair, the massive mop of curls that I'd long given up on trying to wrangle with a straightener.

I slipped a pair of comfy, old sneakers on and gave myself an extra spray of deo; it was hot today, and the last thing I needed was to be the smelly girl too.

I inspected myself. I looked fine. *Sort of.* I looked like me, like I always did. But today I wasn't so sure how well Me was going to go down at my new school.

Bay Water High, where surfing and bodyboarding were

extracurricular activities because the school backed onto the beach. I'd gone to the school's Facebook page a few days ago and scoured their photos, hoping to find someone, *anyone*, who looked vaguely like me. But nothing.

Because it seemed that being gorgeous and thigh-gap thin were prerequisites for being a student at BWH. I was *not* gorgeous. My hair was red and frizzy. My skin erred on the pasty, pale side, with a smattering of cellulite for added texture, and the only gap I had was the one between my front teeth.

She's just big boned, I'd once overheard my mom say to another mother. *It's probably puppy fat, she'll grow out of it*, the other mother had offered up with a look that resembled pity, as if thinking, *Thank heavens she's not mine.* But I was seventeen now, turning eighteen in two months, and I wasn't growing out of it. If anything, I was growing into it more than ever. My phone gave a sudden beep and I looked down at it. A message from my dad lit up the screen and my stomach dropped.

DAD: Good luck on your first day. Thinking of you!

I stared at the message and then left my dad on Read.

"Looooriiii!" My mother's shrill voice came at me again, like a sharp-beaked bird dive-bombing you because you'd stumbled upon its nest.

Oh, that's the other thing you should know about me—my name is Lori Patty Palmer. Of course, when the elementary school bullies got wind of my middle name, which I got courtesy of my great aunt Patty, they had a field day with it.

Move out the way, here comes Lori Fatty Palmer. I could still hear their taunts. My old therapist, Dr. Finkelstein—whose name I always thought conjured up images of impassioned, academic debates in smoky, wood-paneled rooms—said that much of my anxiety stems from the bullying. From the time I'd had food thrown in my face, the time someone wrote "Kill yourself fat bitch" on my locker, and of course, there was the pool . . .

I took a deep breath; just thinking about the pool was making my insides quiver. I'd been so relieved when all of that was over and I'd gone to art school, but now, today, I felt like that person all over again.

Lori Fatty Palmer.

I inhaled deeply and then tried to breathe out all the negativity, like that meditation app I'd downloaded told me to. Breathe in positivity, breath out negativity. *Or was it the other way around?*

Maybe this wouldn't be as bad as I thought. Maybe I was just projecting my own fears and anxieties onto the situation. Maybe I would love it at BWH. Maybe everything would be okay. *Maybe.*

I took another deep breath and the buttons on my blouse strained. (Note to self, no deep breathing today for fear that buttons might pop open.) I walked out of my room, grabbing my pill as I went and throwing it back with a sip of now-cold coffee. I grimaced at the taste. Prozac. I've never gotten used to that melt-in-your-mouth, spearmint flavor even though I've been taking it for years. Why even bother with a flavor? It's not like the taste can disguise what it really is.

2

I arrived at BWH and surveyed my surroundings.

Gorgeous girls with oversized beverages in hand walked past me, sucking on long straws. These were probably the same girls who made those blue, smoothie bowls for breakfast with those cute, star-shaped cutouts of dragon fruit.

Boys with rippling muscles also walked past, oversized beverages in one hand, protein bars in the other. And they all seemed so perky. Smiles, bright eyes, and bushy tails, and I wasn't even inside the building yet. I was walking past a row of perfectly polished SUVs that had uniformly ramped the pavement to drop off the kids. Moms in activewear, gossiping to each other in hushed tones. Dads in suits, looking busy and talking on their phones as they climbed out of their overcompensating midlife crisis Maseratis—*Kinda like my own dad, I guess.* I'd made my mother drop me off a block away from school. I didn't need her causing a spectacle, adding to the overall nail-biting stress of this day.

I pulled the finger from my lips, thrust my head into the air, and tried to look as unfazed as humanly possible. Cool, calm, confident. Breathing in negativity, breathing out positivity, looking for silver linings . . . *or something like that.* I made my way past the cars and found myself at the school entrance, and just as I'd suspected, the cool kids were all standing outside waiting, talking, laughing. Have you noticed how they always seem to move in packs? Like little meerkats. Hyenas. Swarms of bees. I lowered my head again and resisted the urge to bite my cuticle.

A steep flight of stairs rose up in front of me, and I sighed. My body and stairs aren't exactly friends, and the last thing I needed was to be out of breath when I reached the top. That would draw even more attention to me, and I hated attention. At that moment, a girl and a guy walked past me, arm in arm, laughing, looking like a pair of Insta models and taking the stairs two at a time: #couplegoals.

Despite my previous silver lining–laced thoughts, I was beginning to get the distinct impression that I wasn't going to like it here, nor was I going to fit in. I hoped this was going to be worth it. But judging by my brother's first day at school yesterday, it was unlikely. As my mom and I had been leaving the school, he'd burst out of the classroom, thrown himself onto the gate, and tried to climb over it while screaming at the top of his lungs. Let's hope day two would be better.

I made it to the top of the stairs, impressed that my breathing hadn't even kicked up a notch—probably due to all the nervous adrenaline surging through my veins.

“Hey!” someone called, but I didn’t look up. Surely they weren’t talking to me?

But when a foot entered my field of vision, and a body blocked my path to the entrance, I was forced to look up.

Small, cut-off denim shorts. White crop top, exposed flat stomach. Dewy complexion, impossibly long, blond hair. Conditioner-commercial hair.

“Hey, are you the new girl?” conditioner commercial asked, her blue eyes and hair actually glinting in the morning light.

“Uh . . . yes. Lori,” I stuttered, averting my gaze.

“Hi! I’m Amber Long-Innes, and this is Teagan.” She sounded so perky, as if she was high on the sunbeams themselves. I looked from her to Teagan, who in contrast to Amber was olive-skinned and dark-eyed, with the poutiest lips I’d ever seen. Then her lips parted, and she smiled at me. I was almost knocked off my feet, it was so big and luminous.

Okay, okay. I have a confession to make. A big one. As much as I like to mentally slag off girls like this, silently judge and mock, I’m jealous as hell of them. *There, I said it!* Not to mention truly and utterly intimidated. My acerbic, inner sarcasm is just a defense for my outward fears and insecurities. Dr. Finkelstein once explained that defense mechanisms were essential to survival, that many creatures had them. Well, at least I wasn’t a Malaysian exploding ant.

“I’m president of the BWH SRC,” Amber chirped.

“SRC?” I was unfamiliar with this acronym.

“Student Representative Council,” she cooed.

“And I’m VP,” Teagan added.

“My portfolio is HOSS,” Amber continued, tucking a stray strand of hair behind her perfectly shaped ear. She reminded me of Goldilocks, except you could see she didn't eat bowls of porridge.

"And mine's PPC," Teagan jumped in. They talked as if they'd rehearsed this speech many times before, expertly jumping from line to line, like actors on a stage.

"HOSS and PPC?" I asked, when it looked like they'd finally finished the scene.

"Head of School Spirit and Primary Peer Counselor," Amber qualified.

I'd suspected this school was overflowing with teen spirit. Still, I hadn't expected "Spirit" to be an actual thing. The only teen spirit I had was that old Nirvana vinyl that I'd found in a vintage store in Joburg.

"It's our job to show new students around and introduce them to the school."

"Introduce?" I looked into Amber's ridiculously clear blue eyes as panic slid a cold finger down my spine. I tried to push the panic down. I've learned that showing the enemy how you *really* feel is not a good idea. They can, and will, prey on it.

But then Teagan did something unexpected; she pulled me into a hug. "Welcome to BWH, Lori."

"Uh . . . thanks!" I was surprised by what seemed like a genuine show of friendliness. Maybe I'd judged everyone here too soon? *Maybe.*

"Great! We'll do the introduction in assembly first period," Amber said casually, and then they both turned, flipped their hair at the same time (had they rehearsed this move too?), and walked away. I stood there, unable to move, as if the rubber soles of my shoes had melted into the hot concrete. Which was conceivable, since it was scorching today.

"Aren't you coming?" Amber turned, tilting her head and looking at me from a different angle. I wondered if she was thinking, *Nah, still fat from this angle.* I sucked my stomach in quickly in an attempt to appear more streamlined.

"Uh . . . I . . ." Dammit. I exhaled when I realized that the stomach-sucking had caused my voice to rise two unnatural-sounding octaves. "Suuuure." I tried to sound casual even though every cell, nerve, fiber, and muscle in my body wanted to turn around and *run, run, run*!